Praise for
Ministry

A Duch

"Christina Brooke is a bright new star."
—*RT Book Reviews*

"*A Duchess to Remember* surpasses all expectations, leaving you longing for the next installment."
—*Fresh Fiction*

"A delightful, attention-grabbing, sweetly romantic historical read you won't want to miss."
—*Night Owl Romance*

"This is a two-night, preferably one, book. Cecily and Rand's romance is a fun, deceptive, quickstep of a dance."
—*Romance Reviews Today*

Mad About the Earl

"A true historical gem."
—*Romance Junkies*

"[A] version of Beauty and the Beast…that readers will take to their hearts."
—*RT Book Reviews*

"Captivating!"
—*Night Owl Romance*

"A sweet and sexy romance."
—*Dear Author*

MORE…

Heiress in Love

"Each scene is more sensual and passionate than the last." —*Publishers Weekly* (starred review)

"Riveting tale of life, loss, convenience, and heart-wrenching love! Superbly written!" —*Fresh Fiction*

"With this delightful debut Brooke demonstrates her ability for creating a charming cast of characters who are the perfect players in the first of the Ministry of Marriage series. Marriage-of-convenience fans will rejoice and take pleasure in this enchanting read."
—*RT Book Reviews*

"Clever, lush, and lovely—an amazing debut!"
—Suzanne Enoch, *New York Times* bestselling author

"A delightful confection of secrets and seduction, *Heiress in Love* will have readers craving more!"
—Tracy Anne Warren

"One of the most compelling heroes I've read in years."
—Anna Campbell

**Also by
Christina Brooke**

Heiress in Love
Mad About the Earl
A Duchess to Remember

The Greatest Lover Ever

CHRISTINA BROOKE

St. Martin's Paperbacks

NOTE: If you purchased this book without a cover you should be aware that this book is stolen property. It was reported as "unsold and destroyed" to the publisher, and neither the author nor the publisher has received any payment for this "stripped book."

This is a work of fiction. All of the characters, organizations, and events portrayed in this novel are either products of the author's imagination or are used fictitiously.

THE GREATEST LOVER EVER

Copyright © 2014 by Christina Brooke.
Excerpt from *The Wickedest Lord Alive* copyright © 2014 by Christina Brooke.

All rights reserved.

For information address St. Martin's Press, 175 Fifth Avenue, New York, NY 10010.

ISBN: 978-1-250-02935-5

Printed in the United States of America

St. Martin's Paperbacks edition / January 2014

St. Martin's Paperbacks are published by St. Martin's Press, 175 Fifth Avenue, New York, NY 10010.

10 9 8 7 6 5 4 3 2 1

*To Karen, for the friendship, laughter,
and apple crumble*

Acknowledgments

I'd like to thank my editor, Monique Patterson, for her passion for great books and her expertise in helping me bring Beckenham's story to life. My gratitude also to Holly Blanck (I'll miss you, Holly!) and Alexandra Sehulster and to everyone at St. Martin's Press who plays a part in publishing the novels I write.

To my fabulous agent, Helen Breitwieser, thank you for believing in me and my writing and for your friendship, advice, and enthusiasm.

To Anna Campbell, Denise Rossetti, and Victoria Steele, I'm so lucky to have you as friends and colleagues. Thank you for always being there for advice, hugs, and the occasional tough love. And to my dear and talented friends on the Romance Bandits blog, your friendship and support are past price.

Many thanks also to Kim and Gil Castillo for your hard work and attention to detail.

To all the people who read my books and write to tell me how much they enjoy the series (and yes, someday I will tell Lady Arden and Montford's story!), thank you for going on this journey with me.

Last but by no means least, to Jamie, Allister, Adrian, Ian, Cheryl, Robin, and George, who have to suffer through deadline madness right along with me, I love you. Thank you for always being there for me.

Prologue

The tendril of hair that nestled in the Earl of Beckenham's palm was a rare and startling color. The more poetic among her admirers called the shade Titian. But to Beckenham, that seemed too polite a term for such flagrant extravagance. The lone ringlet he held was vermilion shot with gold, a bright corkscrew of flame. Which was appropriate, for its owner was something of a firebrand.

A firebrand who had some explaining to do.

His jaw tightened. His hand closed around the ringlet in a fist. Only one woman in London had tresses this particular shade. His betrothed, Miss Georgiana Black.

The library door opened and she walked in. Her beauty punched him in the solar plexus, just as it always did. A blaze of red hair, expertly coiffed, a glitter of sea green eyes, a luminous glow of pearl white skin.

Her coloring was striking, but no more magnificent than her figure. Miss Georgiana Black had the mouth-wateringly sensuous curves any courtesan would give her soul to possess. In a London ballroom, she was as exotic as a bird of paradise among a gaggle of geese.

And she was his.

Yet these days, it seemed he only ever spoke with her to deliver some reprimand or warning. And each time he did, she behaved worse than before. They couldn't go on like this.

"What is it, Marcus? Couldn't it wait?" Her voice was low, husky. It seemed to wrap itself around him and stroke.

In contrast to the vividness of her features, she was dressed in white from head to toe. Crystals on her low-cut bodice caught the light as she moved toward him, glistening in concert with the delicate constellation of diamonds at her throat. In a practiced gesture, she flicked out her fan and waved it gently to and fro.

In the middle of the Duke of Montford's ball, he'd sent for her to join him here in the duke's library. Doubtless, she was impatient to return to the dancing.

"No, I'm afraid this can't wait," he replied. In the morning, he might be stretched out on a patch of frost-bitten grass with a pistol ball between his eyes. "I want to ask you something." Deliberately, he opened his hand, picked the fiery ringlet from his palm, and placed it on the desk between them. "Would you mind telling me how Lord Pearce came by this?"

She stared at it, her hand lifting instinctively to her own coiffure. "But . . . but that's *my* hair. How could he—?" Her fine eyebrows snapped together. "He did not get it from me, that is certain." She looked up at him sharply. "You think *I* bestowed a keepsake on that libertine?"

No. Despite the obvious implications, he hadn't thought it for more than one second.

But he was furious. With himself for reacting to Pearce's taunts. With Georgie for attracting such insults by her reckless behavior.

In a biting tone, he said, "What other explanation can there be?"

She blinked. "I don't know. But there must be another one, because I didn't give it to him."

Her words were flat, matter-of-fact. They rang with truth. Beckenham wished now that he had not let his temper get the better of him with Pearce. A duel might cause talk, and he needed to avoid providing yet more fodder for gossip about Georgie. He also wished to avoid getting his brains blown out, but that was a separate issue.

"Do you think anyone is going to believe that?" he said.

Her chin lifted. "I don't care if anyone else believes it, Marcus. Only that you do. It is no one else's business, after all."

Air hissed through his teeth as he released a breath. He had to remind himself that she was only eighteen. While her self-possession suggested a lady of more mature years, Georgie retained a sort of schoolgirl naivety. She truly could not see the danger she courted by her flirtatious, headstrong ways.

"Well?" she demanded as if she had the right to feel ill-used. "*Do* you believe me?"

"Yes," he said. "I do."

"Then I hope you punched Lord Pearce on the nose for his impertinence," she said. "And if you didn't, I shall."

He had his cousin Lydgate to thank for the fact that he had not succeeded in choking Pearce to death. However, since the dispute would now be settled by a duel, perhaps he ought not to feel so grateful to Lydgate for prying his fingers free of Pearce's throat. Pearce might not be Beckenham's equal in brute strength, but he was a crack shot.

"I've spoken with your papa," Beckenham said. "He agrees with me that it will be best for you to retire to the country for a while." Just until the rumors died down.

"What?" She looked incredulous. "Pearce has

concocted some ridiculous untruth about me, and *I* am banished from Town?"

He hadn't meant to say this, but the words broke from him. "If you behaved with more propriety, Pearce would not even think to make you the target of such insinuations."

"What nonsense." She snapped her fan shut and tossed it onto the desk. "I cannot help it if men are stupid enough to lose their heads over me or make me the object of their crude bets and jokes."

Her mantrap looks made her susceptible to such behavior; he knew that. It was unfair that she needed to be even more careful than other ladies in her circumstances, but it was a reality. And the truth was, she did not behave as she ought. She took every opportunity to thumb her nose at the arbiters of society. Georgie Black was earning a reputation for being *fast,* a term applied to females whose heedless antics were most likely to end in scandal and ruin.

He'd given up trying to make her understand this. Every time he spoke to her on the subject, he merely goaded her to more outrageous exploits.

Which was why he wanted to take her away from London before she embroiled both of them in scandal. He only wished he hadn't agreed to set the wedding date toward the end of the season.

"Your papa will escort you back to Gloucestershire in the morning," he said. "I will follow in a day or two. I have . . . business to attend to here."

Georgie was a perceptive woman and she caught the slight hesitation. She narrowed her eyes at him. "What business?"

He didn't answer. She ought to know better than to question him about a matter of honor. Dueling was illegal and certainly not a subject for female ears.

She jabbed a slender finger at him. "*What* business, Marcus?"

Her eyes, the color of Mediterranean waters, bored into him. Inadvertently, his gaze flicked down to the glinting curl that still lay on Montford's desk, then back to her face.

Georgie turned white. "You will not meet Pearce over this."

He didn't deny it.

Silks rustled as she rushed around the desk to him. "Don't!" She put her hand on his arm, her eyes wide with fear. "Marcus, you must not give him the satisfaction of rising to the bait. Good Lord, you could be killed."

Hot currents shot up his arm, set off by the touch of her hand. He wanted, with a fierce longing, to pull her into his arms for one last kiss.

Instead, he made himself pick up her hand, remove it from his sleeve, and release it. "You would have me act the coward."

"I'd have you act as a man of sense," she flashed. "As the man I know you to be. You have nothing to prove to the likes of Pearce."

He realized Georgie's eyes held the shimmer of tears. He cut his gaze away. "I will have someone send you word of the outcome."

Her voice shook with passion. "I am not going back to Gloucestershire. And I am certainly not going to let you fight Pearce."

He turned on her. "Do you think you can lead me around by the nose the way you do all those other poor saps who fawn over you? You will not move me on this, Georgie. I can't honorably withdraw my challenge. I don't want to."

She flung out a hand. "What good is honor when you are wounded, or . . . or dead?"

"Your faith in me is most heartening," he said dryly.

"Do you think I want you to kill *him* and have to flee the country?"

She grew shrill in her agitation. He struggled to maintain his calm. "Georgie, I won't discuss this further with you. You shouldn't even know about it."

"Marcus, you must listen to me."

She railed at him then, pounding at his chest with her fists. Tears streaked down her alabaster cheeks; her elegant nose turned an unflattering shade of red.

He took it all in stony silence, wished he'd never summoned her here at all.

She clutched at his lapels, raising herself on tiptoe, but the top of her head still only reached his mouth. Between her teeth, she said, "If you don't call off that duel this minute, our engagement is finished. I mean it, Marcus. I'll not countenance this folly on my behalf."

Deep inside, he felt a stabbing pain, as if jagged shards of ice pierced his chest. But he did not give in to blackmail—whether from a scoundrel like Pearce or from the woman he intended to wed.

"So be it," he said stiffly, removing her grasping hands from his coat, letting them drop. "I'll inform your father that you are now his sole responsibility. I'll wish him joy of you, too."

For a moment she stared at him with a shocked expression. As if he'd slapped her. As if he'd been the one to do the jilting.

Color flooded back into her cheeks. In a low, hard tone that trembled only slightly, she said, "If you die, Marcus, I'll never forgive you."

He gave a crack of bitter laughter. "If I die, I'm coming back to haunt *you*, Georgie Black."

Chapter One

Brighton, England, six years later . . .

Beckenham arrived at his cousin Xavier's Brighton villa travel-weary and famished. After the journey from his estate in Gloucestershire, he craved a bath and a meal and a glass of wine—not necessarily in that order.

He abhorred the hard gaiety of Brighton in the summertime. That was when the Ton descended on the seaside town. By its nature as a holiday resort, the society here was looser, less structured than the London season. Such a laissez-faire attitude was anathema to him, dangerous in its unpredictability.

He wouldn't stay longer than he had to. After dealing with his immediate needs, he'd conduct a pressing matter of business with his cousin tonight and leave first thing in the morning.

From the moment his carriage turned into the villa's drive, he knew that would be impossible.

The flambeaux along the avenue illuminated a scene that caused Beckenham's hopes of a quiet evening to die a quick death. A throng of guests in fancy ball dress strolled down the drive, threading through a mass of vehicles and sedan chairs. All of them with the same destination as Beckenham.

Xavier, Marquis of Steyne, was hosting one of his infamous parties, damn him.

Beckenham sat back against the velvet squabs of his traveling chaise, closed his eyes in resigned exasperation. For several seconds, he contemplated ordering his coachman to turn around and drive all the way back to Gloucestershire.

He found little to entertain him at Xavier's parties and much to alarm and disgust. Masquerades thrown by the Marquis of Steyne were everything that was decadent, subversive, outrageous. It amused Xavier to shock people. Particularly his sober cousin Beckenham.

Oh, yes, Beckenham would give odds that this entire show had been laid on for his benefit. Xavier was being difficult because Beckenham had expressed his intention to take a wife and he wanted his cousin's advice.

An odd choice of counsel when Beckenham's former guardian was the Duke of Montford, famed for making brilliant matches for the members of his large extended family, the Westruthers.

The duke had certainly engineered alliances for Jane, Rosamund, and Cecily to everyone's satisfaction. Not only were they advantageous in every material respect, the parties to the matches seemed covered in bliss.

Beckenham was happy for them. But much as he knew it was his duty to wed and create heirs, he did not wish for that kind of marriage. He wanted a countess who would do her duty without fuss, who was prepared to lead her own life without expecting him to dance attendance on her. A wife who would create no dramas. A wife who would leave him in peace.

Strange as it might seem, Xavier was the only one whose advice he desired in the matter of choosing a suitable countess. Beckenham had sworn off society events in London since Georgie ripped his pride to shreds and stomped on it; the one exception had been to attend Cecily's come-out ball. He did not wish to waste time becoming acquainted with this year's crop of debutantes.

Xavier was both an excellent judge of character and the font of an astonishing depth of knowledge about the Ton and its members. And Xavier would not have any agenda. It would not occur to him to try to make a love match for Beckenham as their female relatives would undoubtedly do. Nor would he attempt to thrust him into a politically advantageous alliance without considering his personal contentment, as Montford would.

Xavier might not have any interest in the subject of Beckenham's marriage, and Beckenham didn't expect him to exert himself unduly. He merely desired Xavier's opinion on which five or so ladies might be best suited for the role of Beckenham's countess.

Beckenham had written letter after letter to Xavier on the subject. All his careful missives had been ignored.

The only way to get his cousin to put his mind to the business was to land on his doorstep and refuse to budge until Xavier bent his considerable intellect to the issue.

So Beckenham didn't turn back. When his vehicle's pace slowed to a crawl, he rapped on the roof for his coachman to stop. He alighted from the chaise and strode through the *carnivale* of guests, a black bat cutting through a bright flock of butterflies.

He did not allow any of the revelers to accost him or deflect him from his purpose. He had no time for such ridiculous fripperies. He wondered that Xavier did, with all the wealth and property under his command.

They'd grown up together as wards of the powerful

Duke of Montford, and Beckenham knew the Marquis of Steyne as well as anyone did. But of all the six cousins who had shared their unusual upbringing under Montford's roof, Xavier was the one over whom Beckenham held the least influence. Convincing Xavier to help him would not be easy.

Reaching the circular drive in front of the house, Beckenham weaved his way through the crawling procession of vehicles and guests. Narrowly, he escaped being set alight by some idiot who had appropriated a flaming torch from its sconce. But he sidestepped that disaster only to be splashed by a gaggle of water nymphs cavorting in and around the fountain.

Polite but firm, he resisted their coquettish attempts to pull him in to join them, and removed their grasping hands from his person with a decided shake of his head. Brushing droplets of water from his sleeve, he ascended the villa steps.

As soon as he crossed the threshold, color and sound assaulted his senses. Music and movement, the blaze of candlelight, silks, velvet, feathers and lace, tinkling glasses, shrieks and guffaws. The scent of a hundred warring perfumes, of beeswax and wine and smoke from men's cheroots.

He glanced about him, wishing very much that he was at home in his library by the fire with a glass of brandy by his side and a book in his hand. The night was young and behavior had yet to reach its inevitable extreme—everyone was still fully clothed, for one thing. Except the nymphs, of course. He suspected those were ladies of the night Xavier had hired for the purpose, so they didn't count.

Xavier's redoubtable majordomo—a sober individual who kept his opinions of his master's habits strictly to himself—greeted Beckenham with an almost imperceptible softening of his black eyes.

"Would you care for refreshment, my lord?"

"Perhaps later, Martin." Beckenham stripped off his gloves and dropped them into his hat before handing the collection to the majordomo. "I want to see my cousin before he becomes otherwise occupied."

Even though Xavier had guests, he might be in one of his retiring moods, eschewing the party for the solitude of his library. One never knew. Xavier could be at his most intellectual and ascetic when hosting an orgy.

The majordomo bowed. "You will find Lord Steyne in the drawing room, my lord."

Not in a retiring mood, then. Beckenham reconsidered. "On second thoughts, would you tell his lordship I'm waiting for him in the library and send some bread and cheese there and a bottle of wine?"

Beckenham preferred not to join the festivities, particularly in Xavier's company. If Xavier was in one of his difficult tempers—and when was he not?—he would be sure to go out of his way to embarrass his sober cousin. He'd invite Beckenham to eat a grape from a naked lady's navel or foist on him some elegant whore whom he'd feel obliged to entertain for the evening so as not to hurt her feelings.

Xavier could be quite diabolically irritating in that way.

It wasn't that Beckenham had no interest in the fair sex. He was a man of strong sexual appetites—and rare skill, if his mistresses were to be believed. Quite how he'd gained the reputation of being an extraordinarily accomplished lover, he didn't know. Perhaps his lovers had been indiscreet. He preferred, however, to bed women of his own choosing, and to do so in private.

With an understanding gleam in his eye, the major-domo bowed again. "Very good, my lord. I shall inquire."

Georgiana Black wondered, not for the first time, how she came to be saddled with such an arrant fool for a stepmother. Papa must have been thinking with the contents of his trousers when he'd wed the woman.

Lady Black was very pretty once, but a life of indolence and spite had thickened the widow's figure and pinched her milkmaid looks. She'd never produced the longed-for male heir, but she had given Sir Donald one more daughter, Violet, who was now seventeen.

Papa had died a little over a year ago, leaving his vast fortune divided equally between his two daughters. Giving in to his wife's urgings, tantrums, and vapors, he'd altered his will, bequeathing his unentailed property in Gloucestershire to Violet alone. A fitting punishment for Georgie, who'd possessed the unmitigated temerity to jilt the Earl of Beckenham and refused every eligible marriage offer since.

The loss of Cloverleigh Manor had been a knife to Georgie's heart on top of the grief attending her father's death. But at least she wouldn't be obliged to live virtually next door to her erstwhile fiancé. She must be grateful for that.

Papa hadn't disinherited her. Indeed, he'd been scrupulously fair in the division of his fortune. A large sum invested in the funds would be Georgie's on her twenty-fifth birthday. Or upon her marriage, whichever came sooner.

While she itched to leave the cloying, vulgar ways of her stepmother behind her, she was inordinately fond of her half sister. She was determined Violet should not suffer through Lady Black's folly. Georgie's twenty-fifth birthday was mere months away, but she meant to delay setting up her own household long enough to see her sister settled and happy.

"Violet is but eighteen, ma'am," said Georgie now, with careful restraint. "You *cannot* have consented to her jaunting about Brighton with those dreadful Makepeaces. Please tell me you did not."

Lady Black stiffened, her hand splayed on the chaise longue as if she'd spring up from her supine position. "Those *dreadful Makepeaces,* as you call them, happen to be dear friends of mine, miss! Yes, and if it weren't for my poor nerves which have held me prostrate on this couch for weeks, I should have gone with them myself. I could do with a bit of gaiety."

Georgie did not doubt her stepmother would have gone if she'd felt equal to the outing. Brighton was England's most fashionable summer resort. The tone of the seaside town was looser, more egalitarian, and certainly more raffish than the rarefied atmosphere of Mayfair. It was the perfect milieu for a wealthy widow who was none too particular about the company she kept.

One thing was certain: Brighton was not a place for a young lady with no one more sensible to guide her than Mrs. Makepeace and her rackety young brother-in-law. Particularly when that young lady was an heiress.

Georgie couldn't believe her stepmother would show such little sense. "Please, ma'am, you must fetch Violet back again. Do you have any idea what trouble the silly girl will find for herself here in Brighton?"

Lady Black's face pinked. "Violet is *my* daughter, and I'll thank you to remember it! She's had no amusement at all since her dear papa died, poor pet."

"Mourning does tend to hamper one's social life," muttered Georgie. She tried again. "Violet is not even out yet."

"All the more reason for her to attend a couple of parties before she makes her debut."

Georgie paced the floor, gripping her hands together. "If it were a case of a few private parties in Bath under appropriate chaperonage, I'd agree with you. But Brighton, ma'am! She'll be ruined before she ever gets to London."

Why couldn't her stepmother see this? Or was it simply because Georgie was the one to point it out that she remained steadfastly blind?

"Violet has a shrewd head on her shoulders," said Lady Black. "She won't do anything she oughtn't."

With careful tact, Georgie said, "Of course not, ma'am. I am more concerned that she will fall prey to someone unscrupulous. She is an heiress, after all."

Her stepmother's eyes narrowed. "Well! If I may be so bold, *you* are scarcely one to cast stones, my dear girl!"

Georgie stiffened.

"Don't think just because you've turned into Miss Prunes and Prisms now that anyone forgets what happened when you were that age. Threw over an *earl,* for Heaven's sake. And look at you now. Four-and-twenty and still a spinster."

"At least I still have my reputation, ma'am," Georgie said quietly.

"By the skin of your teeth!"

"If it becomes known that Violet went to Lord Steyne's masquerade tonight, you may be sure she'll need more than the skin of her teeth to save her," snapped Georgie.

Her stepmother's accusations stung a wound that was still raw. But whatever mistakes Georgie had made in her ignorant, impulsive youth, she'd paid the price. The Earl of Beckenham would never be hers.

She couldn't dwell on that now. She had Violet to

think of. Meanwhile, Lady Black fingered her lace hand-kerchief in a manner that threatened hysterics or palpita-tions or both.

Trying to head off the anticipated tantrum at the pass, Georgie knelt next to the lady. She hesitated, then made herself press her stepmother's hand. "*Please,* ma'am. No good can come of this."

For a scant instant, she thought Lady Black might relent. Then her entire body shuddered, racked by an enormous sob. She buried her face in the scrap of lace she held.

"I told you, my nerves won't stand it," she wailed. "You are heartless indeed, expecting me to drag myself from my sickbed to go on a fool's errand."

Georgie rose to her feet. "If you do not intend to go, I will."

Her stepmother threw up her hands. "Go, then! I'm sure I'm not stopping you."

"Thank you, ma'am," said Georgie, dropping a curtsy. "I'll do my best to bring her home safely."

As she turned to leave, her stepmother called after her, "Just make sure it's only Violet that needs rescu-ing, my girl. Fools rush in where angels fear to tread."

Georgie raised one eyebrow. "And you would be the angel in that aphorism, I suppose?"

Before her stepmother could fully grasp the irony, Georgie murmured, "Excuse me, ma'am. I must dress."

Georgie could only be glad that her mask hid her scar-let face. She had run with a fast set of young people during the season that her betrothal to the Earl of Beck-enham had ended so spectacularly. But even in those reckless days she'd never attended a party like this.

She knew all about the Westruthers, thanks to her

long association with Beckenham. The host of this evening's affair, Xavier Westruther, Marquis of Steyne, was a notorious member of that family. By reputation, he was a shocking libertine, steeped in dissipation. What she knew of him personally, she did not like.

Her opinion of the marquis was not improved when she slipped into his house uninvited that night.

She'd been forced to mock up a costume from the limited wardrobe she'd brought to Brighton. Absent a mask, she'd managed to fashion one by cutting eyeholes into a black lace scarf. The beauty of the scarf was that it covered her entire face, completely obscuring her features.

Her thick, flame red hair was more difficult to disguise, but by dressing it in the style of a generation earlier and dredging it with powder, she'd managed to conceal its exuberance.

She wore her new jade green evening gown because no one would have seen her in it before. With a pang, she realized she could never wear it again after tonight.

Drat that girl! But of course, what did clothes matter when it came to saving Violet's reputation? Violet was clever and good-natured, but her mama's example had given her a somewhat skewed perspective on proper behavior. Heaven only knew what she'd get up to at the Makepeaces' instigation.

Once inside Lord Steyne's villa, Georgie realized how utterly daunting a task she'd undertaken. This was no ordinary ball, where the guests were largely confined to a ballroom and refreshment parlor, perhaps a card room, too.

It seemed as if the entire population of Brighton had overtaken every room in the house and the grounds besides. How would she ever find Violet here?

As she moved upstairs to the second floor in search of her half sister, Georgie suffered several lewd propositions from men who lounged against the wall, accosting passersby. Masculine hands strayed over her person in shocking familiarity.

Georgie was wholly unaccustomed to such treatment. Her frigid stares and icy disdain did not succeed as well as they might in a London ballroom. Stripped of her identity, to these men she was just one more tasty morsel in a banquet of loose-moraled loveliness.

As the rowdy voices grew more boisterous and the attempts to halt her progress more determined, she picked up her skirts and fled down the corridor. Her tormentors, scenting sport, pelted after her with a shout that more properly belonged on the hunting field.

Panic gripped her. What would they do to her when they caught her? Oh, dear Heaven, what madness had brought her here? Where was Violet in all of this? At least Violet had the dubious protection of Mrs. Makepeace and her horrible brother-in-law. Georgie, hoping to get in and out of this party with Violet's and her own reputation intact, had brought no one.

Throwing a glance over her shoulder at the gaining pursuers, Georgie cannoned into a man who had just entered the corridor from a doorway. Aware of a tall figure with a very hard chest, she pressed her palms against him to push away.

It was her host, the Marquis of Steyne.

"Oh, thank goodness," she murmured between pants.

Unlike his guests, the marquis had not donned a costume for this affair, eschewing flamboyant finery for plain evening dress in black and blinding white. A sapphire pin nestling in his cravat glittered as he moved, but the gem was no more intense than his blue, blue eyes. His black hair hung a little long over his brow, but that was the only soft thing about him. The slashing eyebrows, the angular bones of his face, and the strong jaw, not to mention the hard glitter of those pitiless eyes, signaled that he was not a man to cross.

The marquis regarded the men who followed her. One infinitesimal lift of his slashing black eyebrows was enough to bring them skidding to a halt. The merest inclination of his dark head sent them backtracking hurriedly with stuttered apologies.

Recollecting herself, Georgie realized she might well have jumped from the frying pan into the fire. Steyne might have saved her from physical harm, but if anyone at this party was likely to discover her identity, it was he.

With a deep curtsy, she murmured thanks to her savior and made as if to return downstairs.

But his hand on her wrist stayed her. Effortlessly, he drew her back to face him, used finger and thumb to capture her chin and tilt her face to the light.

"Good God, what have we here?" the marquis murmured, lips curling in that cynical, unpleasant smile of his. "A diamond amongst the rough."

Without a by-your-leave, he drew her arm through his in one languid move and began to lead her farther down the corridor. She tried to pull away from him, but his seemingly negligent grip beneath her elbow was too firm.

He turned his head sharply to her, as if scenting a secret on the wind. "I know you, don't I?"

Georgie tensed beneath the guiding pressure of his hand. "I don't think so, my lord."

Of all the bad luck! Xavier, Marquis of Steyne, was not only the one person clever enough to penetrate her disguise but the one person ruthless enough to make use of it in some devilishly unpleasant manner.

Before she could decide how to get away from him without making herself more intriguing, the marquis had drawn her out of the corridor, into an empty bed-chamber.

Georgie cast an apprehensive glance at the opulent bed with its canopy festooned in crimson swags of silk brocade. Were it anyone else but Lord Steyne, she'd kick him in the shin and run. She'd worn sturdy shoes for that very purpose.

But his words suggested he might already have guessed who she was. If she ran now and Steyne spoke of her presence here to anyone . . . That didn't bear thinking about. She needed to throw him off the scent.

Adopting her stepmother's mode of speech with a slightly higher pitch than her usual tone, she said, "Oh, la! Fancy your lordship saying as he knows the likes of me."

"Faces often elude me," he mused as if she hadn't spoken, "but when a woman with a figure like yours crosses my path, I don't forget."

His gaze bored into her, as if he might penetrate her mask by the sheer force of his will. Such was the power of his personality, she almost believed he'd succeed.

She thought he might try to remove her disguise by more prosaic methods, but he stepped back the better to scrutinize her body, in the way that one might view a life-sized painting at an art gallery. He did it with a kind of focused attention that made her flush hotly. She could not help suspecting he stripped her naked in his mind.

Georgie dearly wished she could box his ears. Instead, she must play the part of a female who liked being surveyed in such an insolent manner. Why else would a woman come to this place if not to be ogled and groped? Ugh!

With his raven-black hair and vivid blue eyes, Steyne was ridiculously handsome, but she'd always found his style of male beauty cold and unappealing.

Unfortunately, he appeared to like what he saw in her, for he smiled. "I can't place you, it's true." He tapped one finger to his lips. "I don't think I've had you before."

Casually, he moved to the door. Looking back at her, he added, "Which will make this all the more interesting, won't it? And here I'd thought to be thoroughly bored tonight."

He turned the key in the lock, drew the key out, and pocketed it.

Alarm rang through Georgie's body. She did her best to tamp it down but her voice shook. "I'm not here for the, er, entertainment. I'm looking for someone."

Again the flashing smile that did not reach his eyes. He bowed. "Well, my lovely, you've just found him."

As Steyne reached out to her, she backed away. There was a steely glint in his eye that told her he would not give up on this seduction easily. Lord, why didn't she run away when she'd had the chance? She'd always felt safe around Steyne because she'd known Marcus would protect her.

Now, she could not claim such shelter. She realized Steyne's pursuit had maneuvered her toward the bed when she nearly stumbled over the dais on which the bed stood.

Scrambling to get her footing, she fetched up against the mattress. Before she could regain her balance, he put out his hands on either side of her, trapping her between him and the bed.

Her heart raced as she stared into his face. Even through her panic, she saw that his expression did not convey passion or even desire, but merely cool intent.

Did he mean to rape her? Good God, surely not. That was a line no gentleman would cross. She'd scream her head off if it came to that, reputation or no. But for now, if she could just turn him away without fuss, that would be the better solution.

Steyne reached into her coiffure to finger her powdered curls. "What color is your hair, my glorious girl?"

If he discovered that, the game would be up.

Desperate, she said the one thing that might halt this rake's progress. "No, you must not, my lord. I . . . it was Lord Beckenham I sought in your rooms tonight. I'm—" She swallowed hard. "I'm under his protection, you see."

She knew Beckenham wouldn't be here, but she could still say she looked for him, couldn't she? That she'd thought he might attend a party given by his cousin. Never mind that he loathed Brighton and never set foot in the place.

That stopped the marquis in his tracks. His black eyebrows drew together. "Under *Beckenham's* protection, you say?" He cocked his head. "How extraordinary."

He stared at her hard, then pushed away from the bed, watching her through narrowed eyes as he retreated.

She'd taken a huge risk implying she was Beckenham's mistress, but if it made Steyne let her go, it would be worth it.

Suddenly, his mouth curled into the first genuine smile he'd given her. "Well, well. The sly dog," he said, laughing softly.

With a courtly bow, Steyne said, "My compliments

and my apologies, Miss, er . . . It seems I have been importunate."

She simply stared at him, disconcerted at his abrupt change of front, unable to believe it had been so easy to arrest his advances. She couldn't detect from his demeanor whether he'd recognized her. She thought not. She *hoped* not.

Georgie rose and shook out her skirts. "Then if you've finished importuning me—"

Steyne held out both hands, palms toward her. "Oh, no, my dear," he said in that soft, hateful voice, "I'm not done with you yet."

With an ironic bow, he left the bedchamber, shutting the door behind him.

The room seemed to reverberate in time with her heartbeat. Georgie collected her wits, and hurried for the door.

On the other side of the oak panels, the key turned in the lock with a loud click.

Georgie rattled the doorknob, knowing it would be hopeless. What in Heaven's name was the wretched man up to now? A quick glance around showed no other possible means of escape. She had better search the room for weapons.

She discovered nothing of practical use in the sparsely furnished chamber—not even a fire iron with which to brain her host should he try to ravish her.

The minutes dragged by; she realized how foolish it had been to suppose she could rescue her sister from this kind of peril. Ten to one, Violet enjoyed the festivities, happy as a lark, watched over by her companions. While Georgie was imprisoned in a boudoir by a lecherous marquis with a grossly overblown opinion of his charms.

Fools rush in, indeed. Hadn't Marcus always complained of her impetuousness? It seemed she still hadn't learned her lesson.

The key turning in the lock made her stiffen, her heart bounding into her throat.

Georgie moved as far from the bed as she could manage. Not that it would make any difference to Steyne, but it made her feel better. She snatched up the Chinese vase from the mantel, tested its weight. Too delicate to do any damage and probably priceless into the bargain. She set it down again.

But the tall, dark-haired figure who entered was not Lord Steyne.

It was his cousin, her former fiancé. Marcus Westruther, Earl of Beckenham.

He stood there for what seemed an age, silhouetted against the doorway. She couldn't see his features clearly in the shadows but she didn't have to. They were as sharp and clear in her mind's eye as they had ever been in the flesh.

The shock of seeing him again suspended her faculties. Her lips parted but no sound came out.

Emotion flooded her chest, a swirling mass of reactions that could not be separated into constituent parts. The strength and tumult of her feelings made her lightheaded.

What could she say to him? She'd avoided a meeting between them for years, and now, to see him in such fantastical circumstances . . . Could anything be more disastrous? She dreaded to imagine what he'd think if he discovered her identity.

Ought she simply tell him the real reason she was here?

Could she trust him? Instinct told her yes. He was the most solidly dependable person she'd ever known.

But why on earth should he help her, even if she told

him her troubles? He'd washed his hands of her years ago.

She'd rejected him as a husband, dealt a severe blow to his pride, made them both the talk of the Ton. As far as Beckenham was concerned, there could not be a more unforgivable crime than that. He was a man who prized honor and loyalty above all other qualities.

So she waited in the silence. She would follow his lead.

Her awareness of him was so heightened that the slight tilt of his head as he studied her made her heart zing about her chest like a firework. She heard nothing but her own breathing. The unruly hitch in it seemed to echo in the silence.

He moved into the room, then closed the door. "I hear you've been looking for me."

His deep voice resonated through her body, stirring the embers of a fire that had long lain dormant. *Yes, but never in my wildest dreams did I think you'd be here.*

She didn't answer. Oh, God, it was awful and humiliating and . . . and *wonderful* to see him. She hadn't laid eyes on him since that dreadful night when she released him from the engagement. Almost by tacit agreement, she lived in Town while he'd largely kept to his estate. She'd heard he attended Lady Cecily Westruther's come-out ball in London last season, but of course she hadn't been invited to that auspicious event. Most pointedly not invited.

And now here he was, with her. In a quiet bedchamber in the midst of a raucous, licentious party. But it didn't feel as if they stood in any kind of oasis here. It felt like the eye of a storm.

Her mouth dried as he reached up a hand to loosen his cravat, flick it open, and pull the long strip of linen from around his throat. Then he walked over to the washstand, where a pitcher of water and a basin stood as if ready for guests.

"Take your clothes off," he said to her over his shoulder. "I'll be with you in a moment."

Chapter Two

The room spun. Georgie put out a hand to steady herself against the mantel. She could not have heard correctly. Surely, she could not.

But she didn't ask him to repeat his words, because she knew very well her ears hadn't deceived her. He'd just told her, bluntly, to undress. Because he thought that they . . . that she . . . Georgie's face flushed with scalding heat.

After Steyne's advances, she ought not to be so shocked. But this was *Beckenham*. Beckenham, who had never once gone beyond the line with her, even when they were safely betrothed.

She'd heard whispers about him over the years, stories rarely told to maiden ladies of Lord Beckenham's reputed prowess in the bedchamber.

Affront at his high-handed manner warred with burning curiosity. Temptation spiked within her. Tonight, she might discover whether the rumors were true.

Heedless of her reaction to the peremptory command, the earl stripped off his superfine coat and tossed it carelessly onto a chair.

Such a casual gesture. As if for him this encounter were the most mundane of occurrences.

A disorienting sensation came over her, as if the world swung upside down on its axis. Could it be true that Beckenham did this sort of thing all the time? He didn't have the reputation of a rake. Indeed, she'd never suspected Beckenham capable of taking sin in his stride.

He continued to undress. Those large fingers unfobbed his watch and set it on the washstand, then went to work on the buttons of his waistcoat. She quickly shut her eyes. But listening to him remove his clothes was almost as tantalizing as watching him.

Silk slid against cambric. A hush of cloth and a soft clack of buttons as the waistcoat joined his coat . . .

She opened her eyes again, hussy that she was, helpless to stop herself. She saw that he had indeed shed his waistcoat and was deftly undoing the ruffled cuffs at his wrists. He pushed his shirtsleeves up strong forearms before plunging his hands into the basin of water.

The intimacy of standing here in a bedchamber with the Earl of Beckenham as he performed his ablutions made Georgie ache for what might have been. If only she hadn't been so rash, so stupid. If only he'd loved her. If only he'd understood.

She knew a corrosive, blinding hatred for those women who had enjoyed him.

He belonged to her. He always had.

He splashed his face—once, twice, and dried it with a towel. Then he pulled his billowing shirt over his head in one deft movement. She ought to look away, but she couldn't. She was too awestruck by the solid, beautiful strength of his back and shoulders as he vigorously rubbed at his torso with a wet flannel.

Things were moving too fast for her reason to catch up. Dimly, she knew she ought to leave, and do it now, before this went any further. But threading through such self-preserving logic was a dark thrill of excitement. And a deep, powerful longing that had been inside her, suppressed, unacknowledged, ever since they'd met.

Georgie remembered—oh, how *well* she remembered—the firm, smooth texture of Beckenham's lips against hers. He'd set her alight until her entire body was incandescent with longing for him. She'd burned to make him lose that awe-inspiring control. Yet, throughout their courtship, his kisses had been gentle, unthreatening. The air of danger that clung to him tonight was foreign to her.

Perhaps he reserved his true passion for females of quite a different sort?

The thought stiffened her spine.

Instead of explaining herself, or even making a hasty exit, she drawled, "My lord, such stories of your expertise abound. Yet, I find that tonight, you lack finesse."

For a fraction of time, he froze. Then he laid the flannel down. Slowly, he turned. The gleam of candlelight slid along his bare skin.

His dark eyes glinted. "Is it finesse you want, sweetheart? I thought you were here for something quite different."

She scarcely heard him. She couldn't speak. What lady wouldn't lose her self-possession when faced with a shirtless Lord Beckenham?

She noticed everything about him. The breadth of that imposing chest with its sprinkling of dark hair, its flat brown nipples. The muscles in his arms, the taut, hard stomach.

And he was wet. She didn't know why that made a difference, but it did.

She dragged her attention to his face. Beckenham had a nose that on another man would seem large. On him, it resided in easy proportion among the rest of his strong features. Brown eyes that could warm to chocolate, but now glittered like jet. He had dark hair and a long face with two deep furrows bracketing his mouth. His jaw tensed as the silence stretched between them.

Another thought occurred to her. Obviously, he hadn't expected her to be here. He hadn't recognized her thus far. Who, exactly, did he think she was? Or didn't he care?

Her throat constricted. She didn't want to think of him with someone else. Even now, the notion sliced through her like a blade.

"Madam?" he prompted, moving toward her. "Do you tell me I am wrong?"

She couldn't find it in her to reply. And he wasn't wrong, she realized. That was the Devil of it. She so badly wanted him to kiss her, her lips throbbed with the need. She wanted—oh, all sorts of things. Things she didn't even know how to express.

Most of all, though, she wanted to teach Lord Beckenham a lesson—with what justification she did not know. She had wronged *him,* not the other way around.

She played with fire, no doubt about it. No matter how much she'd teased and flirted in the days of their courtship, he'd never lost his temper, nor his iron control. He had always been stern, even forbidding, but he'd never made her feel unsafe.

Tonight there was an edge—a sexual edge—to him that seemed alien to his character. Or at least, to what she thought she knew of his character.

How well had she known the Earl of Beckenham, after all?

Perhaps all the whispers behind fluttering fans were justified. That in the bedchamber, Lord Beckenham had no equal.

Inwardly, she shivered. Could the gossip be true?

Georgie did not feel safe, standing here alone in a dimly lit room with the Earl of Beckenham.

But she could not walk away.

When Xavier told him an unknown woman in this house had claimed his protection, Beckenham hadn't believed it for a moment. Another of Xavier's stupid games. He'd snatched the key his cousin dangled from his fingers and charged off to release the female from her temporary prison.

He hadn't bargained on Georgie.

The instant he saw her, he'd known. The knowledge had fallen on him like an avalanche, held him frozen in the doorway, gaping like a fool.

What the hell was she doing here? Was she part of an elaborate plot of Xavier's devising?

And why had she claimed Beckenham's protection tonight—if indeed she had done so? His whole body tensed. If Xavier had forced his attentions on her, Beckenham would tear him limb from limb. . . .

But no. Georgie did not seem to have suffered at Xavier's hands, or anyone else's. She was composed, even if her beautiful breasts rose and fell a little too rapidly. That reaction was not surprising, given her predicament.

Still the same Georgie, even in disguise. The lace mask covered all of her face except the glitter of her eyes. Even her wide, sinful mouth was obscured, the scallops of her lace mask edging around that determined chin.

She'd powdered her hair—a crime against nature, but understandable in the circumstances. No lady would wish it to be known she was here tonight. Particularly an unmarried one. That scorching hair would have identified her immediately.

What a foolish risk she'd taken, attending this bacchanal. He ought to persuade her to leave, escort her to her lodgings. But his gentlemanly instincts didn't stand a chance. They were like a child's toy sailboat against a raging ocean of anger and bitterness and frustration and desire.

His gaze lowered. That lush, rounded body still gave him sleepless nights.

Something about the way she stood there, so mysterious and alluring and . . . and *confident,* damn her, made him furious. In this house, at this party. *God.* It made him want to tear the world apart.

Through all that farce of an engagement and its aftermath, he'd clung to his original vision of the girl he'd known all her life. Her presence here tonight turned that vision on its head.

As he watched her, she put up a hand to touch the soft skin behind her ear. It was a gesture so typical of the old Georgie that his rage and desire flared until they forged a steely purpose.

Clearly, Miss Georgiana Black was here at this scandalous gathering because she wanted a man to seduce her.

Let that man be him.

He gave no indication that he knew her. If she wished to behave like an aristocratic harlot, let her discover how harlots were treated by the fine gentlemen who frequented parties like this. With deliberate crudeness, he told her to undress.

Say something, damn you!

He waited for her to put him in his place and stalk from the room. She knew who he was, even if she thought her own identity secret.

She said nothing. From offense? Shock? What? Her silence drove him mad.

He bought himself time by washing, but his hands shook and his body hardened like an adolescent's on his first encounter. Now he'd set foot on this path, he could barely breathe for wanting her.

And then she spoke. *You lack finesse.*

She indicated her wish for a polite seduction. He didn't feel polite. But he was intelligent enough to realize she hadn't said no to the seduction part, just to the manner of it.

So she'd heard about his reputed skill as a lover, had she? Some primal part of him relished the idea. He was on his mettle now, even as he knew this encounter would not be at all like those others. Those women were as pale and insubstantial as ghosts when compared with the vibrancy of Georgie Black.

Water cooled his bare skin, but inside him the flames licked higher. His mouth dried as he walked toward her. So many fantasies. So many times during their courtship he'd held himself in check because she was a virgin and he was an honorable man. They'd be married soon and then he could have her every night if he wanted. And every morning, noon, and afternoon, too.

Those dreams had been shattered when she broke their engagement.

But *tonight* . . .

Oh, yes, he thought grimly. Tonight, he'd make every one of them come true.

"You haven't undressed," he said in a graveled voice. "Shall I do it for you?"

Georgie's mind whirled as her pulse beat hard and fast. Things were moving too quickly for her. If she didn't stop him soon, it would be too late.

She shook her head. "No, I—"

"But first, a kiss." Slowly, he reached out and slid a fingertip between the edge of her lace mask and the line of her jaw.

"Don't," she cried. Her hands flew up; she gripped his bare wrist to stop him revealing her face. If he discovered who she was, she couldn't imagine what he'd do.

Would he be furious, scornful? Perhaps he wouldn't be at all surprised. She didn't know which reaction would be worst.

But she couldn't risk it. Couldn't risk him seeing her and walking away.

"Such vehemence." Beckenham's head angled slightly as he studied her. Then he brought up his other hand. His fingertips traced her jawline; his thumb stroked beneath her chin. "I won't take it off. I'll simply . . ."

Gently, he peeled the lace upward, exposing only her mouth. "There."

Cool air washed over her parted lips. She swallowed hard, released her grip on his wrist.

He slid his fingers into her powdered hair, cradled her head in his palms. A shiver ran down her spine.

He bent toward her until his words feathered over her lips, warming them. "The unknown is always more exciting, don't you agree?"

Before she could reply, he took her mouth, commanded it as no man had ever done before.

Her heart seemed to swoop down to her toes, then zing back up to start a frantic beat in her chest. This was no polite expression of affection but a carnal act of possession. She felt the warm, wet slide of his tongue, the thrust of it into her mouth. She gasped, but a rush of excitement swept her shock away.

Almost without her volition, her hand slid up to caress his nape, urging him closer still. His body was damp. He tasted of wine and smelled of the soap he'd used—a faint citrus scent she knew would remind her of him for the rest of her life.

With a groan, he lashed one arm around her waist and pulled her against him.

He kissed her deeply, hard, long.

His palm skimmed up her side; then his hand closed, firm and possessive, over her breast.

Georgie gave a soft, helpless moan. She ought to stop him but the feel of his hands on her was so sublime, she wanted it to go on forever. He tugged at her bodice, pressed kisses to the swells of her breasts, bit them gently, made her dissolve in his arms, whisper an incoherent plea.

Her desire for him was dangerous, mindless, visceral. She knew she needed to stop his emotionless assault before he went too far, but her rebellious body demanded more.

This was her one chance to be with him. The notion pounded through her, crowding out logic and caution.

Marcus knew more of her body's secrets than she knew herself. Every touch was sublime torture. With each caress her need for him became greater, until it all but consumed her. She could never get enough of this, not if they stayed here in this chamber together until the end of time.

He was everything she'd ever wanted. Everything she'd dreamed. She fell into his kiss, into his heat and hunger. When he slowed his pace, she cried out in protest. God forbid she'd have time to think about the wisdom of this encounter, about consequences.

Her gown loosened, then whooshed to the floor. He turned her, kissed her nape with exquisite attention as his hands reached around her to cup and fondle her breasts. Tiny thrills skidded through her. When he grazed her sensitive skin with his teeth, she bit back a cry.

His lips drifted over her shoulder, his hands rubbing her nipples through corset and chemise.

Her legs seemed to melt in the hot, heavy night. She couldn't stop the pleasured moan that escaped her. Georgie leaned back against him, relishing the feel of his thumbs flicking, circling, rubbing her.

She didn't want to feel this deeply. Even as he made her body sing beneath his hands and lips and tongue, her heart ached. There would be no more of this after tonight. No more of him for her, ever.

The hardness of his erection pressed against the small of her back. His breathing was harsh and hot in her ear as he continued to play with her breasts. There were no whispered endearments, no murmurs of encouragement. She supposed he didn't waste words on the women he took so casually to his bed.

Suddenly, the man undressing her, seducing her without love or tenderness or any sentiment at all, seemed a stranger. And she was a stranger to him tonight. He did not know he did all this to his former betrothed, to Georgie Black.

She turned in his arms but before she could speak, he took her mouth again, wildly, and whatever she'd meant to say flew from her consciousness. He slid his lips down her throat, bit down, setting off explosions of pleasure that radiated through her body. She threw her head back and cried out his name, her fingers digging into his shoulders.

He froze. Then he muttered an oath into her shoulder.

Confusion scattered over her. "What is it?" she whispered. "What's wrong?"

"Damn it to hell, it's no use." The suppressed violence

in his tone shocked her more than the fervor of his lovemaking.

Beckenham swung away from her, raking both hands through his hair. She thought he might speak, but he shook his head, snatched up his clothes, and strode to the door.

He was leaving her. After all this, he simply walked away.

Grief at losing him once more plunged through her. Before she could stop herself, she called after him, "My lord!"

He halted, looked back.

Her voice came out as no more than a whisper. "Don't go."

She stood there, half-naked before him, more vulnerable than she'd ever felt before. Begging him to stay.

He stared at her in silence; then his fingers gripped the doorknob. "Get dressed and leave this place," he said tightly. "You don't belong here."

Oh, Marcus, she thought.

The door closed quietly behind him.

Chapter Three

Beckenham had actually stridden several paces down the corridor before he recalled he hadn't even put on his shirt in his haste to get away from her.

With a biting oath, he ducked into the next bedchamber he came across. The room lay in darkness, its heavy brocade curtains drawn. He groped for a chair on which to throw his belongings, then began to dress.

Marcus, she'd said. She was the only one who'd ever called him that. Even his cousins, as dear to him as brothers and sisters, had always referred to him by his title.

Marcus. How completely she'd undone his furious resolve with that one small word.

The mere recollection of the husky timbre of her voice as she'd said it abraded all his nerve endings, sent a hot spear of lust through his vitals.

He pushed his shirttails into his trousers, trying to ignore the powerful erection that strained to break free. He wanted her fiercely. That had never changed—would never change, he suspected. He'd been right to avoid London society, avoid *her* all these years.

He was not a man given to melodrama; he'd often cursed his own weakness and folly for never attempting to be in the same ballroom as the woman who'd rejected him. Now he knew such extreme caution had not been in vain. He couldn't be in the same county as Georgiana Black and resist her siren's lure.

But no matter the strength of his attraction to her, he'd never, not once betrayed his own notions of gentlemanly behavior while they were betrothed. The shock of seeing her tonight in such an unlikely and suggestive setting had unbalanced him, sublimated his desire and transformed it to fury. Fury had brought a sense that he was somehow entitled to slake his lust upon her.

What he'd done to her tonight was wrong. So wrong, in fact, that he could only be glad she'd kept up the pretense of anonymity. Better she think him a conscienceless rake than the alternative.

Shame twisted inside him like a whiplash. He'd acted like a man possessed. Were he to hear of another man behaving as he had tonight, he'd condemn him without pause.

Beckenham finished buttoning his waistcoat and donned his coat. He had no hope of tying his disheveled cravat, so he didn't make the attempt. At least the bedchamber allotted him was on this floor. He'd reach it without having to go through the more heavily populated public rooms of the house.

And wasn't that just his luck? When he arrived in his bedchamber, he found his cousin awaiting him. An orgy raged on downstairs, but Xavier eschewed it so he could meddle in Beckenham's affairs.

He bit out an ugly curse. His own ramshackle appearance made it all too clear what had transpired in that quiet, airless bedchamber mere corridors away.

"Back so soon?" Xavier regarded him with evil delight glinting from those sapphirine depths. "Ought my commiserations be offered to you or to the lady?"

He sent his cousin a fulminating glare.

Xavier smiled wolfishly. "Dear me. Your reputation as the greatest lover ever seems to have suffered a beating tonight."

"Go to hell."

Damn it, but Xavier was enjoying this. Giving him neither answer nor explanation, Beckenham crossed the room and poured himself a drink with an unsteady hand. The brandy caught fire in his throat, warmed his belly. His skin still burned in the aftermath of that lascivious kiss.

One glance in the glass above the fireplace told him he looked as disheveled and bedeviled as he felt. A dark flush burned across his cheekbones. His hair was wild where she'd plunged her fingers through it; his shirt was open, his cravat hanging limp and bedraggled around his neck.

The ache in his groin was beginning to subside, thank God.

Beckenham drained the glass and poured himself another.

"Do you know who that was?" he asked gruffly, not looking at Xavier.

There was a long pause. So long that Beckenham turned to see if he could read his cousin's thoughts on his face.

If Xavier knew he had just been with Georgiana Black . . . His mind blanked at the thought. If anyone knew or even suspected what they'd done in that stuffy bedchamber, she would be thoroughly ruined.

And he . . .

He would have to marry the one woman he'd never wanted to see again.

The dark blue eyes gazed into his for several seconds. It occurred to Beckenham that Xavier scrutinized him keenly, as if searching for an answer in his face.

Finally, Xavier said, "No. I do not know who that was."

Relief washed over Beckenham like a ten-foot wave. A current of something else eddied at the edges. Something he did not want to identify.

He struggled to keep his tone even. "You said the lady asked for me. What, precisely, did she say?"

There was another hesitation. His gaze shot to Xavier, who gave a slight shrug of his shoulders. "She said she was under your protection."

"Singular phrasing. What made her say it?" He frowned. "Did you manhandle her?"

"How delightfully you express it. At least give me credit for ceasing my attentions the instant your name came up. I never poach on my dear cousins' preserves."

The burning need to beat his cousin to a bloody pulp seized him. It took Beckenham several deep breaths and another hit of brandy to restrain that animal impulse. Georgie had evinced no sign of distress, nor any sign that she'd been assaulted. He ought to let Xavier's behavior pass.

He ground out, "In future, I'll thank you to stay out of my affairs."

"The lady attempted to entrap you, I gather," said Xavier. His tone was dry. "Might as well try to compromise a saint."

"I wonder you lent your hand to it if you thought her purpose was to entangle me," said Beckenham harshly, with a good deal of censure.

Damn, he sounded like a prig. And a hypocrite, to boot. If he was so deuced moral, why hadn't he turned and left as soon as he'd set eyes on her? Or better yet, exposed her masquerade, read her a lecture on the dangers of a gently bred female appearing at such a bacchanal, and escorted her home?

Self-disgust added its might to the maelstrom of emotions swirling inside him.

He'd drawn back because she'd said his name. But even before that, his conscience had niggled at him. That elusive quality of sweetness in her kiss. The soft gasp—of surprise?—when he'd touched her . . .

Then, he'd been too aflame to examine her response, or to care about the innocence that characterized it. From the reputation she'd gained for shocking behavior, from her sheer presence here tonight, he assumed she'd garnered ample experience in the years they'd been apart. And yet . . .

Realization washed over him. Good God. He'd left Georgie Black alone in this house. What the *hell* had possessed him?

Slamming down his glass, he crossed the room to the clothes press and rummaged for a new neck-cloth.

"What now?" wondered Xavier. "Will the legendary lover join my poor party after all? The ladies will riot."

"No." He drew the strip of linen around his neck and fumbled briefly with its folds. He'd never cared much for fashion, and his cravat was not the work of genius, but it would serve. He donned his waistcoat and coat, combed his fingers through his hair in a cursory attempt to tame it, then tweaked his cuffs and turned to go.

"Just remembered something," he said curtly as he strode to the door.

He'd remembered that he was a gentleman.

Beckenham spent the next hour in a fruitless search for Georgie. He'd half expected to find her in plain sight, flirting outrageously—or worse—simply to show him she was not a woman to be trifled with and cavalierly dismissed.

Yet unless she'd found another bedchamber for her activities or lurked somewhere in the shadows of the grounds, he was forced to conclude she'd left the party altogether.

His conscience smarted. Despite her boldness in attending this affair, Georgiana Black was the lady he had once intended to take as his wife. He ought to have set aside his personal turmoil and seen her safely home.

He must find out where she stayed in Brighton and make sure she'd reached there without mishap. There was no getting around that obligation.

Again, his damnable conscience tugged at him. He'd been alone with her in a bedchamber amidst a scandalous masquerade. He'd kissed her, touched her. God, he could still feel the soft, luscious weight of her breasts in his palms. . . .

If a lady falls in a locked bedchamber and no one sees . . .

Ah, but he'd seen, hadn't he? And even if she never spoke a word of it to anyone, even if no one ever discovered what Beckenham had done to her that night, *he* would know.

His mind shied from the inevitable conclusion.

No. He would not act precipitously. He must think before he acted, sleep on it, perhaps. He gave a grim smile at the mere thought he'd get a wink of slumber this night.

Now, he must find her and return her to her lodgings safely and discreetly.

Then he would consider his next move.

For once, luck had favored Georgie. After much fruitless searching, she glimpsed her stepsister preparing to enter the Makepeaces' carriage on the drive outside the villa.

She hastened toward them. But when she saw who accompanied the small party, she halted with a crunch and skitter of gravel.

The worst oath she knew hissed from her lips. Lord Pearce bowed over her sister's hand.

Pearce. The man who'd destroyed her happiness. The man who'd stirred up a world of trouble between her and Marcus with that cursed lock of hair.

He stood there, a little over average height, elegant, with that dangerous air that lent spice to his stunningly handsome looks. He was not as tall, nor as broad-shouldered and muscular as Marcus. In fact, he was less of everything.

Yet when she was eighteen, Lord Pearce's world-weary cynicism had intrigued her. His clear interest in her and the audacity with which he'd expressed it had been a balm to her pride. A pride wounded by Becken-ham's seeming indifference.

Lord Pearce only wanted her fortune, of course. Even at eighteen, she'd been shrewd enough to realize that. He'd not managed to take her in with his devilish charm, though his goads had so often pricked at the wildness in her spirit.

She'd flirted with him, led him a merry dance while always keeping a weather eye cocked for Beckenham's reaction. She hadn't been quite as fly to the time of day as she'd thought herself, however. As cleverly as she'd guarded her virtue, Pearce had ruined her life all the same.

He'd departed hastily from England six years ago; she'd hoped never to see him again. Now he'd returned. For what purpose?

It would be fatal to alert Pearce to her own presence

at this party. Dangerous for him to see her sister here; yet, what was done couldn't be helped. At least Violet had the sense to keep her mask on. Her plain domino obscured her gown completely and its hood covered her hair.

Georgie watched only long enough to ensure that Pearce did not climb into the carriage with Violet and her chaperones. She motioned to a footman and desired her own conveyance to be called.

When at last the hired carriage appeared, Georgie picked up her skirts and hurried down the steps of the villa.

Pearce remained standing where she'd last seen him on the drive, watching the scandalous cavorting that took place in the fountain with a pensive air.

Of course he would not recognize her. Not in this light, in this disguise.

Still, she hurried past, giving him as wide a berth as she might.

Her heart beat hard in her chest until she reached the safety of her carriage. When the door smacked shut behind her, she sank back into the squabs. A warm, intoxicating sense of relief poured through her body.

Without turning her head, she watched Pearce through the window from the corner of her eye as the carriage lurched into motion.

With that self-satisfied smirk she'd grown to fear as well as loathe, he raised a hand to her in salute.

Georgie tried to think rationally, but the twin shocks of seeing her sister with Pearce and that smug gesture of recognition made her brain clamor.

Oh, surely he had not known who she was. That quick, confident wave of the hand might well have been an impersonal gesture made on the spur of the moment to an unknown lady.

Her insides twisted. If Pearce had recognized her and spread tales of her presence at that shocking party . . .

In going to Steyne's villa, she'd meant to do nothing more than rescue her sister from indiscretion. Instead, she'd encountered the two men she'd hoped never to see again.

Her agitation had transformed to self-righteous anger by the time she finally swept into her sister's bedchamber.

Violet, the little minx, was already abed, nestled under coverlet and sheet. She lay on her side and her hands were palm to palm, tucked under her cheek. A slight smile curved her pretty pink lips. Her pale hair flowed over her shoulder like a river of corn-silk. She must have told her maid not to bother papering it, nor even braiding it tonight.

Another person might have been disarmed by the sight. Georgie was tempted to shake her tiresome sister awake.

How dared she look so innocent, so fresh and untroubled after what she'd been up to this evening?

Fear made Georgie's anger spike. If Pearce had decided to make Violet the object of his attentions, the chit didn't stand a chance. She was a clever girl, but she was no match for a man of Pearce's experience.

If only she might be certain that no evil consequences would come of this night's work.

Frustrated and furious at himself on many levels, Beckenham headed back to the villa. He'd combed the house and the grounds without gaining another glimpse of Georgie. Perhaps she'd taken his advice after all and left.

He cursed the evil genius that had brought him here tonight. He'd made a series of bad decisions since Xavier had come to him with the tale of an unknown lady seeking his protection.

He'd traveled to Brighton to ask Xavier's advice on a suitable bride, not to entangle himself with the one woman in England he absolutely could not wed.

The thought had occurred to him more than once during his search: He ought to make reparation for his behavior tonight. If Georgie had been any other lady, he would feel obliged to propose marriage. It was what any honorable man would do.

He had always considered himself an honorable man. No matter how uncomfortable it might be, he followed the path his conscience dictated.

His conscience shouted at him, demanded that he swallow his pride—a huge bite, that—and at least ask the question. An honorable man would not picture himself spurned for the second time and cringe away from that image like a whipped cur. An honorable man would not rely on Georgie's false assumption that he hadn't recognized her. He would not hope that no one else was the wiser about that interlude, that Georgie's reputation did not need rescuing, after all.

An honorable man would not seek a different wife with a view to escape.

He couldn't bring himself to accommodate the notion of proposing to Georgie again, so he focused on finding her, on seeing to it that she was safe.

He rounded the fountain, refusing certain favors from the importunate nymphs for the second time that night. That's when he caught sight of her, hurrying toward him down the steps, the skirts of her gown caught up in one slender hand.

His heart gave a hard jolt. But no, she wasn't heading for him, but toward the chaise that stood waiting on the drive between them.

As if turned to stone, he watched her until she was obscured from his sight by the carriage that stood between them. She entered the carriage and settled herself against the squabs.

The vulnerable line of her throat made his chest contract with a painful longing. He had a crazed impulse to run after the carriage as it moved forward, to open the door and swing himself inside. He'd resolved to see her home, hadn't he?

But when the chaise rolled past, it revealed another familiar figure, one he'd hoped never to set eyes on again.

Lord Pearce, the blackguard, raising his hand to Georgie in farewell.

Chapter Four

Violet rolled her eyes. "We were with Lord Pearce for mere minutes, Georgie. He barely spoke to me. Besides, he is quite old, you know."

Georgie snorted. "Yes, he must be all of thirty-five."

"Well, that seems old to me," said Violet.

"Did—did Lord Pearce mention me?" said Georgie, trying to sound offhand.

Violet shrugged. "He said he was one of your beaux. Oh, and he mentioned your hair."

Oblivious of the way Georgie stiffened, Violet's gaze flicked up to Georgie's crown, where her abundant curls piled in an ordered riot of astonishing brilliance. "He is right, of course. It's magnificent."

Georgie repressed a grimace. Her cursed hair was the source of more trouble than Violet could imagine.

"He's quite charming for an older person, isn't he?" said Violet idly. "One can see why he has such a dreadful reputation. Mrs. Makepeace told me all about him."

"Speaking of reputations," said Georgie a little more sharply than she intended, "it was badly done to go to

Steyne's house with the Makepeaces. You must have guessed how it would be."

Violet's countenance seemed to sparkle. "Indeed, I guessed." She clasped her hands together. "And it was beyond even my wildest imaginings. I shouldn't think anything I might see during my London season could compare. But how foolish to suppose the Makepeaces would not take good care of me, Georgie. Mrs. Makepeace wants me for her brother-in-law, so you may be sure she kept me safe from other men."

"But not, I take it, from Harry Makepeace."

"Oh, pooh! I can deal with Horrible Harry any day of the week." Violet gave a tiny yawn. "It was prodigiously entertaining, though, G. You should have seen how lavish—and how lewd—Steyne's party was."

Georgie gave a small shudder. She'd not told her sister that she had indeed seen for herself. That episode was best forgotten. "I can only guess. And beg you not to repeat a word of what you saw to anyone—most of all to your mama."

"You must think me a complete cod's head. Of course I won't." Violet rested her chin in her hand and gazed at Georgie intently. "Have you ever kissed a man, dear sister?"

A sudden surge of memory flooded Georgie's mind. Last night. That endless searing kiss . . .

She cleared her throat. "Good gracious, why do you ask?"

"Did Beckenham kiss you?"

Georgie's breath exploded from her. *"What?"*

"When you were engaged, I mean. Did he kiss you?" Violet frowned. "I quite thought it was permissible for betrothed couples to kiss."

"It is. I mean . . ." Georgie sighed. She'd never spoken

to anyone about intimacies between her and Beckenham. Georgie answered honestly. "Yes." A sweet stab of pain shot through her. She swallowed hard. "When we were betrothed, we kissed."

Violet's stare seemed to pin her to the wall. "You did? What was it like?"

"Well, er . . ." Georgie struggled to recall past the blaze of passion last night had brought. One word came to mind.

"Pleasant," she said finally. Rather an understatement, but Violet didn't need to know that. She forced a laugh. "But then, it was all so long ago, I've quite forgotten."

Yet she had not forgotten the hot, firm press of Beckenham's lips upon hers last night, the deep, sensuous thrust of his tongue. She'd never guessed passion could be so dark, so all-consuming as the emotion that had gripped her in that bedchamber last night.

"Did you ever kiss Pearce?" asked Violet.

"Oh, good God no," laughed Georgie. "I led him a pretty dance but I never let anyone kiss me except Beckenham."

"What about afterwards?" persisted Violet. "After you jilted him."

"Violet, don't be vulgar," said Georgie. "The proper expression is that we decided we wouldn't suit."

Another eye roll greeted that statement. "Whatever you say, G. But did you kiss anyone after you gave Beckenham his congé?"

Her sister was like a dog with a bone. Rather belatedly, Georgie wondered whence these questions emanated. "Did a man kiss you last night?" she demanded.

"No," said Violet. "But I expect perhaps someday one might wish to, don't you think?"

"Oh, undoubtedly." Georgie eyed her sister, all blue eyes and flaxen curls. "My advice is—"

Violet heaved a heartfelt sigh. "I know, I know. I should not let any man kiss me unless we're engaged."

"I wasn't going to say that," said Georgie. "My advice is that if you don't wish to find yourself speedily betrothed to the man in question, don't get caught."

Violet's pretty mouth was agape. Then she broke into a peal of laughter.

Georgie reached forward and affectionately tapped her sister's cheek. "I never said I was a saint, my dear. I don't expect you to be, either. But I do expect you to be clever."

She took her sister's chin in her hand. "And I think you know that dallying with Lord Pearce in any shape or form is not at all clever. His brand of vileness is beyond the understanding of a lovely girl like you. He would ruin you if he could. Do not grant him the opportunity to try."

It was almost noon when Beckenham went down to breakfast. He expected to encounter a great deal of detritus from last evening's party, including several languishing, unclad bodies on the way.

He'd reckoned without Martin's ruthless efficiency. The place was spotless and silent, but for the chimes of a hallway clock and the muted cry of gulls.

The welcome scents of breakfast pleasantly assailed his nostrils. Cooked meats, eggs, fresh bread. His stomach growled, reminding him that he hadn't eaten more than a few bites of the repast Martin arranged for him the previous evening.

A series of images flashed before his mind's eye. Georgie, soft and firm and round. Responsive, willing, pliant, searingly sensual. That low, husky voice trembling with emotion, begging him not to go.

And Pearce waving good-bye to her with that smug, knowing smile on his face.

Pearce's presence and the familiarity of his gesture to Georgie had set off an explosion of conjecture in Beckenham's head.

What was Pearce doing back in England after all these years? Did he intend to pursue Georgie once more?

As he approached the breakfast parlor, he heard masculine voices and hesitated, listening. He was in no mood for polite company. But he identified two voices, both well known to him. One was Xavier. The other was another cousin, Andrew, Viscount Lydgate.

"Good God, Andy," drawled Beckenham, taking in his cousin's elegance. "Your sartorial splendor is quite blinding this morning."

Lydgate rose and strode toward him. "Beckenham!"

The blond Adonis gripped Beckenham's hand and wrung it, clapped him hard on the back. "By Jove, you're a sight for sore eyes." He cast a humorous look back at Xavier. "Quite a party last night, wasn't it?"

Xavier, who was dressed for riding, bent a penetrating stare upon Beckenham. "Yes. Quite. But our cousin didn't partake of the, er, more public amusements, did you, coz?"

Beckenham's jaw tightened. "As you say."

The glint in Xavier's deep blue eyes abraded Beckenham's conscience. Did he know? Had he guessed Georgie's identity?

Beckenham felt the lively curiosity of Andy's regard.

"Speak plainly," Beckenham said, bracing himself. "Don't keep the boy in suspense, I beg, or put him to the trouble of nosing out the truth."

One of Lydgate's most tiresome habits was an uncanny ability to discover secrets other people would prefer to keep hidden. The girls used to call him the Idle Intelligencer when they all lived together with the Duke of Montford.

"Very well, then," said Steyne with a slight bow. "Our estimable cousin had a close encounter with a shady lady last night."

Lydgate grinned. "So did I. Most delightful it was, too." He glanced from one to the other. Beckenham's nerves vibrated like the tines of tuning fork. "And this is remarkable because . . . ?"

Xavier's gaze locked on Beckenham's. The tension became a churn in Beckenham's stomach. He was almost certain that Xavier hadn't recognized Georgie. His cousin had denied knowing her the previous evening. But at least now he'd know. That choice piece of information was so rich, Xavier couldn't possibly resist the urge to torment him with it.

Xavier's thick lashes veiled those midnight blue eyes. He touched his mouth with a napkin and set it aside. "Only because Beckenham cut me out for the privilege of spending time with the lady in question."

Relief poured through Beckenham like a sluice of cool water. Gruffly, he managed, "Not so remarkable, in fact."

But Lydgate's openmouthed astonishment said otherwise. He addressed Xavier. "And you . . . let him?"

Xavier merely shrugged. "It was the shock, you see."

Did Beckenham imagine it, or was there irony in the gaze Xavier leveled at him?

Damnation! He imagined veiled meanings that weren't there, because he felt guilty. He should not take his cue from Xavier on this. He should discover where Georgie was lodging, march over there, and ask her to be his wife. He would do it and receive her inevitable rejection as a penance for his sins last night.

"But you must be famished after your, ah, exertions, Becks." Xavier indicated the grand array of chafing dishes set out on the sideboard. "Have at it, why don't you? Martin ordered what he thought you would like."

One of Martin's uncanny talents was to anticipate a guest's every desire and whim, so Beckenham wasn't surprised to find several of his favorite dishes.

He filled his plate, then sat down with his cousins at the table. The slow churn in his stomach had subsided a little but he couldn't quite reclaim his appetite.

"Becks is bride hunting," Xavier said to Lydgate.

Lydgate choked a little on his ale, set the tankard down. "No! Damn me but you're full of surprises this morning." He straightened in his chair, eyes widened. "Not the Shady Lady?"

"Most definitely not," agreed Xavier. "Beckenham wants a quiet, dutiful bride who won't give him any trouble. Someone *biddable,* no doubt." The last sentence was said with something of a sneer.

Beckenham focused on his plate. His wish for a bride seemed to belong to another century.

With an effort, he hauled his mind out of the quagmire of his encounter with Georgie. "I wouldn't have put it quite so crudely."

"Women," said Lydgate darkly, "are nothing *but* trouble. If there's one out there who isn't, I haven't met her."

Beckenham didn't agree. "You will admit that your experience of virtuous ladies is limited."

Xavier's lips curved in an unpleasant smile. "Lydgate's right. It is a wife's duty to make her husband's life as hellish as possible, as far as I can see. The docile ones are usually hiding their claws until the wedding

band is securely upon their pretty fingers. The beauties
are vain and far too demanding, the bluestockings are
dead bores. . . . Need I go on?"

Lydgate tilted his head. "Never knew you were such
a misogynist. I love women," he said on a sigh. "I can
find something to admire in the worst of them. That's
my curse."

"Yes," Beckenham said. "Your total lack of discrim-
ination was a factor in my decision to ask Xavier's advice rather than yours." He cocked an eyebrow at the
marquis. "You cannot recommend even one lady to me
as a suitable bride?"

Xavier curled his lip. "I leave the matchmaking to
our former guardian."

"Why *haven't* you asked Montford?" said Lydgate.

"I'm not interested in shoring up the Westruther
dynasty." Beckenham shrugged. "Besides, Montford
washed his hands of my affairs after the debacle with
Georgie Black."

That was the only time Beckenham could recall
thinking the duke was a complete cloth-head. Any reasonable man could see Beckenham had no choice but
to accept his congé with good grace. Montford had
thought otherwise, mocking him for his stubborn pride.
Which just showed how skewed the duke's thinking had
been. Montford deplored vulgar scenes and scandal; he
ought to have been wishing the fiery-haired termagant
good riddance.

No matter how well-matched their inheritances, the
Earl of Beckenham and Georgiana Black were wholly
unsuited to be husband and wife.

"At all events," said Beckenham, "I refuse to have
Montford's Machiavellian fingers dabbling in my marriage."

Lydgate regarded him with patent envy. "At least the

two of you no longer have ties to him. I'm still waiting to come into my fortune. That won't happen until my twenty-fifth birthday. And a more clutch-fisted—" He broke off, his sculpted mouth tightening. "But never mind that. What qualities do you wish for in a wife, Becks? Perhaps we may start there."

Inwardly, Beckenham cursed. If Lydgate made this his project, he wouldn't let up until he saw Beckenham leg-shackled to the perfect woman. Despite his vagaries, Lydgate was as much of a romantic as any of the female cousins. He would try to orchestrate a love match and drive Beckenham insane in the process.

Xavier tossed down his napkin and rose from the table. "Lydgate, the thought of you playing Cupid is almost as nauseating as the thought of Beckenham with a biddable wife."

"Are you going for a ride?" said Beckenham, hoping for an excuse to escape. And, if he must be honest, hoping to put off his interview with Georgie. As well give her his head for washing.

"Already been," said Xavier briefly. A slight smile of perfect understanding touched his lips. "Excuse me. I have business that cannot wait."

He went out, leaving Beckenham to eye Lydgate warily.

His cousin looked like a Greek coin. His gold locks perfectly ordered in the windswept style, his nose as straight as his perfectly white teeth. A hard chin and strong jaw spoke of determination. The blue eyes—a lighter, sunnier blue than Xavier's—glinted with speculation.

Lydgate had his elbows on the table, his chin propped in his hands. He stared at Beckenham intently. Beckenham could only imagine the thoughts running through that fertile, quick mind.

"There's more to the story of the shady lady than either of you will admit, isn't there?" Lydgate said softly.

The attack was so unexpected, Beckenham drew breath with a betraying hiss.

Before he could speak, Lydgate held up a hand. "No, don't lie to me." His tone had turned serious, with an edge to it. "I don't pry into your business. If you don't want me to know, so be it."

Beckenham relaxed slightly. "The lady in question—"

"—Is a lady," Lydgate cut in. "That much, I'd deduced. Fear not, cousin. I won't try to guess at more than that."

You could trust Lydgate on occasion. This, Beckenham decided, was one of them. "Thank you."

"Don't mention it, old fellow." Lydgate tapped his tankard with one finger, his forehead creased. "Leave the question of your bride with me. I'll come up with a short list of possibilities and see that you get the right invitations over the summer. At a house party you have better opportunity to see how the young lady conducts herself in a natural setting, where she's comfortable. The season can make the loveliest girl appear a ninny if she's not properly schooled."

House parties. Beckenham nearly sank his head into his hands. Dear God, not that. But if he must hunt for a bride, it would be better than doing the London season, he supposed.

"Even so, you'll want to do the season before you decide, just to be sure you don't miss any of that year's crop of debutantes," continued Lydgate as if he'd heard his cousin's inner prayer.

Beckenham groaned. "That's months away."

Lydgate eyed him balefully. "If it were up to you, the girl would be delivered to your doorstep, wrapped in brown paper and tied up with string."

With a gleam of humor, Beckenham said, "The idea has its merits."

His cousin balled up his napkin and threw it at Beckenham's head, then raised his eyes to the frescoed ceiling. "How can one work with such a boor?"

"Work" seemed to be the operative word. But Beckenham saw the force of Lydgate's argument. Finding his countess was a task that required careful thought and strategy. If one had to spend the rest of one's life in a lady's company—and in her bed—one ought not approach the matter cavalierly.

He couldn't help reflecting on the life he would have had if Georgie had not thrown him over. What if every night were like the last, only it didn't have to end so abruptly, so painfully?

He shut down that line of thought. Regardless of their combustible passion in the bedchamber, they were wholly unsuited in every other way. He ought to thank her for being farsighted enough to set him free.

There was too much emotion and tumult, too much history there. Their marriage could never be the smooth path he desired, but a rocky, winding road that took them to the heights only to plunge them into despair.

After years of tussling with the snarled and decaying legacy his grandfather had left him, he'd finally reached the stage where his life was orderly and calm. He could only guess at the chaos Georgie Black would bring.

Anger flared. She'd asked for him last night. More than that, she'd walked into his arms, willing and wanton, impetuous as ever, never considering the risk she took. She was at least partly responsible for the tumult inside him now.

But his own recklessness—so wild, so uncharacteristic—stung more. The merest press of his lips to hers had sent him spinning out of control.

Who was he fooling? He'd lost volition the instant he'd laid eyes on her. She could do that to him. She had that much power. A very dangerous woman, indeed.

The one consolation in this mess was that he'd wrenched himself back from the abyss. Had he taken her, there would be no question at all that they must wed now. Thank God for the self-control that had returned when he'd needed it most.

When she'd said his name.

With an inward shudder, he tried to shake off the remembered thrill of her lips brushing his ear, whispering to him.

No. *No!*

It was no use. He couldn't pretend last night hadn't happened. His conscience would give him no peace until he did what honor demanded.

He would pay his addresses to Georgie. She would reject him. He would do his duty and that would be an end to it. Then he could get on with the far more comfortable task of choosing a proper wife.

Beckenham started as Lydgate snapped his fingers in his face. "Becks, have you listened to a word I've said?"

Clearing his throat, Beckenham snatched up his napkin, pressed it to his lips. "My apologies. I was woolgathering." He cleared his throat and added awkwardly, "I do appreciate your assistance, Andy."

Mollified, Lydgate said, "Save your thanks. You won't feel too grateful when the matchmaking mamas start hunting you down."

Appalled, Beckenham let his napkin fall. "I hadn't thought of that."

Lydgate shrugged. "Nothing to be done about it. If you reappear on the scene after such a long absence, there's bound to be only one conclusion. You're one of the most eligible bachelors in England, besides Xavier."

"And you." Beckenham eyed Lydgate. "I hear the young ladies and their mamas find you most maddeningly elusive."

Lydgate sobered. "It takes some doing, staying one step ahead of the dear creatures. Lord, I could tell you some stories that would curl your hair."

Beckenham cocked his head in inquiry.

"*Entrapment,* my dear fellow," said Lydgate darkly. "The most ingenious methods. There was one incident a few years ago. . . ." Lydgate paled, clearly aghast at the mere thought. "But Rosamund came to my rescue. Dear girl, Rosamund."

"You'd do better to confine your attentions to professionals," observed Beckenham.

Lydgate's blue eyes danced. "But where's the fun in that? Paying a woman for her favors don't interest me."

"You like the chase," said Beckenham. Which he, most certainly, did not.

In the months after Georgie had given him his congé, he'd gained himself quite a reputation with the ladies of the Ton. What had driven him, he knew not. But by the time he'd realized his existence was fast careering out of his control, he'd developed and honed his skills in the boudoir to a fine point. His emotions remained curiously detached from these adventures, however, and he finally realized it was dishonest to promise with his body what his heart could not hope to match.

Wiser now by far, he preferred his relationships with women to be clear-cut and uncomplicated. Any mistress of his was compensated handsomely for her company. It was a business transaction, nothing more.

Lydgate's love life resembled a skein of wool after a cat had played with it: tangled beyond hope of unraveling.

"I do indeed." A reminiscent smile played over Lydgate's mouth.

Beckenham suppressed a groan. The threat of a London season was certainly an incentive to pay his addresses to one lady or another before the end of the year.

The betrothal itself had been the simplest and most straightforward aspect of the entire business with Georgie. Beckenham had known Georgie's family all his life. She stood to inherit her father's property, a very desirable collection of acres with a handsome manor house that had once been part of Winford, Beckenham's estate.

Montford had settled it with Sir Donald that these acres would one day be rejoined to the Winford estate through his marriage to Sir Donald's elder daughter. Beckenham couldn't remember a time when he hadn't known he would marry the foxy-haired girl from Cloverleigh.

He hadn't taken much notice of Georgie, growing up, besides judging that she was a bruising rider, as fearless and skilled on horseback as any boy her age. In fact, it wasn't until she let down her skirts, put up that glorious hair, and took the Ton by storm in her first season that he truly saw her for the beauty she'd become.

He broke off. Damn it to hell, why did his thoughts continually return to her? He ought to focus on what Lydgate was saying.

"House parties. Let me think. We need an itinerary."

Lydgate produced a notebook and pencil and made several jottings, a small furrow between his sleek eyebrows. "We'll begin with the Malbys in Norfolk and work our way down England from there."

Ah, hell, thought Beckenham. *I'm in for it now.*

Chapter Five

Dear Lizzie,

    I hope my letter finds you well and that you are not being driven to distraction by poor Dartry. He is a sweet man and will make a kind and generous husband, but oh, Lizzie! I wish you might love him. Truly, it is the most delightful and painful state. . . .

    I cannot believe G has prevailed upon Mama to send me back to the Bath school next term, until it is time for the Season. She was scandalized that I went to a certain party last night and rung such a peal over me! But I cannot regret it, for dearest Lizzie, He was there. He has followed me here from Bath, just as he promised . . .

The hour was not late enough for the promenade along the Brighton shore to have become a crush. Grateful that so few of her acquaintances were up and about, Georgie inhaled deeply of the wild, salted air. She needed to scour her soul after the passion and humiliation of last night.

So much bittersweet yearning in that kiss. He must have felt her need for him, her desperate craving. How could he not? She'd begged him not to go, after all.

Shame flooded her. If only she'd thought before she spoke, her pride might not be as tattered as her youthful dreams.

A few paces behind her, Georgie's maid heaved a dramatic sigh. Smith did not approve of Brighton, nor of walks along the seafront.

Georgie adored physical exercise, needed it as an outlet for an overabundance of restless energy. Violet was still abed after her outing last night, but if Georgie had to stay cooped up in their rooms with her ailing stepmother one second longer, she'd thought she'd explode.

"I've a pebble in my slippers," grumbled the maid. "And this breeze quite destroys our coiffure, Miss G."

By "our coiffure," Smith meant Georgie's coiffure, of course. The maid's hair was plainly dressed, scraped mercilessly back from her forehead and tucked beneath a lacy cap. Not even a tempest would dislodge a single iron gray strand. But Smith was as proprietary about the body she dressed as a little girl with her favorite doll. Or an artist with his masterpiece, perhaps.

If not for the fact that Smith truly *was* an artist, Georgie wouldn't have put up with her admonishments nor her complaints on these walks. But Smith had attended Georgie since her come-out, and sartorial magnificence such as the plain-spoken dresser could produce was worth any amount of grumbling. Besides, Georgie was sincerely attached to her dour woman and delighted in teasing her.

Georgie lifted her chin to gaze out over the pebbled beach below. "Oh, look. Someone is taking one of the bathing machines. I might try that one day."

That successfully diverted Smith from her own troubles. She glowered down at the shore, where several carriages lined up, ready to drive patrons into the sea for a spot of private bathing.

"Not while there is breath in my body, you won't, Miss G," she said. "Those ladies have no shame."

"But it is all perfectly innocent," said Georgie. "They are fully gowned, and besides, no one can see."

"No one but the gentlemen who rent telescopes for the purpose of looking," said Smith darkly. "And when they are wet, those garments outline every curve and cranny. Mark my words, Miss G—"

Georgie laughed. "Calm yourself, Smith. I was jesting, of course." She didn't tell her maid she thought being dipped in the ocean fully dressed must be the tamest sport possible, besides making one appear rather ridiculous.

Nor did she mention the many times she'd escaped her room at Cloverleigh on a hot July night for a bareskinned bathe in the lake. Some things were best kept to oneself.

A nude bathe in the ocean, now . . . That might be interesting. But even she wasn't reckless enough to try it. Not in Brighton, where one could never be assured one was quite alone.

"I beg you won't relay your opinion to my stepmama," she said, a slight smile curving her lips. "I heard the doctor prescribe a course of sea bathing for her only yesterday."

"Hmph!" said Smith. She had no great opinion of Lady Black. Not that she'd ever say so, but Georgie knew her well. "Does that mean we'll be stuck here for the foreseeable future?"

"No, it does not," said Georgie. Every tall, dark-haired gentleman she saw made her heart give a hard thump until she made sure it wasn't Beckenham. The sooner he left Brighton, the better. "If my stepmother wishes to remain in Brighton for the summer, she may do so. Miss Violet and I will leave for Lady Arden's as planned."

She'd like nothing more than to remove Violet from the sphere of the Makepeaces and their ilk immediately but that was impossible. She meant to remain vigilant, for she wasn't entirely satisfied with Violet's innocent denial of kissing. Something was putting a glow in those pretty cheeks. Or someone. Please God it wasn't Pearce.

She knew better than to believe Pearce would let bygones be bygones. If he was back in England at all, he would seek revenge. If he'd decided to wreak that revenge through Violet, Georgie would shoot him through the heart.

She returned to their lodgings invigorated, if not sanguine.

Having allowed Smith to tidy her windblown appearance, Georgie walked into the parlor to find her stepmother sitting upright in a straight-backed chair. Lady Black's avid, curious gaze was trained on a tall, dark-haired gentleman who stood at the window, his hands clasped loosely at his back.

Georgie halted on the threshold, her mouth ajar.

Today, the Earl of Beckenham was dressed in buff trousers and a dark blue swallow-tailed coat. The rig was practically a uniform for the well-tailored gentlemen of the Ton, yet there was no mistaking the identity of the man inside those garments.

Georgie threw a look of inquiry at her stepmother, who made a face and gave a faint shrug of her shoulders. How long had Beckenham been here before Georgie arrived? What on earth could he have found to talk about with Lady Black?

Georgie forced herself to recover her poise, pitching her voice low. "Lord Beckenham. To what do we owe this honor?"

He turned. His dark gaze took her in slowly, from her chip straw hat to her kid half boots. Disapproval, perhaps even censure, radiated from his grim features.

Georgie resisted the urge to put a hand up to her hair. Such a self-conscious gesture would place her at a disadvantage from the start. Besides, she knew she looked as perfect as Smith could make her. Her gown was white muslin made up high at the throat and trimmed with pale green ribbons below the bosom and at the narrow flounce. Expensive, perhaps, but as modest as anyone could have wished.

Beckenham's presence here today must mean he had penetrated her disguise last night. But why hadn't he said something?

Was it her mistake or did his bow seem to contain a hint of irony? She curtsied with the proper deference, batting away her fear. She refused to betray her inner turmoil by a flicker of an eyelid. His face remained impassive as granite, but then perhaps he wasn't experiencing turmoil at all.

Beckenham glanced at Lady Black, who still regarded him with the expression of a dog who is unsure whether it will be given a bone or a boot in the ribs. Despite her bumptious ways, Lady Black had always been wary of Beckenham, whose demeanor made it clear he did not suffer fools gladly.

Georgie's stepmother rushed into speech. "I was just saying to Lord Beckenham how honored we are to receive him today. Are we not, Georgiana?"

"Indeed," said Georgie, lifting her brows. If he wanted to be rid of her interfering relation, he would have to do it. She was rarely thankful for her stepmother's presence, but on this occasion, she had no wish for privacy.

"It is a fine day," said Beckenham. He glanced out the window, as if to ascertain whether conditions had changed since last he'd looked.

"Oh, yes, indeed," Lady Black gushed when Georgie merely curled her lip at the inanity. "We have been most fortunate in the weather. I was just saying to my girls— was I not, Georgie?—that the climate here in Brighton is so salubrious, I might be tempted to take my dear Dr. Wilson's advice and try the sea-bathing cure."

Georgie could almost hear Beckenham's mental dismissal of such remedies as "quackery."

Reading disapproval on Beckenham's stern features, Georgie interposed. "Indeed, my lady, I might well be persuaded to join you."

The crease between Beckenham's brows deepened. Gracious, he was so predictable. If they were still betrothed, he would caution her against putting her body on public display.

Some devil prompted her to add, "Though I daresay it won't be as stimulating as bathing in the lake at Winford."

She had mentioned to him once that she and her cousins used to take moonlit swims in the lake on his estate in the hotter months. Why she sought to remind him of it now, she wasn't entirely certain.

Actually, she knew very well why. She was not only hurt but piqued at his rejection of her last night. It was easier to deal with the pique than the pain.

Beckenham's reaction was all she might have hoped. To anyone else, he appeared politely interested, but she knew the signs he held his anger and disgust on a tight rein.

His lips were stiff as he said, "Dutiful of you to accompany your stepmother. But might I suggest another form of exercise? I'd thought to take you for a drive."

Lady Black exclaimed at his kindness and condescension but Georgie barely heard him for the roar in her ears.

He thought he could waltz back into her life after a six-year absence and demand she go driving with him? As if nothing had happened!

She inclined her head. "Thank you, but I have a previous engagement."

"What previous engagement?" said Lady Black. "I'm sure it's the first I've heard of it."

Dark eyes glittered dangerously down at her. She felt the force of his anger, making his physical presence seem larger and more threatening. But she'd never been one to back down from a fight, nor did she bend to bullies. His attitude made her even less inclined to go anywhere with him.

"You look as if you wish to read me a lecture, Lord Beckenham," she said, ignoring her stepmother's betraying remark. "I don't take kindly to lectures, or have you forgotten?"

"You are mistaken," he bit out. "What right have I to ring a peal over you?"

"An interesting question." One that she'd flung at him more than once during their engagement.

Honesty compelled her to admit he'd had reason and right on his side more than once during that time. If his severity had been tempered by any open expression of regard, perhaps she might have borne it better.

Then again, she'd been an ungovernable chit. Perhaps no approach would have mollified her.

Perversely, curiosity raised its head. Why had he come here today if he didn't mean to chastise her? He must have a compelling reason to break the habit of the past six years and seek her out. What did he want to say to her now that he couldn't very well have said last night?

Suddenly, she had to know. He knew she was the lady in the mask. Of course he did. Why else would he be here?

She wasn't sure she wished to provide a spectacle for their peers by driving about Brighton with him, but if he wasn't concerned by this, she supposed she needn't be.

With the abruptness for which Lady Arden had always chastised her, she said, "Oh, very well, then. I shall change and be with you directly."

She made as if to leave, but he held up one hand to stay her. "What you are wearing is perfectly adequate."

"But I have already appeared in public in this gown today," she objected, making her eyes wide and innocent. "I should disappoint all of those dowagers who shake their heads over my extravagance if I went out in it again."

She couldn't blame him for his impatience. He'd likely murder Lady Black if he was forced to endure her company for another hour. He knew Georgie's habits too well.

"I'll give you ten minutes," he said. And he actually took out his watch as if to time her. "Then I'll come to fetch you."

"How shocking," Georgie mocked, but her pulse had kicked a little when he spoke to her so. Curse her penchant for domineering men!

"Don't test me," he said. "You, of all people, know I never make idle threats."

She flexed her brows. "And you, of all people, must know that I always treat a threat as a challenge."

The slightest hint of a smile played about his mouth and made tiny creases at the corners of his eyes. "It is fortunate then, that either way, I shall be the winner."

Surprised into a peal of laughter, Georgie swept from the room.

Good gracious! Beckenham *flirting*. Whatever next?

Beckenham didn't know how he managed to keep his emotions in check throughout that maddening exchange. Only years of training in self-discipline stopped him from scooping Miss Georgiana Black up, striding downstairs, and tossing her into Xavier's curricle willy-nilly.

Did she really think he was here on a polite social call? Far be it from him to fathom the diabolical workings of that woman's mind, but he could have sworn she truly believed he hadn't recognized her last night.

As if he'd be standing here now if he hadn't, his patience nearly worn to a snapping point with the voluble nonsense her stepmother spouted. That had been perhaps the sole issue on which he and Georgie had thoroughly agreed. Her father had been mad to wed the silly widgeon.

Why Georgie herself hadn't married long before now, if only to get away from her irritating relative, he didn't know. Perhaps her engagement to him had put her off the estate for life.

Perhaps she'd been waiting for Pearce's return.

That notion slipped into his mind like a poisoned dagger slid into flesh. He did his best to dismiss it. She was sincere in her low opinion of Pearce. He'd have wagered his life on that at the time of their parting, and nothing had occurred since to change his mind.

Jealousy was an unattractive and quite futile emotion. It hadn't been jealousy that made him so furious with Pearce over that lock of hair.

If he'd been a jealous man, Georgie's antics with her many admirers would have driven him insane. Instead, he'd thought of them all with the irritated impatience one feels about a cloud of gnats.

He checked his timepiece. The ten minutes were almost up. He experienced a stirring of interest in making good on his threat.

As his hostess rattled on, he wondered what he'd find. Images of last night scorched his brain. In his revisionist imaginings, Georgie's fiery hair had been unpowdered, unbound, bright, and luxurious.

He didn't know whether to be relieved or sorry when, precisely twelve minutes after she'd left the room, Georgie reappeared.

He'd expected her to evince chagrin at his blatant attempt to control her, but she sent him a look that sparked with good humor and said, "Ah, you are a gentleman, my lord. You gave me two minutes' grace."

He narrowed his eyes. Had she waited those extra minutes, tense with anticipation, to see what he would do? She hadn't dared wait longer, though, had she?

That made him feel almost cheerful.

The change of raiment had, of course, been a ruse to help her collect herself. Whatever she wore, she was stunning. He suspected sackcloth might do just as well, for no embellishment could surpass her exquisitely lovely face, nor the worst-cut garment disguise those abundant curves. She'd never seemed to understand this, taking such elaborate pains with her appearance, he'd wondered if she truly knew how beautiful she was.

But of course she did. Before Lady Arden had launched her on the Ton, Georgie hadn't given a straw for what she looked like, hacking about the estate in an old riding habit and a floppy, broad-brimmed felt hat.

Her first London season had changed her. Irrevocably, it seemed.

"Shall we?"

He offered his arm and she placed hers upon it. But only after a slight hesitation, as if she were wary about touching him.

He was unsure what to make of that.

She couldn't feel, as he did, that the slightest contact between them was like two wires conducting a current.

He experienced a jolt of it, but managed to cover his body's reaction by bowing a farewell to Lady Black.

Outside, Georgie seemed to glow.

He remembered that about her now. While the London season had tried to turn her into some variety of hothouse flower, she'd always belonged in the wild, happiest outdoors, no matter the weather. He'd wager neither Pearce nor her other myriad swains knew that about her.

But he couldn't let himself think along those lines. Certainly, as her neighbor and as the man who had been betrothed to her for many years in addition, of course he might claim to know her better than most. It didn't alter his extreme reluctance to become entangled with her again.

Beckenham flipped a coin to the boy who had been walking his horses up and down the street.

When he'd helped her up into the curricle, Georgie raised her sleek eyebrows. "What, no tiger?"

She still held his hand, her eyes laughing down at him. He rather thought she enjoyed her superior position.

"Not today," he answered. Of course not. He needed to be quite alone with her. "This is not my vehicle. I borrowed it from my cousin."

"Which cousin?" she asked as he swung up beside her and let the ribbons run through his gloved hands.

"Steyne." Was she feigning ignorance or had she encountered Lydgate last night? That was not a pleasant thought. Lydgate was damnably nosy, not to mention quick-witted and tenacious. If he had the merest whiff of intrigue, he wouldn't rest until he'd discovered all the details.

"Oh, yes," she said. "I remember now. Your esteemed cousin owns a house here, doesn't he?"

He shot her a quick glance. So that was her game.

Now that they were alone, he need not beat about the bush. "You must know that he does, for you were at his house last night."

She did not betray herself by a flicker of an eyelid. So, she had put those twelve minutes to good purpose, then. He admired her composure even as he deplored the necessity of exposing her lies.

She tilted her head. "I have never visited Lord Steyne's house before, to my recollection. Indeed, I hear the marquis throws shocking parties. Not at all the thing for an unmarried lady. Or a married one, come to that. Which, as you might correctly surmise, would not be considerations that often deter me. However, it so happens that kind of party doesn't appeal to me."

Did she realize how close she came to babbling?

She folded her hands in her lap. "Indeed, Marcus, I wonder that *you* would—"

"Come now, Georgie. You'll catch cold if you play that game. You were there. I saw you." *Touched you. Kissed you. Held you in my arms.*

"I assure you I was not. You must have mistaken me for someone else."

How could he? There was no one else like her.

Frowning his impatience, he said, "Let's have done with this charade, shall we? I knew it was you the instant I walked into that bedchamber last night."

That silenced her. He glanced down and realized she'd chosen her hat to good purpose. When she regarded her lap with a slightly bent head, he could see nothing except her chin and the delicious curve of her lower lip.

That lower lip had been all his last night. The rest of her, too. If he'd been insane enough to take her up on the offer.

Perversely, he was beginning to wish he had. Then their path would be clear now. No escape. He would have neither time nor luxury to consider how disastrous their union would be.

What sort of iron will must he have exerted to tear himself away from her last night?

The thought gave him a stab of regret. Honor could be damnably tiresome sometimes. Most of the time, in fact.

"You are mistaken," she said in a strong, clear voice. "I might also tell you that I resent the aspersion you make free to cast on my character, sir." She waved a graceful hand. "This talk of lewd parties and bedchambers. You must think me sunk low indeed to accuse me of such behavior."

A bold counter, he'd give her that. But then, she'd never lacked audacity.

He might play along with her ploy and forget the incident. Another man would clutch at the straw she offered him.

But having once decided upon a course of action he knew was right, Beckenham never allowed himself to be swayed by uncertainty or base cowardice.

He would propose. She would reject him. Then they could go on as before, and he would know he'd done his duty.

In a low tone, he said, "Don't play innocent, Georgie. I know it was you."

He observed her closely, had an impulse to whisk

that charming bonnet from her head and toss it into the street for the horses to trample.

She evinced no reaction at all. Which of course spoke volumes. Not that he had an iota of doubt on the matter, but if she truly was innocent, his accusations would have produced a reaction of some sort. Fury, most probably. He'd never known a woman with such a temper.

"As I said, my lord, *you were mistaken*." She put the faintest emphasis on the final words, and he received her message loud and clear.

She wanted him to take the hint, accept the lie, and leave her be. Damn her. She knew he'd like nothing more than to forget the entire incident.

She offered him the craven solution. If he took it, he would know himself for a coward. Worse, she would know it, too.

He wished, with sudden exasperation, that she'd make it easier for him, admit to her presence and let him get on with this damnable proposal. But when had anything that involved Georgiana Black been easy?

She left him in the awkward position of offering to right a wrong she refused to acknowledge they'd both committed.

"I know not why you seek to continue this pretense," he said, checking his horses to let a dray lumber past them, "but I must tell you that I am not so easily diverted from my purpose."

"No," she said a little wistfully. "You were ever a steadfast type, were you not? Some might call it stubborn. Or pigheaded, perhaps."

He ground his teeth.

She sighed, and in the voice of one humoring a child, said, "Very well, in the interests of concluding this delightful interview as soon as possible . . . let us pretend—

for argument's sake, you understand—that it was indeed
I at this party, in this bedchamber, with you."

She fanned herself a little with her gloved hand.
"Goodness, I'm all aflutter just thinking of it."

His frustration fired to anger. "Do you think this is a
jest, ma'am?"

"Oh, the very cream of jests. However," she continued, "let us pretend that all of this happened and it is
not a figment of your imagination. What then?"

Her mocking tone stripped any desire to couch his
proposal in terms that might make it acceptable to her.

"Obviously, I must offer you my hand in marriage,"
he snapped. "For an intelligent woman, you are remarkably slow today."

Finally, she gave him the full view of her face. Shock
etched across her features.

For a bare instant, her plush lips quivered.

Then she laughed.

Threw her head back and laughed. A throaty, husky
sound that filled him with all kinds of vengeful, thoroughly bawdy thoughts.

The struggle to keep his hands to himself, com-
pounded by the frustration of bowling through populated
Brighton streets, fully occupied with steering his strong-
willed cattle, made the pressure build inside him until he
bit out, "I take it your answer is no."

Her chuckles ended on a long sigh. "Oh! My dear
Lord Beckenham, you *vastly* underrate your charms if
you think that."

Georgie wished she might capture the expression on
Beckenham's face in her sketchbook. Ludicrous in its
horrified disbelief, devoid of the iron control he'd hith-
erto displayed.

She was so utterly irate, she'd needed the short interval of appalled, well nigh hysterical laughter to marshal her resources.

If a less pleasant task than proposing to her had confronted Beckenham in the past six years, she doubted it. He couldn't have shown his distaste more clearly if he'd written it in fireworks in the sky.

So of course, she refused to oblige him and give him the short sharp refusal such an ungracious, insulting proposal demanded.

She would punish him. It was only fair for the utter humiliation he'd put her through.

"That is, of course, a most elegantly expressed and advantageous offer, my lord," she observed. "I am so overcome, I can barely find the words to reply."

He met her limpid gaze, and a gleam of understanding showed. He'd never been slow on the uptake.

"You flatter me," he said briefly.

"On the contrary, my lord. It is rather you who flatter me. Not many ladies may say they've been engaged to an earl *twice*."

Truly, what woman could resist?

Even now, she was sorely tempted. She might well have given in to weakness and accepted him if the manner of his proposals hadn't utterly lacerated her pride. Reminded her, if she'd needed reminding, that he'd never thought of her as anything more than a duty. A tiresome one, at that.

But for a few heated minutes last night, there'd been no thought of duty, had there? If he had indeed known it was she all along.

Oh, her head ached with the permutations, the implications. And what did he think her reasons might have been for allowing him such liberties? Did he think she'd done it to extract this proposal from him?

Beckenham had always been singularly unaware of his devastating effect on women. Would he believe she'd been unable to resist him? That there'd been no guile on her part when she let herself be swept up into the maelstrom of his passion, no logical thought in her head at all.

Unlike Beckenham, Georgie had never been ignorant of her own charms. She'd flexed her power over men like a fairground strongman flexed his muscles. She still received declarations of undying devotion on a weekly basis. Her house was always as full as a flower market of the posies and bouquets her admirers sent her.

But her feminine charms had never brought her the things she most desired: true love and a purpose in life.

She'd lost any chance of the first when she fixed her sights on a man who would never return her regard. The second, she'd lost first to her father's indifference, then to Lord Beckenham, and finally, to her sister.

The wholly unwelcome notion popped into her head that Beckenham might still want that inheritance. Was that the reason his proposal had come so swiftly? An unpalatable thought. She might choke if she had to swallow any more insults today.

With only a slight hesitation, she said, "You know I don't stand to inherit Cloverleigh any longer, don't you, Marcus?"

The words came out in a rush, sounding a little breathless. How irritating that she should be so anxious for his answer.

"Yes, I did know it," he said. "My offer springs solely from my wish to do the honorable thing. Your reputation if anyone discovered what had happened between us—"

"*Nothing* happened between us." That came out too sharply. Something large and merciless seemed to be crushing her skull.

He drew rein, and the curricle came to an abrupt stop.

Turning in his seat, he said fiercely, "Did you really think I wouldn't know you? Anywhere, in any guise? Even with a mask and hair powder, I recognized you immediately. Why did you do it?"

She swallowed hard. "I don't know what you're talking about."

His hands flexed; the horses shifted restlessly. She knew he dearly wished to shake her. She wanted him to. She longed to feel his hands on her again, even in anger. The thought filled her with fury and shame.

After last night . . . Oh, she'd thought she was safe from him at least, if not from Pearce.

But he'd known her from the very start. Why, then, had he spoken to her in such a manner, kissed her like that? Touched her in ways she blushed to recall? He must have been driven by . . . What? Rage? Disgust, probably. A wish to teach her a lesson she'd been too overcome with longing and excitement to learn.

One thing was certain. At least for a brief space of time, there'd been no mistaking his desire.

She burned to ask him what had made him stop, but that would mean openly admitting her part in the business. Instinct told her if she maintained her denial, he would eventually accept her rejection of his suit. Perhaps not with a clear conscience, but he'd leave her be.

If she admitted her part, he'd demand answers she couldn't give him. He might feel obliged to act in a way that would force her to accept his hand in marriage. She'd no doubt he'd succeed. He could be ruthless when his honor was at stake.

There was another tack she could take. It rather turned her stomach, but she grew desperate. "If I were this mysterious masked woman," she said, "do you think you are the only man I met in a dark bedchamber last night?"

His face hardened to stone. "Yes. I do think it."

She forced a spurt of low laughter. "Oh, my lord. You are too trusting of mysterious masked ladies."

"I am, am I?"

She nodded. "Really, I don't think there's any more to discuss, do you? I reject your proposals, my lord. I would thank you for the honor you do me, but since you accused me of wanton behavior in the same breath, I find it impossible to do so."

In a low, hard voice, he said, "My proposals were honorably made. I do not deserve that they be thrown in my face."

She dismissed that with a wave of her hand. "Don't be absurd. You came here today with the utmost reluctance. You paid your addresses in such a manner that any woman with an ounce of backbone must refuse. Do not attempt to take the high ground now and act as if I'm a fool to say you nay, my lord. You don't want to marry me any more than I wish to wed you."

His face froze. Then it relaxed as he set the horses in motion again.

She ought to feel triumphant. Instead, her chest was at once hollow and filled with pain. She couldn't resist a final shot. "You have salved your conscience by making the offer, misguided though it was. You may return to your normal, well-ordered existence now, Lord Beckenham, with your precious honor intact."

Chapter Six

Beckenham said no more as he guided his horses back to Georgie's lodgings.

Well, she'd rejected him. As he'd known she would. He ought to be relieved. Now he could go on with his plans for marrying a nice, quiet lady who would slip into the steady stream of his nice, ordered life with nary a ripple.

The interview with Georgie did not go at all the way he'd expected. For one thing, she'd denied the entire event took place.

He didn't doubt for an instant the lady in the powder had been Georgie. No other woman came remotely close to her in physical appearance, but it wasn't just that. It was the way she held herself, her voice, the proud tilt of her head. The bright flare of passion that fired inside him when he held her in his arms. The sense of rightness edged with the thrill of excitement, of danger.

No other woman had ever affected him this way. The very air had crackled between them like a storm in the heavens.

She must have felt it. Yet here she sat, as cool as a cucumber, calmly rejecting his offer of marriage.

It rankled, damn her.

"I'll take you back to your lodgings," he said.

"Yes, I believe I shall need to lie down to recover from the shock," she said in a caustic tone that was more hers than the temptress's coo she'd briefly assumed. "Honestly, Marcus, you make me wonder sometimes."

"Yes, you might spend an hour or so devoted to serious reflection," he said, conscious of a wish to irk and confound her as much as she did him. "I won't take your negative for a firm answer."

The words were out of his mouth before he knew he'd meant to say them.

She gasped, clearly as surprised as he was. "You may very well do so. I shan't change my mind."

"Perhaps Lady Arden might change it for you." Satisfaction at the hunted expression that crossed her face burned in his chest. "When she hears about last night."

"You would never be so ungentlemanly as to spread such a falsehood about me far and wide."

"There are so many erroneous assumptions in that sentence, it is difficult to know where to begin to refute them," said Beckenham as he expertly feather-edged a corner. "It is no falsehood to report what transpired between us last night to your kinswoman. As for spreading the tale far and wide, Lady Arden has your best interests at heart. She is also discretion itself."

Georgie fixed those sea green eyes upon him. "You want this? You truly wish to wed me after what happened six years ago?"

She was right. He must be insane to force the issue. He did *not* wish to be betrothed to her. He'd come here to satisfy his honor; that was all.

A blinding flash brought insight. His overpowering desire was not to wed her, but for her to acknowledge what had transpired between them last night. That it was all her—those searing kisses, the press of her lush body against him, the cries of pleasure. He wanted her to admit out loud that he could have taken her then and there if he'd wished.

"I'll call again tomorrow to have your answer."

She glared up at him, her irises glistening turquoise in the strong sunshine. "Are you proposing to cross swords with me on this, my lord? Precisely to what lengths are you prepared to go?" She gave a mocking laugh. "Ought I to be flattered?"

"It was not my intention to minister to your vanity," said Beckenham.

"Oh, I acquit you of that, believe me."

"Nevertheless, I will call again tomorrow." Anticipation gripped his belly at the thought.

"I will not be at home to you, whether you call tomorrow or Doomsday," she declared.

"Now, why would you make such a claim?" Beckenham wondered. "When you know I will come up and fetch you if you deny me."

"Do that, my lord, and I shall have one of my footmen throw you out."

Beckenham laughed. A hoarse, rusty sound. "You are most welcome to try."

Georgiana paid meticulous attention to her appearance that evening. She was only attending a dinner given by some rather tedious connection of her father's, then doing the rounds of various entertainments. There was zero likelihood of Beckenham attending any of these, but for some reason, Georgie felt more self-conscious tonight than she'd been at her come-out ball.

Smith, perhaps sensing Georgie's mood, had outdone herself. Well, what could not be achieved when one possessed the fortune and taste—and, one might say, boldness—to dress precisely as one pleased?

To the surprise of everyone, not least herself, Georgie had never accepted any of the many advantageous offers of marriage made her. That meant, when she finally reached the ripe old age of twenty-five—only a few months hence—she would inherit her fortune outright.

Her trustees had warned her this would make her the subject of unscrupulous fortune-hunters. She was well aware of the fact; she'd swept many such leeches from her skin with a well-practiced flick.

"You are fire and ice tonight," drawled a soft, deep voice in her ear.

Georgie turned her head to meet a pair of clear green eyes in a face that might have belonged to a poet, rather than a villain. High cheekbones, a brow many would call noble, a slightly aquiline nose. Thick sable locks styled in the latest mode. A full-lipped, sensitive mouth that belied the nature of a satyr.

Lord Pearce. Of course. Her mind had been filled with Beckenham, but it was far more likely she'd meet her less congenial nemesis tonight. He'd returned from exile and clearly meant to let the Polite World know it.

The heat of his body, the puff of breath at her ear . . . His nearness implied an intimacy that disgusted her.

She shifted to put a more polite distance between them, regarding him coldly. "Fire and ice?"

She knew what he meant. Her white silk gown overlaid with a silver lace robe was cold in its purity, her brazen locks a stark contrast.

"How unkind of you to make fun of my hair, sir."

"You mistake me. The fire is in your eyes." Pearce's gaze swept over her, as mocking and practiced as a connoisseur viewing a fraudulent masterpiece. "Yes, there is a distinct dash of challenge in their sparkle to-night. What poor devil has had the misfortune to incur your displeasure, hmm?"

She put up her fingertips to cover a small, false yawn, distantly glad they did not tremble. "I cannot imagine what you mean. I am the most even-tempered creature alive."

"A manifestly false observation," said Pearce.

"Oh, I assure you," said Georgie. "Were my temper as hot as my hair, by now I should have fetched a fruit knife from the supper table and driven it through your tiny black heart."

He threw back his head and laughed, making several heads turn. His mirth spoke of pure enjoyment. "Oh, my dear Georgiana, how I've missed you."

He always called her "Georgiana," not Miss Black or even Georgie or G. It set her teeth on edge. But she didn't reprove him for using her name so familiarly. Best to ignore than rise to the bait.

She dearly wished she had the reckless courage to carry out her threat with the fruit knife. Instead, she murmured, "Lady Arden will be looking for me. Excuse me, sir."

Bestowing a vague nod of farewell upon him, she moved slowly through the crowd, head held high. Aware of the trail of gossip she left in her wake.

"There you are, my dear," said Lady Arden as Georgie reached her side. The older lady fanned herself languidly. "Such a crush. Every year I vow never to return to Brighton, and every year, here I am again."

A statuesque beauty of mature years, Lady Arden was elegant tonight in bronze silk. A matching turban set off the toffee highlights in her hair and brought out the brandy of her eyes.

All young ladies of the Black clan made their debuts under Lady Arden's aegis if their anxious parents could possibly secure her. Lady Arden was a matchmaker unparalleled amongst the Ton. Combining taste and judgment with a certain elegant ruthlessness, Lady Arden's success in arranging advantageous matches for her charges was legendary.

Which was why she found Georgie's single state, the sole blot on her gilt-edged copybook, wholly unacceptable.

She brought forward her latest protégée, a young lady who blushed and curtsied. "You know Miss James, of course."

"Yes, indeed." Georgiana smiled down at the petite, rather shy debutante who was some sort of relation to both herself and Lady Arden. "How did you enjoy your first London season, Miss James?"

She chatted amiably, seeking to relax the poor little chit. Despite the girl's months on the Ton, she looked as nervous as a church mouse.

All the while, Georgie felt Pearce's regard like poisoned darts pricking at her shoulder blades.

What was he up to? She ought not to have run away from him before she'd discovered more.

And she had run, hadn't she? In the most craven manner. She marveled at her eighteen-year-old self finding Pearce so compelling. What had possessed her?

Then, his drawling insouciance had seemed thrilling. Now, she knew that his sleekly handsome exterior hid a ruthless self-interest that far exceeded his professed devotion to her.

Merely letting herself be seen talking to Pearce was enough to set tongues wagging. If Beckenham called on her again tomorrow as he'd vowed to do, there'd be even more fodder for gossip.

What were the odds that both men should come back into her life at the same moment?

Ah, but of course. With her luck in matters of the heart, that was almost a certainty.

Beckenham called up to Lady Black's rooms on three separate occasions the following day. He was unsurprised that Georgie was denied to him. He would have been rather disappointed if she'd let him get the better of her too easily.

He didn't make good on his threat to fetch her himself. Georgie would have been clever enough to absent herself today, and he would only look a fool storming into an empty chamber. Quite apart from the gossip such behavior would cause.

However, he'd discovered from Georgie's stepmother that they were engaged to dine with friends at eight, and that later they were to attend the Marstons' ball.

Knowing Georgie's habits, he calculated to a nicety how long she would take to make herself ready for the evening and called when he knew she must be home to dress.

Of course, when he inquired, he was told neither Lady Black nor Georgie were at liberty to receive him. The servant who gave him the news pressed her lips together in disapproval at the strange hour he'd chosen to call.

"Smith, isn't it?" he said.

The dresser gave a slight start of surprise. "Yes, my lord."

He clasped his hands behind his back. "You are Miss Black's personal maid, are you not?"

"Yes, my lord."

"Be good enough to inform your mistress that if she

does not present herself to me here in ten minutes, I shall go up to her."

The dresser made a choking sound. Then she regarded him with a sapient eye. "My mistress would box my ears if I carried such an message to her."

He gave a bark of laughter. "Tell her to box my ears if she wants to commit violence against anyone."

Of course Georgie would never box a maid's ears, nor would the redoubtable Smith stand for such treatment. They had a singularly egalitarian relationship, which was odd considering Georgie looked down her nose at many members of the *haut ton*.

The maid gave a nod that held the barest hint of . . . What? Approval? "I shall deliver your message, my lord."

He chose a farming periodical from the selection on the table and settled down to wait.

And she kept him waiting. A full twenty minutes passed before the answer came.

Smith, staring straight ahead with a wooden cast to her countenance, stated, "My lord. My mistress desires me to say that she will not come down in ten minutes or at any other time. She also said to inform you that she is in her bath, so don't say you weren't warned."

The brazenness of it surprised him into another laugh, even as the image the words conjured in his mind made blood race to his groin in a hot, thick rush.

Georgie, all pink and cream loveliness, water beading over her shoulders as she sponged soap over one slender arm. Her long legs bent, knees peeping from the water like smooth white hillocks. Pink, taut nipples and rich, creamy mounds of—

The maid cleared her throat.

He dragged his mind back to the present. "Is that so?" He thought for a moment. Then he slowly uncoiled himself from his chair. "Perhaps you'd better announce me," he said gently, and gestured for the maid to precede him.

With a choked sound that might have been an outraged protest or a smothered snort of laughter, the maid hurried off.

Beckenham followed at a more leisurely pace. But instead of pursuing the bustling maid farther along the corridor, he made a right turn at the stairs.

As he walked out of Georgie's lodgings, he whistled a soft, jaunty tune. He wondered how long it would be before she would realize he'd left.

"You at a ball, Becks?" said Lydgate. "Now, this, I must see."

He'd settled himself in the dressing room attached to Beckenham's allotted chamber with a brandy and a critical expression.

Beckenham groaned inwardly. What uncanny sixth sense had led Lydgate to be at home still when Beckenham had rung for his valet, Beckenham did not know.

Dressing for the ball didn't take long. He'd brought suitable clothing, for Xavier always made a point of dressing for dinner, even when he dined alone.

Beckenham nodded to his valet to leave the pile of cravats on the table beside him and said, "Thank you, Peters. You may go."

"I often go to balls," said Beckenham, deciding to be difficult. The longer he kept Lydgate arguing, the more time he had to think of a reasonable explanation for this singular departure from habit tonight.

Oddly, he found that his hands shook when he tied his cravat. He tied it the same way every time but now he couldn't seem to get it right.

For an instant, he held out his hand flat, palm down,

and watched it tremble. Then he stripped off the crumpled neck-cloth and picked another from the pile.

"Country balls are not the same," said Lydgate, unfolding his long, lean body from the chair and approaching Beckenham at the full-length looking glass. "Here, let me."

Beckenham growled and shook him off. Annoyance lent him the necessary determination and he tied his cravat with his usual neat propriety, if not with flair.

Lydgate sighed. "You look as somber as an undertaker. At least use a jewel or something to liven it up a bit."

Beckenham grunted. "Sorry, I left my tiara at home." He picked up his black evening coat. "Help me with this, will you?"

Lydgate muscled him into the close-fitting coat. "Your tailoring is all it should be, at all events," he muttered.

"Weston makes all my coats," Beckenham said indifferently. He gave a slight smile. "I do listen to you on occasion, Cousin."

"Listen to me now, then," said Lydgate seriously. *"Don't do it."*

Startled, Beckenham frowned. "What?"

"Don't make another play for Georgie Black."

Beckenham suppressed the oath that rose to his lips. He ought not to be surprised. "The Idle Intelligencer has not been so idle it seems."

"So you don't deny it."

Beckenham shrugged. Why bother? They would all know soon enough when he became betrothed to Georgie Black once more.

It had occurred to him that the circumstance would create a sensation both in his family and among the Ton. But the more he'd considered the matter, the more he'd known it absolutely must happen.

That's what he'd been waiting for all these years. Another chance.

This was no longer about the joining of bloodlines or estates. She must believe the latter at any event, for she had not inherited Cloverleigh. This was about . . .

He frowned. He wasn't entirely sure what it was about. Only that he had to have her. He wouldn't let her slip through his fingers again.

"You're too late, Lydgate," he said, straightening his ruffled cuffs. "I've asked Georgie Black to be my wife."

The stunned expression in Lydgate's blue eyes was swiftly replaced by suspicion. "She tricked you, didn't she? She entrapped you at the party. Georgiana Black was the shady lady."

"She did not entrap me. In fact, she has rejected my suit." That last part had been abominably difficult to admit.

It certainly arrested Lydgate's righteous anger. He shook his head. "She's playing a deep game, mark my words."

"My dear Lydgate, if she was so determined to have me, she wouldn't have called off our betrothal all those years ago. She wouldn't have rejected my proposal yesterday."

But he had to convince her to accept him tonight.

He was well aware that his attitude had undergone a complete reversal in the space of that hour or so he'd spent in her company yesterday.

He'd gone from performing an unpleasant duty with the fervent hope—nay, the comfortable conviction— that she'd reject him, to burning with righteous fury when she'd refused to at least acknowledge what had happened between them.

He'd wanted to see some sign of how deeply that

encounter had affected her. Surely it must have thrown her into chaos, as it had him. How could it not?

And then . . . He didn't know when, but somehow that emotion had transformed into a steadfast desire to turn back the clock and right past mistakes. He *wanted* her to say yes. He wasn't so perverse or so shallow that he wanted her only because she didn't want him.

And she *did* want him. That trembling, husky voice still echoed in his head, begging him not to go.

He faced Lydgate. "You will not meddle in my affairs."

Regret tinged Lydgate's expression. "No, Becks. I see it is far too late for that."

They arrived at the ball sometime before eleven o'clock. Beckenham ought to have left it later, perhaps, but he didn't want to risk missing her. Ladies like Georgie always kept several engagements each night. She'd once remarked to him that unmarried ladies must feel like traveling salesmen, peddling their wares hither and yon.

He'd thought her pleasantly smug in her own status as his betrothed. He'd liked it.

If only he'd known.

The distance of this house from the town of Brighton itself meant that it would most likely be the final destination of guests this evening. Some would stay overnight; some would be driven back to town in the wee hours by their sleepy coachmen.

Xavier had easily secured Beckenham an invitation. Few hostesses would refuse admittance to an earl. Even fewer hostesses with marriageable daughters would turn away an unmarried earl.

He wouldn't be an unmarried earl for much longer. Not if he had anything to say about it.

Chapter Seven

For the first time that evening, Georgie felt the tension about her neck and shoulders ease the tiniest bit.

She enjoyed dancing and tonight she'd chosen partners for their agility and grace. The waltz, so scandalous to the older generation, had surely been put on earth just for her. She thought of nothing but the dance.

And if every time a tall, dark-haired gentleman entered the ballroom her heart skipped merrily into her throat, that was mere folly. Beckenham never attended society balls. He wouldn't break any of his cast-iron rules for her.

Drifting through the crowd at the conclusion of one of the sets, Georgie spied Lord Pearce. Quickly, she turned and headed in the opposite direction, trying not to appear as if she hurried. Drat her hair. He would spot her immediately.

True to her prediction, Pearce caught up with her in the card room ten minutes later and bowed over her hand. "My dear Miss Black. Were you avoiding me?"

"Why would I do that, sir?" She slipped her hand

from his with more haste than politeness and moved away from him, ostensibly to watch the play.

He followed, of course. "I'd hoped for a word with you alone."

"You won't get it," she said through her smiling teeth. "Good God, sir. Haven't you done enough?"

His voice hardened. "My dear Miss Black. I haven't started yet."

Her stomach clenched with fear but she wouldn't give him the satisfaction of seeing her distress. She lifted her chin and joined in the general murmur of approbation when Mr. Tilton won his hand at piquet.

"Don't you wonder why I'm back in England?" he said. "My aunt, bless her, is about to cock up her toes. My obscenely rich, horribly high-in-the-instep aunt."

"Indeed?" she said. "I would commiserate but I suspect you will be more likely to celebrate."

"Oh, yes. For she intends to leave her entire fortune to me."

She hissed out a breath but her tension wouldn't ease. "I cannot conceive what interest you think I have in your fortunes."

He raised his eyebrows in gentle disbelief.

After a pause, he said, "I'd always thought to return to see you comfortably wed with a gaggle of children around you. I am glad it is not so."

She stared at him incredulously. He didn't have the unmitigated arrogance to believe she'd waited for him, did he?

"You never did anything that smacked of the commonplace," he added in a curiously husky tone. His gaze ran over her. "I thought you a pearl past price when you were eighteen. I'd never have guessed you'd grow even more ravishing with time."

She was too accustomed to flattery to blush and bridle at this sentiment. How like a man to think all he need do was praise a woman's appearance for her to melt at his feet.

"And yet, I fear I cannot return the compliment, Lord Pearce. *You* are quite dreadfully commonplace, you know."

Unperturbed, he said, "Oh, not commonplace, surely. Obvious, perhaps. Your beauty is so dazzling, my dear, no red-blooded male could fail to remark upon it."

Beckenham had not remarked upon it, she thought. And didn't know whether to be resentful or grateful for the circumstance.

Now she came to think of it, not even when she'd stood with Beckenham in that quiet, fraught bedchamber had he made one allusion to her appearance. Granted, she'd worn a mask, but the Marquis of Steyne hadn't been so reticent a few minutes earlier, had he?

Perhaps Beckenham didn't admire her style of beauty. A lowering thought.

"So solemn," said that hateful, mocking voice. From the corner of her eye she saw Pearce draw his snuffbox from his pocket. "Are you afraid of me?"

She sniffed. "You forget who bested whom in our last encounter, my lord."

He turned the snuffbox in his fingers. "I would rather call the result of that last contest a draw. And unlike you and my lord Beckenham, I have one last card to play."

The blood turned to ice water in her veins. How could she have overlooked that?

"Yes, I see you remember."

The hard knot in her chest tightened. "You'd seek to ruin me."

"Not if you give me what I desire, my dear."

She forced herself to ask. "And what is that?"

He laughed softly. "Now, now. Such things ought not to be rushed. All in good time."

He took a pinch of snuff and dusted his fingers. "I must compliment you on your charming sister, my dear."

So he had known who Violet was at that awful party! Georgie wasn't controlled enough to conceal her reaction. "Stay away from her," she hissed. "If you hurt her, I will make you wish you were never born."

"I was fortunate enough to meet Miss Violet at—" He tapped his lip thoughtfully. "Now, where was it again? Oh, yes, now I recall. It must have been in Promenade Grove. Or was it at Pavilion Parade, with that dragon of a maid of yours? A vast pity Miss Violet is not out yet. She will take the Ton by storm."

"I refuse to discuss my sister with the likes of you, my lord."

Georgie could barely move her lips. She felt as if she'd been sculpted from ice. She didn't know whether to believe him ignorant of Violet's presence at Steyne's villa. Pearce was the sort of man who didn't miss anything. The mere fact her sister's name crossed his lips was an affront.

Had he met Violet often in Brighton without Georgie's knowledge? That could well be the case. Even though Violet wasn't out in society, she went for walks with her friends and took part in harmless entertainments like picnics and day excursions with other young ladies and gentlemen of her age. All under strict chaperonage, of course.

But she knew from experience how adept Pearce could be at eluding and confounding chaperones.

The suspicion that he meant to use Violet to hurt her grew.

He glanced around him at the card tables. "The play

here is remarkably dull. Shall we return to the ball-room, my dear?"

Georgie's mind seethed with possibilities. What did Pearce want from her? If she knew that, she might discover how he meant to go about achieving his ends. If he still desired to wed her, he would not publish the letter. If he wanted something else—revenge, perhaps—he need have no such scruples.

He held out his arm to her with smooth, confident expectation. She didn't want to touch him but prudence forced her to comply. Laying her fingertips on his arm was like stroking a coiled viper.

Pearce looked down at her with a glint in his eyes. "Smile like you mean it, dear Georgiana."

Gritting her teeth into the semblance of a smile, she replied, "May you rot in Hades, my lord."

He laughed as if she'd made some irresistible witticism. "Oh, undoubtedly. But I believe I shall enjoy myself considerably before I meet my fiery fate."

She had no doubt he'd enjoy himself by punishing her for what she'd done to him all those years ago. But if tonight's conversation were anything to judge by, he intended to play with her first. He meant to take pleasure in a slow, drawn-out torture.

Had she been stupid to give him that kind of power? At the time, she'd seen no alternative. She'd made her decision with nary a thought for herself.

No, that wasn't the case. She'd considered the consequences and decided she could bear any punishment Lord Pearce meted out.

Now she would reap what her eighteen-year-old self had sown. Older and wiser, she was no longer certain she could bear such a bitter harvest.

She could only guess what he intended, what her choices might be. Ruination, certainly. Marriage to

Pearce. Or did he no longer care about wedding her, now that he was to inherit a fortune? Would he insist on taking her as his mistress instead?

Worse than any of those unpalatable alternatives, did he mean to court Violet? Georgie knew—none better!—how beguiling Pearce could be.

Perhaps, she thought, rather desperately, she might at least distract him from Violet. There was only one way she could think of to do that. She must let him get close to her again.

And just when Beckenham . . . *Beckenham*.

The thought of him stopped her heart. She could not allow him to be drawn into this mess a second time. History repeating itself with a vengeance.

Thank God she'd refused him outright during their drive yesterday morning. When he pursued her so doggedly all day, she'd wavered. If only he'd court her properly, she'd thought. No, not court her. *Woo* her like a lover instead of treating her like a tiresome obligation.

The hot spike of excitement she'd experienced when a panting Smith scurried into her bedchamber to tell her Beckenham was on his way in to see her bathe that evening had been deliciously intense. She liked flirting with Beckenham. She'd never been able to coax him into such risqué frivolity when they were betrothed.

Perhaps, she'd said to herself, if he'd only bend, just a little . . . If she could see a way to make him fall in love with her . . .

But now such wistful daydreams had been shattered by the hateful man beside her.

Her pride raged at being obliged to endure his company a second longer than she wished. Over the past year or so, she'd become accustomed to ordering her life largely as she pleased, with no man to stymie her. No Papa, no Lord Beckenham. Even her trustees were easily handled. She had only to bat her lashes and smile and they would do whatever she wanted—within reason.

Now she must submit to a more ruthless tyrant than any of them might have been. To think that once upon a time, she'd found Lord Pearce's smooth dangerousness rather thrilling. Now he took on the grim, sadistic aspect of a jailer.

Fortune did not favor her. As soon as they reentered the ballroom, the musicians struck up for the waltz.

Without a word to her, Pearce slid an arm around her waist and drew her swiftly into the dance. As one who had the right.

As soon as he entered the ballroom, Beckenham's gaze flew to Georgie like iron filings to a magnet. She was dancing with Pearce. Damn him to hell!

"So it's true our friend is back," said Lydgate as if he'd read Beckenham's mind. "Thought he'd never show his face again."

"You underestimated his gall."

Lydgate might be abreast of the latest news, but Beckenham had made his own inquiries about Pearce. The dog had returned to his kennel, all right. Hoping to get his hands on a sizable inheritance.

After six years, it seemed everyone was prepared to forget Pearce's transgression. At least until they knew whether he'd succeeded in securing his aunt's fortune. Despite the veneer of gentility, the Ton was a venal, fickle lot.

"I suppose you've heard about his aunt," said Lydgate. "Rich as Croesus, so they say. Holed up in Bath on her deathbed, besieged by adoring relations."

Beckenham nodded. He didn't care about Pearce's

prospects. He was far more interested in the way Georgie seemed to hang on Pearce's every word.

The years rolled back. He remembered other nights, in other ballrooms, where he'd propped himself against the wall, watching Georgie and Pearce waltz. All that raw emotion flooded back. He wanted to pummel the smiling villain into a bloody pulp.

How dare he so much as speak to her? How dare he touch her hand?

Beckenham had believed Georgie when she told him there was nothing between her and Pearce all those years ago. Now, watching them entertain each other, he began to wonder. How had Pearce come by that lock of hair?

But Georgie was no liar, and she'd denied all knowledge of the incriminating ringlet. Call him gullible, but he still believed her version of events.

That didn't mean he was happy to see her whirling down the floor in Pearce's arms, looking delighted to be there.

As they spun past, Beckenham had a fierce urge to thrust his hand out and yank Pearce away from her by the absurdly high collar of his immaculately cut coat.

"From what I hear, it's by no means a foregone conclusion where the aunt will leave her fortune," Lydgate was saying. "That's why Pearce felt he had to come back here to turn her up sweet. Rumor has it the old lady is very haughty and as shrewd as she can stare. Not pleased about his fall from grace over the duel. She won't see him, so he's come to Brighton to lick his wounds and regroup."

Beckenham had a fair idea of the reason Pearce was in Brighton now. Well, whatever the case, he could forget about trying to get his hooks into Georgie.

The waltz ended and the two of them were swallowed by the crowd.

"Hold this, will you?"

Beckenham shoved his glass at Lydgate—who muttered something about not being a damned footman—and headed in Georgie's direction.

He spent some little time searching the throng before he saw Georgie. Alone now, she moved with her usual grace but in an inexorable fashion toward the ballroom's entrance.

Without appearing to hurry, Beckenham lengthened his stride to catch up.

As if she knew he followed her, Georgie darted a glance over her shoulder. Alarm flared her nostrils, widened her eyes. Her entire body seemed poised for undignified flight.

The reaction was brief. She appeared to collect herself sufficiently to stand her ground and make a regal curtsy as he bowed deeply to her.

He held out his hand. "My dance, I think."

She hesitated, then rewarded his bold assurance. Her fingers trembled a little as she placed her hand in his. He saw the defiance in her glinting smile.

"You seem very cozy with Pearce tonight," he muttered as he led her back to the floor.

"How on earth can one be cozy in the midst of a crush like this?" Her voice was light, a little shaky.

"Oh, I think you know precisely how. You waltzed with him."

She nodded, not meeting his gaze. "I have danced with many other gentlemen, too."

And not just this evening. No doubt she'd danced with hundreds since she'd last taken the floor with him.

The feel of her in his arms, even with the regulation distance between them, was so all-consuming, he could scarcely think straight. He might almost pity those other poor sods who would never in their lives get closer to her than this.

Her scent drifted to him, light and floral but with the merest hint of some exotic, smoky note. The flagrant femininity of her flooded his senses.

He'd known many women intimately, yet he felt as if he'd lived without the mere sight of one for the past age. Nothing compared to his hand clasping Georgie's, his arm around her waist, the top of her head tantalizingly close to his lips.

"I must suppose you know the reason I'm here," he said.

She looked up. "Yes. But I wish you had not troubled yourself. My answer has not changed, my lord."

Something plummeted in his stomach. "Nevertheless, indulge me with a stroll on the terrace."

He realized the request had come out as more of an abrupt order, but he was put out by how much more welcoming she'd been toward Pearce. With Pearce, she'd laughed and flirted and tossed her head.

Her eyes narrowed, presumably at his tone.

He rephrased. "My dear Miss Black, you appear a trifle overheated. Might I escort you to the terrace to take the air?"

Her lips twitched. Then she gave a rueful sigh. "Very well, my lord. Since you ask so nicely."

They did not linger on the terrace for long. Moonlight streamed through the trees, making shifting patterns on the soft turf beneath their feet. A number of couples had accepted the invitation provided by paper lanterns that lined the walks throughout the garden to lose themselves for a minute or an hour in the sylvan setting.

Georgie slipped outside her own body to watch herself

with Beckenham, desperate to capture and remember the perfection of this moment. A quiet interlude with the man she . . . With Marcus. The fresh, ocean-washed air seemed sweet with promise, tantalizing. She might still turn back from her purpose, fling herself into his arms, sob out the whole story, beg him to keep her safe.

His solid, large presence beside her invited her trust. But trust had never been the problem between them. She'd trust him with her life. She simply did not trust him with his own.

It didn't help to tell herself that until that day, she'd no hope of ever having even this much from Beckenham. Somehow, it seemed doubly cruel that any chance they might have had together would be snatched from her a second time.

Perhaps she'd been wrong all those years ago. Perhaps she ought to have behaved like a lady and let him fight that duel. If she had, he might have won it by shooting Pearce in the shoulder or some such civilized method, while Pearce's shot missed. They would both have lived, honor satisfied, and she would have wed Beckenham as planned.

But at the time, the affair had seemed momentous to her, a clear-cut matter of life and death. Had that been mere vanity on her part? What girl doesn't dream of men fighting over her? How her friends sighed and exclaimed over it when they'd heard. But she'd always been a practical woman, impatient with such fancies.

Afterwards, Lady Arden had accused her of deliberately engineering the situation.

She hadn't meant to do it, but that didn't lessen her culpability. Perhaps it made it worse. Stupid, stupid girl!

She still thought that Pearce, at least, had held a deadly purpose in provoking the challenge. And her intervention had achieved its aim, hadn't it? Beckenham was neither dead nor living in exile as an escaped murderer. They'd been free of Pearce for six years. If it hadn't been for this aunt and her fortune, they might never have seen him again.

But no matter the rights and wrongs of her behavior, she couldn't go back and change the past. And even if Pearce hadn't returned, she couldn't accept Beckenham.

He didn't love her, and that was that.

In a quiet stand of trees, Beckenham stopped and suddenly, she was in his arms. A shiver of longing and desire ran through her. How could the strength and warmth of him feel so utterly perfect, when everything else was all wrong?

He bent his head toward her, but all of a sudden she couldn't go through with that part of her plan. She'd wanted to give him a disgust of her by playing the wanton, but she wasn't strong enough to let him kiss her. Not tonight. Or ever again.

She gathered all her strength and pressed her palm to his shoulder, holding him at bay. "Marcus, I meant what I said. I will not marry you."

He stilled. Then his arms slowly dropped to his sides. It seemed to her that he paled, though that could have been the moonlight. "Why not?"

She couldn't tell him the truth, so she made herself give a careless shrug. "I'd be a fool to marry. I want for neither position nor fortune. In a very few months I shall be my own mistress. I find I like that idea very much."

"You cannot mean it," he said, incredulous. "You wish to remain a *spinster*?"

She laughed, though she felt the reverse of mirthful.

"You say that as if it's a dreadful fate. Don't you see how I should loathe being at any man's beck and call?"

"Our marriage would not be like that."

She snorted. "Oh, would it not, Marcus? The first instance of defiance and you would be quick to show me who was master."

He fell silent for a time. Then he said, "You cannot deny the passion between us. At least be honest about that. It *was* you at Steyne's villa, wasn't it?"

How fortunate he couldn't see her blush. She made herself give a throaty laugh. "Yes, it was I. Of course it was." She waved her hand. "There. I've admitted it. Make of it what you will, I am sure I do not care. But cease all this nonsense about marriage. No one knows what happened between us that night. There is no need to make a martyr of yourself over it."

"It is not martyrdom to act as a man of honor," Beckenham began.

If she heard one more word about his confounded honor, she'd scream. "Answer me this, Marcus. Do you—?"

She broke off. She'd almost asked him if he loved her. But she couldn't bear to see the look of pure astonishment on his face at the very notion.

Instead, she said, "If you had not met me at Lord Steyne's that night, it would not have occurred to you to propose to me. Would it?"

"But I did," he said with irrefutable logic. With a touch of impatience, he added, "Come now, Georgie, it's not like you to be missish."

She gasped. "Missish?" To require that her husband love her, choose her as a bride freely, with no suggestion of duty or obligation?

His brows drew together. "I'm offering a practical solution to our difficulties. I compromised you. What else are we to do but get married? It's not as if my situation in life has altered since you accepted me the first time."

"So you are saying we should just pick up where we left off, is that it? How prosaic."

If she weren't so humiliated and furious, she could have flung herself on the ground and sobbed. Good Lord, could the idiot not see what she wanted from him? What she'd always wanted?

She'd retrieve her tattered dignity if it killed her. "I cannot marry you, my lord. Thank you for the honor you do me, but the answer must be no."

"Georgie, I need a wife," Beckenham said. "It was my intention to look for one. In fact, I came to Brighton to . . . Well, never mind that. But it seems to me as if our meeting again like this was somehow . . ." He shrugged uneasily, as if the notion didn't sit well with him. "Fated, I suppose."

Her heart smacked against her ribs, as if trying to escape her chest.

He captured her hand, gazed down at her with those serious, dark eyes that never failed to melt her a little inside. "Marry me, Georgie. Let's forget the past. Let's forge a future together."

His hand enveloped hers in a strong clasp. They both wore gloves, yet the gesture felt searingly intimate. It spoke of all she could never have from him.

Georgie gathered every last vestige of courage within her and drew her hand away. "No, Marcus. The past cannot be undone." How she wished it could be wiped like chalk from a slate. "I will not marry you. That is my final word upon it."

His jaw was set so hard, she thought it might crack. There was a fierce look in his eyes, as if he'd been forced to accept defeat in an unfair fight. Then he stepped back with a short, sharp nod. "So be it. If that is your final word."

Georgie turned and left him in that quiet grove, her head as high as a queen's. But the lights from the ballroom took on a nimbus through a sheen of hopeless tears.

Chapter Eight

Beckenham sighted the target, took aim, and fired. A splinter on the left edge of the playing card exploded into the air.

Not good enough. He was off his game this morning but he'd put a hole through that pip if it took him all day. He reloaded and took aim again.

"Your pistol throws to the left. Try mine," said Xavier, offering him an ornate ebony-handled dueling pistol.

Beckenham shook his head. "It's a poor tradesman who blames his tools."

He'd deliberately chosen the old pistols from his coach to give himself the added handicap. He needed something that required all his concentration, so his thoughts wouldn't return constantly to her.

They both took another shot. Xavier, relaxed, annoyingly negligent in his deadly accuracy. Beckenham, vibrating with suppressed emotions, wound tight as a spring.

Damn her! Damn *him* for being so ridiculously hopeful that she'd accept him. What idiot wouldn't have learned his lesson and let her be?

Lydgate moaned softly from his prone position on the lip of the fountain. "Barbarians. I wish you wouldn't. Not at this hour."

Xavier sent him a mocking glance. "Deep doings last night, coz?"

Beckenham picked up another pistol ball. "Go away if you don't like the noise."

"No," said Lydgate. "Not until you tell me what happened last night."

"Nothing happened." He wasn't about to share his folly with anyone, least of all his cousins.

He squeezed the trigger, obliterating Lydgate's next remark with the explosion of the pistol. The shot went wide, and the acrid stench of gunpowder filled his nostrils.

"What did you say?"

Lydgate raised his voice. "I said something happened between you and Miss Black at the ball. You might as well tell us what it was. And Pearce dancing with her, too, for all the world as if they were old friends."

"I always rather liked Georgie Black," drawled Xavier. "She seemed a little less pointless than most of her ilk. At least, no one could describe her as *biddable*."

Lydgate snorted. "Between virago and milksop there is a happy median."

Beckenham sent Lydgate a warning glance but said nothing. He didn't trust himself to speak of her. He just wanted to forget.

"I hear Pearce has been called back to his aunt's. They say the end is nigh." Xavier smiled faintly. "They also say she has the constitution of an ox and merely wants to throw her avaricious relations into a flutter." He paused. "One wonders the lengths Pearce would go to secure his fortune."

"What? You suspect foul play?" said Beckenham.

"If there is, I shall know it," said Lydgate.

Xavier dropped his pistol arm to his side, regarding Lydgate critically. "You never fail to amaze me. Why should you care about Pearce's aunt?"

Lydgate put his hands behind his head and stared up into the blue summer sky. "It never hurts to know things."

"Perhaps you might busy yourself finding me a bride rather than prying into matters that don't concern you," Beckenham tossed over his shoulder.

He felt, rather than saw, his cousins exchange significant looks.

"Oh, that's back on, is it?" said Lydgate. "Right-ho. I'll have an itinerary ready by the end of the week."

Beckenham cursed under his breath. He wanted to leave Brighton and never return. Now he'd have to endure both Brighton and his cousins' company for another seven days. As long as he avoided seeing Georgie, he might just manage to retain what sanity he had left.

"Oomph." Her maid grunted as Georgie inadvertently elbowed her in the chest.

"Oh, Smith, I am sorry," said Georgie. "It's so close and dark in here, I can hardly see what I'm doing."

They struggled in an awkward embrace inside one of Brighton's famous bathing machines, attempting to change Georgie out of her gown. Georgie cursed under her breath and swept her hair away from her neck so Smith could unbutton her gown.

Remaining in Brighton while she knew Beckenham stayed at the seaside resort also was a bitter torment. On the one hand, the raffish gaiety of the place threw Georgie's desolation into high relief. On the other, the mournful cry of the gulls seemed to echo the emptiness inside her.

Lady Black seemed determined to try every cure Bath offered before they left the town to stay at Lady Arden's country house. Georgie knew that vapor baths and sea bathing were no more likely to cure her stupid melancholy than they were to cure her stepmother's nervous complaints, but the amusements enjoyed by her peers in the seaside town held little appeal. And besides, at balls and parties and picnics she routinely ran into Pearce.

He hadn't made any further mention of that confounded letter, but the threat of it always hovered between them, forcing Georgie to be civil. If he'd hoped such tactics might eventually win her over, he didn't know her very well. The feeling of submitting to his will, even if it only meant exchanging pleasant words with him when they met, was abhorrent to her.

She was grateful that here, at least, they would be safe from running into Pearce. No men were allowed in the vicinity of the women's bathing machines.

Her stepmother was already being dipped into the sea, if various squawks and exclamations heard over the pound of the waves were anything to judge by. Violet was ready and waiting for her turn, sitting on the step of the wagon with her face lifted to the sunlight and spray.

After another few contortions, Smith managed to dress Georgie in a generic yellow bathing costume and turban they'd hired for the purpose. Georgie plucked at the neckline and sniffed the voluminous garment suspiciously. She didn't like the idea that someone else had worn this before her. And no wonder these burly, redfaced women were required to dip one into the surf. One would surely drown under the weight of one's skirts otherwise.

She thought of the lake at Winford and those daring

moonlit swims, bare-skinned and free. But Cloverleigh was no longer hers. If she ever swam nude in a lake again, it would not be on Lord Beckenham's estate.

No. Even when Violet finally inherited Cloverleigh, Georgie would stay away.

Smith finished tying her turban and said, "There, Miss G. Mind how you go."

"Why don't you come in with us, Smith?" said Georgie.

"Me, miss?" The maid eyed her as if she was cracked. "You won't catch me going in there. Nor manhandled like a sack of grain by those old harridans."

"I can't say I blame you." She was beginning to regret her own decision to join in.

Georgie seated herself next to Violet on the edge of the bathing machine, curling her bare toes over the step.

Her sister had a dreamy, pensive look in her blue eyes. With a dart of fear, Georgie wondered if she thought of Pearce. Violet couldn't be smitten with him already, could she?

Georgie had no way of knowing how many times they'd met. She'd warned the maids never to leave Violet alone when they went out walking with her, but she hadn't wanted to raise the subject with Violet again for fear of goading her into contrary behavior.

She forced lightness into her tone. "What are you thinking of, my dear? You look far away."

"Hmm?" Violet turned to focus on her. "Oh, nothing." She nodded toward the wailing, splashing figure of her mother. "I think she must feel very poorly to subject herself to this."

The stocky woman charged with "dipping" Lady Black in the ocean spoke to her in a firm, matter-of-fact tone, as a nanny might to a child. But it made no difference. Lady Black whooped and shrieked out her complaints. The water was too cold. The salt stung her eyes. She was sure to catch her death, and so on, until a rogue wave reared up and smacked her in the face, knocking her turban askew.

"I don't think I'll go in after all," Georgie said to her sister, raising her voice a little above her stepmother's hysterics. "I was right. The entire process is simply too undignified." She put her hand up to her head. "And this turban itches in a most suspicious manner."

With a surge of revulsion, she plucked it from her head and tossed it back to Smith, who caught it as deftly as she did everything else.

Then Georgie turned back and took Violet's hand in hers. "Darling, I want you to tell me if you are happy."

Violet gave a tiny start of surprise. "Happy? Of course I'm happy. Why shouldn't I be?"

A wispy blond ringlet had escaped Violet's head-dress and Georgie tucked it back inside with a gentle finger. "You seem distracted lately. Not quite yourself. In fact," she added carefully, "ever since that night at Lord Steyne's—"

"Good gracious, is that all?" said Violet, laughing. "Nothing of the sort. It is merely that I—I wondered if I might rather stay with Lizzie for the rest of the summer while you go on to Lady Arden's."

Georgie's brow furrowed. Lizzie lived in Bath. And Bath was where Pearce intended to return to await his aunt's demise, if the gossip was true. "But we mean to plan your come-out next season. Lady Arden would think it quite odd if you were not there, too."

Violet looked so downcast that Georgie said, "Could not Lizzie accompany us to Lady Arden's, perhaps?"

That didn't cheer her sister in the least. Violet shook her head. "Lizzie is to be married soon and there are all manner of preparations to be made. She will not be permitted to leave Mr. Dartry, in any case."

"Ah, of course," said Georgie. She hesitated, wondering how to ask about Pearce without mentioning his name. "You do not mind that your friend is to be married before you, do you?"

"As if I would be so petty," said Violet. She was silent for a time. "Only, it does seem to bring home the fact that I am old enough to have a husband of my own, doesn't it?"

Choosing her words carefully, Georgie said, "Is there any particular gentleman you have in mind for the role?"

Violet threw Georgie a laughing glance. "Of course not, silly."

But Georgie noticed that her sister's lips were compressed rather tightly when she returned her attention to her miserably wet mama.

Beckenham ran his gaze over the list of eligible ladies his cousin provided, two weeks later than initially promised. "I know some of the families, but I'm not acquainted with any of the girls."

"Well, if you hadn't lived like a hermit these past six years, you would be," responded Lydgate. "Some of them only came out in the spring, of course. Why the frown?"

Beckenham glanced up from the list. "Doesn't madness run in the Maxwell family?"

Lydgate ran the feather of his quill between his fingers. "Eccentricity, yes. Madness, no. Never fear. Miss Jennifer Maxwell doesn't seem to have a tendency to wear a flowerpot on her head instead of a hat or anything like that. You'll have the opportunity to observe her when you meet her at Petridge Hall."

"No. She won't do." Beckenham took up his pen and

drove a straight, uncompromising line through the unfortunate young lady's name.

"Bit harsh, old fellow," protested his cousin. "I mean, after all, who doesn't have a few lunatics in their family? What about poor Uncle Pemble? He used to hide in the water closet when it was time to go to church on Sunday. And when Aunt Winifred did manage to drag him there, he howled like a dog through all the hymns."

Lydgate didn't mention Beckenham's own grandfather, and for that, Beckenham was grateful. It had been his life's work to erase the damage the third earl had done, both to the estate and to the family name.

Unimpressed, he replied, "I'm not keen on the stable, Lydgate. I'm afraid Miss Maxwell will not do."

Lydgate held out his hands, palms facing outward. "Say no more. Miss Maxwell will be dropped from the list. Any other objections?"

Before he could reply, Xavier strolled in. Wearily, he drawled, "You two *still* here?"

Beckenham lifted the sheet of paper on which Lydgate had written out his itinerary. "Now that I have what I came for, I'll remove myself."

"What's this?" Xavier plucked the paper from Beckenham's hand and frowned over it. "Ah."

He glanced at Lydgate. "You've been hard at work, I see." He turned the page over, as if looking for something that wasn't there. "But how remiss of you, Cousin. You left out the most obvious candidate."

Lydgate straightened, darting a glance at Beckenham, who shrugged. "Have I? And who might that be? Not Georgie Black."

"Of course not. The younger sister. Miss Violet Black, of course."

Beckenham snatched the paper back. "*Violet* Black? Are you mad? The girl is an infant."

"On the contrary," said Xavier. "About to turn eighteen, and as different from her spitfire sister as she can be. Out next season but I think you could persuade Lady Arden to give you first right of refusal."

"You speak as if the girl's a piece of land," Lydgate protested.

"And isn't all this simply a form of commerce?" said Xavier, flicking a dismissive hand at Lydgate's list. "Forgive me. I'd no idea your sensibilities were so delicate."

Beckenham said nothing. He only vaguely remembered a quiet little fair-haired child playing with dolls at Cloverleigh Manor years ago.

The prospect of courting Georgie's sister made his stomach churn. "No. She's too young."

"Besides the fact she's *Georgie Black's sister,*" Lydgate pointed out.

Xavier's next words arrested him. "She inherits Cloverleigh, did you know?"

Beckenham's hand tightened on the shaft of his pen.

He did know. Cloverleigh was not only a very tidy, lucrative estate, it had been part of his own lands once upon a time. His grandfather had been a madman, a gamester and a wastrel who'd lost a massive sum to Georgie's grandfather in a game of deep basset. The old villain had paid his debt by carving off the unentailed portion of his estate.

Beckenham's guardian, the Duke of Montford, was the one who had convinced Georgie's father that an alliance between Georgie and Beckenham would be advantageous. Without a son to inherit, and only a distant relative living in the Americas next in line for that honor, it seemed reasonable for Sir Donald Black to make Cloverleigh Georgie's dowry.

Of course, the broken engagement put an end to

Beckenham's hopes of making his estate whole again. But now, there was a chance. . . .

No. He couldn't do it. Lydgate was right. He couldn't court Georgie's sister.

"Out of the question," he said. "It would be awkward in the extreme to wed the sister of the lady who jilted me."

Worse, he'd be obliged to see *her,* wouldn't he?

A fierce longing gripped him. Despite Georgie's rejection at the Marstons' ball, he still couldn't get their heated encounter on the night of Xavier's party out of his head. The soft, smooth feel of her skin, the way she'd trembled under his hands, shuddered at the touch of his mouth, his tongue.

A good thing he was sitting at Xavier's desk, because the hard, hot bulge in his trousers would betray him otherwise.

Why couldn't he purge Georgie Black from his thoughts?

The task was made more difficult because he heard about her in Brighton wherever he went. Even on a short walk on the seafront at an unfashionable hour, he'd come upon a crowd of gentlemen coming to blows over a spyglass, of all things. He wouldn't have paid them any heed, except that one of them had the infernal impudence to jostle him.

The young buck begged Beckenham's pardon, which won him a reprieve from a fist in the face. Upon Beckenham's inquiry as to the reason for the affray, the young buck told him word had it that the divine Miss Black currently inhabited one of the bathing machines below.

Thus, the heated argument about who should have a turn at the spyglass for the purpose of a rare and stimulating sight.

Refraining from picking the group of youths up by

the scruffs of their necks like a litter of puppies and pitching them into the sea, Beckenham had stalked away without a word. Worse, he'd been obliged to exercise considerable restraint to stop himself glancing hopefully toward the bathing machine in question.

This ridiculous obsession must be curbed immediately. He did not doubt that marriage to another lady would cure him. He was not the sort of man who panted after another woman once he'd committed himself.

For that matter, he probably dwelled more than usual on his scorching encounter with Georgie because he hadn't bedded another woman since that night. It wasn't healthy to go without for so long.

And yet, the thought of seeking a lover in Brighton was strangely abhorrent.

He realized Xavier was speaking and switched his attention to the present.

"As I've said to you before, it is immaterial to me whom you marry, but my sources tell me the girl is exactly what you're looking for. And she brings the land with her. From a practical standpoint, you couldn't do better, if you ask me."

Beckenham was about to point out that he *hadn't* asked Xavier, only to recall before the words were out of his mouth that, actually, he had. That's why he'd come to Brighton in the first place, only his initial purpose seemed a matter of a lifetime rather than weeks ago.

Xavier tilted his head, his lazy gaze oddly penetrating. "If you wish, I'll arrange with Lady Arden for an inspection of the merchandise. If you don't like what you see, no harm done."

Beckenham swallowed an objection to Xavier's boorish phrasing as he realized his cousin meant to deride his own businesslike approach.

He was forced to see the merit of Xavier's argument. He'd long ago convinced himself it was his duty to retrieve what his grandfather had lost at the gaming tables. That was why he'd agreed to marry Georgie, after all. He ought to take the chance to restore his estate while he could. If Violet married another man, the opportunity would be lost forever.

Beckenham possessed a vast fortune and impeccable lineage. He didn't need his bride to bring anything with her save a good family name and an agreeable disposition. But Cloverleigh . . . Yes. That was certainly a powerful inducement.

In his mind's eye, Georgie mocked him for his pompous deliberation.

Somehow, that settled it.

"Very well," he said. "Thank you for the recommendation." Putting Miss Violet on the list did not mean he would definitely marry her. But he'd be a fool not to at least consider the girl who inherited Cloverleigh as a bride.

Xavier appeared thoughtful. "I'd say I'm happy to be of service if I didn't feel so much like a horse trader. Either that, or a pimp."

He smiled, made an ironic bow, and headed for the door.

"You know, Lydgate, I find myself positively avid for the day when the great Marquis of Steyne must finally wed," Beckenham remarked while his cousin was still in earshot.

Xavier turned, his long fingers gripping the doorknob. Silkily, he said, "Why Beckenham, how kind of you to take an interest in my nuptials. But I believe I shall manage the business of a bride without help from either of you."

With a slight smile, he left the room.

Lydgate gave a dramatic shiver. "Can you imagine it? I wouldn't like to be in *that* poor girl's shoes. He's a handsome devil but a damned cold fish."

"Why didn't Montford ever choose him a bride?"

But that was a question even the Idle Intelligencer couldn't answer. "Let's get on with this, shall we? Now for the itinerary."

Beckenham sighed. "Must we?"

Lydgate moved to stand next to Beckenham and leaned over the desk so he could spread the closely annotated parchment before them. "It's all mapped out for you. I propose we begin with Hendon. Three of the ladies on your list will attend that party, so you will kill three birds with one stone, so to speak."

"Which ladies?" said Beckenham.

"Miss Priscilla Trent, Miss Jane Harrow, and Lady Elizabeth Fanshawe."

None of these ladies were known to him. "Very well, then. I trust you can procure us an invitation."

"Consider it done," said his cousin. "But not 'us,' Becks. *You.* I have other fish to fry."

Beckenham raised his brows. "Another of your schemes, Andy?"

For once, Lydgate's breezy aspect turned cold. "Best you don't know, old fellow."

Beckenham turned to eye him steadily. "You'd tell me if you ever need—"

"What? Am I an infant running to his cousin to kill the big bad wolf?" Lydgate scoffed.

"You are assisting me with my quest," said Beckenham. "I only offer a helping hand with yours."

The fire in Lydgate's eyes died to a smolder. "Now you make me feel ungracious. Thank you. I know I can rely on you in a pinch. Always could." He shook his head. "It won't come to that, however. I'm best when I work alone."

This work, Beckenham surmised, was risky. He wasn't sure if Lydgate would do anything downright illegal, but from what he'd let fall over the years, the work he did was dangerous. If he were caught, no one would come to his aid.

No one but his very powerful family.

Yes, that counted for something. That counted for a lot.

He passed the list back to Lydgate. "Very well. Let's put everything in train."

"I can't help feeling I'm assisting in a travesty," sighed Lydgate. "Do you truly want a bloodless, calculated alliance? What about falling in love?"

A sudden, excruciating pain locked around Beckenham's chest.

He lowered his gaze to the paper Lydgate held. "Love?" he snorted. "Love is for poets and dreamers, Lydgate. My marriage will have nothing to do with love."

Chapter Nine

Lady Black held up a scrap of paper she had torn from a newspaper advertisement as their carriage drew up opposite the Star and Garter. "Listen to this, Georgie. It says shampooing or the Indian medicated vapor bath is a cure to many diseases and giving full relief when everything fails; particularly rheumatic and paralytic, gout, stiff joints, old sprains, lame legs, aches and pains in the joints."

Georgie kept her skepticism to herself. Of all the cures Lady Black had tried, this was hardly the most outlandish. It was, perhaps, the most exotic, but that might make it more interesting.

Taking her silence for doubt, Lady Black shook the paper in her face. "*When everything fails,* Georgie. And if the King patronizes this Mahomed fellow, then I am sure he must be good enough for me."

In spite of herself, Georgie was curious about the methods employed by the latest charlatan to induce their monarch to part with his money. She didn't promise to partake of whatever strange techniques might be used there, but she wouldn't mind taking a look.

The building was an unremarkable structure, save for the large lettering that covered one story: MAHOMED'S BATHS. ORIGINAL MEDICATED SHAMPOOING; HOT COLD DOUCH & SHOWER.

The interior of the establishment was breathtaking— quite literally. The air was as moist and sultry as a sub-continental clime, redolent of scents that were as foreign to Georgie as the murals of jungle scenes and brightly plumed birds that covered the walls.

A very dapper brown-skinned gentleman greeted them with a wide smile. "Ladies, welcome, welcome! What a pleasure and an honor it is to have you here."

He introduced himself as the proprietor of the establishment. Mr. Sake Deen Mahomed was dressed in a sober English style, rather than in a manner befitting his surroundings. But his colorful personality more than compensated for the lack of flamboyance in his attire.

Mr. Mahomed saw Georgie eyeing the battalion of crutches, back braces, and walking sticks that adorned one wall of the foyer.

He laughed. "Miss Black, you are astonished at my decorations. I do not wonder, for it is an amazement, is it not? After taking my special vapor baths and sham-pooing treatments, my clients no longer have need for such aids. They throw them away. This—" He waved a hand at the wall of medical apparatuses. "—this is a testament to the efficacy of my unique methods. The Turkish baths? Pah!" He dismissed the Turkish baths with a happy sneer. "My remedies are formulated from the ancient medicines of India. Passed down through generations of healers. To me."

This last was said with a flourish so full of good-natured conceit that Georgie grinned back at him.

Mr. Mahomed listened to Lady Black's myriad symptoms with a thoughtful air, then handed her a list of treatments, recommended some of them, and waited with attentive courtesy while she perused and debated with herself.

When Lady Black finally chose the vapor bath, shampooing, and a massage, Mr. Mahomed clasped his hands together in the manner of someone restraining his applause. "My lady, you are as discerning as you are gracious."

He looked up and beckoned to a neat English woman dressed in a plain flannel gown. "Polly will take care of you. She is trained in every procedure. I myself personally have seen to this. You are in excellent hands with Polly."

Georgie found herself so delighted and amused by Mr. Mahomed's ebullience that she also agreed to every procedure on her stepmother's list.

By the end of it all, she felt wonderfully renewed, her body so relaxed, she might have melted into the floor. There was something immensely pleasant about having one's head massaged. She'd never known that before. She emerged feeling revitalized and clean and deliciously scented.

Considering her stepmother's similar state of bliss, she understood why Mahomed's Baths had become the rage. Georgie even persuaded Mr. Mahomed to sell her a couple of vials of his precious medicated "shampoo." She still did not believe in the curative effects of these treatments, but if they might take one's mind off one's woes even for a short time, the exorbitant price was worth it.

Whatever its effect on her physical health, the visit to Mahomed's left Georgie in a more positive frame of mind in which to contemplate her future.

On long walks by the sea, she made plans. She could not have Beckenham, but that did not mean her life was over. There were any number of ways a single woman of good fortune could make herself useful in the world. And of course there would be the excitement and activity involved in launching Violet on the Ton next spring.

The pressure of worrying about Violet's possible romance with Pearce had eased a little, since Georgie knew him to have left again for Bath. She'd taken the extreme and regrettable precaution of keeping an eye on Violet's mail, but all Violet received were letters from her school friends and various relatives, so that was all right.

Georgie wasn't complacent, however. She knew there would be a reckoning with Pearce but until that day, she would need to plan for life after her twenty-fifth birthday.

She returned from one of her seafront promenades to hear voices in the drawing room.

Her stepmother appeared on the landing. "There you are, Georgie. Come and hear the news."

She hesitated before following. News usually meant a visit from Mrs. Makepeace, whose company she routinely avoided. Ever since she'd heard of Beckenham's sudden reappearance in Georgie's life and his equally sudden disappearance, Mrs. Makepeace had cross-questioned Georgie until she'd felt like the accused in a murder trial.

It was not Mrs. Makepeace but Lady Arden who called on them today.

She rose and embraced Georgie warmly. "My dear," she said, drawing back and searching Georgie's face in that disconcertingly sharp way she had. "Does the sea air not agree with you? You look peaky."

"I am well, thank you, my lady." Georgie accepted a cup of tea and sat facing the window as the other ladies settled themselves. "News? What news, pray?"

Lady Black sat upright on her couch, wide-eyed and

pregnant with what was presumably the latest gossip, her customary languor fallen away.

She clasped her hands to her breast. "Beckenham! Oh, it is too good to be true."

Georgie hoped she had not betrayed herself at the mention of his name. Beckenham had left Brighton without a word to her. What else had she expected?

Georgie made an effort to look politely interested. "What about the earl?"

"You haven't heard?" Lady Arden smiled blandly. "I had not thought to be first with the news. You and Beckenham appeared so . . . cozy at the Marstons' ball."

"You were mistaken, ma'am," was the only response Georgie gave to that piece of sophistry. "Lord Beckenham and I were civil to each other, as the occasion demanded, nothing more."

Georgie knew Lady Arden sought to draw out the suspense, but of course her stepmother was a stranger to the subtler forms of social torture.

"The Earl of Beckenham is going to take a wife," burst out Lady Black.

"He has embarked on a tour of England," said Lady Arden, smoothing her skirts. "Acquainting himself with all the eligible ladies in the country, if you please."

Suddenly, Georgie felt as if she stood in the middle of a blizzard, her vision clouded by whirling flurries of white. Her insides turned to ice.

"They say he is fêted and fawned upon wherever he goes," Lady Arden continued. "My sources tell me he is beginning in the north and working his way down England. Rather like a king on his progress, don't you think? I trust none of his poor hosts will bankrupt themselves to entertain him. He was ever a man of plain tastes."

Both ladies watched Georgie closely, perhaps expecting her to rend her clothes and wail.

"What do *you* think is the meaning of this sudden start, Georgie?" asked Lady Arden.

Georgie swallowed hard. Seconds ticked by before she could force herself to say, "A timely decision. Lord Beckenham must be nearing thirty, I would suppose." She knew to an hour how old he was. "It sounds like an efficient way of going about finding a bride," she managed. "Lord Beckenham is nothing if not efficient."

She took a hasty sip of tea, scalding her tongue, then looked up at her companions. They both watched her. She hoped she'd managed to pull the wool over their eyes, but Lady Arden's eyes missed very little.

Belatedly, Georgie realized the significance of that avid expression on her stepmother's face.

Oh, no. Lady Black had been given false encouragement by Beckenham calling on them in Brighton. She intended to throw Georgie's hat into the ring, offer her up as a candidate. That's why Lady Arden was here.

Deliberately, Georgie set down her cup and saucer on a piecrust table beside her. "Ma'am, I know what you're thinking," she began a trifle unsteadily, "but pray, I beg you, put it from your mind."

"And what do you think you have to say to it, my girl?" demanded her stepmother with a snort.

Georgie blinked. "My lady, my betrothal to Lord Beckenham is firmly in the past. I could not possibly throw my cap at him now."

"You, Georgie?" Lady Arden blinked, putting a hand to her breast. "Oh, my darling girl. Have no fear. I wouldn't dream of putting you forward as a prospective bride a second time."

"My goodness, no," Lady Black tittered. "One might say *that* chicken's neck is wrung."

One might, if one were a vulgar, hateful baggage, thought Georgie savagely.

She fought to regain control over her emotions. But the heavy blow of hearing Beckenham would marry, coupled with the dawning notion about the precise cause of her stepmother's excitement, held her speechless.

"We mean Violet to have him, of course," said Lady Black. "And there's not a moment to lose."

Georgie gripped the arms of her chair hard.

Violet . . . Violet and Beckenham . . .

Now the whirling was not around her; it was inside her brain. She even felt a little light-headed, but good Heaven, she was—she was *damned* if she'd faint now.

"Violet is very young," Georgie managed, a scrape in her throat.

"Older than you were when you became betrothed to Beckenham," said Lady Arden briskly. "Eighteen and thirty. Very nice. Eminently suitable. And of course, she has the added advantage of Cloverleigh."

Georgie's gaze shot to her stepmother. Had she planned it all along? Had this been the reason she'd urged Papa to change his will and leave his estate to his younger daughter?

No. She couldn't credit Lady Black with so much foresight.

But what did that matter now? And what would Violet have to say about this?

"There is no time to lose," Lady Black reiterated. "We must return home to pack at once for an extended stay in the country."

"My dear Dorothea, there is no need for such haste," said Lady Arden with a smile. "I believe we shall not chase after the earl all over England."

Thank God, thought Georgie. How humiliating that would be.

Her stepmother opened her mouth to protest, but Lady

Arden held up her hand. "Nothing disgusts a man so much as the feeling he is hunted."

She tapped a slender fingertip to her lips. "I shall think of a way to present our dear Violet in the best possible light. But you *must* leave it to me, Dorothea," she adjured with a severe look at Lady Black. "And do not go running off to tell all and sundry of our plans. You will only be made to look foolish if they do not bear fruit."

Lady Arden rose and shook out her skirts, signaling her intention to leave.

As Georgie curtsied to her, Lady Arden grasped her chin, tilting her face upward. "You had your chance with him, my dear."

And you threw it away.

Georgie didn't need Lady Arden to say the words. She said them to herself every single day.

"But I do not wish to marry Lord Beckenham," said Violet. "He is yours."

That night, the two sisters snuggled under the covers together in the big tester bed in Georgie's chamber. They often talked like this, making plans, sharing secrets until the candles guttered, long after Lady Black had retired to bed.

Lately—ever since that night at Steyne's villa, in fact—there'd been a certain level of constraint, Georgie thought. But perhaps she was imagining it out of her own guilt. She did not mean to share all her secrets with Violet, did she?

Tonight, Georgie's heart was wrung with conflicting emotions. Despite her love for her sister, she experienced a corrosive, shameful envy of Violet and all that might be hers.

After a silence that was perhaps a trifle too long, she

made herself shake her head in reassurance. "Dearest, he is not mine. He never really was, not in that way."

She reached out and smoothed back a lock of hair from her sister's brow, tucking it behind her ear. "Beckenham is a good man, darling. He would make—" She drew a deep breath. "—an excellent husband."

"Then why did you give him up?" asked Violet with an oddly penetrating stare.

A very good question, indeed. "We did not suit," said Georgie.

Violet's nose crinkled a little. "That is one of those polite social phrases which means precisely nothing."

"In this case, it is the truth. Lord Beckenham's character is so very different from mine—steady, honorable, straightforward." *Autocratic, unemotional, rigid.*

She sighed. "He grew impatient with my foibles, my headstrong ways. I took delight in driving him to fury, I admit."

She stroked Violet's hair. "But he would adore *you,* my dear."

What man wouldn't adore Violet? Sweet, pretty, and agreeable, with enough intelligence and spirit to make her interesting, but not so much spirit that she was labeled a termagant.

Despite her recent accidental foray into Lord Steyne's den of vice, Violet did not flout convention or indulge in outrageous exploits. She did not flirt or challenge or argue. True, Violet could be quietly obstinate at times, but it was Georgie's habit of violently and openly opposing his slightest efforts to control her that Beckenham detested. Besides, he ought to have a wife with a bit of backbone, not some chit who wouldn't say boo to a goose.

"Lady Arden says she will bring me out in society early, before the season, so I may meet Lord Beckenham." Violet shifted a little on the pillow, so she could look directly into Georgie's face. "He is quite . . . old," she ventured. "Don't you think?"

"Old?" Georgie snorted, feeling oddly annoyed. "He's not yet thirty."

She used to embroider him samplers with silly corruptions of famous aphorisms on them for his birthdays. He'd received each of them with a slightly baffled laugh.

She sighed.

Violet slid a glance at her. "So you don't think the disparity in our ages is a bar?"

"Of course not." Georgie did her best to plaster a smile on her face. She flicked Violet's cheek with a fingertip. "Silly. It's not as if he's in his dotage. You could do far worse, you know. In fact—" She forced herself to say it. "—I couldn't have chosen a better man for you myself."

"You told me he was the stuffiest, most pigheaded brute in the world."

Startled, Georgie said, "I said that?"

Violet gave a decided nod. "Yes. You always spoke as though you hated him."

"I never hated him." Georgie knew her voice sounded hollow. "My criticisms were unjust. You know what my temper is like. We did not deal together, but that did not blind me to Lord Beckenham's many excellent qualities."

She wished Violet were not quite so perceptive, that she would not stare as if to silently challenge every assertion Georgie made. Unable to maintain her front much longer, Georgie lowered her gaze and fingered the coverlet.

Violet rolled onto her back. "Lady Arden is talking of persuading Lord Beckenham to hold a house party of his own. A short list of ladies would be invited to compete for the honor of his hand in marriage."

"What?" said Georgie. "That is monstrous." And so like Lady Arden to know what would most appeal to Beckenham. It was a masterstroke.

Violet sighed. "Oh, she will not couch in those terms, of course. And she will prevail, I have no doubt."

"So that is why Lady Arden is so confident nothing will be decided until the end of this ridiculous tour Beckenham is making," said Georgie. "You have to hand it to her. She is magnificent in her ruthlessness."

Violet raised herself on her elbow and clutched Georgie's hand, looking suddenly intent. "You will come with me, won't you, G? You would not leave me to deal with Mama and Lady Arden on my own."

She couldn't think of anything she'd like less. "No, darling. It wouldn't be wise."

Violet's delicate hand gripped her wrist in a surprisingly firm hold. "But I need you."

Georgie shook her head. "People would gossip. You know how they are."

Violet's grip on her hand tightened and the mulish look she so seldom wore settled over her delicate features. "You've never bothered what people have said about you before."

Georgie slipped her hand from Violet's grasp and touched the tip of Violet's nose. "But I do care for what they might say about my sister."

"But—"

"I am not going with you, and there is an end to it, Violet. Indeed, it is high time for me to set up my own household. My twenty-fifth birthday is not far away and I believe I may talk my trustees into loosening the purse strings in anticipation."

Violet didn't relent, and Georgie dug her nails into her palms to stop herself shouting a refusal. Oh, this was too much for her to be expected to bear!

Why had she felt compelled to plead Beckenham's cause with Violet? Let Lady Arden and Lady Black get on with their schemes. Georgie need have nothing to do with it.

Wasn't it enough that she'd been forced to give up Beckenham without everyone conspiring to marry him to her sister?

"Violet, you will have your mama and Lady Arden. That is quite sufficient, I should think."

There was a long silence.

"Lord Beckenham is very handsome, isn't he, G?" said Violet, almost idly, into the semidarkness.

Georgie cleared her throat. "Very."

She realized now that she'd been wrong in her suspicions that Violet had a tendre for Pearce. Wonderful. That was wonderful news.

Violet twirled a lock of hair around her finger. "With my fair looks and Beckenham's dark coloring, we *would* make a fine couple, would we not?"

"The finest."

"And there is Cloverleigh to think on, of course," mused Violet. "The earl is known to be an excellent steward of his lands."

"That is true." Georgie doubted whether Violet remembered much about Cloverleigh. She'd never evinced interest in visiting the place or inspecting her holdings, relying on her trustees to do what they thought best.

"Then, too, Papa would have been pleased at the alliance," Violet added. "In fact, now I come to think on it, Papa most likely left me Cloverleigh for that very reason."

The acid burn in Georgie's chest made breathing

difficult. A measured reply was out of the question. If Violet had purposely set out to emotionally eviscerate her, she couldn't have done a better job. Knowing her sister had no such intention only made it worse.

"I think you are right," said Violet at last, as if Georgie had spoken. "Lord Beckenham would make a perfect husband in every particular. I shall be pleased to go, after all."

Impulsively, Violet hugged Georgie. "Thank you for advising me. Without your blessing, I could not possibly have agreed to this. Goodness, I am so excited and yet I believe I shall sleep like the dead tonight. Can I stay in here with you?"

There was nothing Georgie wanted less, but she said, "Of course, sweetheart," and used the excuse of blowing out the candle to remove herself from Violet's embrace.

She lay there, staring up at the canopy overhead. She trembled uncontrollably, as if it weren't the height of summer at all.

With a sleepy sigh, Violet said, "And you truly do not mind."

Georgie made herself say, "I would be happy to see you wed to such a man."

"Well, if Lady Arden has her way, I will be," said Violet on a yawn.

And as they both were well aware, Lady Arden could be a very determined woman, indeed.

Chapter Ten

Dear Lizzie,

Do you remember how cast down I was that I am obliged to go to Gloucestershire on a matter of family business? Now, I am so happy, I could dance several jigs, for He is following me there.

Can you believe it? Even with all of his obligations and worries, He counts them for nothing if he cannot be close to me. I could not fathom how he will do it, but he told me I should trust him to find a way. . . .

Two months later . . .

As their chaise rumbled through the gates of Beckenham's country estate, Georgie's heart drummed harder than the rain on the carriage roof. The knuckles of her clasped hands grew white.

How had she come to agree to this fiasco? Did she truly think she could bear to stand by and watch while all those ladies—including Violet—vied for Beckenham's favor?

She rather wondered what the earl himself would make of the process. Another man would preen at the attention, but Marcus . . . No, he was not a man given to preening. In all likelihood, such a surfeit of adulation would make him distinctly uncomfortable.

The thought cheered her slightly, until she recalled that be he never so impatient with toadeaters, he was still a man. Ladies could be extremely clever about making a man feel like a god.

And what if he showed preference for one of these ladies? Worse: what if he fell in love with one of them? With Violet? Her body gave a shudder of revulsion at the thought.

"Thank you for coming with me," Violet said for perhaps the thirtieth time since they'd set out. "I feel so much better, knowing that you will be here and I needn't face them all quite on my own."

"Only for you would I even contemplate it," said Georgie, striving to keep the grim note from her voice. She tugged at her gloves a little more forcefully than necessary.

If it were not for her stepmother's sudden nervous collapse, she would not have set foot in this house, nor taken part in such a demeaning charade.

No matter in what terms Lady Arden delicately couched it, everyone knew the root cause of this invitation to Beckenham's country seat. The Earl of Beckenham wished to take a wife, and to choose her with the least inconvenience possible. The matchmaking mamas would parade their charges for Beckenham's scrutiny like cattle at market.

Nothing could have been more unfortunate than Lady Black's sudden illness. Georgie knew it was genuine. Nothing less than total incapacitation would have induced her stepmother to be left behind on this venture.

The excitement of anticipating this house party was undoubtedly to blame for her recent hysterical episode. The doctor had diagnosed nervous exhaustion and sent her to take the waters in Bath.

Knowing how hopeless it would be to expect a quick recovery or any exercise of willpower on her stepmother's part, Georgie offered to remain behind to nurse her. Violet, too, had argued that they ought not leave her mama if she was feeling so poorly.

But Lady Black insisted that with her brother's wife to tend her and with dear Dr. Wilson at her beck and call, she had no need of them. Indeed, her poor nerves couldn't stand the mere thought of Violet throwing away such a golden opportunity.

So, here Georgie was, preparing for day upon day of exquisite torture.

Beyond the massive wrought iron gates, the drive to the house was a long and winding one, lined by ancient oaks. One last turn and Winford burst into sight, a great monolith against the lowering sky.

Georgie leaned forward to peer out the window. She'd thought the house couldn't be as grand as she remembered, but if anything, her memory had downplayed its magnificence.

If Beckenham had intended to signal what a great honor he would bestow upon his future countess, he couldn't have gone a better way about it than to invite the candidates here. What woman wouldn't wish to be mistress of such a house?

Georgie would wager the place ran like clockwork, too. No fear that his lordship had allowed the estate to sink into rack and ruin as his grandfather had before him. The grounds and exterior of the house were a testament to that. Neatly tended gardens and sloping lawns bordered by woods. The ivy that sprawled over the bricks of the great stone edifice was well tamed, the windows sparkling clean, the gravel drive raked just so.

"Goodness," said Violet. "It seems larger than I remembered. Which is strange, for I was only a child when I saw it last."

Six years ago, Violet had been twelve, or thereabouts. Did Beckenham remember her? Probably not. Young men didn't tend to take much notice of little girls.

"You must call at Cloverleigh while you are here," Georgie reminded Violet.

"But it is tenanted," Violet objected. "I should not wish to intrude."

"You must write to them and ask," said Georgie. "In fact, you might request Lord Beckenham to accompany you. He has more than a passing interest in the place, and your prospects there will set you apart from the rest of them as nothing else can."

Violet opened her eyes wide. "You mean he will not be instantly smitten with my beauty and charm? I must, instead, lure him with my inheritance. How disappointing."

Georgie's gaze sharpened, but the twinkle in her sister's eye reassured her. Perhaps she'd imagined the dry, cynical note in Violet's voice.

"Of course he will be smitten," Georgie replied. "But men like Beckenham are never guided solely by their personal wishes, Violet. From a practical point of view, Cloverleigh is a singular and powerful inducement. He wishes to regain the lands his grandfather lost."

Had it been vanity on her part to expect more from him than a practical marriage all those years ago? Probably. Well, if she had any vanity left, it would be effectively trampled out of her by the end of this delightful sojourn. Once again, she cursed her stepmother's frailty. She felt like a caged bear on its way to a baiting.

The carriage crunched to a halt before she was ready. Thunder rolled overhead, as if to echo her foreboding.

"Hmm. No afternoon ride for me, I fear," she said, glancing at the rapidly darkening sky. "What a pity. I'd looked forward to renewing my acquaintance with the estate."

She'd looked forward to some form of escape from the trial by social intercourse that awaited her. In fact, she'd sent their horses ahead of them for this very purpose.

The humiliation of standing by while Beckenham weighed his marriage options was nothing to the pain of it, and every excruciating moment would be underscored by slighting comments and gossip from the other ladies present, particularly their mamas.

A footman, smart in hunter green livery, opened the carriage door and let down the steps. Another footman held an umbrella, waiting to hand them down.

Georgie gestured to Violet to precede her, gathering all her resolution to face what came next. What was the point in fighting the inevitable? She was here now and must make the best of it. If there was one thing Georgie abhorred, it was people who wrung their hands over what couldn't be helped.

If she must assist in this farce, she would do everything in her power to see to it that Violet won Beckenham. As long as she decided marriage to Beckenham would be best for Violet, that was. She hadn't quite made up her mind to that yet.

"No rest for the wicked," quipped Violet sotto voce as they entered the hall to find Lady Arden awaiting them.

"And just what, may I ask, in the name of all creation are *you* doing here?" Lady Arden eyed Georgie up and down.

"Good afternoon to you, too, ma'am," said Georgie, dipping a curtsy.

Lady Arden's bright gaze flicked to Violet. "Where is your mother, child?"

"Did you not get her letter?" said Violet, removing her bonnet and shaking the water droplets from its brim. Rain pelted down outside now. A gust of wind blew into the hall before the footman heaved the heavy door shut.

"Farrago of nonsense," said Lady Arden. "I could not make head nor tail of it for all the crossed lines and blotches—tearstains, one must suppose. If I had, you may be sure I'd have posted up to Bath and fetched Violet myself." She blew an exasperated breath. "Well, come along. Now you're here, Mrs. Paynter will take you up."

Having seen Violet settled in her apartment next door, Lady Arden swept in to Georgie's chamber.

Deducing from the spark in her eye that Lady Arden wouldn't allow the presence of a servant to stop her speaking her mind, Georgie nodded a dismissal at Smith. "I'll see you when it's time to dress for dinner."

"Now, you must tell me the meaning of this," said Lady Arden as soon as the door shut behind the maid. "I suppose that stupid, indolent woman decided she was too ill to travel."

Georgie thought it best to ignore the insult to her stepmother. "Lady Black would have given much to be here, ma'am. She truly is unwell."

"Then why didn't the silly woman send some other relative to chaperone Violet?" Lady Arden pressed her fingertips to her temple as she paced. "Good God, this is an awkward state of affairs."

"Believe me, no one is more sensible of that fact than I," said Georgie. "Do you think I wish to be here, at *such* a party? I feel like Banquo's ghost. The specter of the bride who might have been."

That made Lady Arden laugh. "I always liked you, my girl. Such a pity you and Beckenham didn't stick."

Georgie said nothing.

"But you are cold." Lady Arden grasped Georgie's hands in hers and chafed them. "Let us get you out of these damp things, shall we?"

"There's no need," protested Georgie. "I am merely a trifle damp." She wished her relative would say her piece and leave her be.

"Nonsense. I never had a daughter, you know. Or a son, for that matter." With brisk efficiency, she helped peel the gown from Georgie's body, then set to work on her corset strings while Georgie shed her petticoats.

"There." When Georgie stood only in her chemise and stockings, Lady Arden snatched up a light rug from the foot of the bed and put it about Georgie's shoulders. The gesture had a faint whiff of maternal tenderness about it. Strangely, Georgie felt comforted. A sudden, sharp longing for own mother made her duck her head.

Collecting herself, Georgie perched on the edge of the bed to ease off her stockings. "I will do my best to stay out of the way. You needn't fear I mean to create a scene or add fodder to gossip."

Eyeing her with a judicious air, Lady Arden said, "It is not your nature to fade into the background, Georgie."

Stung, she demanded, "Do you think I would try to overshadow my sister?"

"No, I merely think that any man with a pulse will not waste time with debutantes when you are in the room."

Georgie flushed. She'd promised Violet moral support, but this sort of thing was precisely what she'd feared. "You may be sure that Lord Beckenham is far too high-minded to allow any woman's charms to distract him from his duty."

"Ha! I'd never have taken you for such an innocent, my dear."

This sort of talk merely rubbed salt into the wound. Wasn't it precisely because he was so good at resisting her supposed siren's lure that she was here now playing gooseberry to her sister rather than mistress of this house?

Her looks, such as they were, had only ever brought her grief.

Without a great deal of hope, she said, "Do you want me to leave?"

Lady Arden tilted her head to the side, as if seriously considering the merits of sending Georgie back into the storm. That ruthless streak Georgie had always rather admired in her relative was now wielded against her.

"No," she said at last. "Your sudden departure would cause gossip. Now that you are here, you must show all of the young ladies and their matchmaking mamas that you have no intention of picking up where you left off with Beckenham."

"I shall do my best to avoid his company altogether," said Georgie. That would serve her desires equally well. "Perhaps we could put it about that I caught a chill and cannot come downstairs."

"Craven," mocked Lady Arden.

Georgie sighed. Lady Arden was right. Besides, there was her promise to Violet. She could scarcely provide moral support from her supposed sickbed.

None knew better than she the nasty little claws some ladies hid beneath their gloves. Put them into a situation like this, all vying for a countess's coronet, and it would be a bloodbath.

Her sister had no notion of how vicious her rivals could be, nor how adept they were at hiding their malice from gentlemen they sought to impress. As hostess,

Lady Arden would be too occupied to watch over Violet all the time.

"Do we know anything of the competition?" inquired Georgie.

"But of course, dear. How could you doubt it?" Lady Arden glanced out the window. "All frightfully eligible, pretty-behaved girls. I believe Beckenham stipulated the young ladies must be quiet and docile."

"Did he?" Georgie knew how to take that, she supposed.

"An amazingly bland parcel of ninnies," continued Lady Arden idly. "But I suppose that's what most men want, after all. A pretty young thing to warm their beds with enough sense in her head to run a household and sufficient meekness to obey their every dictate."

Georgie's lip curled. "How tedious of him."

Lady Arden's gaze sharpened. "Do you think he deserves better?"

He needed to be shaken out of his irritating complacency. The kind of female Lady Arden described would never do it.

Violet never would. She banished the treacherous thought.

"If they are ninnies, he will find them dead bores," Georgie observed. "Violet, on the other hand, is intelligent as well as sweet-natured. She is perfect for him."

The words seemed to leave a lump in her throat.

Lady Arden came to her and placed a bracing hand on her shoulder. "Whatever lies between you two is in the past now. I want you to act like Beckenham's future sister-in-law, not his former betrothed."

Georgie met Lady Arden's eyes. By sheer will, she allowed her gaze to reflect nothing save tranquil acceptance. "That is precisely my intention, my lady."

* * *

The flash of flame red hair in the distance, quickly hidden by a large black umbrella, was the first sign that Georgie Black had come to Winford.

Beckenham had taken the gentlemen of the party on a tour of his stables, happily unaware of the rude shock in store for him upon his return.

By God, he ought to have known that prime piece of horseflesh, just arrived from the Black household ahead of their party, would be neither Violet's nor Lady Black's, but Georgie's. Not many females were strong enough or skilled enough to control a mare like that.

"New arrivals, eh?" said Lydgate, gesturing with his whip to the carriage on the drive.

"Indeed," said Beckenham, trying to ignore the rush in his blood, the soaring sensation in his chest, even as the rain sheeted down around them.

An oath from Lydgate cut through the downpour. "What the Devil is *she* doing here?"

Giving him no reply, Beckenham narrowed his eyes, staring after Georgie, but it was no good; the house had already swallowed her up. Too late, he realized he hadn't even noticed her companions. One of them must surely have been the sister.

Damn the woman! Hadn't these past months been spent getting her out of his system, once and for all?

Only he still hadn't found the opportunity to ease certain . . . tensions of the body and spirit, and that made him susceptible to . . . Damn it to hell, why did she have to turn up on his doorstep unannounced?

He must have gone through the motions with his guests after that, for later, he couldn't recall a word anyone had said to him. He skulked down in the drawing room for as long as he could before he realized she wasn't going to join the rest of the company before dinner.

He didn't even have the opportunity to cross-question

Lady Arden, who had talked him into the entire charade. He'd thought it an excellent idea at the time. It suited his notions of effectiveness and efficiency. Besides, it meant he could curtail the tedious progression from one house party to the next in search of a bride.

Instead, the most likely contenders all came to him. He would choose a countess by the end of this house party or perish in the attempt.

Sometimes, when he was obliged to listen to Lady Charlotte Cross's prattle, he would happily choose the "perish" option.

He had only himself to blame, of course. He'd drawn up the exclusive list of candidates. They'd been here for close to a week already, save for Violet Black. Though he knew the girl was coming, the thought that Georgie might accompany her hadn't entered his head.

Had he secretly hoped this would happen when he agreed to add Violet's name to the list?

He didn't like to think himself capable of using Violet to get to her sister. That notion was so foreign to his character, he was momentarily disgusted with himself for even letting it cross his mind.

By considering Violet, he did nothing but his duty. Everyone had agreed that a match rejoining Cloverleigh to the Winford estate was highly eligible when it was Georgie who stood to inherit. Why should that have changed now that Violet would get Cloverleigh?

At dinner, Lady Arden seated Georgie as far away from Beckenham as it was possible to be, and yet his every fiber was aware of each breath that entered and left that magnificent bosom of hers. The ambivalence of his feelings put him at constant war with himself.

All through his conversation about horseflesh with Miss Margo deVere, Beckenham thought resentfully of Georgie's lush body, of its ridiculous power over him.

He shifted a little in his chair. No, best not to think of that.

Had Georgie planned to make his possible courtship of her sister as difficult as possible? She seemed to have a deep affection for Violet. No doubt she'd warned the girl against him.

He'd seen at once that Xavier was right about Violet Black. She was precisely the sort of lady he wanted. Calm, sweet, with a quiet dignity that did her great credit.

Pretty, too. As pretty as a rosebud.

His gaze slid back to Georgie, whose beauty was more like a tropical flower. Lush, vibrant. Carnal.

Good God, he needed to stop thinking about her.

Yet he couldn't help noticing that her manner was retiring in the extreme this evening. She'd barely spoken two words to him in the drawing room, where they'd gathered before moving in to dinner.

She wore a watery gray gown, a color he'd never seen her in before. What the Devil was she doing in gray? She wasn't in half mourning, was she?

And the demure way she cast down her eyes and most correctly restricted her conversation to the guests to her right and left made him wonder what game she was playing.

The old Georgie would have commanded the admiring attention of the male half of the table; the envy of the female portion. She possessed an inner fire that drew men like moths.

The old Georgie would laugh that low, husky laugh of hers, make men turn their heads, break off their conversations, lean toward her, forgetting their dinner companions entirely.

Lady Arden, he saw, looked upon Georgie with approval. Had she read her kinswoman the riot act? Was Georgie behaving herself in obedience to Lady Arden's decree?

Perhaps that was it. Perhaps Georgie had been enlisted to *promote* a match between him and Violet.

The notion did not sit well with him. Georgie had more than her share of pride. Surely it galled her to be obliged to take a hand in catching him for her sister.

Unless she didn't care whom he married . . .

Georgie forced herself to ignore Beckenham as much as possible. Which was exceedingly difficult to do, for if ever a man appeared to advantage in evening dress, it was he. There was something about the contrast between the rugged austerity of his face and the clean lines of black and blinding white that set her pulse pattering like a military drum.

No. She had a job to do. She needed to observe the other candidates for Beckenham's hand, analyze their strengths, their weaknesses, and plan how she would knock them out of the running. On Violet's behalf, of course.

Four other young ladies were present, and a formidable opposition they were. Miss Priscilla Trent, Lady Harriet Bletchley, Lady Charlotte Cross, and Miss Margo deVere.

At dinner, she'd noted that Priscilla was a cool blonde with impeccable manners. Lady Harriet was very taking, but no beauty. She had an intelligent spark to her eye, however, and who could say but that Beckenham might take a shine to her? He'd liked her enough to invite her here, hadn't he?

Lady Charlotte Cross was a classic dark-haired beauty. One to watch, Georgie thought. And Miss deVere, despite her unfortunate family background, was attractive and animated. By the small amount of her conversation Georgie overheard, Miss deVere was hunting and horse mad, so her sporting interests would please Beckenham.

Georgie had more opportunity to observe her quarries when the ladies removed to the drawing room after dinner.

Lady Arden dispensed tea. Georgie took her cup with thanks and turned to find Lady Trent, Miss Priscilla's mama, at her elbow.

"So brave of you to come, in the circumstances," she murmured, her eyes shooting sparks, her lips thinly smiling.

Ah, so now it started. "I am no more than a chaperone for my sister," said Georgie. "I see nothing courageous in that, ma'am. Violet is such a pretty-behaved girl, I've practically nothing to do."

"Indeed?" said Lady Trent. "One wonders that Miss Violet's mama is not here to lend her support."

"Does one?" Georgie smiled. "I'm afraid my stepmother's health does not permit the exertion. However, Violet is fortunate that our kinswoman, Lady Arden, is here to lend as much, er, *support* as she requires."

That made the stiff-rumped matron poker up. Perhaps she'd forgotten that Lady Arden hailed from the Black family.

"For me, visiting Winford is like a homecoming," said Georgie, warming to her theme. "Violet and I grew up on the neighboring estate, you know. The property will be hers upon her marriage."

She lifted her chin and searched the crowd beyond, pretending not to notice the thunderstruck look on Lady Trent's face. "Excuse me. I must greet an old acquaintance."

Georgie glided away, leaving anger and uncertainty

in her wake. She was beginning to enjoy herself, just a little. She did not doubt the news of Violet's distinct advantage over her peers would be all over the drawing room in seconds flat.

Perhaps she'd made Violet a target for malice, but as soon as they all saw how superior her sister was in every respect, they'd be aiming their poisoned darts at her anyway. Against Violet's looks, disposition, and dowry, those other young ladies did not stand a chance.

The only fly in the ointment was Georgie herself. She knew in her bones that Beckenham was too decent to fail to consider her feelings on the matter. Her presence here was most unfortunate. If she'd stayed away, he would have been able to put her out of his mind and do his duty to marry Violet and reclaim the estate his grandfather had lost.

Whatever the case, it might be to Beckenham's benefit to marry Violet. Georgie still needed to reserve judgment about whether Violet would be happy as Beckenham's countess. She must not lose sight of that. Violet herself seemed content at the prospect, but what did eighteen-year-old girls know, after all?

Seeking a respite, Georgie took her tea to where the Dowager Marchioness of Salisbury surveyed the gathering with a gimlet eye and seated herself beside her.

Here was a friendly face, if not an ally. Lady Salisbury wore an impressive purple turban that complemented the gown she wore. Smack in the middle of the turban perched a brooch containing the largest diamond Georgie had ever seen.

The old lady caught her staring and leaned toward her. "Paste, m'dear! But don't tell anyone. I'm pockets-to-let, and hoping Harriet has enough gumption to snare this earl before the entire family sinks under debt."

Georgie blinked at being made the recipient of this startling information. "It is a very fine copy," she murmured. "One would never know."

"Aye." The lines around Lady Salisbury's lips deepened as she pursed them. "But it's not as if all of London don't know the state we're in, baubles notwithstanding. The Abbey is falling in a heap. Poor Salisbury is at his wits' end."

"I am sorry to hear that," said Georgie. The notion that one lady in particular truly needed this marriage depressed her.

She sought for a more cheerful subject. "Lady Harriet is pretty."

"She's passable," said the dowager. "As clever as she can stare. If the gel can be brought to keep her nose out of a book long enough to set her cap at Beckenham, I shall have done my duty. Her mama is worse than useless," she said, indicating a gaunt female who sat alone sipping her tea and looking as if she'd rather be elsewhere. "*Bluestocking.* Good God, what use is booklearning, pray, when your house is falling down around your ears?"

Well, she could not let Lady Harriet have Beckenham, but perhaps she might persuade Lady Arden to make her a match. Georgie was still lending her ear to the dowager's woes when the gentlemen joined them.

Viscount Lydgate, Beckenham's cousin, made a beeline for them. "Good evening, Lady Salisbury. And Georgie Black. Well, well, this is a sight for sore eyes. How do you do?"

She rose and curtsied. With a flashing smile, he bowed elegantly over her hand and led her to an alcove set a little apart from the company.

She felt a hard, dark gaze upon them as they settled

themselves. Did Lydgate mean to flirt with her? His manner was certainly flirtatious. She received this signal with a sinking feeling. She supposed she ought to set up a flirt here to deflect attention from her former engagement to Beckenham. Now, presented with the perfect opportunity, her heart wasn't in the business.

She'd been mistaken, however. Lydgate did not wish to flirt with her. Once out of earshot, a note of steel entered his voice. "I am surprised to see you."

"No more than I am to be here, believe me," she replied. "You don't think I came because I wanted to watch him choose a wife, do you?"

He searched her face. "Perhaps you came to ruin his chances."

She felt a spurt of anger. "Whatever you might think of me, I would never injure my sister. It is for her that I agreed to come when her mother would not. I couldn't let her undertake such a journey alone."

He didn't look satisfied.

Impatiently, she said, "I don't know what you think I might do, anyway."

"Your mere presence is enough. I saw him watching you at dinner."

Her heart beat faster. "You are imagining it. You are mistaken."

"On the contrary. I happen to have extremely keen powers of observation. And I know Becks very well." Lydgate looked deeply into her eyes and gave his killer smile, as if he were paying her an extravagant compliment instead of accusing her. He raised her hand to his lips and murmured, "Do not disappoint me, Georgie. He deserves to be happy."

After what you put him through.

The unspoken words hung on the air. She flushed

and would have responded, but he made her an elaborate bow and walked away.

She sank down on the window seat and turned her head to stare out. A mere sliver of tangerine sun peeked from between thick gray clouds. Twilight mellowed the undulating landscape, turned the lake a mysterious violet.

She loved this countryside. She'd been brought up to believe she'd own a piece of it for herself one day, but that dream had died with the dissolution of her engagement.

Still, it was home, the repository of too many joyous memories of youth to discount. Some of those memories included Beckenham.

"A fine prospect is it not?" said a deep voice behind her. She turned and her breath hitched at the sight of Beckenham towering above her. Heat spread through her body like wildfire.

"Yes," was all she managed to say.

His sober regard traveled slowly over her body. "I trust you had a tolerable journey."

"Yes. Tolerable. Thank you," she murmured. What was wrong with her? Georgie Black, tongue-tied before a man? Her friends would laugh themselves sick if they could see her.

Belatedly, she asked, "And you? I hear you have been traveling these past months."

He shrugged. "House parties here and there." He would not discuss his marriage plans with her. Perfectly reasonable, under the circumstances.

She swallowed hard, acutely aware of his nearness, of the way the other guests slid them furtive glances under cover of their own conversations. Her reaction to him made his attentions almost too excruciating to bear. He did not touch her or regard her with any particular warmth, yet the memory of his passionate exploration of her body at Steyne's villa hummed low inside her.

She found herself staring at his hands.

"Would you care to take a stroll with me on the terrace?" he asked her.

Astonished at the very idea, she jerked her attention to his face.

Oh, he was very much in command of himself, wasn't he? As if he'd never stroked her in intimate ways, kissed her wildly. As if he had not renewed his proposals to her in Brighton, taken her into his arms with something like tenderness at the Marstons' ball.

She felt the heat rise to her cheeks and mentally slapped herself for allowing those thoughts to take possession of her mind. With a faint grate in her voice, she said, "I don't think that would be wise, do you?"

His grim mouth quirked upward. "I expect I can control myself for a few moments while we enjoy the fresh air." He held out his arm to her.

She shook her head with a quick glance toward the rest of the company. "Please, Beckenham. You must not single me out like this. You must pretend I am not here." She gave a smile that she hoped didn't show the hurt. "For I'm not, you know. Not for the reason they are. I am a chaperone."

"A mere chaperone? *You*, Georgie?" But he let his arm fall by his side.

Didn't he think her respectable enough for the task?

Her temper had always been volatile; he'd lit the fuse. With a glittering smile, she shrugged. "I am sure I'll find my own entertainment while I'm here. There are enough gentlemen to go around, after all. Particularly as all the young ladies are setting their caps at you."

She lifted her chin at the flash of anger in his eyes,

waved a careless hand. "You may go back to your bride-hunting, my lord. Don't concern yourself with me."

His brow lowered and his jaw set as hard as the helmet on a suit of armor. "I am to ignore you? Very well, then. That is easily arranged."

She watched him go, her pose erect, outwardly serene. Only she knew about the ache in her heart and the burning sensation behind her eyes.

Beckenham rose the next morning with a savage need for punishing physical exercise. A pity Lydgate was no early riser; he could do with a bout of punching the living daylights out of someone.

Lydgate was not up to his weight, but he more than made up for that fact with science and skill. And a few dirty tricks Beckenham had learned to watch for.

But there was no doing anything with Lydgate before midday, so a bout of boxing was not an option.

With a growl in his throat, Beckenham threw on his riding clothes and strode down to the stables.

"Saddle Demon," he ordered the stable hand. "No, stay. I'll do it myself."

The sleek black stallion was called Demon for a reason. Beckenham had bought him from a northern baron who had a good eye for horseflesh but no idea how to break them in. Nor did he believe in gelding horses, probably as an affront to his own manhood, Beckenham thought.

Consequently, Demon was half wild. Beckenham had thought to spend many solitary, patient hours this summer training him.

So much for that resolution. This business of finding a bride seemed to consume all his time.

This morning, he felt the need for something half wild between his legs. The irony was not lost on him, and that lent his resolve all the more steel.

Having reassured the restive beast with a few soft, rough words and saddled him, Beckenham led him out of his stall.

The stallion tossed up his head, skittered sideways, snorted displeasure with the bridle. Beckenham gave him a firm, clear, "Settle down," and led him into the paddock.

A brilliant blue sky overhead made him wish he did not have a house full of guests. He could ride forever on a day such as this.

Assuring himself that his mount had indeed settled down, he set his foot in the stirrup and climbed into the saddle.

The stallion instantly reared, protesting at his weight. He was ready for that, however, and kept his seat. "There, you brute. Stop that now."

Horsemanship was all in the knees, the pressure on a flank should be sufficient to guide a horse. A good rider never used a whip or a spur.

Respect for the magnificence of the beast was, in Beckenham's opinion, as essential as a firm hand on the rein.

He let Demon dance and sidle, greeting his spirited attempts to eject him from his seat with calm commands to settle down, quiet down.

When the horse seemed marginally quiescent, he urged him to a walk.

Progress was slow and the setbacks numerous, but by the end of an hour's work, Beckenham realized his own simmering frustrations seemed to have lifted somewhat.

He returned Demon to his stall for a rubdown, rejecting the stable hand's offer to do it for him. He believed that part of training a horse was getting close to it. What could be closer than grooming?

The stallion nudged him insistently. He'd learned early that after he worked, he earned a treat. This time, an apple Beckenham had filched from the kitchens.

He produced it, smiling at the slightly comical frill of the horse's lips, his toothy grimace as he munched.

Beckenham stroked the velvet nose and wiped his hands of the sticky combination of equine slobber and apple flesh.

Satisfaction warmed him. "You'll do," he told Demon. And for the first time since Georgie Black had arrived at Winford, he thought he might do, too.

George stood on the south lawn, transfixed. She was on her way to the stables, when she caught sight of a man on a horse. The man, of course, was Beckenham. He'd chosen a mount with several devils inside him, by all appearances.

The very first thing the naughty imp did was to rear up, hooves flailing like a warhorse bent on destruction. Fear made Georgie want to close her eyes but she couldn't look away. Surely even Beckenham couldn't keep his seat.

But he did, by God! He did!

Georgie felt a surge of triumph and pride run through her at his skill. Immediately, she was vexed with herself. How could she view that skill as if it were somehow hers?

As if *he* were hers.

He hadn't been hers for six years. Yet, returning to this wonderful country where she'd been born made her feel as if that horrible London evening had never been. For as long as she could remember, while living here, Beckenham had been hers. She'd had the right to take pride in his horsemanship.

As he had taken pride in hers.

The notion made the ache in her chest deepen.

Perhaps it was reckless of her, but she couldn't find the will to walk away. She allowed herself to watch him handle that wicked mount with sincere admiration and pleasure.

When he was done, she continued her journey to the stables. It seemed petty and wrong not to tell him how much she had enjoyed that skilful display.

She arrived in time to see him talking to one of his grooms.

She'd made no sound, but he seemed to sense her as soon as she entered the stable block, for his head shot up and his eyes narrowed.

Dismissing his groom, he came toward her. "Meeting someone?" he growled.

All notion of expressing her admiration for his horsemanship flew from her head. She let one corner of her mouth curl in a sensual smile. "But of course."

His face darkened, if that were possible. "You will confine such improprieties to somewhere other than this house."

She opened her eyes wide. "I shall keep your strictures in mind. If I decide to obey you, I will let you know. Miracles do happen, after all."

"Who is it?" he demanded. "What poor unfortunate has been unlucky enough to be snared in your toils?"

She laughed. A rusty, reckless sound. "Why do you speak in the singular, my lord? There is more than one unattached male under forty at this party."

"Ma'am. I'd no notion your requirements were so particular."

She shrugged, letting his biting sarcasm glance off

her armor. "Married men are *such* a bore. And I am a great admirer of youthful vigor."

Good God, what possessed her to say such things? Clearly, she was out of her mind. If she didn't stop herself, she'd make a blunder. Then he'd realize she didn't know what she was talking about.

She wanted to shout at him that *she* wasn't the one who kept mistresses or openly attended scandalous parties. *She* didn't have a reputation to rival Casanova's. She wasn't the one who took amorous encounters in her stride.

The memory of him walking out on her at the villa that night was so painful that she winced and turned her face away. "Let's have done with this. I came down here to have my horse saddled for a ride. That is all."

Silence. Then he said, "Where is your groom?"

"I never ride with a groom in the country, Marcus. You know that."

"True enough," he muttered. "How many times have I told you what a foolish and dangerous habit that is?"

"Too many," she said. "It is not your place to scold me anymore, Beckenham. It never was."

"As your host, I have some right to see that my guest is safe, I think. It would be my responsibility if you were brought home on a door."

"If I am brought home on a door, you may scold me to your heart's content," she answered, trying to brush past him.

He caught her elbow in a firm clasp.

Fire raced through her. She gasped, stared up at him. "Let me go."

"If you won't take a groom, you'll have to accept my escort."

She tugged to free her arm, but he held her fast. "I don't have to accept anything. Let me go."

She read the implacable expression on his face. "Oh, very well, then," she said, tugging her arm again.

He released her. "Good. I'll saddle our horses."

"I'll take the groom," she snapped.

And strode away from him, the skirts of her habit swishing about her legs.

Chapter Eleven

Grimly determined, Beckenham found Georgie's side-saddle and hefted it, ignoring the fact that several of his servants had stopped work to enjoy the show.

"If you so much as touch my Daisy, I'll break your fingers," Georgie hissed.

With an ironic bow, he held the saddle out to her and dropped it into her arms.

She received the heavy piece of tack with a muted "Oof!" Juggled it, staggered, then straightened. Murderous darts flew from those magnificent eyes.

"Thank you," she said witheringly, and stalked off, and he lost a few seconds in reluctant admiration of the way she moved.

She readied her steed in record time; he was faster. They left the stable yard together, but on reaching open country, Georgie let the mare have her head.

Damn, the woman could ride. She wore a severe habit in funereal black with only the smallest concession to femininity in the soft plume of a feather that curled over its brim.

On another lady, the costume would have been somber. On Georgie, it was stunning. The black only served to contrast with that bright hair, her flawless white skin, so delicate as to appear more translucent than the filmy gauze cravat she wore at her throat. And the cut of that garment . . . The figure-hugging masculine tailoring only emphasized the womanliness of her lush curves.

He wondered, briefly, whether it took the strength of two maids to assist her into that cunningly constructed little jacket. No member of the dandy set had ever worn a coat so exactly molded to his form.

He did not attempt to overtake her; he knew where she headed. He was well acquainted with the volatility of her temper and knew she'd be calmer for the exercise if he let her go now. He'd deserved a dose of her wrath for his base accusations.

Those accusations had not been the work of a gentleman. They'd been absurd. He didn't know what had come over him.

Yes, he did, though. Jealousy, pure and simple. He'd hated watching her flirt with Lydgate last night, even though he knew there was nothing serious in it.

She did not so much as glance around to see if he followed. She galloped that chestnut mare of hers across fields and paddocks, scrambled up a rise lined with poplar trees, and reined in.

He urged his mount on with a click of his tongue but kept his distance when he reached the ridge alongside her.

The vista beyond that ridge was one that had been in his family since Edmund Westruther, the first Baron Beckenham, had accepted his title and the gift of this land from a grateful king.

Cloverleigh Manor.

For more than a generation, this part of the estate

had been out of Westruther hands, frittered away by Beckenham's grandsire.

Now Beckenham had the chance to reclaim it.

That chance might come only once in his lifetime. He was fully alive to the possibility that if Violet Black married another man, as of course she would if *he* didn't wed her, that man would wish to hold on to such a valuable piece of property. It was handsome enough and lucrative enough to become a gentleman's principal seat.

Once the land was entailed on the next male heir, it would be well nigh impossible to retrieve it.

The old anger flared. Against Georgie, for ruining everyone's plans to see his estate restored. Against himself, for allowing matters to spiral out of his control. By jilting him, she'd thrown away what he suspected was just as valuable to her as it was to him.

Reclaiming this land was his duty. But it had never been his home as it was hers.

He gazed down at the neat, redbrick Elizabethan manor, with its well-kept lawns and surrounding farms and fields. There was a simplicity to its beauty, as if it were a woman with marvelous bone structure and flawless skin who needed no adornment.

No fancy, man-made lake or follies or naturalistic landscaping here. Just an honest, solid, handsome house set like a gem in the midst of glorious Gloucestershire country.

He allowed his mount to sidle next to her Daisy.

"Magnificent, isn't it?" she said softly. As he'd predicted, the temper seemed to have seeped out of her during that hell-for-leather ride.

She turned to him, cheeks flushed, sea green eyes sparkling, wisps of red hair corkscrewing around her face.

"Magnificent," he agreed.

He tore his attention away from her. Stupid to feel his pulse pick up, his breath catch. Georgie Black was magnificent. There'd never been any denying that fact.

She was also headstrong, careless, impulsive, and quick to anger.

And not the wife for him.

She rejected you twice, you fool! How many times did he need to tell himself that?

But that night at the Brighton villa, she hadn't rejected him. And she'd known who he was, even if she didn't know he'd recognized her.

She'd called him Marcus. She'd begged him to stay.

Difficult to believe this strong goddess of a woman had actually spoken those words to him. Georgie Black had never pleaded for anything, except his forfeiture of that ill-fated duel.

Abruptly, he said, "I never fought Pearce, you know. He didn't show up."

He watched her closely, but the only sign she gave in response was a certain tautness about her neck and jaw.

Finally, she turned her head to face him. "I know that."

"How did you know?" He'd broken the first promise of his life by not sending her word of the outcome.

"Do you think I could rest until I knew?"

She had not answered his question, he noticed. Ah, well, the duel had been kept very hush-hush on his side, but who knew how many people Pearce had told?

Not that any man would boast of failing to come up to scratch for an affair of honor.

He frowned, but before he could question her further, she said abruptly, "You ought to marry Violet. She inherits Cloverleigh, you know."

"Yes, I do know." He hesitated. Despite the obvious underlying reason for this house party, it made him distinctly uncomfortable to discuss his marriage with his former betrothed. The woman to whom he'd proposed only a handful of months ago.

In fact, since Georgie's arrival, whenever he tried to picture marriage with one of the ladies Lydgate had selected, his mind flew back to that scene with Georgie at the villa. He couldn't get it out of his head.

She leaned forward and patted her mare's neck. "You needn't feel awkward about it, Beckenham. What's between us is ancient history."

She paused, then said with some difficulty. "I want you to be happy. I desire my sister's happiness above everything. I believe you might both be well content with this match."

Her voice had grown a trifle husky, but he barely noticed that. "You want me to marry your sister," he said flatly. "Yet you did not wish to wed me yourself."

Saying the words was more difficult than he'd expected. He waited for her answer with a tightening in his gut.

She gave a twisted smile. "Oh, but I am a contrary female. I'm fully alive to the fact that you have all the excellent qualities any sane woman might wish for in her husband. And I know you will take good care of Cloverleigh. That is very important to me."

Perversely, he felt the reverse of flattered.

In her shoes, he'd be . . . Why, if Lydgate or Xavier intended to marry Georgie, he'd . . . His horse tossed his head and danced skittishly backwards. Beckenham loosed the rein a little.

"It is unfortunate that I have been obliged to come here," she went on. "But if you find it awkward to court my sister out of consideration for my feelings, let me assure you that such consideration is unnecessary."

"Shall we go?" He found the need to change the

subject. So much reasonable plain-speaking was a little too much to stomach at this hour.

Before she could answer, he urged his steed on, cantering easily down the gentle slope to the pastures below.

It was a world of *do you remember,* and *what might have been.* With every step closer to the house that had been her home for eighteen years, Georgie felt the clutch in her chest grip tighter.

They said an Englishman's home was his castle. The attachment of a man to the land he owned and cultivated was as natural as breathing.

But what about women? Georgie's love for this countryside was as deep as ever her father's or Beckenham's had been.

At least, she told herself, Cloverleigh would be Violet's. At least it had not gone to some long-lost cousin in the Americas. That made it even more imperative that Violet marry a good man who knew how to husband the land as well as he knew how to husband a lady.

She might have chafed at Beckenham's autocratic nature, at his self-appointed position as her keeper, but she'd never entertained the slightest doubt that he had her best interests at heart. Violet, with her sweet temperament, would find him the perfect husband.

An image of Beckenham kissing Violet the way he'd kissed her at Steyne's villa made her close her eyes and rush into speech.

"I hear there is a new bailiff," she said. "What is he like?"

Beckenham's lips set in a stern line. "I do not hold with his practices. I wrote to the trustees about it six months ago but I received short shrift."

"Ah. My esteemed stepmother's brother and his faithful dog. You know, Beckenham, I would not say this to anyone but you. But I often think that my father must have been suffering from moon madness to marry that woman."

He shrugged. "Perhaps he was lonely."

"Perhaps he wanted a male heir." That notion had always hurt her too deeply to express. She did not know why she brought it up now.

He glanced at her. "I gather it was Lady Black who urged him to leave the property to Violet."

"He did not need much urging. He was in such a rage with me over our broken engagement, I think he would have tossed me out of doors but for the love he bore me."

"He did you a great disservice depriving you of Cloverleigh."

Of course, Beckenham understood this about her as no one else ever would, not even Violet. He knew because he felt that same pride of ownership, of belonging, on his own land. He knew because he knew her.

Regret for her father's actions tinged his voice. She did not want him to pity her.

"You may be sure that I am left well provided for. I also inherit my mother's fortune. Assuming, of course that my esteemed trustees haven't gambled all my money away on 'Change or siphoned off the capital to line their own nests."

His brows drew together. "You must demand a full accounting upon your majority. That's not far off."

"Oh, be sure that I will," said Georgie. "But my trustees are dears, and as honest as the day is long. Violet's, on the other hand . . . Well, I had Mr. Moreton's measure from the outset, not to mention that lickspittle solicitor's." She glanced at Beckenham's face, noted his grim expression. He had their measure, too. "I positively look forward to your dealing with those gentlemen when you are Violet's husband."

He threw her an irritated glance. "I've not offered for your sister and she has not accepted me. I wish you would stop treating it as a foregone conclusion."

She opened her eyes wide. "Surely you would not act in a manner contrary to good sense and judgment merely to spite me?"

By tacit agreement, they reined in some distance from the house. He glanced at her. "I don't like the idea of taking what should have been yours."

She reached over to place a hand on his arm. "Please do not think that way. I do not begrudge Violet or you. But I do begrudge Uncle Moreton the running of the place until Violet either marries or reaches the age of five-and-twenty. Particularly if this bailiff is not up to scratch, as you seem to think."

A muscle ticced in Beckenham's jaw. Gruffly, he said, "Of course they were right; it is none of my business."

She paused. *Courage, Georgie!* "You must make it your business. You must marry Violet."

He made no comment for a long time. Then he said, "I hear there's a new tenant at Cloverleigh."

"I suggested to Violet that she ought to call," said Georgie. "Yet she is young and feels diffident about intruding. Perhaps you might accompany her."

He was silent for a time. Then he said, "No. It is not my place to do so. Besides, I believe the tenant is a single gentleman and will only remain at the house for the summer. It is hardly worth her making his acquaintance."

He nodded his head toward Winford. "Shall we return?"

"Of course," said Georgie. "You must not neglect your guests."

He did not seem in any desperate hurry. He turned his head to look at her and it seemed to her that he read in her eyes everything she felt. The warm feeling of homecoming tinged with a poignant pain of regret.

He set his horse in motion. "Shall we visit the bluebell wood before we go back?"

Half her childhood had been spent in that wood. With an instinctive need to brace herself, Georgie nodded. "I should like to do that if we have time."

They entered a fairyland full of mystery and shadows, ancient gnarled trees with massive roots that lifted out of the ground like monstrous tentacles. Shards of sunlight streamed through gaps in the canopy above, and the dust motes swirled and danced within them like tiny fey folk.

In places, the wood was dark and cool and damp with verdigris lichen and emerald moss sprawling over tree trunks and the ground. A stream ran through, the water icy even in summer, clear enough to see every smooth rock and pebble beneath.

A carpet of leaves and damp earth underfoot, a sense of stillness so complete, it was as if humans had never set foot in this wood before now.

Silently, they halted. Georgie took the fecund forest air deep into her lungs. With a pang, she realized she might never visit here again. If Violet married Beckenham, it would be too painful.

Beckenham slid from his horse and moved to help her dismount, but she was too quick, swinging herself down from the saddle without assistance and dropping to the ground.

She didn't trust herself if he put his hands on her. Whatever her resolutions might be as far as marrying her sister to her former fiancé, she was afraid that all he had to do was touch her and she would fall. Even if that touch consisted of the wholly impersonal act of lifting her down from the saddle.

Georgie found a few straggling late bluebells in a patch of sunlight. Delighted by the distraction, she picked one and before she knew what she did, she had stood on tiptoe and threaded it through Beckenham's buttonhole.

He watched her gravely. Some strange light in his expression made her cut her gaze and turn quickly away to resume her explorations.

When he had seen to the horses, he said, "Speak frankly, Georgie. Do you truly not mind if I court Violet?"

How could she answer that question frankly? "I *want* you to marry her, Beckenham. I told you that."

She managed to say it without her voice breaking. She looked him in the eye, too. If nothing else, she could be proud of herself for that.

At eighteen she'd blazed a trail through life, doing as she wished, taking what she wanted, without ever counting the cost. She'd learned her lesson when she'd lost the most important thing of all.

Now she did not treat her boons so cavalierly. Georgie Black had grown up.

His face darkened. He strode toward her, took her by the arms as if he would shake her. "Is it nothing to you, then? Do you not feel the slightest qualm about delivering the man you were to marry to your sister?"

She wanted to scream at him to let go, let go of her. In every sense of the word.

I never wanted to come back here, to see all I've lost.

The sudden fierce resentment she felt toward her father, toward even her sister—innocent Violet who had never asked for any of this—shocked her to the core.

The old Georgie rose up inside her like a phoenix from the ashes. She thought she'd destroyed that tempestuous, selfish little beast, but here Beckenham was, holding her, his big hands wrapped around her upper arms, mere inches from her breasts.

If he had not been holding her, she would have staggered back.

Her body swayed toward him.

He stared down at her. In a graveled whisper, he said, "See if you won't regret this."

His mouth crushed down on hers in the most satisfyingly brutal way. His arms lashed around her, holding her so tightly, her breasts mashed against his broad chest.

She felt the heat in him, the ravenous hunger. His tongue invaded her mouth and she welcomed it, dueled with her own.

He backed her against a tree, kissing her all the while. She felt the hard scratchiness of the bark behind her as she rested her head against it.

They were close enough now that her booted feet stood between his; her stomach pressed against the growing erection his breeches did nothing to disguise.

The notion excited her. She wanted to climb up his body, get inside his skin. The urge to undress him there, in the forest cool, became overwhelming. She wanted to see all of him, not just his chest and back, magnificent and muscular though they were.

Everything.

He was a fever inside her. His hands moved to her rump, lifting her, rubbing her against him. The act was so carnal, so frank in its intent that she could scarcely believe Beckenham was the man doing this to her.

But he wasn't doing it out of passion, she realized. He thought he was punishing her, didn't he? Teaching her a lesson for not falling to pieces over the mere prospect of him courting her sister.

Violet. She wrenched her mouth from his. "No," she panted. "This is wrong."

"But it feels so very right to me." His lips diverted to her throat, drifting over sensitive skin, pressing pulse points. Oh, dear Heaven, she loved it when he did that!

Violet. Dear God, what was she doing?

In a sudden frenzy, Georgie shoved at Beckenham until he released her.

His breath came in pants; his dark eyes burned like coals. "A bit late to turn missish, my dear."

"I am not missish! I am merely recollecting the reasons why kissing you is a terrible idea."

She brushed at her riding habit, and wished she could brush away their encounter as easily as she removed twigs and bark.

He made her crazy. She made him insane. This could not go any further.

"Don't tell me you didn't enjoy that," he said with a fierce look. "You were right there with me, Georgie."

She wished he didn't call her by her first name. She wished they'd resumed formality when they'd dissolved their engagement. And wasn't she clutching at straws?

Honesty was her trademark. She used it. "I am attracted to you. I always have been. We . . ." She sighed. "This cannot happen again."

She saw the precise point where his face turned to granite. "Let's go back. It's getting late and my guests will be down to breakfast soon."

"Yes. And might we forget about this, ah, interlude?" she said, striving for a light note. "I am heartily ashamed of myself."

"I will not speak of it again, certainly," he said. He had not said he would forget.

Silently, she waited while he collected their horses and followed him out of the glade.

He slowed his pace to walk beside her. "It was a pity you came back."

They were cruel words, but spoken without heat. They were not meant to hurt her, merely to state a fact.

She nodded. "I wish to Heaven I had not."

But if she had not, she wouldn't have set eyes on him again before he married. For some reason, she didn't think she could have borne that, either.

At least she would have that kiss to remember. At least she would have that.

Pathetic, stupid, but there it was.

She gave a sudden, ripping sob, then laughed, to try to cover it. "Let's leave this place. I am always fey when I come here."

"Titania," he murmured.

"Ha!" she said, more at ease deflecting compliments than dealing with genuine emotion. "Was Titania a carrot-top, too?"

His dark eyes seemed as mysterious as the shadows in the wood as he stared at her. "I have always imagined her so."

Struggling for levity, Georgie responded lightly, "She was a troublesome female, as I recall."

He inclined his head in assent. "She led the faerie king a merry dance. Then she fell in love with an ass."

"Because the faerie king gave her a potion to teach her not to flout him," she countered. "*I* should not forgive him so easily."

"The poor fellow was desperate, I expect. Men commit every kind of folly when . . ." He broke off. "At all events, the affair ended happily."

"I wonder," said Georgie. "In my experience, people don't change that much, particularly strong-willed characters like those. My guess is they reenacted that same comedy over and over, tormented one another until the end of time."

Beckenham fell silent.

The parallels were obvious. She was constitutionally incapable of being a biddable wife. She would have given him no peace.

Violet, however, was perfect for him.

But she could not convince him of that with words. She must *show* him how superior Violet was to all those other debutantes. How much better she'd be for him than Georgie ever was.

As they rode silently back to the house, Georgie began to plan.

Chapter Twelve

"You spent the morning cavorting about the countryside with the one lady at this gathering you ought to avoid."

Lydgate curled his lip in disgust and tossed Beckenham the pair of gloves he'd taken down from the wall of Beckenham's purpose-fitted boxing saloon.

Beckenham caught them, wondering what Lydgate would say if he knew about that kiss.

Beckenham was an enthusiastic pugilist, and one of his few indulgences beside his stables was converting the outbuilding next to the bathhouse into an appropriate place for all kinds of indoor physical activity.

The walls were lined with racks of equipment, from shuttlecock rackets to cricket bats to boxing gloves, bows and arrows and foils.

He pulled the boxing gloves onto his hands. "Less talk, more action, Lydgate. I'm going to black those pretty blue eyes of yours."

Lydgate gave a dramatic shudder. "Not the face, dear coz. Anything but the face."

Beckenham knew he didn't have a chance of hitting

Lydgate's face unless Lydgate allowed him to. On Beckenham's good days, they were fairly evenly matched. Beckenham's weight and power against Lydgate's superior agility.

Today was not going to be one of Beckenham's good days.

If he'd cherished any illusions about that, their first, rather one-sided bout left him in no doubt.

Panting, he said, "It was a chance meeting. Besides, we spoke only of my courting Miss Violet."

He punctuated the sentence with a right aimed at the shoulder, which Lydgate easily dodged.

"And?" said Lydgate, shifting his feet and boring in with a one-two feint and punch that smacked Beckenham in the ribs.

With a grunt, Beckenham drove through the pain to land a blow to Lydgate's chest that sent him staggering back a pace. Lydgate's eyebrows twitched together, and the light of battle joined gleamed in his eye.

Answering his cousin's question, Beckenham forced out, "Says she wants me to marry her sister. Says I'm the man to run Cloverleigh to her satisfaction."

Lydgate danced back, dashing his arm across his forehead to wipe away sweat. "Generous of her."

"I thought so." It had been generous. Even the sweetest-tempered female, which Georgie most assuredly was not, would have found it difficult to say those words.

She was capable of that kind of quixotic generosity, he found.

"So you'll fix your interest with the sister?" Lydgate persisted. He bore in with a few jabs toward Beckenham's smarting rib cage, but it was mere flourishing; he didn't have his mind on the fight.

Beckenham shrugged. "It does seem like the perfect solution."

And Georgie didn't mind. Didn't mind at all. Encouraged him, in fact.

Damn her.

They finished the bout and Lydgate took himself off, presumably to meddle in someone else's affairs. Beckenham went to the bathhouse and indulged himself in a long, hot soak, before entering the fray once more.

Georgie entered the drawing room, where the ladies gathered that afternoon. She intended to while away the time before dinner with a gothic novel she'd managed to unearth in Beckenham's austere library.

Tempted though she was to curl up in the window seat of that dark, masculine cave and stay out of sight, she had a duty to Violet to protect her from the cats. Quite apart from that, she refused to hide herself away as if she had something to be ashamed of.

"I suppose you do not embroider, Miss Black," said Lady Charlotte, interrupting a particularly stirring passage between the star-crossed lovers in Georgie's novel.

"Hmm? Actually, I do embroider. Just not at this moment," said Georgie. She closed her book. "I cannot imagine why you should suppose otherwise. Isn't every young lady taught such things?"

Lady Charlotte smiled. "I simply thought . . . You are known to be such a keen sportswoman."

"Am I?" Georgie opened her eyes wide.

"Indeed." Lady Charlotte used sharp little white teeth to snip off a thread. She raised her voice a little, so the others could hear. "In fact, I propose we set up an archery tournament tomorrow, so that Miss Black might show us her skill."

Hmm. Georgie's gaze flickered to Violet, whose fingers tinkered idly at the pianoforte. "Thank you, but I believe of the pair of us, my sister is the superior archer. She will represent the family." She raised her voice a little. "What say you, Violet? Will you give Lady Charlotte here a contest with your bow?"

"Indeed. I'd be delighted," said Violet serenely.

Butter wouldn't melt, thought Georgie with smug satisfaction.

Looking a little discomfited, Lady Charlotte said, "I shall speak with Lord Beckenham about the arrangements."

"Splendid," said Georgie.

Unbeknownst to Lady Charlotte, she could not have chosen a milieu to set off Violet to better advantage.

While she was no great horsewoman and she could not bring herself to fire a pistol, Violet had a precision of eye that made a sport like archery second nature to her. What's more, she looked ravishing in profile. Georgie knew just the right hat she should wear for the occasion: a cunningly wrought little piece that slanted rakishly over one eye.

Well done, Lady Charlotte, Georgie thought. The girl was shrewd enough to know that as a sports enthusiast, Beckenham would take a keen interest in the event.

Georgie glanced over at Lady Arden, who sat at the escritoire, writing letters until the pile at her elbow seemed to grow monstrous. The business of matchmaking and meddling was never done, it seemed.

Lady Arden was like a sparkling spider at the center of an intricate web of relatives, allies, and persons who owed her a favor. Georgie knew that had she desired, her kinswoman would have arranged an eligible match for her.

She wasn't damaged goods; she still had a very generous dowry, thanks to her mother's fortune. Gentlemen proposed to her regularly, either in fits of mad passion or with a clearer eye to the main chance.

She'd never been tempted. She intended to rub along with her stepmother until her twenty-fifth birthday, when she'd inherit the fortune her irate papa had not been able to bring himself to deny her. She'd always intended to set up a permanent household of her own in London. Now, she rather thought London would not be far enough from Winford for her comfort.

The gentlemen arrived then, freshly changed after a fishing expedition, and all pretense of interest in embroidery or music was promptly abandoned by the ladies.

Lady Charlotte said, "Will you join us, Lord Beckenham? Do sit down."

"No, thank you. I'm about to take the gentlemen on a tour of the estate. Dull stuff to do with the new drainage system. Not a subject for ladies, I'm afraid."

Beckenham hadn't so much as glanced in Georgie's direction since he'd entered the room.

In other circumstances, she would have insisted on going with the men. She'd vastly prefer riding about Winford, learning about new farming methods, to sitting quietly in the midst of all this repressed animosity. As it was, she opened her book again and began to read.

Lady Arden held up her hands for silence. "My dears, I have a proposition to make. Whenever I am hostess at a house party, I like to make my guests sing for their supper, so to speak. Ordinarily, this takes the form of a concert or a little embroidery project that will keep the ladies occupied and useful while the gentlemen commit various atrocities on the local wildlife."

She smiled, as there were titters from the assembled young ladies.

"This time, I have arrived at something quite different. In the lake, there is an island with a grotto. Man-made, of course. The interior of the grotto requires a little something in the way of decoration."

She gestured to the three footmen who flanked her, holding large baskets and pails and various other pieces of equipment. "Here we have a collection of seashells I had delivered. You, my dear ones, will be covering the walls with these shells."

"Oh! I have seen this before, at a house in Ireland," said Lady Harriet, clapping her hands.

Lady Charlotte looked doubtful. "Mama will kill me if I break my nails."

Lady Arden stared at her. "Then you'll have to take care, won't you? Come along, girls. I'll show you the way and then you may continue."

Georgie longed to escape the suffocating tension in the drawing room. This seemed too rich an experience to miss.

"What on earth?" she murmured to Lady Arden as they left the drawing room.

"I like to set challenges for my ladies," she explained. "Being a countess is not all about keeping one's nails pretty. You need to be prepared to roll up your sleeves on occasion. We'll see which of them shows her mettle."

"But I thought you were completely for Violet, my lady," said Georgie, puzzled. "Don't tell me you are impartial in this."

"I expect Violet to pass this test with flying colors," said Lady Arden serenely. "But remember that I also have my family to consider. It is an excellent opportunity for me to assess brides who might be eligible for my boys."

By "her boys," Lady Arden meant the gentlemen from the Black family whom it was her duty to marry off successfully. She had no children of her own.

"Dear ma'am, your name ought to be Machiavelli," murmured Georgie, smiling.

Lady Arden sighed. "My talents are quite wasted," she mourned. "Had I been a man, I should have been Prime Minister."

"But where would the fun be in that?" said Georgie.

Lady Arden laughed. She wielded an enormous amount of power through her family and social connections. Everyone knew it. Even the Prime Minister.

The ladies piled into two little boats, each rowed by a footman, with the third footman bringing up the rear with the equipment.

With much giggling and fluttering, the ladies allowed themselves to be handed out of the boats, onto the sloping bank of the man-made island.

The grotto looked cold and dank, a perfect setting for hoary tales and hermits. They waited outside while the footmen unloaded supplies and lit lamps. Then they ventured in.

The space was surprisingly large, cold and cavernous, and oddly damp.

"You expect us to cover the entire thing by the end of our stay?" demanded Lady Charlotte. Heavens, but the girl was tiresome.

"Many hands make light work," quipped Lady Arden. "If you are the stuff of which countesses are made, you will have it finished by the time you leave this house."

The implication was akin to a threat. Georgie bit back a smile.

Miss Margo deVere, game as a pebble, said, "Right-ho! Will you show us how it's done, my lady?"

"But of course." Elegant as a rose, Lady Arden set out the tools of their craft. "I have sketched out a design you may follow if you wish, or you may each design your own panel of wall and do it that way."

She nodded to a waiting footman and he stepped forward with a pail full of gray slurry and a box full of tools. Lady Arden selected a trowel and held it up. "This is what you spread the mortar with, do you see? So. Select the shells you wish to use."

She took a handful and set them down on the stone table in the center of the room. "Now, get up some of the mortar on your trowel and spread it thickly on the surface. Then you simply press the shells down into the mortar. Work quickly, and only spread as much mortar as you think you'll need for the shells you have to hand, otherwise, the mortar will dry before you can press them in."

She demonstrated, quickly making an attractive pattern of shells on the table itself.

"It's like a mosaic," said Lady Harriet. "I have seen sketches of Roman mosaics my father brought back from Pompeii. Only they were done in tiny tiles."

"Precisely," nodded Lady Arden. "I think it will be best if each of you work on your own panel, so that I may judge how well you do."

She roughly divided the irregularly shaped room into sections and handed the ladies chalk. "You can mark out your design on the wall with the chalk, or you may do it freehand if you prefer."

She looked over at Georgie. "Might I leave you in charge here?"

"Of course. Is there a trowel for me? I believe I shall finish your work on the table here, if I'm to stay."

"Certainly, my dear. I'll leave you to it, then." She smiled at everyone. "Enjoy yourselves."

Georgie seated herself at the little stone table and

sorted through her allotted shells. As she worked, Georgie kept an assessing eye on the girls. Violet stared at the wall with a thoughtful brow before drawing some tentative lines. Then she shook her head and wiped them away with a cloth.

Miss deVere had already begun mortaring and sticking shells in a cheerfully haphazard design that somehow seemed to work quite well. Lady Harriet was making a very detailed, very pretty sketch of a lion that Georgie doubted could be easily translated with the materials to hand, but she would like to see the poor girl try.

Miss Trent had chosen to fill out her space with a geometric pattern that was simple yet effective. Lady Charlotte made no attempt to put forethought or effort into the task. Her work was desultory, punctuated by sighs and complaints.

Beckenham was no fool. He'd write down Lady Charlotte as a baggage before too long. She was the kind of girl who could not help but show her true nature. Some men wouldn't see past the enchantingly pretty face, with its dark eyes and rosebud mouth, but Beckenham wasn't one of them.

Marcus would be far more attracted to Miss Trent's dignified gentleness. She was precisely the sort of colorless female he was looking for. She would never give him an iota of concern. She would agree with everything he said, having no decided opinions of her own.

Of course, even Miss Trent could not compete with Violet. Georgie's sister had wit and strength of character that Miss Trent lacked.

She didn't think it was pure bias on her part. Violet truly was the best candidate for the position of Beckenham's countess. But that would count for nothing unless Violet would be happy with the match. She must not lose sight of that.

Dear Lizzie,
He is here! He came, just as he said he would. . . .

"Well, my dear? What do you think of him?" Georgie had dismissed her maid and was fixing diamond drops into her ears. The little gems swung, catching the light as Georgie glanced up into Violet's reflection in the looking glass above her vanity table.

"You were right, Georgie, I like Lord Beckenham very well," said Violet. "At least, the little I have seen of him."

"Do you like his looks?" Georgie said, swiveling on her stool to take Violet's hands in hers. "Do you find him attractive?"

How could Violet fail to be drawn to all that hard masculine virility?

Violet's cornflower blue eyes shadowed a little. "He is certainly handsome," she allowed.

"But?" prompted Georgie. She had a very odd feeling in her stomach.

Her sister shrugged. "He does not set my maidenly heart aflutter. But I suppose my heart is scarcely in question here."

Georgie did not let herself feel the emotion that threatened to well up inside her. She needed to do what was best for Violet. Her own feelings did not matter. She chose her words with care.

"Sometimes one may grow to care for a gentleman in time. And Beckenham is a good man, Violet."

"So you keep saying." With a rueful smile, Violet sighed. "I do not have high hopes of him choosing me over the other ladies. They are so accomplished, so rich and well-bred."

"And what, pray, has all that to say to anything?"

demanded Georgie. "You are the daughter of Sir Donald Black, and if that was good enough for him six years ago, why should it not be good enough for him now?" Georgie rose and shook out her skirts. "Besides, you have a distinct advantage over the other young ladies."

"My dowry," said Violet glumly.

"Your sweetness of disposition," corrected Georgie. "Believe me, a man like Beckenham does not wish for a troublesome shrew like Lady Charlotte to wife."

"Lady Charlotte is a cat," agreed Georgie. "But I like Lady Harriet and Miss Trent, too, though she does tend to poker up on occasion."

"Very high in the instep, the Trents," Georgie agreed.

"Margo deVere is jolly company," said Violet.

"Jolly." Georgie nodded. "Aye and a madcap hoyden if ever I saw one. You may be sure that Beckenham has more sense than to marry into that barbaric family. Do not allow her to lead you into mischief, Violet. I've seen her kind before."

She hesitated. "I rode to Cloverleigh Manor with Beckenham this morning. Or rather, he followed me for he would not let me go alone without a groom."

She found that she was proud of the way she did not betray to Violet any sign of what had happened in that cool, quiet glade on the way home. Truly, that kiss had been a mere expression of pent-up feeling. It would not happen again.

"Oh?" Violet's tone was disinterested. "I suppose I should have done that. Truly, Georgie, I wish to Heaven Papa had left Cloverleigh to you. I have not lived there since I was a little girl. I barely remember it. I have no connection to the place."

This was not the first time Violet had expressed the sentiment. "I think it would be wise for you to take an interest," said Georgie. "If you wed Beckenham, you will have more than Cloverleigh to deal with."

Georgie turned away, ostensibly to fetch her wrap from where Smith had laid it out on the bed. The wrap was a gauzy film of nothing, and would keep her no warmer than air. But the night was sultry, after all, and what did comfort matter when it came to fashion?

"Yes, of course, you are right." Violet seemed to brace herself. She lifted her chin. "I shall endeavor to make you proud."

Heedless of crushed silks, Georgie hugged her sister. "I know you will, dearest. I just hope that you will be happy, too."

They mingled in the drawing room before dinner. Beckenham found himself in a strange mood. Edgy, dissatisfied. He'd taken the other gentlemen fishing in the lake and then on a tour of the estate, but his mind had been preoccupied. He'd spent the greater part of the afternoon wondering about Georgie and what trouble she might be stirring up.

Yet she appeared to have passed an entirely blameless afternoon decorating the grotto with the other ladies. He'd seen her enter the house, a trifle dusty and disheveled with a gray smut that he thought must have been mortar on her nose.

She looked young and fresh and . . . rather sweet.

Sweet? Georgie? Good God, he must be heading for early senility.

Though he conversed politely with his guests, he never failed to be aware of her as she stood in a corner, sipping champagne and conversing with Lord Trent.

She was dressed fashionably but rather soberly once again, in dark blue silk with a neckline so modest, he wondered if the gown was indeed hers or one she'd borrowed from one of the matrons. However much she might retire from the hub of conversation, she could not escape her admirers.

First one, then two, then three and four gentlemen gravitated toward her, until it seemed that he was surrounded by females and the men had all decamped to her side.

He was obliged to admit she did nothing to seek masculine attention. In fact, she eventually excused herself to cross the room and sit with the old Dowager Marchioness of Salisbury. Seemingly pleased with her company, she settled in for a long prose until the dinner gong sounded.

They did not stand on ceremony when it came to seating everyone. Lady Arden had decided that it was more important for Beckenham to converse with his prospective brides than to observe the rules of precedence.

She had, however, placed Georgie as far away from him as possible.

Ha! Did she think he was in any danger from Georgie? Yes, he might have kissed her that morning, but he blamed his uncharacteristic actions on the atmosphere, the sense of stepping back in time.

Of course, he had never kissed her like that in the old days. . . .

"Lord Beckenham, might I compliment you on your cook?" said Miss Trent, at his left. "An old retainer, I gather."

"Indeed," he replied. "Mrs. North has been with us since I was a boy. Thank you, I shall tell her you approve."

He wondered what his redoubtable cook would make of Miss Trent. Not a bad-looking girl, but a little stiff for Mrs. North's taste. Still, a calm reserve was not unattractive to him. If a little dull at times, at least Miss Trent would never subject him to excesses of emotion.

He glanced down the table at Georgie, who could not help herself, it seemed. She was laughing. Despite her efforts to appear sedate—so as not to take the shine out of her sister, he suspected—she could not help but draw masculine admiration with that full-throated, husky chuckle of hers.

His gaze flicked to Miss Violet, wedged between Lord Trent's bulk and the young Lord Hardcastle.

She seemed prettily animated tonight, responding to Hardcastle's sallies with smiles and the odd blush here and there.

Miss Violet Black was a charming girl. He hoped to know her better over the course of the next couple of days. He could wish Lady Arden had thought to place her next to him this evening.

Miss Trent still waxed lyrical over his domestic arrangements, asking him all sorts of questions he could not answer. He left household affairs in the capable hands of his housekeeper and took an interest only on the rare occasion that something went awry.

Perhaps Miss Trent attempted to show him how competent a householder she would be. He didn't doubt it but he discovered a sudden wish for more than a chatelaine in his countess. Not that he could have said what that extra something might be.

Would Miss Violet provide it? He glanced at her again. Lively, pretty, and no goosecap if he were any judge of the matter. Perhaps she would suit him, just as Georgie said.

And of course, there was Cloverleigh Manor.

The next remove was on the table before Lady Charlotte claimed his attention.

"I was shocked, my lord, to discover Miss Black had landed on your doorstep uninvited," she was saying.

Startled, and more than a little annoyed, he said without inflexion, "Were you?"

He eyed her wineglass, which now stood empty. Perhaps he ought not to judge her too harshly. Perhaps he ought to order her some lemonade instead.

In a milder tone, he said, "I assure you, Miss Black was indeed invited, Lady Charlotte."

She picked up her goblet, eyed its dregs blankly, as if she could not remember having drunk every drop, then set it down again. "No! You cannot mean that you would consider Miss Black for a bride. Particularly after . . . Well, *you* know."

He raised an eyebrow.

She leaned forward, whispering loudly, "She *jilted* you."

A footman with a decanter of burgundy stepped forward to hover at Lady Charlotte's elbow, but stepped back at Beckenham's slight shake of the head.

Oblivious, Lady Charlotte continued, "The most shocking thing! I'd no notion until Mama told me last night, for of course, Miss Black is *so* much older than I."

She laughed in a manner she might have thought was pretty but which curdled Beckenham's stomach.

"Of course, everyone knew you were well shot of her," she confided.

"I was?"

"Oh, but *yes*!" Lady Charlotte widened her eyes. She leaned toward him, a trifle unsteadily. "It's Mama's belief that Miss Black is no better than she should be, no matter what airs and graces she tries to assume. Everyone knows what a wild past she has."

"Do they?" He regarded this low-minded little brat with distaste.

"Her sister is hardly better," continued Lady Charlotte recklessly. "You can tell these things immediately. See how she blushes and bridles at Lord Hardcastle's flirting. Quite shocking."

Much more of this, and he'd punish this arrogant little upstart in a way both of them would regret.

"Excuse me," he said abruptly, and turned from her to resume his conversation about the properties of beeswax with Miss Trent.

He was furious, he realized. If Lady Charlotte had been a man, he would have been sorely tempted to call her out. But she was an eighteen-year-old spiteful little vixen, who had imbibed too much of the heavy burgundy Beckenham had been foolish enough to approve for this evening's meal.

She deserved a severe set-down. Indeed, he felt a burning need to defend Georgie's honor. Yet the more reasonable part of him could see Lady Charlotte wasn't herself.

He let it pass, but he seethed for the rest of the meal.

Later, when he finally managed to get Georgie alone, he said to her, "Watch out for Lady Charlotte and her dear mama, won't you? They want to discredit Violet and they mean to do it through you."

Georgie gazed at him, her eyes glinting with anger. Then she shrugged. "As yours is the only opinion that matters and you know everything there is to my discredit, I trust you will not let it prejudice you against my sister."

He regarded her thoughtfully. "The old Georgie would have bowled up to Lady Charlotte and asked her what she meant by slandering her name."

She smiled. "I'm wiser now, I hope." She raised her brows at him. "Did you tell me of it so you could watch me scratch Lady Charlotte's eyes out? How disappointed you must be."

His gaze flickered over her; then he looked over to the pianoforte, where Hardcastle turned the pages for Violet, who played and sang a sentimental ballad.

"You restrain yourself for Violet's sake," he said.

"She is very dear to me." Carefully, Georgie added, "Did you think I would come at all to such a party if she was not? She begged me to accompany her when her mother fell ill. I didn't see how I might refuse her. I am sorry that it makes it awkward for you."

It was awkward. It was . . . maddening, too. He met her gaze and wished, fervently, that the rest of the company would fade away and leave them quite alone.

Chapter Thirteen

The house party went on for several days with little variation in theme. Beckenham thought he'd managed to acquaint himself well enough with all the young ladies present, but he was no closer to deciding on which of them would make the most suitable bride.

His first instinct was to blame his indecision on Georgie's unsettling presence, but that wasn't altogether fair. True to her word, she'd taken pains to remain in the background. He'd scarcely exchanged a handful of words with her. No, it wasn't Georgie's fault; he couldn't help feeling that none of the ladies present was the right one.

Violet Black was something of an enigma. She was perfectly pleasant company, but he always had the impression that her thoughts were elsewhere. A more conceited man would have been piqued. As it was, he supposed he was glad she didn't seem to have formed any silly tendre for him.

Indeed, he'd taken care to avoid inviting any young lady who seemed disposed to think herself in love with him. How awkward and tiresome that would have been.

He was not a man who enjoyed society or parties as a rule. Rather perversely, given the stated purpose of this gathering, he'd taken advantage of the bad weather to escape to the outdoors, where matchmaking mamas and delicate young ladies wouldn't follow.

Georgie was a hardier creature, and he'd often looked out for her, galloping her mare over the meadows, but since that morning they'd visited Cloverleigh, she'd never appeared.

Today, to escape a proposed game of charades, he'd ridden out into the drizzle with Hardcastle and Lydgate. However, part way through the afternoon a stiff breeze had blown the rain clouds away, bathing the landscape in sunshine. They were just returning when he spied a party of three riders up ahead.

Like most members of her family, Miss Margo deVere looked as if she'd been born in the saddle. With her was Miss Violet Black, and . . .

Beckenham's jaw tightened. "What the hell is he doing here?"

"Who is he?" said Hardcastle, craning his neck to see.

Lydgate merely said, *"Ah."*

Beckenham shot him a furious glance. "What do you mean 'ah'?"

Lydgate straightened in his saddle. "My dear fellow—"

"Don't you bloody *my dear fellow* me. You knew, didn't you?"

But the parties met then and there was no further opportunity for conversation.

"Lord Beckenham." Removing his hat, Lord Pearce made an elegant bow, his thick, waving hair tousling romantically in the breeze. He greeted the other gentlemen in turn.

One glance at the ladies told Beckenham they were impressed. Miss Violet's blue eyes sparkled and her cheeks were prettily flushed. Miss deVere emitted a rather gauche giggle.

Beckenham only gave a curt nod in response. "Miss Black. Miss deVere. Misplaced your groom, did you?"

Smoothly, Lydgate interposed before the ladies could reply to the abrupt accusation. "Were you returning to the house? May we join you?"

Without waiting for a response, Lydgate performed some magical equestrian maneuver whereby Beckenham found himself riding with Pearce, Lydgate partnered Miss deVere and Miss Violet and Lord Hardcastle brought up the rear.

"What charming young ladies," murmured Pearce. "I believe they stay with you at this house party of yours?"

"Those ladies, charming or no, are not your concern," said Beckenham. He'd have to tell their chaperones to keep a closer eye on them if Pearce was in the vicinity. "What are you doing here? Just happened to be passing, I daresay."

"Why, no," said Pearce, his brows lifting. "I'm the new tenant at Cloverleigh."

Beckenham silently cursed Lydgate. He'd wager his cousin knew all about it. Why the hell hadn't he told Beckenham instead of letting him discover it this way?

"Oh? I'd heard someone by the name of Sanderson had taken the house."

"That would be my man of business," said Pearce.

So the cur had deliberately concealed his identity. Had he thought to meet Georgie in secret while she was here?

"Actually, I have yet to inhabit the place, truth be

told," Pearce said. "I've spent most of my time in Bath."

"Toadying to your aunt."

"Protecting her, rather. My dear Beckenham, you would not credit the things people will do when such a large sum of money is involved."

Mendacious rubbish. Pearce would eat all his avaricious relatives for breakfast. He'd certainly sell his own mother for the chance at such a prize. Beckenham didn't doubt he'd prevail, by fair means or foul. Foul, most likely.

"Well, I'm sure I wish you joy of your inheritance," said Beckenham. "But don't imagine Miss Black will fall into your arms whether you win a fortune or no."

Pearce turned his head. "You wound me, my lord. Do you think I don't know her better than that?"

"What I think doesn't bear repeating when there are ladies present," Beckenham bit out. "Stay away from her, Pearce."

"Loath as I am to appear to obey your commands, I fear I shall be obliged to do so for the present." Lord Pearce gestured in the direction of Cloverleigh. "I merely came to see that the household was in order before I return to my relative's deathbed. I cannot afford to be absent for too long. Her health is rapidly deteriorating."

"If you value your own health, you will not come back here."

Pearce's green eyes glinted with malice. Softly, he said, "Do I scent a challenge?"

The gall of him, to bring that up! "I only duel with gentlemen," said Beckenham. "I'm afraid you no longer qualify."

A nasty smile curved Pearce's lips as they reached the crossroads. "Has she never told you what happened that night? Do you really think I was scared to meet you all those years ago?"

"Strangely, Pearce," Beckenham said, "I don't think of you at all."

With a touch to his hat brim, he led his party in the direction of Winford.

After the persistent showers of the past week, to Georgie's pleasure, the weather suddenly turned. The day was so fine, in fact, that the proposed jaunt to the village led to some exclamations about the heat and the injurious sunshine. However, once Lord Beckenham chose to accompany them on the excursion, the ladies braved the elements gladly.

After this abrupt change of face, a flurry of activity ensued as they all donned bonnets and gloves, armed themselves with parasols and reticules.

"We shall buy ribbons and lace," said Georgie. "Our hats could do with a new touch."

"You are forever giving our hats a new touch," said Violet with a chuckle. "Too many times I have planned what to wear only to find I don't recognize my own bonnets anymore."

It was some sort of compulsion, Georgie admitted as they all set off in a giggling, fluttering phalanx to explore the village.

Beckenham, Georgie saw with satisfaction, strolled with Violet on one arm and Miss Priscilla Trent on the other. Miss Trent appeared to be monopolizing his attention, however, while Violet's attention seemed miles distant.

Georgie frowned. If Violet couldn't hold her own against *one* of these ladies, how would she stand out in the crowd?

Miss Trent paused in her discourse then, and Beckenham turned his head to address a remark to Violet. The darling girl turned her head to smile up at him in the sweetest fashion. If that did not make him melt on the spot, she didn't know much about men.

A voice beside her said, "They make a handsome couple, do they not?"

She saw who accosted her. "Lord Lydgate. Yes, indeed they do."

He offered her his arm. She took it, a little surprised at the hard strength she felt beneath his dandified blue coat.

Lydgate slowed their pace—deliberately, she thought—until they were still in sight of the other members of the party but out of earshot.

Hoping to forestall anything he might say, she forced out, "I hope they make a match of it—Beckenham and Violet, I mean. The earl could search the length and breadth of England and never find a lovelier girl."

When she glanced at him, his face wore a pleasant expression, but his eyes quizzed her.

"Do you disapprove?" she asked.

He tilted his head. "The match seems eminently suitable. It may interest you to know that Beckenham rejected the notion at first."

Indignation bridled within her. "What? He thought Violet beneath him?"

"Pray, come down off your high horse, ma'am. Of course not. Is that likely?"

She shook her head. "Then I don't understand."

He spread his hands. "Out of consideration for your poor hurt feelings, of course. How galling to have a mere sister supplant one as Countess of Beckenham."

Her hand tightened on her parasol. "Did he say that?"

"Not in so many words. But you know how he is. A gentleman to the core."

Beckenham pitied her! She'd been afraid that would happen. Good God, she could sink into the ground with embarrassment. She could light up the sky with incandescent rage.

She controlled her emotions. "The match has my wholehearted support. I told Beckenham as much. Not only do I wish to see Violet happily settled, but I desire to see Cloverleigh Manor in good hands."

"None better than Beckenham's."

"Precisely."

"Then I take it I can assume you will not do anything to scupper your sister's chances?" said Lydgate.

"I'll be as obnoxious to the earl as you could wish."

Lydgate nodded in satisfaction. "That should do it. Oh, and you might consider setting up a flirt while you're here."

She wrinkled her nose at that. "I could pretend to flirt with you."

Lydgate laughed. "Heaven forbid! You are so charming, my dear, and I am so susceptible. I should undoubtedly lose my heart to you."

"What nonsense, Lydgate. It is well known you do not have a heart to lose."

"Try Hardcastle," he recommended.

She looked ahead, to where Lord Hardcastle bent to listen to Lady Charlotte's prattle.

"But he is just a boy," she protested.

"Your senior by one or two years, I fancy," said Lydgate. "And he was making your sister the object of his gallantry only yesterday. A fine chap, but he don't have a feather to fly with, more's the pity. Looking for an heiress to tow his estate out of the River Tick."

She recalled her fear that Violet might be pining for Lord Pearce. She hadn't entirely shaken off that suspicion, so it was with mixed emotions that she contemplated a new romantic interest on the horizon.

Surely Georgie would have noticed if Violet showed any preference for the young man. Whatever the case, Hardcastle would not do for Violet.

"Well," said Georgie. "I am glad you pointed him out to me. I shall certainly do my poor best to detach him from my sister."

They reached the village outskirts then, and the group clustered around Beckenham, who was pointing out various attractions. "The King's Head is reportedly haunted by a lady who waited for her lover so they could fly to Gretna Green. The lover never appeared and the lady took her own life in the attic room. On the anniversary of her death, she walks and wails for her lost love."

The female contingent gave a collective sigh.

Georgie drawled, "Heavens, Lord Beckenham, I'd no notion you were such a romantic."

She arched a brow at him, then moved past him to take Hardcastle's arm.

Addressing her new captive, she said, "Now, my dear sir, you must advise me on a purchase I need to make."

A little startled, as well he might be, the young man said, "Oh. Yes. Yes, of course, Miss Black. Happy to oblige. A matter of importance, I apprehend?"

"Of *vital* importance, sir."

She turned to wave Beckenham on. "Pray continue, my lord. You won't mind if I skip the lecture, will you? I'm a native of these parts myself, you know."

Beckenham's expression darkened, if that were possible, but he inclined his head and turned back to the rapt attention of his audience.

Black looks from Beckenham. How that brought

back the past, Georgie thought as she walked toward the draper's shop with Hardcastle in tow.

"Ma'am, I confess to the liveliest curiosity," he said. "What is this matter of vital importance?"

"Ribbons," she said, thrusting thoughts of Beckenham from her mind. "I need to purchase ribbons and lace. You shall help me decide."

He laughed, and his lingering smile lit his frank gray eyes in the most attractive way. He was not handsome, precisely, but he had a pleasant countenance that could be called handsome when animated. That engaging look made her think, *Lydgate was right. You are dangerous.*

Harmless flirtation was good for the soul, Georgie thought as she and Hardcastle exchanged witticisms and pleasantries.

"I forbid you to buy this," he said, holding a length of white lace out of her reach. "Appropriate for a spinster's cap. Not for the adornment of the divine Miss Black."

She reached for it, grinning. "Give it to me! How did you become the arbiter of lace, pray? And might I remind you that I *am* a spinster?"

He laughed at that. "A less spinsterish lady I've yet to meet." He lowered his tone. "You ought to be decked in exotic silks and emeralds, not white lace. No, never lace."

"How silly." She was about to continue the argument when the shop bell tinkled and Hardcastle looked up, past Georgie's shoulder.

His pleasant, teasing expression vanished, swiftly succeeded by the look of a starving man at a banquet.

She turned to see Violet enter the shop.

Georgie glanced back at Hardcastle. Oh, dear Lord. She ought to have known. Lydgate's instincts were never wrong.

Whether or not Violet returned Hardcastle's regard

was impossible to tell. She was certainly animated in his company, but Georgie could not fault her sister's manner, nor her conversation.

Not a creature of reticence, Hardcastle couldn't keep the light of longing from his eyes. Such helpless devotion could be seductive in its own right. He was a personable young man and might well win his way into Violet's affections if nothing happened to prevent it.

Rather sorry for him, but seeing no help for it, Georgie redoubled her efforts and managed to monopolize Hardcastle for the rest of their visit to the village. She kept him fully occupied the entire way home, too.

From her salad days, she had learned and refined upon the arts necessary to hold a man's attention. She employed every single one of them to keep Hardcastle by her side and laughing.

Several times, she was aware that Violet observed her with a puzzled, almost wary expression. *You will thank me one day, my dearest love. He is not the man for you.*

Equally, she noticed that Beckenham sent her one hard, disapproving stare before he turned back to his conversation with Violet.

By the time they reached the house, Georgie was exhausted, and wished for nothing but a hot bath to cleanse her soul.

Flirting! The woman whose lips had been locked with his only days before was now smiling her cat-in-the-cream-pot smile up at young Hardcastle, as if her whole happiness depended upon him. So much for his concern that Pearce might worm his way into her good graces once more.

If she so much as let Hardcastle touch her hand, Beckenham would . . .

He stopped himself. This kind of thing was precisely what had caused all the trouble in the first place. He ought to be glad she no longer held any power over him, that her rash behavior no longer reflected on him as her betrothed.

Titania and Oberon, doomed to play out the same jealousies time after time.

Yes. She'd been in the right of it, rejecting his proposals. For once, Georgie had acted with a more level head than he.

A low thrill of husky laughter floated to him as he strove to make polite conversation with Miss Violet.

He'd discovered common ground with Violet in their mutual admiration of Gothic architecture. She questioned him about the history of the small but beautiful church that perched on a gentle rise by the village green.

But he lost the thread of that interesting conversation upon hearing yet more evidence that Georgie was hell-bent on beguiling Hardcastle.

It was like a dirty joke, Georgie's laugh. Men turned themselves inside out to entertain her, just so they could hear it. And fantasize about where else they might hear her laugh that way. Sprawled naked on tangled sheets during a lusty bout of sex.

Was she even aware that she had this effect on men?

He'd never given her the least indication of how greatly he'd hungered for her that way. Not until the night at Xavier's villa.

She'd said there was no hope for them. People didn't change; she was right about that. He accepted it. But for her to immediately switch her attention to Hardcastle made him want to reach down that blameless young gentleman's throat and rip his lungs out.

Bad enough that Pearce had landed in the vicinity. Did she need to enslave every man who came her way?

Beckenham couldn't help it. When another low laugh rolled toward him, he turned his head sharply to stare at Georgie and her swain.

She looked so young and fresh in sprigged muslin with light green ribbons and a straw hat that tied under her chin with a big, silly bow.

Yet she was clinging too close to Hardcastle's arm, leaning on it as if she didn't have the strength to walk without his support.

He snorted in disgust.

As if she heard him, she turned her bright, amused gaze on him. Their eyes met; he saw a distinct challenge in hers. She lifted her chin at his frown and huddled even closer to her companion, if that were possible.

Beckenham snapped his head forward and redoubled his efforts with Violet.

In her gentle voice, she asked him whether he intended to watch the ladies' archery tournament.

It sounded like dull work to him, but he was never discourteous. He'd already discovered that enduring tedium was one of the principal duties that fell to the lot of a host.

"Indeed," he said. "I am looking forward to it."

"I believe the competition will be fierce," said Violet.

"Oh?" he said, taking a keener interest now. "What is the prize?"

With a mischievous smile, Violet said, "There will be a fat purse for the winning. But the real prize is your notice and admiration, my lord."

Startled, he said, "Mine?"

"Why, of course," said Violet. "That is why we are all here, is it not? To win your approval. The tournament will be rather like one of those medieval affairs where the knights vie for a lady's favor," she added thoughtfully, "only in reverse."

A rush of heat made itself felt on his cheeks. Was he—damn it all—was he blushing?

"And what form should this prize take?" he asked warily.

"I don't know! Perhaps . . . perhaps a kiss?" She said this with a wicked little grin that reminded him so much of her sister, he instinctively turned back again to glance in Georgie's direction.

Still plastered to Hardcastle's side. The young man was smiling. As well he might be, with all that lush loveliness pressed against him.

Grimly, Beckenham thought of a tournament he might propose among the gentlemen. One that would be too bloody for the ladies to witness. The winner would be the last man still standing.

He decided, most uncharacteristically, to do some flirting of his own.

"Who is in this tournament?" he asked casually.

"The younger ladies," said Violet. "Of course, if Georgie joined in, there would be no contest. She's a first-rate archer. But she declined to compete." A small cloud seemed to descend over her brow. "I suppose Georgie has other fish to fry."

Beckenham was arrested by her expression. The glance she shot over her shoulder at the two cooing doves dawdling behind the rest of the party told its own tale. Did she disapprove of Georgie's flirting as much as he did?

More common ground there, then.

Impulsively, Violet said, "You ought to bestow your favor on me now, before I go into battle."

He forced a laugh. This sort of talk made him distinctly uncomfortable but he'd resolved to flirt, hadn't he? "But I don't wear any ribbons or such. Perhaps a handkerchief. . . ." He felt in his pocket.

Violet smiled up at him with the most winning expression. "Might I have the bluebell you wear in your buttonhole? Where on earth did you find it at this season?"

He hesitated but a moment. "Why, of course."

He halted, squinting down at his buttonhole. He'd forgotten about it. Peters must not have noticed when he'd brushed the coat. The flower was more than a little wilted now.

"Let me."

Before he could stop her, she reached up and placed her palm on his chest to flatten the lapel while she plucked the bluebell from its snug little resting place.

He felt a twinge of guilt. Violet's gesture seemed to shatter, finally, any rapprochement he might have reached with Georgie.

They'd halted, allowing the rest of the party to overtake them. They were the focus of attention—how could they not be? But he found he didn't mind.

He sensed, rather than saw, Georgie's approach. Indeed, his attention was so focused on Georgie and her reaction to this silly byplay that the sight of his buttonhole blossom disappearing into Violet's bodice did little to arouse his interest.

"Oh, *well done*," murmured Georgie as she strolled past them, still clinging to Hardcastle's arm.

He was not certain if she'd addressed the remark to him or to Violet. But the cool, amused unconcern in her voice sparked his ire.

He barely heard a word Violet said to him after that. He could not wait to get Georgie Black alone so he could give her a piece of his mind.

Chapter Fourteen

Georgie had done her best to remain close to Hardcastle's side, but at the last minute before they entered the house, his attention was caught by Violet, who stumbled a little on the steps to the terrace and had to be supported.

Hardcastle moved with a swiftness that told Georgie, at least, that he'd been aware of Violet the entire time he was exchanging flirtatious nonsense with her.

The look he gave Violet as he helped her regain her balance confirmed Lydgate's prediction and Georgie's worst fears. Whatever Violet's feelings, Hardcastle was a man well on the way to falling in love. Good God, she must do something. But what?

Watching the two of them intently, Georgie started when Beckenham gripped her elbow.

"Will you come with me, Miss Black?" he said formally. "I'd like to show you the, er, rhododendrons we were speaking of earlier."

Rhododendrons?

"Certainly," she said calmly. She was in for a scold. Might as well get it over with.

Just to tease him, she added, "Shall I ask Lord Hardcastle to accompany us? I believe he has a great interest in rhododendrons."

"I think not," said Beckenham through his teeth.

"Very well, then," she murmured. "I'm sure your rhododendrons are nothing short of spectacular."

He didn't rise to the bait, just cast a hard, impatient glance at her as they left the terrace by the side steps and took the path that led to the shrubbery.

As soon as they were well out of earshot and somewhat screened from the house by the aforementioned plants, he rounded to face her.

"Was that edifying display for my benefit, or are you seriously contemplating taking Hardcastle as a husband?"

She laughed. "For your benefit? Well, you could say that, although you have quite the wrong end of the stick there, my friend. Marcus, do be sensible. If I wanted to make you jealous, I should not have chosen that boy as my instrument."

Hearing her refer to Hardcastle as a boy seemed to calm him somewhat. She found she didn't like that reaction. She found that although it had not been her intention to make him jealous—she'd learned her lesson about that six years ago—she was intrigued by the violence of his reaction. That never-quite-doused spark of rebellion inside her did not want to let him off the hook so easily.

It also occurred to her that it would not be wise to explain to him the true reason she'd monopolized Hardcastle. Beckenham might do his best to appear unswayed by emotion, but she knew he looked for any excuse not to offer for Violet. Duty to his estate still warred with compassion for Georgie in his breast.

He was well aware that marrying Violet was to offer

Georgie an affront. If he had the merest whiff that Violet's affections might become engaged elsewhere, he would instantly retreat.

"*Are* you jealous, Marcus?" The question was a direct one, calculated to throw him off balance, to stop him from delving deeper into her motives.

From the murderous expression on his face, it worked.

"I will not afford that question the dignity of a response," he said harshly. "Are you so lost to propriety that you cannot see the damage you do to your own reputation when you act in *such* a way?"

"Oh, pooh!" she said, laughing. "A little harmless flirtation while walking with a large group of respectable ladies and gentlemen in broad daylight? Come now, Beckenham. You must know that one can be far naughtier than *that* before one risks serious injury to one's reputation."

"Your past ought to show you the dangers of such behavior. You play with fire, Georgie. Sooner or later, you'll be badly burned."

She shrugged. The worst had already befallen her six years ago. She'd been burned, all right, reduced to ashes by her own reckless stupidity.

She'd never deserved him, but for the space of their betrothal, she'd managed to fool the gods somehow. She'd never quite trusted her good fortune. That distrust had prompted her evil genius to test her luck, time and again.

Until her luck ran out.

And still she cursed herself for her stupid pride. She ought to have begged forgiveness, crawled to him, implored him to take her back. If her temper had not got the better of her, if it weren't for what happened after the night she'd ended their engagement, she probably would have. She'd been reckless and stupid but she'd never been blind to the pure gold she had in him.

She'd turned wild in her grief and rage, but that phase had not lasted long. He was not to know it, for he'd never returned to London society after that, but her behavior in recent years had been exemplary. Indeed, her acquaintances in Town would have stared in disbelief to see her behave the way she had toward Hardcastle today. Her reformation was the one reason Lady Arden hadn't banished her from society altogether.

Clearly, Beckenham brought out the worst in her. She'd wanted to distract Hardcastle from his pursuit of her sister, true. But she'd done it with unwonted zeal, had she not?

She realized, now that the accusation was made, that she'd more than one motive for her actions.

Instead of sobering her, the notion made her resentment flare.

How dared he judge her over a stupid, innocent dalliance? After what they'd done together at Lord Steyne's that night. After the reputation he'd forged for himself since they'd parted.

"I don't know what gets into you." He was pacing now, hands clasped behind his back in what she recognized from bygone days as his "lecturing mode." "Last night you behaved as properly as anyone might wish, yet today you've transformed into a veritable Delilah."

That stung. Particularly when the only man she'd ever played Delilah for was Beckenham himself. And look how that had turned out. She couldn't even tempt the man to sin when she stood there, half naked and willing, before him.

"You are overreacting," she said, struggling for calm, feeling the temper rise in her like the pressure in a geyser before it blows. "It was a harmless flirtation."

"Surely you, of all people, know that flirtation is never harmless," Beckenham said.

Her anger was so great, it nearly masked the hurt inside her. Anger was a far easier emotion than pain. She clung to it, fed it.

How dared he be so damnably self-righteous? He'd been at Steyne's party that night. She'd never seen anything like it, never even dreamed of such debauchery. Yet he was there, openly participating, without even the hint of a disguise. How was it that he, a man, could be present at such an affair with impunity and yet she, a lady, was called to account for harmless flirting?

"If you will not think of yourself, think of how this behavior reflects on your sister," he was saying now. "Would you wish her to behave as you did today?"

She sent a significant glance at his empty buttonhole. "I think she does well enough for herself in that department, don't you?" she said dryly. "And it did not seem to me that she earned your disgust for it."

"Do not think to turn this around on me," he warned. "You let your passions guide you into dangerous waters, Georgie."

"Hardcastle? Dangerous?" She laughed, but it was a hollow sound. "He is a pussycat and you know it."

She saw now that he was undergoing some sort of internal struggle. Did he hold himself back from striking her? Kissing her again as he had in the wood? What?

"At least my passions, as you call them, are honestly felt," she flung at him. "What of your passions, Beckenham? Is this cold-blooded manner of selecting your future bride truly your wish? Or are you afraid that if you let yourself be guided by your passions, you will be in danger of repeating the past?"

The stunned look on his face told her quite clearly he was not as self-aware as he expected her to be.

Caution stirred within her. If she didn't stop goading him, he would marry some cold fish like Miss Trent. That would never do.

"You are mistaken," he said icily. "I know what I owe my name and my estate."

"What about to *yourself*?" said Georgie. "What about your happiness, the happiness of your wife?" That last word scraped in her throat.

"The two are not mutually incompatible. Why else would I submit to a house party like this if not to get to know the ladies in question?"

He made an impatient gesture. "That is beside the point. I am making a request of you as your host, if nothing else. Do not continue down a path that will be sure to earn you the contempt of every right-minded person present. That is all I have to say to you on the subject."

Through the haze of her fury, she managed a small yawn. "Thank goodness for that. You are quite tedious, you know, when you become self-righteous."

"Thank you," he said witheringly.

"Don't mention it." She dropped him a curtsy and swept from the shrubbery, half blinded by the film of red rage before her eyes.

He thought she'd behaved badly today? He hadn't seen anything yet.

Beckenham strode into his library, not stopping until he hit the brandy decanter. Lydgate was before him, he saw, at ease with the newspaper and a glass of amber liquid at his elbow.

"My dear fellow," Lydgate said.

Beckenham held up a hand as he sloshed brandy into a glass. "Don't start," he said grimly. "Not until I've drunk this."

He tossed down the liquid fire, reflecting on reason number seventy-six he was glad he had not married Georgie Black. He would have turned into a sad, blithering drunk by the time the honeymoon was over.

Honeymoon . . . The word conjured images he'd fantasized into being more than once in that endless betrothal. Dear God, she made him insane.

He poured himself another drink and threw himself into the chair by Lydgate's.

His cousin quirked an eyebrow. "Can I guess?"

Beckenham transferred a moody gaze to his brandy. "I suppose you might." He sighed. "I read her a lecture, which I had no business doing. Now she is ripe for murder. Or worse." *Ruination*. Thank God she didn't seem to know about Pearce's arrival at Cloverleigh. That would set the cat amongst the pigeons.

"The lecture would have been on the subject of . . . ?" Lydgate trailed off with a questioning lilt.

"Oh, you can't have been blind to that ridiculous display on our jaunt to the village."

"What, with Hardcastle?" Lydgate shook his head. "My dear Becks, you might be awake on every other suit, but you are a clodpole when it comes to that woman."

That made Beckenham straighten. "What? What do you know of the matter that I don't?"

Shrugging, Lydgate sipped his brandy. "I dropped a word into her ear that I noticed her sister seemed to be the object of Hardcastle's fond gazes. She moved into action immediately. Presumably, to—"

"—Distract Hardcastle from pursuing her sister and thereby ruining my chances with her," Beckenham finished.

An overwhelming relief flowed through him, swiftly followed by chagrin. "Oh, balls," he said tiredly.

"You raked her over the coals for it, didn't you?" said Lydgate. "She is not my favorite person in the world, but at least I can give credit where it's due. She did it for her sister, and possibly for you, too. She genuinely wants the two of you to make a match of it."

Beckenham felt a grim sort of heaviness descend on his chest.

What did his cousin know about it? He wanted to question Lydgate further but couldn't bring himself to do it. "Ah, hell. I owe her an apology, it seems. Not but what I think she ought to trust to me to cut Hardcastle out with Violet if I wished to do so."

"Since when have you ever cut out another gentleman to win a lady's favor?" said Lydgate amused. "No, not you. You would simply stand there, arms folded, and look brooding and wait for your natural air of impenetrability to entice the lady to your side."

That surprised a short laugh from Beckenham. "What nonsense is this?"

"Oh, come now. Surely you are aware of your effect on women." Lydgate shook his head. "I've seen it often and often, in the old days. There I would be, exerting all the charm and wiles at my disposal, practically turning cartwheels to get some sweet little thing to notice me, and a mere brooding glare from you would draw her like a moth to a flame."

"You are ridiculous."

"Now, of course," said Lydgate with a gleam in his eye, "your reputation as a lover of legendary skill precedes you."

Beckenham felt himself redden. "Damn you, Lydgate. Will you have done with this nonsense?"

"Have it your way." Lydgate drained his glass and set it down. "This crop of young ladies might make very good wives, but they are extremely dull sport for a gentleman determined to remain a bachelor. Now that I have given them the once-over and set everything in train, I must depart."

A twinge of something very like panic flickered through Beckenham. "Must you?"

"Duty calls. I ought not to have stayed this long."

Lydgate spent some time creasing the paper to fold it precisely in half and cast it aside. "Do you mind if I give you a word of advice, dear fellow?"

"Not at all." Beckenham rarely followed Lydgate's advice, but it was usually entertaining to hear it.

"Don't have Lady Charlotte. She's a spiteful little cat."

"I'd gathered. Is that all?"

Lydgate hesitated. "Don't offer for Miss Violet."

Startled, Beckenham said, "I thought you were angling for the match. What have you against the girl?"

"Oh, nothing in the world. No, but I think," said Lydgate deliberately, "that you ought not to make that particular connection."

Beckenham still didn't understand. "True, her mother is not the most genteel of ladies, but her birth is perfectly respectable."

"I am not talking about the girl's parentage, damn it," said Lydgate. "I'm talking about her sister. Georgie Black is a walking temptation, Becks, and you know it. Best for you to stay away. Good Lord, her mere presence here ought to tell you she is as close to her sister as can be. Imagine the family gatherings. Those *will* be cozy."

"You've changed your tune," Beckenham remarked, refusing to be drawn on the kind of temptation Georgie presented. "You overrode my doubts on the subject to invite Miss Violet here in the first place."

"Yes, but I didn't think that woman would turn up,

did I? *And* I hoped that by now you'd have her out of your system."

"You make her sound like a disease."

He knew what Lydgate implied, but he'd never been in love with Georgie Black. Committed to her, yes. Infuriated by her headstrong ways, but in love?

No, he was not a romantic. Men like him did not fall in love. They made sensible, dutiful matches to increase their estates and strengthen their bloodlines. Created more wealth to pass on to future generations. They did not marry out of tender emotions.

Most certainly, they did not marry to slake a wild lust.

He was honest enough to admit he felt lust in abundance for Georgie Black. What man could not?

"I can manage my own affairs, thank you, Lydgate. I appreciate your efforts on my behalf, but—"

"You want me to take my advice and shove off," said Lydgate cheerfully. "Well, and that's what I'll do, old fellow. Just do me a favor and think about what I've said. You're as canny a man as I've come across at fixing other people's messes. But you're just a little blinkered when it comes to messes of your own."

Chapter Fifteen

Savagely, Georgie attacked the bodice of her most striking evening gown with sewing shears, needle, and thread. How fortunate that she'd bought several lengths of pretty lace trim at the village shop today in defiance of Hardcastle's advice.

Contrary to Lady Charlotte's assumptions, Georgie was a clever seamstress. It was the work of a few moments to cut a deeper scoop to the bodice of the evening gown and finish it off with a border of creamy scalloped lace.

The gown was a muted coral pink, which ought to clash shockingly with her hair. Yet, somehow, it looked just right with her Titian locks, complementing them instead of clashing.

The cut of the bodice skimmed low across her breasts, allowing them to plump up enticingly. She was never in danger of showing nipple, of course—that would be too outré even for her, though she knew some dashingly fashionable ladies thought nothing of it.

But to a man's mind, there was always the enticing

possibility of seeing more than was decent. And that hope was the reaction she wished to evoke.

The gown was far less shocking than most you would find at any London ball. The difference, she thought, was that her breasts were so ample. She'd always taken care never to put them so evidently on display.

Her sister's reaction when they met before dinner that night told her she'd achieved the effect she sought.

"Georgie!" Violet exclaimed, flushing. "You look . . ."

Georgie fingered the ornate gold cross she wore suspended at her neck. "Do you like it?"

"Well, I . . ." Violet blinked. "It is . . ."

"Good," said Georgie, tucking her hand through Violet's arm. "If *you* are speechless, only think how Lord Hardcastle will feel. I do like him, don't you?"

"Yes, indeed I—But you, Georgie? I did not think you came here in search of a husband."

"A husband? Me?" Georgie laughed. "What should I want with a husband? Besides, poor Hardcastle hasn't a feather to fly with, you know. He's a fortune-hunter looking for a rich bride."

"Is he?" said Violet indifferently. "I hope he may find one. He is quite an amiable gentleman." She hesitated. "I wish you would not flirt with him so openly, though, Georgie."

All at once, Georgie wanted her bluebell back. "Do you?"

"It . . . it made you the target of some unkind remarks," said Violet.

"And yet, on our walk, I saw you flirt very prettily with Lord Beckenham," said Georgie, trying to keep the edge from her tone.

Violet wrinkled her nose. "I like him, but he is more like an older brother or, or a father than someone I could imagine marrying—" She broke off, laughing. "You should see your face, Georgie. What did I say?"

Georgie shut the jaw she'd allowed to drop open. "Pray do not ever let him hear you say he is like a father. He is not yet thirty."

"Well, and I'm only eighteen," said Violet a trifle sullenly.

"What did you do with the bluebell?" demanded Georgie.

"Bluebell? Oh, I forgot about it," said Violet carelessly. "It must be tangled up in my gown." She glanced at Georgie. "Why do you ask?"

Georgie shrugged, struggling to contain a spurt of unjustifiable anger toward her sister. "No reason. I thought you might have plans to wear it at the archery tournament."

"Mmm, no, I don't think I shall, after all," murmured Violet, checking her exquisite reflection in the looking glass.

Not trusting herself to speak, Georgie held her peace.

Beckenham tugged at his cravat as he went down the stairs to the drawing room. He'd rehearsed the apology he meant to make several times in his head while his valet fussed over him. Now that it came time to deliver it, he wanted to get it over with as soon as possible.

He was trying to devise a pretext by which he might get Georgie alone before dinner to deliver the teeth-clenching words of regret, when he clapped eyes on her.

Georgie.

Dear God!

His first reaction was animal and raw, a surge of blood and heat straight to his groin, a dryness in his mouth. The strong beat of his pulse took up residence in his ears. He couldn't breathe.

She wore a gown that reminded him of wild strawberries. Those white, mouthwatering mounds of her breasts looked like generous dollops of cream, waiting to be licked. He knew, without knowing how he knew, that the color of that dress was the precise color of all her womanly flesh: her nipples, the soft, intimate parts of her that he'd always longed to explore.

She was a sensual banquet laid out before him. He wanted to spread her on the dining table and feast.

He stood in the hall, unmoving, as if sculpted from marble like the Greek gods that surrounded him, until a soft, masculine rumble sounded in his ear. "Magnificent, ain't she? What I wouldn't give to get my hands on those."

The speaker was Lord Oliphant, Lady Charlotte's father.

Beckenham felt the old rage rise up in him, and his fists clenched. Too late he recalled that what was on display for his delectation could also be seen by any number of other men. And they would not be slow to express their appreciation.

More than express it, if given half the chance.

Too late he realized that particular display was not even made for his benefit.

All intention of asking forgiveness for misjudging her that afternoon flew from his brain. No matter what her motives were, she went too far this time.

With an effort, he stopped himself seizing the raddled roué beside him by the throat and stepped back to let the older man precede him into the drawing room.

The storm brewed all night long. Though he made no attempt to speak with her, Beckenham was a dark mass of clouds gathering, crackling with electricity, ready to burst over them both.

Georgie lifted her chin. She looked forward to the coming confrontation. Relished the prospect.

She did not need to encourage the men to dangle after her. The only one who did not ogle her shamefully was Hardcastle. The one man who ought to be the focus of her attention.

But she was too angry to care about Hardcastle just now. Even the startled look Lady Arden sent her did not dull the edge of her fury.

How far might she push Lord Beckenham without doing anything at all? She knew her attitude was perverse, even self-destructive, but she could not seem to stop herself.

And what did she have to lose, anyway? Violet would not marry Beckenham, but someone else would, and then Georgie would have to fly far away, live on the Continent. Africa, perhaps. Somewhere she would not have to witness him making a family and a home without her.

She knew she was in trouble when Lady Arden touched her elbow as the ladies left the gentlemen to their port.

"My dear Georgie. I can tell from the glitter in your eyes that this evening will not end well for you. Have a care, my love."

She had the strangest urge to throw herself into Lady Arden's arms and sob her heart out, the way she'd done six years ago, when she finally accepted that all was lost between her and Beckenham.

But she couldn't do that now. "You need not be concerned, my lady. I shall retire early tonight." There was a distinct pinch between her eyes. "In fact, I shall retire immediately. I have the headache."

Lady Arden nodded briskly. "Yes, perhaps that is best. Things often look different in the morning."

Georgie did not retire immediately to her room, however.

The dowagers had insisted that the doors and windows to the drawing room remained closed. Consequently, the room had been stuffy and hot.

Feeling the need for fresh air, Georgie slipped out onto the terrace through the long window in the library.

She contemplated the folly of what she'd done. Her temper had always been her downfall, and tonight was no exception. She'd intended to draw all eyes—most particularly, Beckenham's.

She'd wanted to provoke a confrontation. Too late to realize there was nothing left to say. They'd been over this time and again.

"Waiting for someone?"

The harsh voice startled her. She jumped, swung around, her heart hammering.

Beckenham. He hadn't lost time following her.

She swallowed. "I suppose I was waiting for you."

The honesty of that answer struck her. Yes, she had been waiting for him. She hadn't quite given up hope of divining his reaction, of feeling it.

"Flattering," he said. "And here I'd thought all of this . . ." He let his gaze run slowly down her body. "All of *this* was for young Hardcastle."

She looked at him straightly. She'd never liked games. She wouldn't play this one any more. "I told you. He is a boy."

He joined her at the balustrade, braced his hands shoulder width apart upon it, and stared off into the distance. Then his head snapped around and his glittering dark eyes bored into hers. "Sometimes I wonder if you know how very—" He sighed, gestured at her. "Georgie, your, you—" He shook his head, as if frustrated that he could not put into words what he wanted to express.

"What?" she demanded. "You need not scruple to say it, since you've insulted me quite comprehensively already today."

"Look at yourself!" he ground out. "Deliberately provocative, putting everything on show. Inviting all kinds of lewd comments. Lord Oliphant even—" He broke off. "Never mind."

She raised her brows. Men made lewd comments about her whatever she wore. Tonight, she'd taken command of her feminine power and wielded it as a weapon.

She shrugged. "What do I care for the opinions of a parcel of old rakes?"

"It's not just rakes." He pushed away from the balustrade and turned, shoving fingers through his hair. He swung back. "A man can't help but think of making love to you whenever he looks at you."

He broke off, as if horrified at his own frankness.

They stared at one another.

Her heart beat frantically. She swallowed hard. Did that mean that *he* found her alluring?

Yes, it must. It did.

And yet, he'd had no trouble resisting her that night in Brighton, hadn't he?

Something tore inside her. For years, her better self had waged war against a nature that was passionate, sensuous, with the Devil's own temper.

At eighteen she'd let her passions reign—and what a mistake that had been. In the intervening years she'd subdued them, repressed them, until it was second nature to deny her impulses.

Now, the passionate, sensuous, Devil-tempered creature flamed up inside her, laying waste to coherent thought.

"Do *you* want to make love to me, Marcus?"

The words, a husky whisper, spooled between them like an invisible thread.

He looked away. She saw the convulsive movement in his throat. "I told you. It's a normal reaction for a red-blooded male when he sees a woman like you looking like this. Pure biology."

It took all her courage to maintain her confidence in the face of that statement. "Oh, I don't think so," she whispered. "I don't think it's such an impersonal reaction as that."

He lifted his gaze to the sky, as if searching for an answer in the stars. Another convulsive movement in his throat.

Her evil genius made her push him to acknowledge it. She wanted, suddenly, to get him as hot and bothered as he'd made her in the villa that night.

That's what Delilahs did, wasn't it? Or was that a Jezebel? She'd never paid an awful lot of attention to the words men used to describe the women who held power over them.

Anger flared again at the castigation. *Delilah*. She'd tempt him, all right. She'd make him surrender his power to her, just like Samson did.

"What would you do to me, if you could?" The husky words caressed, abraded, stirred Beckenham's blood to fever pitch.

The part of him that had been growing ever more interested in this conversation hardened to a painful rod.

He couldn't pinpoint when his righteous indignation had spiraled yet again into lust laced with fury. But he verged on doing something reckless, out here in the privacy of the night.

She was wanton, staring back at him with those

amazing eyes, like a calm exotic sea. But no, they were not calm, those eyes. Angry little sparks flew from them like lightning bolts.

She was furious. Well, damn it, so was he.

Rage made her reckless. She'd asked him what he would do to her. He posed the corollary. "What would you like me to do?"

Her color fluctuated in a delicious wash of pink. It only emphasized the smooth creaminess of her skin, the utter brilliance of her eyes.

Those breasts. God, he wanted to plunge his face between them, fill his hands with them, lick them all over until she screamed. And that hair. He'd drag his fingers through the fire of it while he loved her until she forgot her own name.

She had nothing to say to his question. Why would she? They were speaking of his desire, after all.

He closed the distance between them. Panic flickered in her eyes, but she stood her ground. She had her back to the balustrade. There was nowhere for her to go.

Yes, she was so angry, she would kiss him merely to punish him, to show him that he was not the one in control.

He found that he didn't give a button about control, about mastering her physically or in this battle of wills between them.

He just wanted her. And he was tired of denying himself.

Had she been here only a few days? It felt like a century that he'd struggled against this need. For six years they'd been apart. And not a day had passed in that time when he hadn't thought of her, desired her.

Now she was here, making suggestive remarks. That perilously low-cut bodice begged him to finish the job and free her magnificent breasts to the balmy night air.

One day you'll discover you're not such a damned paragon. You're made of flesh and blood and base carnal instincts. Just like me, just like your grandfather, just like every other man. . . .

Pearce's words came to him suddenly, out of nowhere. He'd come close to choking the life out of the cur for saying them, among other things.

Suddenly, he stepped outside himself and took a long hard look. If he took Georgie now, as he'd had every intention of doing, he'd be no better than the rest. He wouldn't deserve her any more than they did.

It struck him that she didn't know her true worth or she wouldn't fling herself at him like this.

"Don't," he said quietly, willing his desire-crazed body to calm down.

She blinked. "What?"

Her emotions swung on a pendulum; he saw it in her face. She didn't know whether to be furious or relieved.

His certainty grew. "Don't behave this way. It isn't honest. It isn't you."

That's what had always inflamed him, he realized now. He wasn't jealous of any of those men who slavered over her body, extolled her beautiful face. He'd been angry at her for holding herself so cheaply as to flirt with them, for seeking to manipulate men with the only power they allowed her.

What they never saw was the strength, the wit, the godawful temper, willfulness, the compassion and courage that made up the woman. They never saw past her spectacular looks.

He ignored the siren call of her body and gently, almost reverentially, touched her cheek. "You don't need to pretend with me."

Her face threatened to crumple, but only for a second.

She stared at him, an expression that was almost fearful in her eyes. "I don't know what you—"

He kissed her. Slid his fingers into her loose, luxuriant coiffure; framed her face with his hands; and took her mouth with his.

Her scent dizzied him. Desire rampaged through his body like a baited beast but he beat it back, used all his considerable will to keep his lips gentle, to draw out her response.

And just like that, it was as if he'd slashed the ropes tethering a balloon to the ground. His whole spirit lifted, soared high and bright. Filled with an extraordinary sense of rightness, even as the flame of his passion for her burned ever brighter.

He felt her initial gasp of surprise, the uncertainty in her response. Leashing the straining lust inside him, he kept the kiss soft, almost languid in its slow, gentle rhythm.

On a shuddering sigh, her mouth clung sweetly to his. Her hands slid up his coat lapels and twined together at his nape.

She'd never know what it cost him to keep his own hands where they were, not out of respect for her maidenly virtue, but because he wanted to show her this was about more than animal instincts and carnal pleasure. So much more, he couldn't find the words. He'd have to tell her with his kiss instead.

He was the one who drew back first, touching his forehead to hers, sliding his hands to her slim shoulders. "Georgie," he murmured against her lips. "Marry me."

She went still.

"We belong together, Georgie," he said. "Don't deny it. Don't lie to yourself."

Moments passed before she found her voice. "But

I . . . Marcus, what about . . ." She made a helpless gesture back toward the house.

"I don't want Violet. I don't want any of them. It was a stupid, ill-conceived business from the start." His hands tightened on her shoulders. "I've always wanted you. I think you know that."

She drew back, just a little, and he let his hands fall to his sides. He didn't try to stop her, just tensed for her reply.

Georgie pressed her fingertips to her temple, as if prodding her brain to action. "I'm sorry. I cannot answer you now. I cannot think."

The disappointment was like a physical blow. He'd hoped for her enthusiastic, impulsive acceptance. He'd wanted to take her to bed tonight, to claim her, body and soul, for his own. He'd give himself over entirely to her pleasure, be her slave, be the best lover any woman had ever known. Show her how vital she was to his happiness.

Happiness. Had he ever even hoped to be happy?

She bit her lip. Her fingertips touched behind her ear in that way she had when she was deeply troubled.

Abruptly, he said, "Whatever your answer, I won't marry Violet. Or any of them." *Or anyone at all.* "Don't allow loyalty to your sister to sway you."

"No," she whispered. "No, I won't."

With a convulsive swallow and a clipped nod, she slipped from between his body and the banister and moved past him. A strange melancholy clung to her graceful, elegant figure as she returned to the house.

His voice, hoarse with emotion, probably didn't reach her. "Say yes, Georgie. Please, say yes."

Chapter Sixteen

Oh, that kiss.

In bed later that night, Georgie pressed her fingertips to her lips. She'd never known Beckenham was capable of such tenderness. Even now, simply recalling the aching sweetness of the way his lips had molded to hers, she nearly melted into the sheets.

That kiss had told her he knew her, inside and out, that he cherished her, that he . . . That he loved her? Was she deluding herself to read so much into a physical act?

Men, she knew, tended not to connect physical acts with tender feelings of any kind.

But try as she might, she couldn't be cynical about it. She'd begun by attempting to dominate him, to use his evident desire for her against him.

His response hadn't been a matter of tactics. He'd called her bluff, dared her to be truthful, authentic in a way no one had ever demanded of her before. If that kiss had been an honest expression of his feelings, she'd be every kind of fool to say him nay.

She hadn't delayed her answer to torment him. She'd

been bowled over by his words, brought to her knees by his kiss. He'd been right about her, she realized, and that hurt more than she could ever admit.

Her father had spoiled her as a child. Giving in to her blandishments, he'd treated her like a son, taking her with him wherever he went as he carried out his duties at Cloverleigh. His pride in the land, his love and sense of responsibility for the people who worked it, had infused her blood.

As the years passed and her stepmother did not produce a son, Georgie had accepted gladly that Cloverleigh would be her responsibility one day.

Then came the news: She was to be betrothed to Lord Beckenham, who lived on the neighboring estate.

The day of her betrothal, her father's attitude changed. She was to stop careering about the countryside like a hoyden and learn to act like a lady, like a future countess. She would make her come-out one day. She must do her utmost to be a credit to the earl.

Suddenly, decisions were taken about the estate without even the pretense of discussing them with her. Her father set her at a clear distance, rebuffing her attempts to persuade him to change his mind, punishing her acts of defiance.

She'd been devastated. Not only because he'd dismissed her from a role she loved, but because her father seemed determined to forget all about her. Now she was a girl again, she'd become a creature of no importance.

And this quiet, dark-eyed young man who was to be her husband seemed no better. Reticent to the point of brusqueness, the cares of the world on his broad shoulders, he did not seem like the sort of man who'd treat her as an equal when it came to matters of business.

She knew Marcus had had much to bear from his

grandfather while the old earl had lived. Even she'd heard tales of drunken rampages and mindless, twisted violence. And those were the stories people in the district had thought fit to repeat to a young girl.

Marcus was determined to continue his former guardian's work, putting his grandfather's estate to rights. She honored him for it, knew that he would husband her land equally well. But if her own father shelved her like a china doll, what hope did she have that any other man would respect her opinions?

Years passed. Lady Arden swept into her life and taught her everything she needed to know about the Ton. She'd been a late bloomer, physically. But as her body developed interesting curves, she'd learned lessons her mentor hadn't taught her, too. About attracting men, controlling them.

She remembered presenting herself to her papa all decked out in her finery on the night of her come-out ball, hoping her appearance would somehow reanimate his affection for her. He'd barely looked up from his work.

Something had snapped inside her that night. As the gentlemen of the Ton fell like spillikins around her, she'd taken pleasure in playing the femme fatale, enjoyed the heady rush of power her appearance brought.

Only Beckenham had refused to play her game. The one man she'd wanted was the only one she couldn't bring to heel. And in the end, she discovered the kind of power she'd wielded wasn't power at all. Quite the reverse, in fact.

Tonight, she'd committed the folly of trying to use that illusory weapon against Beckenham. If she'd succeeded, she would have ruined any chance they might have had.

He'd seen through her. Dear God, how that had hurt.

She'd thought herself so clever, brilliant and untouchable as fire before he'd called her bluff.

And he'd done it without any assertion of his own considerable power. He'd seen her clearly, and he'd cherished her for who she was.

If that wasn't love . . .

Did it truly matter that he hadn't said the words? Perhaps he never would. Perhaps in time he would say them. She wouldn't try to force him or beguile him into it.

Her love for him was a foregone conclusion. She'd loved him for so long, she couldn't pinpoint when she'd begun. It was simply a part of her, like her heartbeat.

With a hard clutch in her stomach, she remembered Pearce. The letter.

No. She would not let Pearce spoil everything again. She'd tell Marcus. All of it must be open between them now. She didn't think he'd spurn her when he knew the truth. Not if he loved her. Once she and Beckenham were married, Pearce could not injure her in any way that truly mattered.

She stretched, exhilaration flowing through her body, despite the anxiety. Tomorrow, she would tell Marcus yes. She couldn't wait for the morning to come.

As she lay there, wakeful in the darkness, the minutes dragged by. She was so restless, she was almost tempted to slip out and throw herself into the lake. All this nervous energy needed expending somewhere.

Suddenly, the door opened, startling her. Beckenham paused in the doorway, holding his candle, watching her.

"Marcus!" Georgie scrambled up to a sitting position, the covers drawn up to her bosom.

Her eyes were wide with shock, lips slightly trembling. The glorious hair was neatly plaited into a braid.

Her face looked scrubbed clean, fresh as a daisy, her creamy complexion glowing with innocence in the moonlight.

He experienced a momentary qualm. There was no going back for either of them if he went through with this. "Tell me to go away and I will."

"No, don't go." She dropped the covers, held out a hand to him, her smile luminous. "How did you know I've been wishing for you?"

Desire flared as he came into the room. Her night rail was unadorned, made up high at the throat. Prosaic. Out of character, if one considered the inflammatory gown she'd worn that very evening. Only he knew that this was the real Georgie.

Softly, he closed the door, turned the key in the lock.

"I've come for your answer," he said, sitting on the edge of the bed beside her. "I couldn't wait."

"Yes, Marcus." She said it simply, closing her eyes, opening them again. "Of course. The answer is yes."

Beckenham leaned in, capturing the hand she stretched out to him, and kissed her.

His other hand came up to her hair. "I need to do this," he said, tugging the ribbon from the tail of the braid. He ran his fingers through it to loosen and separate the thick strands of fire until they spread and rippled around her face. So soft . . .

"There."

When he moved to kiss her again, she stopped him, her palm pressed flat against his chest. "Marcus, I hate to do this, but before we . . . I—I need to tell you something."

Everything inside him stilled. His body felt the delay as an acute form of torture, but he could not afford to make a misstep now. Not when he was so close to making her his.

"Yes?"

She touched his arm. "I have to tell you the truth about that duel. About Pearce."

There was a sick churn in his stomach but he forced himself to nod. "Go on."

She dropped her gaze. "Yes. Well." She drew a deep breath. "When you would not listen to me about the duel, I became frantic. You see, I knew the ugly mood Pearce was in. I knew he wanted to kill you. I went straight back to the ballroom and found him. I told him that you and I had fought. That our betrothal was over. And that . . ."

She raised her gaze to the silk canopy overhead and swallowed. "I said that I would run away with him, as he'd begged me to do. But that it would have to be the following morning, early, for Papa was taking me back to Gloucestershire on the morrow."

He sat back, stunned. "And he believed you?"

Her mouth took on an oddly grim line. "I can be very convincing. But he didn't entirely trust me, even so. He made me write him a letter."

He frowned. "A letter. What did it say?"

She flushed. "It doesn't matter what it said. I didn't mean a word of it, not about him. The point was to give him something that would prove my intent to fly with him to Gretna Green. He's not stupid. He knew my motive was to prevent the duel. The only way I could convince him I would go through with the elopement was to pen that note."

"A love note, one presumes."

She nodded.

"And he threatened to make the letter public if you didn't follow through."

"Yes."

It was as if he'd separated into two distinct versions

of himself. The one man consumed with rage of such a magnitude, he could have laid waste to entire civilizations. The other considering, calculating, planning what must be done.

"I duped Pearce," said Georgie without any vestige of pride. "I didn't turn up at our meeting place, and by the time he'd realized I wasn't coming, the hour for the duel had passed."

And he'd been oblivious to it all. Beckenham stared at her. Devil take it! Pearce had been blackballed from every club, shunned by his peers, practically hounded out of the country once the news of his supposed cowardice had become common knowledge. All Georgie's doing.

Beckenham ought to be furious with her. If he'd known at the time, he would have found her interference appalling, scandalously reckless, emasculating, impossible to forgive. Now, all he cared about was that she must not suffer for what she'd done.

"What happened to the letter?" Surely all this careful planning had allowed her to retrieve it, also.

"He still has it. I couldn't see a way to get it back without showing my hand, you see. And of course, he left England immediately afterwards. There was simply no time to get it back."

"Damn it, Georgie!" A blistering oath ripped from him. He needed to find Pearce and get that letter, then make him pay.

He made as if to stand, but she caught his wrist. "I don't think he'd use it, Marcus. Not once we are wed. What would be the point?" She gazed up at him with fear in her eyes. "That's if you still want me."

He stared at her. "You sacrificed your reputation. For me."

"I loved you, you see," she said softly. "I always have."

The shock of that revelation, coming hard on the heels of her disclosures about Pearce, froze him in place.

Hoarsely, he said, "Georgie, I—"

She surged up to press her mouth to his. Something broke inside him, and then he was kissing her fiercely, wildly, dragging his lips across her cheek to her earlobe, to her throat. His emotions seemed to expand until they were too large for his soul to contain.

When she fell back against the pillows, she brought him with her, and he knew that he'd do whatever it took to keep her, to protect her, to *love* her until the day he died.

That kiss was incendiary, lascivious, thoroughly consuming, everything he'd dreamed. He shed his robe and flung it away, moved over her, desperate now to be inside her, to show her, to discover for himself all that the act of making love could be.

Georgie writhed beneath him, her slender fingers sliding over his shoulders, plunging through his short hair, kneading his nape. Her breathy pants, her senseless murmurs spurred him on.

"God, Georgie, you're more than beautiful," he said, working at the thin pink ribbon that tied the neck of her night rail. "So much more."

She gasped as the ribbon came loose and he slid her night rail off her shoulders, yanked it down to reveal her breasts.

He lost his mind then, for he was but a man and her breasts were the stuff of fantasies. He set out on a voyage of discovery, first with his hands, his fingertips, gentle touching, caresses, little plucks at the rosy loveliness of her nipples.

As he watched, her eyes closed, her lips parted; she was thoroughly focused on sensation.

He gave in to his desires and used his mouth on her.

She was exquisitely sensitive; her body twisted help-lessly when he suckled her, so he did it some more, making her buck her hips with the force of her pleasure.

Slow down. . . .

Giving her breasts one last, loving caress, he moved down her body, kissed the roundness of her belly, the crease at the top of each thigh.

He slid his lips over her, reveling in the texture of that soft, smooth skin, warm and perfect as new cream. His fingertips investigated her long, slender legs, the sweet rounds of her knees, her inner thigh. A soft, wel-coming moan told him she was ready for more intimate investigation.

He stroked upward, into the wet folds of her sex.

She was lush and hot there, and he kept his fingers moving as he slid up her body to kiss her lips again. He wanted to be close to her, close enough to swallow her reactions, to look into those amazing azure eyes when she came.

He touched her lightly at first, then dipped his finger into her juices and circled her clitoris with a firmer touch until she whimpered, undulating against him. She moaned; then her hand clamped like a vise around his wrist. Her eyes shot open and she convulsed beneath his hand. He smothered her cry with his mouth.

He didn't let her rest or come back to herself after that. Instead, he positioned himself, guiding his swol-len cock to the moist heat of her entrance.

She stared wordlessly up at him, and the vulnerabil-ity in her eyes would have told him she was a virgin even if her body and her untutored responses had not.

He pressed inside a little way, feeling her tightness, knew with an odd mixture of tenderness and elation that he was her first and only lover.

He only wished he could wipe his own past clean.

This act was too important to share with anyone who didn't matter.

He touched her cheek in a gentle caress, but a powerful urge had taken hold of him now and it was all he could offer by way of reassurance. The need for her pounded in his blood, screamed in his head. He drove slowly forward, heard her soft choke of pain.

Realized it was better to get that part over quickly, lunged, and drove home.

The feel of her was everything, all at once. Best for her if he finished quickly, but he'd waited so bloody long for this, the selfish part of him wanted to be inside her for as long as humanly possible.

Which, it turned out, was not going to be very long at all.

After a few careful thrusts, she seemed to pick up the rhythm, lifting her hips to move against him, a stream of talk flowing from her like a light summer breeze. Her enthusiastic participation wound the torture a notch higher.

"Yes, oh, yes," she said. Her hands ran down his back. She scored him lightly with her nails, sending cascades of sensation through his body.

But the light, almost tentative caress of his buttock, the murmur of appreciation that came from deep in her throat, did for him entirely.

With a harsh cry, he exploded into her.

Georgie bit her lip and slid a glance at Beckenham. He lay on his back beside her, chest heaving with the aftermath of a truly earth-shattering experience.

Her mind had shut down somewhere along the way. She'd been a bundle of need and feeling. The way he'd touched her . . . She felt a pang of pleasure low in her belly at the mere thought.

But the sensation of him inside her . . . Ah, that had been extraordinary, despite the momentary pain. She couldn't wait for him to do it again.

Georgie had surrendered to the inevitability that they would repeat this experience. The sooner, the better, in her view. She smiled as Beckenham trailed his knuckles softly down her arm. On a sigh, she turned into his kiss.

A scratch on the door yanked her from the sensual pleasure of Beckenham's caresses. She froze. "What was that?"

"Hmm?" Lazily, Beckenham lifted his head from her breast.

"There's someone at the door!"

"Ah. Just in time to surprise us in flagrante and force you to make an honest man of me."

"Don't joke about it," she whispered, pushing ineffectually at his massive shoulders. The man really was a great lump of rock. "Get up, get up! Where's my wrap?"

She scrabbled around in the bedclothes, batting away his straying hands.

"I locked the door," he murmured, gripping her hips, pulling her back into him. Into her ear, he breathed, "Remain silent and wait for them to leave."

"But—"

Effortlessly, he pushed her down on the bed and picked up where he'd left off. He continued working his leisurely way down her body, murmuring approval as he went.

Georgie gave an inward groan of half frustration, half delight.

Beckenham, relaxed and playful, was an intensely seductive man. She shivered as he blew gently on the skin he'd been licking.

He glanced up at her with a wicked gleam in his eye,

a look she'd never seen there before. Then he moved down, and down further, trailing kisses as he went.

She stifled a yelp when his mouth found her sex. "Ah! Oh, dear Heaven!"

He lifted his head. "Uh-uh, not so loud, Miss Black. There's someone at the door, remember?"

"I think they've gone away." She consigned whoever it was to Hades and lay back, sinking into sinful, heated bliss.

"Miss Black." A frantic whisper carried through the door, reaching Georgie's ears. "Miss Black, you must come quickly!"

"It's a lady. How extraordinary," Beckenham murmured against her thigh.

Georgie shot out of bed so fast, she stubbed her toe and swore, making Beckenham's shoulders shake with suppressed laughter. With a darkling glance at him, she hurriedly drew on her dressing gown and buttoned it.

Clearly, the act of love made Beckenham light-headed. His harsh features lit in a grin of pure enjoyment. He sat there, gloriously naked, without a shred of modesty.

"Lie down!" she reached over and shoved at his chest, which was even harder than it looked. Obligingly, he fell back onto the mattress. "Stay!" she ordered in a hiss.

She yanked the covers over him, so that they covered his face. A muffled voice sounded from the covers, "This is not very dignified, you know."

"Hush!"

Finishing buttoning the robe, she hurried to the door, trying not to look as if she'd just been thoroughly ravished. He'd kissed her *there*! No, she couldn't think about that now.

She unlocked the door and opened it.

Lady Charlotte Cross stood outside.

"Lady Charlotte!" exclaimed Georgie, darting a quick glance up and down the empty corridor. "What on earth are you doing up at this hour?"

"Oh, thank Heavens, Miss Black." The girl grabbed Georgie's hands and tugged. "Quickly! Oh, you must come quickly. I don't know what to do!"

Chapter Seventeen

Upon hearing the situation, Georgie sent the girl back to her room, refusing her offer of assistance.

"I shall manage," she assured her. "You will risk your reputation as well if you come with me, and given you're the only levelheaded one among the lot of them, that would be a pity."

She held up her hand when the girl would have argued further. "Leave it to me," she ordered. Then she practically slammed her bedchamber door in the girl's face.

"I don't know what you're smiling at," she flashed at Beckenham as she whirled on him.

He had emerged from the covers, looking tousled and manly and delicious, which irrationally made her even more out of temper with him.

His grin widened. *"You."* He clasped his hands behind his head, showing an impressive collection of muscles beneath the smooth skin. "I'm smiling at you, Georgie."

Momentarily, she lost her train of thought. Her mouth actually watered, and the remembered feeling of those strong arms holding her tightly, of them bracing his weight as he drove into her, made her blood heat.

Snap out of it, you fool! There was Violet to think of.

She hurried to the clothes press to find something to wear.

"What was all that about?" Beckenham sounded supremely disinterested.

She glanced up, to see him stretch lazily, more muscles flexing and shifting on that impressive expanse of chest. Good God, was the man determined to destroy her concentration?

She was so unbearably tempted to consign the young misses of this ill-assorted party to their fates. To climb back into that big, broad bed and have that big, broad man all to herself.

But where would Violet be if she did that?

"No, no, no. I will not be tempted," she muttered to herself.

She hunted around, then picked up Beckenham's dressing gown and hurled it at him. "Get dressed," she said. "You're coming with me."

Amazing the way making love to a woman could lead to all sorts of interesting discoveries. Beckenham had known Georgie for years, but he'd never have guessed she'd be so volubly passionate in bed. She talked constantly, a stream of expressive nothings that poured into his ear.

He didn't even know what she'd said. He was constitutionally incapable of listening to talk when he was that far gone. But remembering the *way* she'd said it made him hard again, just to think of the husky tone of her voice.

And she had a streak of prudishness. He'd never have guessed that about her, either.

All lush sensuality during their lovemaking, now she chided him like a spinster aunt. And he'd taken great delight in teasing her. Another discovery, that he could provoke her quite as easily as she'd always provoked him.

He hadn't felt so damned relaxed and happy in . . . Ever, he thought now.

For once, acting on impulse had worked in his favor. The glow of pure masculine satisfaction in taking her, claiming possession over her body, was one he could not seem to shake.

She'd told him she loved him. Had always loved him. He wanted to shout it from the rooftops. Damn, how stupid he'd been not to see it, not to know how he'd felt about her. They'd wasted so much time.

He ignored her demands that he hurry, taking the opportunity to watch her dress. Or more accurately, to see as much of her naked body as he could before she covered it.

First, the stockings. One shapely leg raised on the stool of her dressing table, her hands competently rolling the stocking up over her pretty knee, tying it in place with a garter. Then, the other.

He decided he liked to see her put her hands on herself. There was something sensual about her movements, despite her haste, as if she, too, enjoyed the feel of her skin beneath her fingertips.

Then he decided that he liked watching himself touch her even more.

"Let me help you," he said, finally sliding out of bed.

She glanced up at him, her eyes widening as they took in the full length of him. His cock seemed to have reawakened, but poor beleaguered devil, he'd have to wait. Even Beckenham knew it would be a crime to take her again so soon after the last time. She must be sore.

Still, there was no law against putting his hands on her, was there?

She tied the second garter. "I don't need the kind of help you mean to give me."

He quirked an eyebrow. "Shall I ring for your maid, then?"

"Very funny!" She snatched up her shift.

He caught her arm and drew her toward him. "Indulge me," he said.

Skimming the back of his hand over her shoulder, he pushed the satin dressing gown aside and bent to kiss her clavicle. "I've been wanting to do that all night," he murmured.

She sighed, tipped her head back. "Have you?"

"But of course." Using both hands now, he slid the dressing gown from her shoulders, bent to kiss the plump mound of her breast.

She shuddered, swayed. Then she pushed at him. "No, Beckenham. Violet is in trouble. I must go to her. You have to come, too."

"She is not hurt?" He hadn't thought of that until now. The notion sobered him.

"No, no. She is merely . . . She needs me. Us. It will be best if I explain on the way there."

He stopped interfering with her dressing after that, and soon she was ready and pinning up her hair.

"Where?" he asked her.

"The grotto, I believe."

Startled, he said, "The grotto? At this hour?"

"Never mind that now. We must hurry!"

Beckenham rowed them to the grotto with swift, powerful strokes of the oars. Guiltily, Georgie enjoyed the show. She'd never been so acutely aware of any man's physique before.

It came from the experience of what that body could do to her, she realized. She'd lost more than her virginity in that bed. She'd lost herself in him.

But she'd gained so much more.

Intimacy. A closeness so deep and compelling that it was beyond word or thought to describe. An addictive feeling. One that would be excruciating to forgo.

Difficult to keep her mind on track, to plan how she was going to get Violet and her friends out of this mess with no one the wiser.

She wanted the world to go away and leave her with Marcus, so she might enjoy him to the full.

Some presentiment told her they were not over the worst yet, however. He'd taken her confession about Pearce and the letter far better than she'd expected. After his initial fury, he'd acted as if he meant to do nothing about it, simply let it go.

That wasn't like Beckenham. Her compulsion to make a clean breast of matters had been selfish, she realized now. There would be a reckoning between the two men. Only this time, Beckenham would be shrewd enough to tell her nothing of his plans.

Apprehension blossomed inside her.

"What are you thinking about?" he asked, as if sensing an alteration in her mood.

She prevaricated. "I am a fallen woman," she said solemnly. "And I find that I do not care in the least."

"Enjoy your fallen status for tonight. We'll announce our engagement tomorrow," he said.

She wanted to demand that he not confront Pearce, but she did not wish to ruin his contentment so soon. She'd rarely seen Beckenham so at ease. Never, in fact, had he been carefree enough to tease and make fun. He'd always borne the weight of the world on his shoulders, ever since he accepted his grandfather's tainted legacy and doggedly set about making things right.

Thankfully, they arrived at the little island before her thoughts could grow too morose. Beckenham helped her out of the boat and pulled her to him for a swift, hot kiss before he handed her the lantern and let her precede him up the stairs to the grotto.

A burst of feminine giggles told Beckenham Georgie's information must be correct. Incredibly, the young ladies of the party were inside that grotto at just after two o'clock in the morning. They had, if he were any judge, imbibed an excessive quantity of liquor.

He hung back. "Best if you go first, I think," he said to Georgie. "Make sure they're decent."

"Dear Heavens," she said. "Do you think they might . . . Oh, never mind. Wait here."

He heard another burst of giggles, then Georgie's voice demanding in the most censorious of accents what they meant by their scandalous behavior.

"If anyone finds out about this escapade, you'll be ruined, the lot of you."

The situation was, of course, reprehensible and shocking, but some note in Georgie's voice tickled his sense of humor. Was it—could it be maternal moral outrage he heard? Georgie Black, reading a homily on appropriate behavior.

He heard her call his name and hesitated. "Are they decent?"

"They are fully clothed, if that's what you mean," said Georgie witheringly. "As for *decent* . . ."

He saw what she meant. Draped, sprawled, and lounging like bucks in a brothel on a quantity of imported rugs and cushions, the ladies of his house party had certainly imbibed more of his best brandy than was good for them.

"They must have filched it from your library," said Georgie, clearly mortified. "I do beg your pardon."

Lady Harriet smiled muzzily up at them. "You're together," she pronounced. "I'm so glad."

He could only stifle a laugh when Georgie turned pink. She said hurriedly, "I had to rouse Lord Beckenham in case any of you needed to be carried."

Beckenham sent a significant look toward Miss deVere, who seemed to have fallen asleep or lapsed into unconsciousness, one slim hand gripping the neck of the brandy decanter. "It seems you were right. My presence was not superfluous, after all."

Miss Trent gazed up at him through bleary eyes. "My mama," she pronounced carefully, "is going to kill me."

Beckenham regarded her not without some sympathy, which was really quite gallant of him, he thought, considering this exploit had interrupted a truly magnificent evening. Right now, he could be in Georgie's bed, nuzzling those delicious thighs. . . .

He shook himself, glanced at Georgie. "I'll have to make two trips. We can't all fit in the boat at once."

"If you put Miss deVere in the second boat, I can row that one," said Georgie briskly. "We shouldn't lose any time."

He argued politely with her but to no avail.

She touched his arm, saying in a low voice, "Please, let us not tarry. I have a dreadful feeling about this. If we're discovered, all of their reputations will be in jeopardy. Mine as well."

He gave in, stooping to remove the brandy decanter from Miss Margo deVere's slackened grasp. He slid his arms under her and heaved her up.

She moaned and shifted in his hold, blasting his face with brandy fumes.

Beckenham recoiled with a wince. Excessive inebriation was off-putting at the best of times, but in a young lady . . . He hoped the silly chits would learn their lesson. They would all have very sore heads on the morrow.

He looked forward to that with some satisfaction.

He slid an arm beneath Miss deVere's knees and gingerly picked her up. She didn't weigh much. He jerked his head toward the others. "Can they walk, do you think?"

Georgie bent over Lady Harriet. Gently, she patted the girl's face. "Come, Harriet. You must come with me now."

With Georgie's assistance, Lady Harriet clambered to her feet, then swayed. Georgie supported her with one arm around her waist.

"Miss Trent, can you walk?" She looked down at the girl, who was smiling as if the world was a very happy place.

"Of course," responded the girl with owlish surprise.

After a few failed attempts, that pattern-card of propriety gave a huge, exasperated sigh and rocked forward until she came to her hands and knees. Then she shuffled a couple of paces to the stone table in the center of the room. Planting first one hand, then the other on the tabletop, she inched her way upright and slowly raised herself to a standing position. She tottered, and Georgie quickly reached out to steady her.

Beckenham and Georgie exchanged glances. "Right, then," he said. "Let's be off, shall we?"

Georgie went first, supporting both Miss Trent and Lady Harriet. Beckenham followed with his fair bundle.

When they'd managed to load the boats, Georgie conferred briefly with Beckenham. "The question is," she said slowly, with a glance back at the grotto, "if Violet is not here, where on earth is she?"

"In bed back at the house, if she knows what's good for her," said Beckenham, adding in a graveled undertone, "where I wish we were, right now."

Only by the gleam in her eye did Georgie acknowledge that piece of frivolity. "No, Lady Charlotte said Violet went to the grotto."

He snorted. "Making trouble, as usual."

"I don't know. Why would Lady Charlotte fetch me and not one of the matrons if she meant to cause trouble?"

He didn't have an answer to that. "Check on Violet when we get back, and then you may be easy."

She nodded. Each of them took command of their respective vessels and rowed the miscreants back to shore.

As he rowed, he thought a little guiltily of the expectations he'd raised in the youthful bosoms of these young ladies, not to mention the bosoms of their doting mamas. If cleaning up their mess tonight was the only punishment the universe meted out to him, he might count himself lucky.

And when the rocking motion of the boat became too much and Miss Trent hurled up the contents of her stomach, Beckenham could only be thankful she did it overboard.

The following morning after breakfast, Georgie asked Violet to walk with her in the rockery. A most prosaic term for the glory of a man-made wilderness full of cool, overgrown pathways and the skip and chortle of water cascading over artfully arranged stones.

As soon as she was sure they couldn't be overheard,

Georgie said, "You know, of course, about the bustle last night."

She'd found Violet asleep in her own bed when she looked in on her. The relief had been monstrous.

Her sister ducked her head a little to avoid a low-hanging branch. "Yes. No doubt that is why they were not at breakfast this morning. What will happen to them?"

"Oh, nothing too terrible, I hope. At least, their mamas will probably mete out punishments, but Lady Arden and I hope to keep the matter quiet. The house party is over, however. Everyone is leaving today."

On reflection, she and Beckenham had agreed the incident in the grotto gave him the perfect excuse to bring the house party to a discreet close. Clearly, the behavior of Lady Harriet, Miss Trent, and Miss deVere had tainted the entire endeavor. Lord Beckenham could not be blamed for declining to consider marrying any of the ladies present.

She hesitated. "Violet, why did Lady Charlotte tell me you were at the grotto, too?"

"Oh." Her sister's blue eyes flickered to her and away. "Well, G, if you must know, I agreed to accompany them. It seemed—" She flourished a hand. "—I don't know, as if I would be holding myself above the others if I refused. Even Lady Charlotte was going, initially. She must have thought better of it, too."

Thank goodness Violet had acted with some common sense. "So you did not go."

"You know I did not. I decided it would be too great a risk. Besides, I do not like strong spirits and I knew Margo had filched the brandy. Drinking it was the main purpose of the jaunt."

Georgie had to be satisfied with that, she supposed. One couldn't rely on Violet never to get into trouble, but her sister was an intelligent girl, clever enough to weigh the benefits of a venture against the consequences of getting caught.

Yet there was something about Violet's manner—an unease, perhaps even a furtiveness—that made Georgie suspicious.

A sudden thought occurred. Violet's bedchamber was next to hers. Had Violet heard . . . something last night?

The mere notion made Georgie flush to the roots of her hair.

She cleared her throat. "Violet, there is something I must tell you."

Was it her imagination, or did her sister's shoulders drop, just a fraction, as though in relief. "What is it?"

Georgie spied a conveniently placed stone bench and said, "Let's sit down."

The day had warmed considerably, it seemed.

"Are you well, G?" said Violet. "You look awfully strange."

"Yes. Well." She cleared her throat. "What I'm about to tell you will strike you as rather shocking. Well, not shocking, precisely. Surprising."

Georgie smoothed her hands over her skirts. Her palms felt clammy inside her gloves. She knew, of course, that Violet had most definitely not formed a tendre for Beckenham. That lessened her guilt but only slightly.

"I'm all agog," said Violet. "Pray, do not keep me in suspense."

Georgie licked her lips. She felt a sheen of perspiration on her brow. Why had she chosen to make this disclosure outside, on such a hot day? "First, I owe you an apology."

"An apology?" Violet laughed. "What for?"

"I'm getting to that," said Georgie, a little crossly.

Violet clasped Georgie's hands. "Shall I save you the

trouble, my dearest, darlingest G? You and Lord Beckenham have discovered you are in love—*finally*—and are to be married, as you should have been six years ago."

Georgie felt her jaw drop as her sister went off into peals of laughter.

"Stop it, Violet. It is *not* funny. You knew all this time? But why didn't you say something?" The torture she'd been through, struggling to be fair to Violet, tamping down her jealousy, living with the pain of longing lodged like a huge splinter in her chest.

Her sister sighed and wiped her eyes with her handkerchief, chuckling still. "Oh, G, what good would that have done? There is never telling you anything, is there? Besides, if I'd refused to participate in this charade, how could I have brought you and Lord Beckenham together?"

Georgie felt like an idiot for not seeing it before. She'd been so tangled up in her own angst, she hadn't realized her sister had played her like a fish on a line.

Violet flicked her handkerchief. "Why do you think I participated in this degrading house party? Why do you think I begged you to come with me? True, I did not engineer my mother's illness, but I would have found a way to drag you here even if she'd been able-bodied, I assure you."

The shock of it suspended Georgie's faculties. She didn't know whether to shake her devious sister for all she'd put her through or hug her instead.

She settled on the hug.

"You *wretched* girl!" She laughed, but her eyes brimmed with tears, too. "That business with the bluebell. That night, in my bedchamber back in Brighton, when you said—"

Violet put on a high, light voice, mimicking herself. "With my fair looks and Beckenham's dark coloring, we would make a fine pair. I wonder you didn't strangle me."

They both erupted into giggles again.

"Clever puss! You had me fooled indeed," said Georgie. Her heart felt extraordinarily light. She'd never been so happy to be hoodwinked.

"You cannot know how relieved I am that you have resolved your differences at last," said Violet. "I thought I might have to take extreme measures."

It was on the tip of Georgie's tongue to ask Violet what "extreme measures" might have entailed, but she wisely held her peace.

"So," said Violet as they strolled back to the house, arm in arm. "When is the wedding, hmm?"

"I don't know," said Georgie. "If I had my way, it would be as quick and as quiet as possible. We will attract enough attention as it is."

She picked a leaf off a shrub as they passed it and twiddled it between finger and thumb. "You and I will have to leave Winford tomorrow, I suppose, or it will look rather strange to the other guests."

Violet stopped short, but almost immediately resumed her easy gait. "Why bother about them? Everyone will gossip once you announce your engagement anyway."

"That's true. Still, I want to minimize the scandal-broth as much as possible."

She didn't say it to Violet, but she didn't want to be responsible for tarnishing Beckenham's reputation any more than necessary. Their marriage would be a nine days' wonder, but no more than that, if she could help it.

When she said as much to Beckenham, however, he

wouldn't hear of her leaving with the other guests. He frowned. "Out of the question."

The part of her that always objected to his autocratic dictates fired up, but before she could do more than open her mouth, he smiled at her. "I refuse to be parted from you now. Who knows what trouble you might find before I can put that ring on your finger?"

He'd already sent an urgent message to the Duke of Montford asking him to arrange a special license for them. It would be only a matter of days before they could tie the knot.

"In the meanwhile," he said, dipping his head to nuzzle behind her ear, "you and I shall make up for lost time."

She gasped, abandoning the promptings of her better self to revel in the sensation of his lips cruising over her skin. "Whatever you say, my lord."

He laughed, soft and low, nipped gently at her earlobe. "Who are you and what have you done with Georgie Black?"

"If I am quiescent, it is only because your commands accord with my own inclinations."

She didn't even bother to remind him that it was broad daylight, that they stood in his library, that anyone could come upon them at any moment.

Most of the guests had already left. Only a few of the single gentlemen remained, perhaps a little bewildered by the mass exodus from Winford that had taken place without warning that day.

Georgie was so wrapped up in Beckenham, the entire household could have broken out in purple spots and she wouldn't have noticed. She was vaguely aware of Lady Arden's sharp eyes upon her, but she didn't want to tell her the news. Not quite yet.

That night, Beckenham visited Georgie's bedchamber once more. He immediately took up where he'd been obliged to leave off the previous evening.

His slightest touch set off fireworks in her blood; the expert way he used his mouth on her was almost too pleasurable to bear. He set about loving her with the same intense focus, skill, and dedication that he did everything else. She reached climax so easily, so violently, so many times, she actually thought she might die of bliss.

"I wish I could pleasure you half so well," she told him with a tinge of chagrin at her lack of experience.

That made him laugh so hard, she had to clap her hand over his mouth out of concern that someone would hear.

"I don't see what's so funny," she said, frowning. "You must have had a lot of practice to make you the greatest lover in the history of the world. This is only my second time."

Gripping the wrist of the hand that had covered his mouth, he pinned it down on the pillow next to her head as he rolled to loom over her.

She felt a surge of excitement at the slight restraint, at the dark, intense fire that replaced the smile in his eyes.

"Ah, Georgie, you make me insane with desire just by breathing." He said it a little roughly, as if it was not an easy admission to make. "What we have is infinitely rare. This degree of passion is new for me, too."

Something burned behind her eyes. She'd known deep inside that what lay between them now was special. Hearing it from him made her heart swell in her chest.

He reached down between them, and the broad tip

of his member pressed between her slick folds. As he slid, hot and hard inside her, she finally, irrevocably, surrendered the last piece of her soul to him.

Dear Lizzie,

Pray, do not scold me for failing to write. How do you and Dartry go on? Of course, I shan't miss your wedding, silly. I would not miss it for the world.

I am desolate. He is gone and I do not know if I shall see him again for some time. If he should ask, you will keep forwarding his letters under cover of your own, won't you, dearest? And if worst comes to worst, well . . . No. I refuse to look on the dark side. Something must happen. It has to. . . .

The news of Georgie's and Beckenham's second engagement did not take Lady Arden by surprise.

"Delighted to hear it," she said briskly. "I *could* wish that you'd both behaved so sensibly six years ago. However, I am glad you have finally resolved your differences."

She kissed them both, and Georgie had the vague suspicion that perhaps Violet's hand had not been the only one helping their cause along.

"A pity your papa was such a muttonhead as to leave Cloverleigh to Violet," commented the older lady.

"I am right here, Lady Arden," said Violet, who had been sitting quietly, embroidering in the window seat.

"Yes, yes, I know that. But you cannot be offended, for you take no interest whatsoever in the place."

"I'm not offended," said Violet. "I have never pretended to love Cloverleigh like Georgie does. If I could give it to her, I would, but my trustees won't let me and

I don't inherit until I am married or five-and-twenty, whichever comes first."

"It hardly matters now," said Beckenham with a shrug. And Georgie could tell he meant it.

When his dark gaze rested on her, she felt like the most adored woman in the world. A parcel of land, no matter how beloved, did not even weigh in the balance.

Lady Arden cleared her throat ostentatiously and Georgie gave a guilty start.

"I trust your wedding will not be too far distant," said the older lady dryly.

"As soon as the special license arrives," said Beckenham, still not taking his eyes from Georgie. "Montford will bring it."

"Will he?" Lady Arden said it coolly. There was quite a history between her and Beckenham's former guardian, the Duke of Montford. Georgie didn't know the details, but it was generally accepted that Lady Arden was Montford's long-standing mistress.

Before Georgie could remark, however, Lady Arden clapped her hands together. "Well, thank goodness that's settled. Now, about Violet's come-out in the spring."

Beckenham bowed. "I believe that's my cue to depart."

"Yes, yes, off you go." Lady Arden shooed him with her hand. "I see I shall get no sense at all from Georgie if you stay."

Feeling a little sheepish, Georgie managed not to blush too hard when Beckenham took her hand and kissed it before he strode from the room.

"Georgie, he is smitten," Violet hissed as soon as he was out of earshot. "And so are you! See how she blushes, Lady Arden?"

It seemed to Georgie that everyone must know that

she and Beckenham were lovers. Lady Arden was right. The sooner they were married, the better.

"Very likely," said Lady Arden. "But we are to discuss you, today, Violet. I had word from your mama that she will remain in Bath for the present, but she still wants you to return to school once your stay here is at an end. She doesn't feel her health is equal to chaperoning you at the moment."

"Violet can stay with us," volunteered Georgie.

"Oh, no!" said Violet. "I'm sorry, Georgie. It's a kind offer, but you and Beckenham must wish to be alone."

"Yes, and what's more, Violet needs someone who will keep a strict eye on her." Lady Arden observed Violet thoughtfully. "I've half a mind to take you to Scotland with me."

Violet's face went curiously blank. "Scotland," she repeated, almost as if to herself. "I should like that."

"Well, we'll see what your mama says," said Lady Arden.

She went on to lay out her plans for Violet's debut. What she would wear, the parties she might attend, the people to whom she ought to make herself agreeable. And of course, the eligible bachelors she might wed.

"You are in the capital position of inheriting a handsome property," said Lady Arden. "To a man like Beckenham who already owns a large estate, Cloverleigh would be no more than an additional source of income. It would not be his principal seat. That is something to consider if you wish to make your home at Cloverleigh."

There was a pause. "I haven't lived there for years," said Violet. "I do not think it would matter to me."

Something in Violet's manner was off, but Georgie couldn't pinpoint it. It occurred to her how very adept at prevarication Violet was. She had never betrayed her true feelings about this house party to Georgie by word or by deed. What else might she be concealing?

"So, you are saying we ought not rule out gentlemen of wealth but no property," said Georgie. "Perhaps even a younger son if he has a decent fortune."

She hadn't considered that Violet might remain in the district. They could be neighbors. The thought gladdened her.

"That's right," said Lady Arden. "What we do *not* want, on any account, is a gentlemen whose own estate requires a great deal of capital expenditure."

As the conversation progressed, Violet grew increasingly remote. Disquiet crept through Georgie's body. She must make a point of speaking with her alone about all this.

Eventually, with several matters settled to Lady Arden's satisfaction, it was agreed that subject to Lady Black's approval, Violet would leave for Scotland with Lady Arden immediately after Georgie's wedding.

Later, Georgie taxed Violet with her suspicions in the most tactful way she could think of. "Darling, things seem to be moving fast where you are concerned. Do you find it overwhelming?"

"Not at all," said Violet. "Only, I had thought that you might stand up for me, Georgie."

"Stand up for you? I want nothing but the best for you. You know that," said Georgie, taken aback.

"You and Beckenham are marrying for love," Violet said quietly. "You are so happy, you don't even hear what people say to you half the time. Don't you think I deserve that, too?"

"Oh, Violet," said Georgie, touching her arm. "Of course I do."

How could she have been so obtuse? And how could she possibly urge caution and prudence upon Violet?

When Georgie knew that if Beckenham had been the village blacksmith, she would not have let anyone or anything stop her marrying him.

"Is there a particular gentleman you might be thinking of?" said Georgie.

"No, but it is not beyond the bounds of possibility that one day I might, is it?"

Relieved, Georgie said, "Well, my dear, you may just as well fall in love with a suitable gentleman during your season as with an unsuitable one. You may be sure that I won't let anyone thrust you into a match that will make you unhappy." She hugged her sister. "Why don't we cross that bridge when we come to it? Enjoy your come-out and see what happens?"

Violet gave herself a little shake. "Yes. You are right, Georgie. I will do that. Of course."

Chapter Eighteen

"Georgie, I must leave you tomorrow," said Beckenham. "I shan't be above a night. Perhaps two."

Georgie was cutting flowers for the house, laying them in a boat-shaped basket. She looked up. "Oh?"

She'd appeared so serene, so content as she moved purposefully through the walled rose garden, choosing the best blooms and clipping them efficiently with her shears. Beckenham had watched her for some time.

He drank in the sight of her, dressed in her dimity gown and floppy straw hat. His head filled with the heady scent of roses, senses lulled by the lazy drone of bees. He'd never dared to imagine he and Georgie might fall easily into such everyday domestic patterns.

Beckenham smiled to himself. Calling Georgie Black domestic was like calling a tigress a kitchen cat. But he couldn't deny he enjoyed the way she'd begun to make herself at home in his house.

Now, he said, "My business is unavoidable, or God knows, I'd have put it off."

"Where are you going?" she asked.

He wouldn't lie to her. "Bath."

Her gaze sharpened, but she didn't hurry to give expression to the emotions that chased across her face. She bent to arrange the flowers in her basket, long lashes shadowing her eyes.

He'd assured her he had no intention of challenging Pearce over her recent disclosure, or at all. He'd explained that since Pearce hadn't shown up to their previous affair of honor, the matter could not be revisited, ever.

Besides, a duel, no matter how quietly conducted, would always become common knowledge. He'd grown wiser than his twenty-four-year-old self in the intervening years. Still, she'd been unconvinced until he admitted he meant to get her indiscreet letter back. He'd just have to find another way.

"You said we needed to be clever about retrieving the letter," she reminded him now. "Have you thought of something clever?"

"Perhaps." He frowned, taking the basket from her. "I don't want to raise your hopes. It rather depends on the circumstances. I go to Bath now because Lydgate has written that Pearce's aunt may not last the week."

"You expect him to act against me once that is resolved," said Georgie.

"It's likely, don't you think?"

"I'll come with you," said Georgie, adding yet another rose—this time, a perfect, pale pink bloom—to the heavily laden basket.

He knew refusing her outright would set up her hackles. "How would that look? We are not married yet."

"No matter. My stepmother is staying in Bath for her health. Drinking the waters, you know. Violet and I need only join her there." Georgie made a face. "I must tell her of our engagement sometime, I suppose. She'll be *furious* with me."

He was indifferent to Lady Black's wishes, but he said, "You will have to find Violet a brilliant match to make up for stealing me."

She laughed. "I did not steal you. You threw yourself at my head, and so I shall tell my stepmother."

He took her hand and kissed it. "You cannot steal what was always yours to begin with."

Her features lit with such tenderness, she made his heart warm in his chest. "I just misplaced you for a while?"

"Why am I now feeling like a dropped handkerchief?" he wondered.

"But my *very* favorite handkerchief, at that."

He chuckled, and as they walked on, she tucked her hand in the crook of his elbow.

"I am well aware that you simply burn to forbid me the journey," she said, returning to the subject of Bath, as he knew she would. "I cannot tell you how much I appreciate your forbearance."

"Generous of you." He narrowed his eyes a little against the sun. "Might I ask you—beg you—not to come to Bath?"

"I would not interfere," she said.

"Thank God for that."

"Unless *absolutely* necessary," she added.

The basket dropped to the ground, spilling flowers. He gripped her arms. "This is not a game, Georgie. You of all people should know that. I am prepared to discuss my plans with you. I'm prepared to listen to your opinions. But there is more than this letter between Pearce and me. This time you will stay out of it, do you hear?"

Danger flashed in her eyes, but her lips formed a brilliant smile. "Oh, Marcus!" she cooed. "I do so love it when you turn masterful."

Abruptly, he let go of her and stooped to return the scattered flowers to their basket.

"I'm sorry." Her voice was soft now. He felt her fingertips brush his shoulder, a fleeting touch. "You know how I hate to be left out of things."

He straightened, his lips twitching into a reluctant smile. At least she hadn't flown into a rage. They made progress, it seemed. "You will have to take it as payment in kind for hoodwinking me about the duel."

She bit her lip, then sighed. "In your shoes, I'd have been furious with me," she admitted.

He had been furious. Furious, frustrated at his unwitting impotence. But also deeply, powerfully touched—awestruck, even—that she'd risked so much to secure his safety. Could he do any less for her?

By tacit consent, they turned their steps toward the house and she said no more about Bath.

Gracious of her to concede so quickly. He'd thought to have a fight on his hands. He still wasn't convinced she wouldn't scheme to get to Bath in spite of him, but much as his instinct screamed at him to forbid it, he'd learned to his cost that wasn't the way to go about negotiating with her.

The truth niggled at him like a splinter in his thumb. He didn't want her to go with him because he was afraid. Fearful that in Bath she'd be accessible to Pearce; that until his own wedding ring was on her finger, all manner of things might go awry.

He knew better now than to take her or their betrothal for granted. Every night, he woke in a panic until he remembered she was still there with him at Winford, still his. If only Montford would make haste with that damned special license!

At least, in the meantime, he might act to rid them of the menace named Pearce.

He gave no sign of his inner turmoil, nor of his relief at her reasonableness over Bath.

"You might wish to rest before dinner." He smiled down at her. "I have something planned for this evening that will require all of your considerable energy and attention."

"Actually, I have made plans of my own for us tonight," said Georgie with a glance at him under her lashes.

The husky note in her voice heated his blood. He quirked an eyebrow. "Oh?"

"Meet me in your boxing saloon at midnight," she murmured, taking the basket from him as they gained the terrace, where Lady Arden and Violet were taking tea.

Having expected something infinitely more enticing, he was disappointed. A thought occurred to him and he frowned. "How many times have I told you, Georgie? I will *not* teach you to fence."

"It's nothing like that. You'll see." She flashed him a smile that was at once mischievous and slightly . . . nervous?

That disconcerted him, made him more than a little wary. Georgie, in this mood, was unpredictable. She seemed to have taken his refusal to allow her a role in retrieving her letter in good part; he trusted tonight wouldn't involve some devious plan to punish him for his tyranny.

She refused to be drawn on the surprise she had in store for him. Lady Arden and Violet were within earshot by now, so reluctantly, he held his peace.

Beckenham strode into his boxing saloon at the appointed hour, anticipation flowing through his veins. Uncertainty eddied at the edges, though. He wasn't entirely sure he liked surprises. Particularly when he couldn't quite gauge Georgie's mood.

He'd worn a minimum of clothing, leaving off coat, waistcoat, and cravat in the optimistic conviction he wouldn't be wearing anything for very long.

He glanced about him. The place was cavernous, a little cooler than the sultry summer air outside. Lit with a few branches of candles here and there.

It was also empty.

Or no. Not entirely empty. A chair had been placed in the middle of the bare floor.

He tilted his head to study it. What game was she playing now?

He walked over to the chair and saw a length of black velvet and a note.

The note read: *The blindfold is for you. Put it on.* And as rather an afterthought, the word *please* had been added below.

Hmm.

He reached out to finger the soft nap of the velvet band, tingles shooting up his spine to prickle at his nape.

Intriguing. Definitely suggestive. And yet . . .

He found himself strangely reluctant to obey the playful command.

Again, he looked around. "Georgie?"

No answer. Clearly, she would not show herself until he did her bidding with the blindfold. And then what? His mind reeled at the possibilities.

His heart began to hammer wildly as he picked up the length of velvet. His throat dried and his chest tightened until he could scarcely breathe.

He let the blindfold spool from his hand to puddle on the chair.

"All right, Georgie, you've had your fun." She would think him a poor sport, a boring old stick-in-the-mud, but . . . He swallowed hard. Or tried to. His mouth was lined with sandpaper.

No answer.

She must be hiding here somewhere. He'd find her, damn it. She didn't need tricks like this to arouse him to fever pitch. He didn't need to wear a blindfold for her to drive him crazed with desire.

Then he hesitated. He remembered the trace of anxiety in her face that afternoon, when she'd told him to meet her here. He knew that while inexperienced, Georgie had a deeply passionate, sensual nature. She wanted to explore with him, experiment.

God, he was all for exploring and experimenting. One hundred percent for it, in fact. He had several interesting things in mind, himself.

He just did not want to wear that blindfold.

"Georgie?" His voice was hoarse now. He licked his lips.

Again, silence so deep, it seemed to sing in his ears. She wouldn't come out of hiding until he tied that bloody strip of black velvet around his eyes.

On some strange level, he understood that this was very important to her, to them both. If he refused to play along, it might . . . well, she might take it as a rebuff and become less . . . adventurous, take less initiative in future.

Vulnerability. That's what he'd seen in her face that afternoon. If he rejected this overture, he'd strike at something precious. He wouldn't hurt her for the world.

An invisible band around his chest seemed to tighten as he reached out again for the blindfold. His hand actually shook.

Damn it! Put it on, you fool. What are you waiting for? It was only a blindfold, not a scold's bridle.

He snatched up the length of velvet. In jerky, rough

movements, he pressed the blindfold to his face, tied it in place behind his head. Rather tighter than was comfortable.

The world went black. He knew several moments of acute disorientation, heard the harsh saw of his own breaths. The material seemed to suffocate him, even though it left his nostrils and mouth free. The knot bit into the back of his skull.

He sucked in air, forced himself not to rip the damned thing off again.

His voice was hoarse. "I've done it. Georgie? Georgie, you can come out now."

Courage, Georgie.

She slipped out from behind the door that connected the boxing saloon to a change room. Silently, she watched Beckenham's tall, broad-shouldered figure. She saw with approval that he'd dressed appropriately for the occasion.

She herself had stripped down to nothing but a thin lawn shift for this meeting. Feeling the cool air brush against her bare arms, she padded in bare feet toward him.

Mr. Mahomed's baths had given her the idea. She'd wanted it to be a complete surprise, however, and until she hit on the notion of a blindfold, she'd been at a loss to know how to get Beckenham to the bathhouse without hinting at her plans.

The boxing saloon adjoined the bathhouse by a narrow corridor, purpose-built to allow Beckenham to move from training direct to a hot bath without exposing his overheated body to the cold outside.

On approach, she saw now that Beckenham held himself with an odd tension. She hadn't expected him to react as he had to the simple act of blindfolding himself. But then, he was a man who liked to be in control, wasn't he?

"Marcus," she whispered, making him turn his head sharply in her direction. "I'm here."

He gave a sharp gasp when she touched his shoulder. That pleased her. Determined to take this as slowly as they both might stand, she trailed her fingertips from his shoulder across his chest, until she met warm skin and the scribble of dark, springy hair exposed by the open V of his shirt.

Her desire ratcheted up a notch with that touch. He was hers, all hers, to do with as she wished. Hers to pleasure. Hers to love.

She glanced down. Whatever Beckenham's feelings on the subject of blindfolds, the bulge in his trousers told her without doubt that he was as aroused as she.

He smelled of starch and a faint trace of soap and more than a hint of man. Georgie slid her hand beneath his shirt, explored the hard plates of his chest, caressed the smooth, burning hot skin. She stood on tiptoe and leaned into him, pressed a kiss to the place between his clavicles, saw the hard, convulsive movement in his throat.

He breathed heavily; she felt it, heard it, and yet she thought she might well be the first of them to break. She couldn't wait much longer. Perhaps she might save this sort of thing for another time.

"Come with me," she said.

Taking his hand, she led him slowly across the room and step by step, down the short connecting corridor. He waited, a muscle ticcing in his jaw, while she opened the door.

"Here we are."

Steam greeted them in great rolling puffs. When it cleared a little, Georgie paused to admire her handiwork.

The room was an octagonal shape, with a massive round bath set in its center, built over a hot spring. Murals of bacchanalian feasts covered the walls; the ceiling was a pagan sky filled with angry-looking gods.

The curtains at the massive arched windows were drawn against prying eyes. She'd lit candles everywhere. Their flames were reflected like fairy lights in the pool. On the water's surface floated a myriad rose petals of different colors, from deep burgundy and scarlet through to pink and white. The air was sweet and spicy, redolent of certain preparations she'd purchased from Mr. Mahomed's in Brighton.

With Smith's help, she'd ferried towels, robes, unguents, even fruit and cheese and wine for a midnight feast if they felt so inclined.

The fluttering in her stomach made her think she would not be hungry anytime soon.

She became aware of the labored breathing next to her. A sheen of perspiration lined Beckenham's brow above the blindfold.

"Georgie," he panted. "Georgie I can't—"

He ripped off the blindfold and hurled it from him. With a violent shudder, he leaned a shoulder against the doorjamb and gasped for air.

Chapter Nineteen

Georgie's satisfaction gave way to horror. "Marcus! Marcus, what's wrong? Here. Come here and sit down."

She put her arm around his waist and half staggered with him toward the luxurious divan that had figured largely in her plans for tonight. He sat down hard upon it, ducking his head, wiping the sweat from his brow with his shirtsleeve. "It's all right. I'm fine."

Georgie knelt at his feet, her hands on his knees, her chest cramping at his obvious distress. "I'm sorry! I'm so sorry, my darling. Was it the blindfold?"

He shook his head but it seemed to her that the gesture wasn't a negative, merely an attempt to shake off whatever had descended upon him just now. "Just give me a minute."

Head still bowed, shoulders heaving, he put out his hand to her, clasped her fingers in reassurance. Distraught, she pressed his hand to her cheek.

How could she have so miscalculated? She'd seen he wasn't entirely comfortable with the blindfold, hadn't she? Why had she insisted he go through with that part of it? But how could she have known?

She'd thought his manner indicated leashed desire, not . . . not *this*.

His breathing soon calmed enough that she ventured to put up a hand to touch his cheek. "Marcus?"

Strong arms lashed around her. With a groan, he lifted her to him, kissed her long and hard, in a way that made it seem as if he were holding on to her for dear life, relying on her breath for air. That if she didn't anchor him with her kiss and her body, he'd be swept away by some invisible force.

She didn't understand his reaction, but she'd give him anything he needed, anything he asked of her. She was desperately sorry to have caused him pain.

He pulled her up and somehow, she was kneeling on the divan, straddling his thighs, kissing him back with all the love for him inside her, gripping his face between her palms.

His hands left her hips to fumble at his trouser buttons. Before she could pause to wonder how this would work or what she was supposed to do, he'd found her entrance and driven up inside her, impaling her to the hilt on his thick, swollen shaft.

She cried out at the wonderful feel of him filling her so completely, in such a novel way that she felt him in places she hadn't felt him before.

Riding him was new to her, but after a little guidance she relaxed into the rhythm of it. Despite her concern, Georgie gloried in the feel of him, at the way their bodies worked together, with her setting the pace in the rise and fall of her hips, him grinding into her with his pubic bone on every upward thrust. She reveled in his closeness, at the intimacy of this act, at the sensations that spread throughout her body when he filled her to the brim.

His hungry, frenzied lovemaking had taken her by

surprise. Yet she was so ready for him after all the planning and thought she'd expended on this moment, that her climax overtook her swiftly in a hot, heady rush.

He gripped her hips, steadying her as she convulsed and trembled, her head flung back, abandoned in her wild flight. Then he collapsed with her onto the divan, rolling them until he braced himself over her.

She watched his face, a dark flush high on his cheekbones, his eyes glazed with heat. He clenched his jaw and drove into her, over and over, in a hard, hot slide that seemed to go deeper with every thrust.

Incredibly, she felt the tingle in the soles of her feet again, and the low simmer in her blood as he stoked the flickers of pleasure to a blaze.

This time, when she came she took him with her. With a smothered shout of exultation, he buried his face in her hair, his big body shuddering with release.

When Georgie lay quietly in his arms and his heartbeat had resumed its normal pace and the panic that had closed his throat and the wildness in his body had subsided, Beckenham finally took in their surroundings. "I'm sorry, Georgie. I ruined your surprise."

She shook her head, raising herself to a sitting position. "You haven't. You just delayed it a little." She stretched luxuriously. "And most enjoyably, too."

He ran a hand down her torso as she arched into the stretch. He'd taken her like the veriest brute. He didn't feel *too* guilty about it, however, for it hadn't escaped him that she'd climaxed. *Twice.* Lucky for him that Georgie was a strong woman. She didn't break easily. Not in a physical sense, at least.

Georgie met his gaze. "Will you tell me what happened to you just now? It was the blindfold, wasn't it?"

After a hesitation, he nodded. "It was foolish. I don't

know why I—" But he did know. He did not like total darkness and he liked even less being made to feel utterly powerless in the dark.

He sat up also. "Nothing for you to worry about. I just don't like blindfolds, that's all." He stood. "Let's bathe, shall we? It would be a pity to waste all of this."

He was playing for time; they both knew it. He thought she might insist on knowing everything immediately.

To his relief, after a slight pause, she said, "All right. Lovely."

Thank God she was one of the few women who knew when a man didn't want to talk. She'd get it out of him sooner or later, but she wouldn't press him now.

Georgie had worn only a shift in which to greet him tonight. He hadn't fully assimilated that fact until this moment. Now she whipped it over her head and dropped it on the floor. She moved to the enormous bath, completely and unashamedly nude.

His hands stilled on the waistband of his trousers as he watched her walk with that uniquely feminine gait to the pool. Her hair tumbled over her shoulders, reaching halfway down her back. The roundness of her bottom, the dimples at the base of her spine that winked at him as she moved, made him stifle a groan.

Holding one slender arm out for balance, Georgie dipped her toe in the water to test it. She glanced back at him over her shoulder, a look in those sea green eyes that made his skin hot and tight. "Perfect."

She stepped down into the water, sending rose petals drifting and spinning in her wake.

Beckenham rid himself of the remainder of his clothing in record time. He wasn't far behind her, but he didn't miss the frank look of appreciation she cast his naked body as he moved to join her.

The water was still warm, deliciously so, and the mineral tang of it filled his nostrils as he walked across the tiled floor of the bath toward Georgie.

He caught her around the waist and kissed her, running his hands over the water-slicked smoothness of her skin.

"Will you do something for me?" she murmured against his lips.

"Anything. As long as it doesn't involve wearing a blindfold." If he joked about it, he might feel less like a prize idiot.

She didn't seize on the reference to probe him further, for which he was grateful.

"Sit on that ledge." She indicated a wide step at the other side of the pool.

He obliged, setting his hands on the ledge and pulling himself up to sit facing her. Now they were of a height. The water lapped around her waist, and her navel played peekaboo with him as the water level rose and fell.

Those breasts, half hidden by her thick, bright hair, tantalized him, swung against him as she reached past where he sat to one of the small bottles on the side of the bath.

She poured some of the liquid into her hand, then set the bottle aside.

It smelled of jasmine and spices. She let some of the golden liquid dribble from her hands onto his chest. The contrast between its cool viscosity and his flushed skin made him shiver.

Then she touched him, working the unguent over him in firm, gentle strokes, kneading at muscles, skimming over the sensitive flesh of his nipples, up and over his shoulders, down his arms.

The last of the tension from his fight with the blindfold

faded away. His bones slowly turned to jelly at her touch, even while his gut clenched with the effort of keeping his own hands to himself. She paid particular attention to his muscles, and he knew a moment's gratitude for all the punishment he'd put his body through to keep himself fit for boxing.

"Mmm," she murmured, framing his rib cage with her hands, then working inward, over the ridges in his belly. Languid, soft caresses that made his cock hard as a pole.

She made another appreciative sound at the sight of his member showing its interest in the proceedings.

Georgie glanced up at him, then back down. In a hushed voice, she said, "Can I touch it?"

"Please."

Her fingertips fluttered over his cock, which jerked and hardened further at the contact. She gave a surprised chuckle, but did not let it deter her.

Slippery with unguent, even beneath the water, her hands explored his contours, made him groan as she touched the sensitive head, investigated the ridge beneath. A feather-light fingertip brushed his balls, making them tighten.

She closed her fingers around his cock, until she held him in her fist.

Her voice was husky. "Like this?"

Beckenham's body tensed, fighting the urge to spill in her hand.

"Show me how you want me to touch you," she whispered.

"You're doing a fine job," he gritted out.

"Tighter?"

He squeezed his eyes shut. "Yes."

"Like this?"

"God, yes." He made an involuntary thrust with his hips.

"Now what?"

He gave in and wrapped his hand around hers, showing her what he wanted, everything she desired to know. His chest felt like it might burst and his head spun as he climaxed in powerful, hot jets of seed.

He pulled her hand away from his cock, then he kissed her, reversing their positions, standing to swing her out of the pool and onto the edge so that her legs dangled over the side.

Water sheeted from her body as if she were Venus arising from the waves. Her lovely nipples beaded with moisture, hard and pink and delicious. Kneeling on the step, he tasted each of them in turn, laving, licking, sucking until she'd braced her hands on the floor behind her, thrusting into his mouth, crying out with the pleasure of it.

Then he gripped her thighs and tilted her to him. Spread her wide to his gaze.

She gave a shocked little murmur. "Oh, no . . ."

He glanced up at her. "You are beautiful," he said. "Don't deny me."

Her lips quivered. Then she tilted her head back and closed her eyes.

He took this for acquiescence, sliding his hands up her legs to place them over his shoulders. Then he bent his head and feasted.

Much later, when they lay together in a surfeited daze, her head on his chest, Beckenham said, "I think I know why that happened before. With the blindfold."

She didn't look up at him or speak, just continued stroking his chest.

He'd felt like a damned fool. He owed her an explanation, though. It was time she knew the truth about him, anyway. Not that he'd concealed anything deliberately, but the blindfold, not to mention the forthcoming confrontation with Pearce, had brought it all flooding back. If they were to be husband and wife, she needed to know about the darkness he carried inside him.

"You will have heard of my grandfather," Beckenham began. "Living in this district, how could you not? His . . . eccentricities were stuff of legend."

"Yes. I've heard of him. What was he like?"

He stroked her hair. He couldn't tell her some of the unspeakable things, but he could give her a fair idea. "He used to strip naked in the middle of the night and take his gun out with him. Hunting poachers, he said, though I'm told all he ever shot was ducks. He drank too much, gambled too much. He gamed away Cloverleigh, as you know. He was incomprehensibly extravagant. At the time of his death, he owned seven hundred pairs of handmade riding boots. *Seven hundred.* While some of his tenants struggled to keep their children fed."

She pressed her palm against his chest. "You changed all of that."

Certainly, he had done what he could for his tenants, a process begun by the Duke of Montford when he'd become trustee of the estate. But there were too many wrongs that could never be set right.

After a pause, she ventured, "Did he . . . Did he beat you?"

He shook his head, though she couldn't see him. "He was never violent toward me. Not directly. I was the heir, you see." He'd been lucky compared with the others in that household, compared with anyone in his grandfather's power.

He thought Georgie lay slightly heavier against him, as if that disclosure had eased some of her tension.

"No, there was no physical cruelty. But there was always a cruel edge to my grandfather's exploits. Things were almost bearable when my father was alive, but once he died . . ."

Beckenham swallowed hard.

"The old earl made my mother's life a living hell. Again, not beatings—strangely, that would have been against his code—but cruelty of the mind. Screaming abuse, threats and the like. A stable hand gave Mama a puppy. It was one of my grandfather's hunting dogs, the runt of the litter."

For a moment, he couldn't trust his voice. Then, huskily, he went on. "You should have seen how happy it made her, such a silly little thing. We called him Scamper. In one of his rages, my grandfather picked up Scamper by the scruff of his neck and threatened to throw him in the fire."

"Oh, no! He didn't do it, did he?"

"No, but we thought he would. Only the previous night, he'd forced a bottle of port down one of his horse's throats and killed it. What would a puppy matter to him?" His grandfather had always kept a horse in the house, like a companion animal. One was always dodging piles of manure in the halls.

She shuddered. "What happened to your poor mother?"

He set his jaw. Even now, more than twenty years later, the memory tore a hole in his chest. "She died of a fever. I think in the end, her soul gave out. She struggled hard to stay alive for me. She just wasn't strong enough."

"Poor lady. And poor little boy."

He felt hot moisture seep onto his chest. Georgie's

tears, he realized. But she still didn't look at him, and he was grateful for that. He hated sounding like a puling whiner. He hated being the cause of her tears.

He would get this over with, though, and then never speak of it again. His throat grew tight, as tight as it had when he'd donned the blindfold. "For, oh, perhaps a month, it was just my grandfather and me and the servants. God, I was only five. I was terrified of him. Even though he never raised a hand to me, just being surrounded by all of that unbridled violence and insanity without my mother to turn to was frightening enough."

He swallowed, his throat suddenly dry again. "There was a—a concealed cupboard. A priest's hole, really. Whenever he went on one of his rampages, I would shut myself inside it and listen and wait for the storm to pass. It was very close and very dark in there."

She didn't say it and he knew he didn't need to. That must have been why he'd had such a strong reaction to the blindfold.

A muted wail broke from Georgie then. Her shoulders shook and he held her close while she sobbed, stroking her back and murmuring soothing nothings to her. "It's all right. It's all in the past now." And having finally admitted to her what he'd never said to another soul, he thought he spoke the truth.

She raised her head, dashing at her lovely eyes with the back of one hand, her anger flaring up. "But my parents, your other neighbors, your relatives, why did no one *do* something?"

He reached up and smoothed back her curls, tucking them gently behind her ear, wondering at his good fortune in having such a fierce champion. She looked as if she wanted to hurl herself back in time and shoot the old earl through the heart.

"My grandfather was a law unto himself. No one had

the power or the right," he said. "Until my mother died and the Duke of Montford took a hand. I don't know how His Grace did it. I've always thought he must have threatened the old man with Bedlam if he didn't surrender me. Whatever the case, the duke took me to his estate at Harcourt to live, and when my grandfather died a few years later, the duke became my trustee and guardian and I became the earl."

After a pause, she said thickly, "I'm going to burn that blindfold. I could kill myself for putting you through that."

"Georgie, you weren't to know. How should you? I didn't know myself until the past all came rushing back like that. I am the one who should be apologizing. You made a special evening for us. Thank you, my darling."

He pulled her down to his kiss. When she drew back again, her nose shiny red and her face a little puffy, her eyes glazed with unshed tears, he took her face between his hands and smiled up at her. "I love you."

The words were inadequate to express the complexities of his feelings for her, and yet they were completely and utterly right.

A look of half disbelief, half joy spread across her tearstained face.

"Oh, Marcus!" And then she buried her face in his shoulder and wept in earnest.

Chapter Twenty

Beckenham left for Brighton the following morning, without relenting in his determination to leave Georgie behind.

Any plans she might have had to cajole him, threaten him, or otherwise circumvent his plans might have survived the shocking disclosures of the previous night. They'd died a quick death when he finally related the truth about his history with Lord Pearce.

"What I didn't tell you last night," said Beckenham heavily, "is that Pearce's grievance stems from something my grandfather did."

He glanced at her, not seeming to know how to go on.

"Is the story too delicate for my ears?" she asked, slightly amused at his reticence.

"No, it's not that. Well, it *is* a shocking story, but my hesitation wasn't for that reason. I . . ." He broke off, eyeing her, rubbing his chin with the back of his thumb. "You seem to be taking this news well."

Her brow furrowed. "I don't know what the news is, so how can I—?"

"I mean, about Pearce. He targeted you to strike against me."

"Oh, I *see*," she said on a spurt of anger. "You thought my vanity would be bruised if I discovered he wasn't enamored of me? Good God, Beckenham, why should I care the reason Pearce pursued me? If he'd truly loved me, he wouldn't have coerced me into writing that letter."

When Pearce had transferred his attentions to Violet, that hadn't injured her vanity, either. She'd been too fearful for her sister to consider herself slighted. All she felt for Pearce was loathing and—yes, she admitted it—fear. No matter how strong and clever Beckenham might be, he simply could not comprehend the depths to which someone like Pearce might stoop. She was afraid for him, that his innate goodness would be his undoing.

There was an odd expression on Beckenham's face. After a long hesitation, he shrugged. "Men do strange things in the name of love."

"Men of honor do not do *that* kind of thing."

"I don't know, Georgie." Beckenham stared out across the gardens to the lake. "I used to believe a man's honor mattered more than anything else. Now, I think that sometimes, honor is a luxury a man can ill afford."

She narrowed her eyes. Did he mean to *defend* Pearce's actions? The mind boggled. If that was Beckenham's intention, they were unlikely to find any common ground there.

She turned the conversation back to the matter at hand. "What connection can Pearce possibly have to your grandfather?"

Beckenham cleared his throat. "Well, besides his madness and violence, my grandfather was also very, er, promiscuous."

Randy old goat was a phrase Georgie had often heard to describe the old earl.

"No different from many of his peers, I should suppose," she said with a grimace.

"One difference," said Beckenham. "One significant difference. My grandfather was Pearce's father."

"No!" Georgie said. Then she frowned. "How can that be? Pearce is the firstborn son. He inherited the title."

It was common for ladies of the first rank to bear children who did not belong to their husbands. But to introduce a bastard into the marriage before one had borne a true heir simply wasn't done.

Beckenham looked grave. "Lady Pearce might not have been a willing participant in the act of consummation."

Georgie felt the blood drain from her face. "He . . . he forced her?"

"That's what Pearce believes. Knowing my grandfather, I do not doubt it. No one else outside the family and me knows of it. The elder Lord Pearce acknowledged him as his own son. He didn't discover the truth until later."

"One can only imagine how furious he must have been."

Beckenham nodded. "That is why Pearce needs this inheritance. Old Lord Pearce left every unentailed asset elsewhere. Once he'd acknowledged the cuckoo in their nest as his son and heir, he couldn't change the effect of the entail or keep the title from Pearce. But he *could* make the boy's life a misery and deprive him of all the privileges due to a son of the true blood. He deliberately let the entailed property go to wrack and ruin."

Astonished, Georgie took a moment to assimilate

what he'd told her. "If this is not generally known, how do you—?"

"That night. The night Pearce came to me with the lock of your hair, the story came spewing out of him. It explained why he has always hated me."

"But you didn't do anything! His hatred of you is wholly unjust," she said.

"But none the less potent for that. After all, my grandfather, his parents, all the players in the drama are gone. I'm the only one left to blame."

"I suppose," she said slowly, "that explains why he brought the lock of hair to you, doesn't it? He wanted to force a reckoning between you. Our argument and the broken betrothal were an unexpected boon."

"He chose you in the end, though," said Beckenham grimly. "Believe me, I have not forgotten he missed the duel to run away with you."

She gripped both his hands tightly in hers. "Promise me you will be careful."

He promised, but she knew it was a promise he might be forced to break.

As she waved him off some time later, Georgie thought about Beckenham's words. *Why* had Pearce thrown over the duel for her? Had he imagined himself in love with her? Had he wanted Cloverleigh? Or had he merely decided that stealing her away would cause greater pain to Beckenham than a bullet wound could ever do?

Oh, her mind buzzed with speculation and worry. She was too restless to sit inside and mind her stitches. The day was a fine one, so she went to see if Violet would accompany her on a ride.

She found Violet taking tea with Lady Arden and two young gentlemen, who rose upon her arrival in the drawing room.

"Oh!" said Georgie. "I didn't realize we had callers. How do you do?"

Good Gracious, Lady Arden wasn't letting the grass grow when it came to securing a husband for Violet. Georgie recognized Mr. Wootton and Lord Palmer as two of the most eligible young bachelors in the county.

When Lady Arden had made the introductions and the courtesies had been exchanged, Violet said, "Did you come to collect me for our ride, Georgie? I am sorry to have kept you waiting."

This was said with a meaningful expression, but Georgie simply smiled back at her as she poured herself some tea. "There is no need to rush off."

Setting her cup and saucer aside, Lady Arden said, "Perhaps you gentlemen would care for a canter yourselves? I am sure I should be most obliged to you if you'd keep my dear girls safe. They *will* insist on slipping away from their groom."

The gentlemen eagerly assented, failing to observe Violet's lowering expression.

"By Jove!" said Wootton, rubbing his hands together. "We shall make a merry party, shall we not? Have no fear, Lady Arden. We shall deliver the young ladies safely home."

"You speak as if we were parcels," said Violet, giving a false little trill of laughter that set Georgie's teeth on edge.

Lord Palmer raised his quizzing glass to his eye in a rakish way that sat so ill with his open, youthful face, Georgie stifled a laugh. "And most charming parcels at that."

Being a well-mannered girl, Violet made no further attempt to escape the inevitable. With a covert roll of her eyes at Georgie, she excused herself to change with an air of weary resignation.

Georgie's opinion of their callers did not change, either during the ensuing conversation or when the four of them rode out. The gentlemen, true to their words, kept up such a dawdling pace, Georgie might have screamed with frustration if it weren't so entertaining to watch Violet deal with her admirers.

The gentlemen were so relentlessly patronizing, Georgie couldn't blame Violet for her response. She ran rings around the poor dim-witted fellows, confounding them with insults that were cleverly couched as compliments, appearing to agree with their pompous pronouncements while saying the exact opposite.

Upon their return to the house, Violet smiled and spoke softly and said everything that was polite and correct. As soon as the door closed behind them, however, she gave a primordial cry of repressed fury, ripped off her hat, and stormed up to her bedchamber, muttering all the while.

Georgie lifted the skirts of her habit and followed.

She reached the bedchamber in time to see her sister fling her hat into a chair and fall back onto the bed with a huff that stirred the puffs of blond hair framing her face. "I cannot bear it. I cannot do the season. Not if they're all like that."

"You are being a *little* overdramatic, aren't you?" said Georgie.

"Dramatic?" said Violet. "Do you *know* what that fool of a Wootton said to me?"

"The part about ladies being delicate like little kittens or the part about our brains being smaller and thus less able to reason than men's? I heard every lamentable word," said Georgie. "But they are not all like that, Violet. I promise you."

"I'll wager some of them are worse." She raised her head and let it fall against the bed again with a dull thump.

Georgie picked up her sister's hat and dusted its crown with her hand. "Those boys are raw and silly but essentially harmless. It's the men like Lord Pearce you need to keep at a distance."

Violet raised her head and banged it again. "Ouch." She put her hands up to her hair and yanked out a pin. "I cannot believe you would put me through an afternoon such as we've spent for an entire season," she complained.

"Oh, have some sense, Violet!" said Georgie, suddenly exasperated. "You are not some simple country maid. You are the heiress to an estate with many dependents. You have an obligation to marry the sort of man whose interests dovetail with yours. Someone who will be a good steward of your land."

Violet bit her lip. "I wish to Heaven Papa had left Cloverleigh to you."

"Do you know something, Violet?" Georgie snapped. "So do I! But he didn't, and we must both make the best our lot." She threw up her hands. "Good gracious, just listen to me. Anyone would think you'd been saddled with a millstone around your neck instead of vast wealth, not to mention beauty and brains. Although sometimes, my girl, I question the last part."

Not at all helpful, but Georgie was too angry to temper her words. She swept from the room, feeling for the first time that her sister was a very spoiled young woman, indeed.

Dinner that night was stilted and uncomfortable. Lady Arden's stream of chatter did not make up for the tension between Violet and Georgie. For once, the older lady forbore to interfere, however, perhaps judging it best to leave them to sort out their own differences.

Georgie was too tense even to contemplate making amends with Violet. The knowledge that Beckenham might be carrying out his plans for Pearce at this very moment almost obliterated all else from her thoughts. She made an excuse to retire early, but that was a mistake. She couldn't sleep for worrying.

She woke late the following morning, having only managed to fall into a restless slumber shortly before dawn. In a bid to clear her head, she went for a solitary ride, ignoring Beckenham's demands that she take someone with her. She hated dragging a busy groom hither and yon at her whim.

She roamed the verdant countryside of Winford, feeling the fresh air and the sights and sounds of the fields and lanes calm her spirit. Upon crossing into Cloverleigh land, she stopped now and then to speak with one of the tenants.

They seemed surprised and pleased to be remembered, and she realized she'd been away from here for far too long. As she asked after their children, wives, husbands, and farms, Georgie wondered if Violet would ever be at ease here with these people. She didn't know how she might bring about a transfer of loyalty to her sister. Perhaps it would be for Violet to prove herself first.

The tenant farmers were a circumspect lot, but upon direct questioning, there were a few disparaging remarks about the bailiff Violet's uncle had installed at Cloverleigh. Everyone would be happy once Violet was married to a decent man and the reins were out of her uncle's hands.

"I'll make my sister aware of your concerns, Mr. Hedge," said Georgie. "She will take the matter up with her trustees and we'll see what may be done."

"Aye, but we'd rather have you, Miss Georgie, if you don't mind me sayin'." Mr. Hedge, who had always treated her in a fatherly fashion, shook his woolly head and regarded her beneath beetling brows. "A vast pity you and his lordship—" He stopped abruptly, coughing, halted by an elbow in the ribs from his wife.

Georgie laughed and leaned down toward the couple. In a conspiratorial murmur, she said, "As to that, dear Mr. Hedge, you may be the first in the district to wish us happy. For the second time, mark you!"

There was much jubilation at this news. Accepting an offer of hospitality from the delighted farmer and his wife, she found herself sitting down to a meal with them and their family. They dined at noon, unlike the Ton who took their main meal in the evening, and when Georgie eventually took her leave, she nearly groaned with happy repletion.

As she rode along the ridge that overlooked the red-brick mansion that had been her childhood home, she saw a curricle bowling up the drive, a man in fashionable dress driving it.

The new tenant, she assumed. The one who hadn't spent a lot of time at Cloverleigh since he'd hired the house on a short-term lease.

Upon returning to the house, she stripped off her gloves and stopped at the terrace to greet Lady Arden.

"Where have you been, child?"

"Oh, all about," said Georgie cheerfully. "I visited some of our tenants and dined with the Hedges."

"Did you not think to take Violet?" said Lady Arden. "She must be introduced about the place. I know your stepmother loathes the country, but she's been derelict in her duty keeping Violet away all these years."

Guilt made a flush creep up Georgie's throat. She had done nothing to persuade her stepmother to return.

A little ashamed now that she had slipped out that

morning without requesting Violet's company, Georgie said, "Did Violet eat breakfast?"

"No, she didn't. I believe she claimed she had a headache and hasn't come down all day." Lady Arden watched Georgie closely. "Did something happen between you two yesterday? You were like a pair of icebergs at dinner last night."

"Oh, we had a silly argument. Nothing to be concerned about," said Georgie.

She hoped she spoke the truth. She wanted to make it up with Violet, but she wouldn't retreat from anything she'd said. More than ever, she believed Violet's duty was to the Cloverleigh estate.

"I'll go up and see her, shall I?" she said, rising. "She might come down for tea."

It wasn't at all like Violet to sulk, so Georgie was rather surprised that no one had seen hide nor hair of her sister all day. By the time Georgie scratched on Violet's door, it was past three in the afternoon.

When no answer came, Georgie called softly, "Violet?"

But there was no response from within. On a sudden rush of presentiment, Georgie turned the handle and pushed open the door.

The bedchamber was empty, the bed made.

A note lay on the coverlet, addressed to her.

"What are you doing here?" said Beckenham as Lydgate strode into the private parlor Beckenham had hired for his use at the York Hotel in Bath.

Without waiting for an answer, Beckenham lifted a finger to the waiter who had been laying out his breakfast at the table in the window embrasure. "Set another cover for his lordship, will you?"

Lydgate waited until the servant had withdrawn, then sent Beckenham a stern look. "Don't cozen me, Becks. I came to find you of my own accord. Been hearing things. Terrible things."

He all but shuddered, making Beckenham debate silently with himself whether to punch Lydgate's lights out now or wait until he'd stated his purpose. He decided on the latter.

"Sit down, why don't you?" He indicated the chair opposite him.

Mud splashed Lydgate's boots, and the disarray of his hair seemed to be the product of actual wind, rather than the fashionable style known as the windswept.

Beckenham raised his brows. "Am I to take it you rode here *ventre à terre* to stop my marriage? Did Montford order you to intervene?"

"She's not here, is she?" He glanced about him as if he expected Georgie to be hiding under the sofa.

"She is not."

"Well, that's something." Lydgate tossed his hat and gloves onto an occasional table and sat down. He nodded toward the jar of ale in Beckenham's hand. "Pour me some of that, will you? I need it."

Beckenham complied, leaning over to fill Lydgate's tankard.

"Much obliged." Lydgate drank deeply. "No, of course I'm not here to stop your marriage. Why should I want to? *I* happen to think you're cracked, but it's not my affair when all is said and done."

"That has never stopped you interfering before," murmured Beckenham.

Lydgate held up his hands, palm out. "No. I shan't dance at your wedding. But if you're determined, far be it from me to try to dissuade you."

"I love her," said Beckenham shortly. The last thing

he usually shared with his cousins was this kind of mawkish sentiment, but for some reason, he wanted them all to know. Lydgate would spread the word.

Lydgate observed him intently. Then a smile slowly spread across his face. "By Jove," he said softly. "Don't that beat the Dutch?"

Beckenham cleared his throat and gestured with his knife toward Lydgate's plate. "The bacon's very good."

Seeming to snap out of his reverie, Lydgate obligingly addressed himself to the bacon. "I take it you're here to ask the uncle's permission to marry?"

Beckenham frowned. "Who? Oh, you mean the stepmother's brother. I forgot he lived here. No, I hadn't considered asking anyone's permission."

Which departure from correct behavior made Lydgate lift his brows. He didn't comment, however, but said, "What, then?"

Beckenham set down his fork. "I have business with Pearce that must be conducted before the aunt's demise."

He stated it coldly, aware of how brutal he sounded. Even Lydgate blinked.

But he couldn't let some misplaced sense of delicacy stop him carrying out his plan. The stakes were too high to allow himself the luxury of scruples this time.

He needed to get that letter from Pearce. Using Pearce's Achilles' heel as well as the imminent death of a relative to achieve his ends stuck in Beckenham's throat. But if that's what he had to do to rule a line beneath that episode with Pearce once and for all, he would do it. He would die for her. Breaking his own moral code ought to be nothing to it.

Slowly, Lydgate said, "So you would jeopardize his chances of inheriting unless he does whatever it is you want him to do." He looked at Beckenham over the rim of his tankard. The tranquil blue stare made Beckenham uncomfortable.

Beckenham didn't let his gaze waver. "That's the size of it."

"You know something to his discredit. Besides running from the duel, I mean."

Beckenham gave a brief nod.

Tilting his head, Lydgate's long fingers toyed idly with the saltcellar. "Do you mean to fight your way through the relatives to her deathbed to murmur some noxious tidbit into her ear?"

The implied criticism was justified, but he could survive Lydgate's scorn. He could survive anything, as long as he didn't lose Georgie. "A word to her man of business would be sufficient, I expect."

"Ah." Lydgate touched his lips with his napkin and set it beside his plate.

"Something wrong with the fare here?" said Beckenham.

Lydgate smiled coolly. "I find I've lost my appetite."

"I have to see him." Beckenham was frowning, shrugging away Lydgate's disapproval. "So far, he's fobbed me off. They say he's attending his aunt's sickbed, but he cannot be there every hour of the day, can he?"

"One would suppose not," said Lydgate. He reached for his tankard. "He means to keep you kicking your heels here."

"I tried bribing one of the aunt's servants but it was no use. They were a closemouthed lot."

Lydgate stood. "Good God, will you listen to yourself?" The suppressed violence of his tone indicated just how far Beckenham had fallen.

Beckenham stared stonily back at him. "Don't tell me you haven't done worse."

A muscle ticced in Lydgate's jaw. "Maybe I have. But we're not talking about me."

Beckenham stood also, braced his hands on the table, and leaned in. "Oh, yes. I'm cast as the noble fool in all our family dramas, am I not? The sort of prig who'd sacrifice everything, everyone he loves, for his honor."

Lydgate flung out a hand. "No one else shoved you in that role, Becks. You carved it out yourself, through sheer will and a deep-seated goodness that few of us can even pretend to. Look what you came from! Even that upbringing couldn't bend you or make you less than you were. Don't let her do this to you."

But Lydgate had it all wrong. Georgie would be just as horrified as Lydgate if she knew what he was about to do. The thought made him hesitate, but only for a second. Once he had eliminated Pearce's threat, they could be happy.

"Take care, Lydgate," he snarled. "You speak of my future wife."

His cousin's blue eyes flashed, then cooled to ice. "That's how it is. I see."

With his usual, elegant, unhurried gait, he moved to collect his hat and gloves. Then he turned back. "Ah. Now I recall the reason for this visit. I came to tell you Pearce is no longer in Bath. He left yesterday."

"What?" Beckenham strode forward so swiftly, he knocked his chair backwards. Rage flew through him. "Why the hell didn't you say so before?"

A discreet cough from the doorway made him turn his furious gaze toward the servant who stood there. "What?"

The man coughed again, nervously this time, and said, "There's a gentleman to see you, my lord."

He held a card on the silver salver. Lydgate strolled

over, picked it up, flicked it into his fingers to pass to Beckenham.

Impatiently, Beckenham waved the card away. "If it's not Lord Pearce, I won't see him."

"My lord, he says it's urgent. The gentleman is—"

"I don't care if it's the king himself downstairs, I'm on my way out. I've no time for callers."

As the servant scurried from the room, Beckenham turned his glowering gaze on his cousin.

"Tell me everything. Everything you know."

Dear Georgie,

   Do not be angry with me, dear one. I swear I have not run away in a fit of spite. I have thought of a way to give each of us what we most desire and I could not wait another moment to put my plan into action.

   Pray do not be alarmed for my safety or my whereabouts. I have gone to Mama. By the time you read this letter, I shall be in Bath already, so do not put yourself to the trouble of following me. I shall write to let you know I am safe and well.

   Your loving
   Violet

"What shall we do?" said Georgie when Lady Arden had read the letter.

"I must go after her, of course," said Lady Arden, pursing her lips. "Tiresome girl! What on earth does she think she'll achieve in Bath?"

"Shall I go with you?" said Georgie.

She shook her head. "No, you are staying put in this house until you are safely wed to Beckenham, my girl. I won't have this betrothal botched a second time. I'll be back as soon as I've made sure the chit arrived in one piece."

Lady Arden made swift preparations for departure. On inquiry, they discovered that Violet's horse was missing from the stables.

"Do you think she rode to Bath?" said Georgie anxiously. "She did not take anyone with her."

Her blood turned cold at the thought of a young girl like her sister riding all that way alone.

Lady Arden said, "No doubt she hired a carriage in the village. I'll inquire at the inn."

Before Lady Arden left, she said, "Something I should warn you about before I go. The new tenant at Cloverleigh . . . Have you any idea who that is?"

Impatience gripped Georgie. Why was Lady Arden wasting time with such trivia? "No, I never caught his name."

"It's Lord Pearce. Take good care not to go too far from the house while I'm gone, won't you?"

With that, Lady Arden swept out of the house.

Stunned, Georgie turned to climb slowly back upstairs.

Pearce. Good God! He was the man she'd seen driving up to Cloverleigh in his curricle this afternoon. No wonder he'd looked oddly familiar.

Confound the man! What was he doing here, and not in Bath? Where was Beckenham? Had he not met with Pearce yet? Would he be close behind?"

Georgie's mind reeled. Why? Why take over the tenancy of Cloverleigh and never make one attempt to approach her?

She clutched the banister hard. Had it been Violet Pearce wanted to see?

Had he succeeded?

Might Violet have given Bath as her destination when

she really meant to travel only as far as Cloverleigh? That would explain taking her horse.

On a sudden impulse, Georgie shot up to her sister's bedchamber and found her little escritoire.

Violet's traveling desk was locked but a hurried application of Georgie's penknife soon took care of that.

The usual accoutrements of the writing desk were all there: quills, parchment, ink bottles, blotter, sand . . . Several small bundles of letters, none of them from any man.

One bundle, tied with red ribbon, was in Violet's friend Lizzie's hand. Georgie tugged at the ribbon, fumbling a little as the notes cascaded from the pile.

Hesitating but a second, she snatched up the top letter that slid from the pile. She needed to read only one of them to realize her worst fears.

Georgie knew all the secret ways into and out of the house at Cloverleigh. Taking care that no one saw her, she crept into the house that night.

She'd set her groom to keep watch over the house all day, asking him to inform her immediately if Pearce left.

At dusk, the groom brought the news that his lordship had given the servants two days' leave, but that he hadn't gone anywhere himself.

That convinced Georgie. He had Violet. He meant to compromise her thoroughly, then shame the family into agreeing to let them wed.

She waited until darkness swallowed the landscape and a full moon rose to shine with a brightness that made everything seem eerily enchanted. The delay was excruciating. But if she stormed the house in broad daylight, there would be no containing the scandal. Perhaps it was too late to contain the scandal even now.

If only she hadn't argued with Violet like that! She

couldn't help concluding that their disagreement had been the catalyst for this flight.

She frowned as she stole down the narrow servants' corridor. How on earth did Violet think marriage to Pearce would solve their problems?

Georgie held her breath as she opened the false panel in the library wall a fraction.

The room was lit by a few branches of candles. Pearce sat alone in an armchair with a glass of what looked like brandy at his side.

Where was Violet? Georgie knew a moment's indecision. Should she try to find her elsewhere in the house? She could be anywhere. Besides, perhaps it was time for a confrontation with Pearce. Best if she said her piece to him without Violet's interference.

She straightened her spine and pushed the door wide.

Pearce looked up, his rather disheveled dark locks falling in an attractive tumble about his brow. She could appreciate the sheer beauty of him, even if it did not attract her.

His eyes widened in surprise. Then they took on a gleam of masculine satisfaction that made her furious.

"I'd no idea it would be this easy," he said softly.

"Where is she?" Georgie bit out the words, her fury rising along with her panic. "What have you done with her?"

He rose to his feet, bowing. "My very dear Georgiana. Have you lost your sister? How careless of you."

"You might have guessed I am not in the mood for frivolous nonsense tonight, sir. If you hand Violet over to me, we will go quietly back to Winford. No one, not even Beckenham, need be the wiser."

"Do you think I'm afraid of Beckenham?" said Pearce, setting down his glass and walking toward her. "You, at least, know why I didn't meet him that morning."

"You have my letter," she said with a bitter taint to her voice. "Why did you need Violet, too?"

"You are very sure of yourself," he observed coolly. "What makes you so certain it's you I want?"

She straightened her spine. She could do this. She moved closer to him. The very idea of casting out lures to him bucked her pride, but she'd do anything to save her sister.

Anything.

She shrugged, never taking her eyes from his. "A woman knows these things, Lord Pearce." She didn't know it, but she counted on reawakening the passion he'd once felt for her. She despised herself, knew she betrayed Beckenham, even though it was only a pretense. But this was Violet! She couldn't let her sister consort with this man.

Fire blazed in those ordinarily cold gray eyes, a heat she recognized as desire.

He reached for her but she backed away, wagging a finger at him. "I want to see Violet. I want to know she's safe and unharmed first."

He stood there, shaking his head. At what? At her?

"Where is she?" Georgie couldn't seem to moderate the sharpness of her tone.

So much for feminine wiles.

At first, he did not answer. Then he said, "Upstairs, in her old bedchamber. She's unharmed and unmolested. We won't disturb her, I think."

Her heart stopped in her chest.

"Don't look at me like that," he ground out. He strode over to her, took her chin in a firm grip. "I am not the monster you think me."

She jerked her head away. "Only a monster would ruin an innocent girl to punish her sister." The words had the flavor of melodrama, but that's what this was, wasn't it?

Suddenly, his earlier words sank in. Dear God, she'd been wrong. Violet had *not* come here to Cloverleigh after all. Pearce was bluffing.

When Violet had last lived at Cloverleigh, she slept in the nursery. That suite of rooms had been shut up, its furniture placed in storage in the attics. She couldn't sleep there even if she'd wanted to. Not to mention how unlikely it was that Violet would demand her narrow old nursery bed.

Still, Georgie must not act until she was absolutely sure. She made herself listen to what Pearce said.

"My behavior was not exemplary, I admit. But what of you, my lily-white dove? You flirted and teased and led a man on until he believed . . ." He broke off, his eyes softening from bullet hardness to mercury. "Whatever you think, I have done all of this because I love you. I never stopped, you know."

That made her laugh, a harsh, hoarse sound. She thought of the letter, of his veiled threats in Brighton. "Love! You know nothing of love."

For several seconds, she thought he might strike her. He restrained himself. Then he said, "Oh, and you do?"

Yes. She knew that love was not selfish or cruel. Love did not mean forcing the other person in any way, nor manipulating them.

Something he saw in her expression made his own turn ugly. "You don't seriously imagine yourself in *love* with that damned prig, do you? After what happened last time. Good God, he flaunted his stupid wife hunt under your very nose!"

She would not discuss Beckenham. Any mention of him would be inflammatory.

"If you loved me, Lord Pearce, you would not try to coerce me. You would let me and my sister go."

The sneer on his face faded. "You will have to resign yourself to a night here, I'm afraid, my darling. I will coerce you if there's no other way. The matter is of some urgency, as I understand it. Montford is on his way here with a special license."

Sick horror turned her stomach. "I will never marry you."

"Then I'll take you as my mistress," said Pearce. "Don't fool yourself. Beckenham won't want my leavings."

"Are you sure *you* won't be taking *his*?" she flung back at him.

In an instant, she regretted her furious riposte. He seized her in a rough grip, dragged her against him and sank his mouth onto hers.

Revolted at the contact, she fought like the tigress Beckenham called her, tooth and nail. The prospect of rape became very real as he used his superior strength to subdue her. She was twenty times a fool for coming here alone, yet again risking her reputation to save a sister who didn't need to be saved.

"Is it that you are jealous of your sister, Georgiana?" he murmured, planting kisses all over her face. "Don't be. I never cared for her. I didn't take her. She's not here. You can search the house if you don't believe me."

"I believe you," she said.

"It's just us. Me and you. You'll see how good we can be together."

She sighed. Relaxing against him, she offered her mouth to his.

As he took it hungrily, she reached out to the sideboard, feeling until her hand hit the base of a decanter.

His tongue plunged into her mouth; his hand closed over her breast. She gripped the slender neck of the decanter just as the door burst open and Beckenham erupted into the room.

The decanter dropped to the floor as Beckenham yanked Pearce away from her and planted a fist in Pearce's face.

Pearce crashed into two enormous globes, sending the celestial heavens spinning off their axis. He dashed a hand at his bleeding lip and glowered up at Beckenham from his position on the floor. "Déjà vu, eh, Beckenham?"

Beckenham yanked at the bottom of his coat, making it snap back into order. But he wasn't looking at Pearce. He gazed at Georgie, love and fear in his eyes. But not a trace of the disgust she deserved. "Are you all right? Did he hurt you?"

"I'm well. In once piece. I came to get Violet, only she's not here."

He frowned. "Violet's in Bath. I saw her this morning."

"Oh, thank goodness! Oh, Marcus, I'm so sorry."

"Don't be." He glanced at Pearce. "I've been every kind of fool."

Pearce watched them through narrowed eyes, the sluggish trickle of blood from his lip almost black against the pallor of his chin. "Well, well," he said softly, getting to his feet. "I see the two of you have kissed and made up. How very bloody nauseating of you."

"I've come for that letter, Pearce." Beckenham could scarcely drag his eyes from Georgie to bother with the blackguard, but it had to be done.

He wanted to pull Georgie into his arms. She'd

been through a frightening assault, but she looked magnificent. Another woman would have collapsed in hysterics or cowered in shame, but not she.

Despite her dishevelment and the reason for it, Georgie Black stood tall and proud and fiery as an avenging goddess.

"You won't get it," Pearce spat. "If you marry her, I'll make you a laughingstock, Beckenham."

I'll kill you first.

Pearce seemed to read his expression, for he laughed, a harsh crack of a sound. "If anything happens to me, I've left instructions to publish the letter in every scandal sheet."

Beckenham gritted out, "It might save us both some time if I make one thing clear, Pearce. No matter what you do or when you do it, dragging Georgie Black's name in the mud will not change two things: First, that I love her. Second, that she *will* be my wife."

Pearce got to his feet. "I don't believe you." He turned his head to look at Georgie, whose face was brilliant with emotion. "Don't believe him, Georgiana. He'd say anything to have you, but you'd soon find out that his damnable pride will always get in the way. The high and mighty Lord Beckenham will not take a ruined woman to wife."

Damn the fellow, but he had a glib tongue. He almost had Beckenham questioning his own motives.

"Hmm?" She flicked a gaze at Pearce. "Oh, are you still spouting nonsense, Pearce? I am not an insecure eighteen-year-old anymore, my lord. You can't sway me by planting doubts in my head. I no longer have doubts about Beckenham's love for me, you see."

Shame washed over Beckenham at the thought of his younger self. A man too full of puffed-up conceit to admit his regard in case Georgie took advantage of it some-how, used her power over him to make him her slave. Too full of pride to stop her when she left him.

He couldn't fail her. After that brutal interview with Lydgate, he'd almost talked himself out of playing the last trump card in his hand, but he would do it now. Not for himself or his own pride, but to spare Georgie the scandal of that letter becoming public.

He opened his mouth to make the threat. He'd even rehearsed it in his head the entire way from Bath. *The let-ter, Pearce, or I'll whisper your terrible secret in your dy-ing aunt's ear. See how you go securing her fortune then.*

Too late, he found he couldn't say the words. Not with Georgie standing there, looking at him as if he'd hung the moon and the stars for her. Not even without her to witness. Not even to spare her could he lower him-self to such a despicable act. How could he live with himself, threatening to expose a man's undeserved mis-fortune? A misfortune his own grandfather had perpe-trated.

And yet, how could he fail Georgie so miserably? There must be another way.

Almost gently, Georgie said, "I love Lord Becken-ham and he loves me. We will be married, Lord Pearce, whether you publish that letter or not."

Beckenham's gaze switched to Pearce, and surprised an expression of such agony that he thought he must have been mistaken.

But then all the pieces suddenly fell into place. From the start, every choice Pearce had made pointed to one thing.

When he'd been offered the chance to wreak revenge on Beckenham in the duel, had he taken it? No. He'd agreed to fly away with Georgie instead. Even though he must have been aware the entire arrangement was a ploy to save Beckenham.

He'd been duped, disgraced, forced to leave England.

In Bath, once again, he'd been offered an impossible choice. Leave his wealthy aunt at a critical moment, a choice that might well lose him a fortune, or take the opportunity of Beckenham's absence to win Georgie before she became Beckenham's forever.

His way of showing it, of courting Georgie by treachery and blackmail had been all wrong, but in his own way, he loved her.

"You never intended to use that letter, did you, Pearce?" said Beckenham abruptly.

Pearce's eyes glittered. "What? Are you mistaking me for your honorable self, Beckenham?"

"Oh, I would never do that," said Beckenham. "But I think I'm right about you, all the same."

He held out his hand to Georgie. "Come, my dear. Let us leave Pearce to wreak whatever revenge he may."

If she was puzzled or surprised, she hid it well. "Of course, my lord."

She swept Pearce a curtsy and they turned to go.

"Do you want to know what's in that letter, Beckenham?" Pearce's voice ripped through the room to them.

He felt Georgie stiffen.

Beckenham turned. "Not particularly. But I suppose you mean to show me."

His heart pounded. He'd not imagined he might push Pearce to hand the letter over. It seemed too good to be true. Until he realized this was a last-ditch effort on Pearce's part to cause a rift between him and Georgie.

Very well. If that's how he means to play . . .

* * *

Georgie gripped Beckenham's arm hard. *Don't do this,* she pleaded with him silently. *Don't read it and ruin everything between us.*

The things she'd written! The things Pearce had made her write!

No man could overlook or ignore such sentiments penned by his wife to another man.

She addressed Pearce. "You don't keep that stupid note on your person, surely." Her tone was annoyingly shaky.

"But of course he does," said Beckenham. "What man wouldn't treasure a love note of yours, my dear? Even one penned under duress."

True to Beckenham's prediction, with a sneer at Beckenham, Pearce put his hand into his waistcoat and drew out a rather tattered-looking piece of parchment.

Georgie had an urge to fly at Pearce, to rake that smug, smiling face with her nails. To snatch those lurid, false words and hurl them into the fire.

Would Beckenham take the opportunity to destroy it? She prayed he would do so without even glancing at the contents.

But no. Of course he took the letter and bent his head to read.

She let her hand drop from the crook of his elbow. Felt the space between them grow wider and colder with every heartbeat.

The time that followed must have been mere minutes. Seconds, even. To Georgie, they stretched out forever. Her heart hammered in her breast. Her palms were clammy. She felt acutely the needle prick of Pearce's gaze upon her. The weight of Beckenham's silence.

She sent Pearce a glare that could have razed cities. Then she caught it. Emotion mirrored in the set of his jaw. In the tightness of his sensual mouth. And most of all, in his eyes.

She would not call it love. She refused to dignify what he felt for her with that name. But there was something. An outward manifestation of some deep feeling, and that shed new light on the past.

All those thoughts and impressions flowed through her mind in an instant. She shook it off. She couldn't think about it now.

She was so acutely aware of Beckenham's every movement while he read. He gave nothing away.

What must he think of her? To have even thought those things, much less written them down, was shocking in itself. He would be disgusted with her. Worse, perhaps he might believe she'd truly meant them.

At the time, Pearce had ordered her to make it convincing, but she'd been eighteen and known nothing about the sort of activities she'd described. Had she succeeded too well in making it seem authentic?

Beckenham rubbed the side of his mouth with the back of his thumb. A sudden noise came from deep inside his chest. Then another.

She thought she couldn't have heard properly, but the sound came again.

"What's so funny?" she demanded as Beckenham threw his head back and roared with laughter.

"'You are the greatest lover ever,'" he read out. "Your prose, my sweet Georgie. It is simply priceless."

She blushed, too relieved to take umbrage at the criticism of her literary style. "I was only eighteen. And I really had no idea what I was talking about."

Beckenham's amusement was the final straw. Pearce had turned his back to them, leaning his forearm against the mantelpiece.

Incredibly, after all that had passed between them, Georgie found it in her heart to be a little sorry for Pearce. Not too sorry, but enough for her to wish to apologize for the role she'd played. She'd thought him impervious to heartache all those years ago. If she'd known his feelings were genuine, she would never have flirted with him as she had.

Georgie made as if to move toward Pearce, not sure what she'd say. Beckenham gripped her hand to stay her.

Wordlessly she looked up at him and he shook his head.

"Best leave him."

She knew then that Beckenham understood.

The second they were out of sight of the house, Beckenham took her into his arms.

"Oh, Marcus!" She wanted to sob with relief, laugh with joy. Kiss him, draw him down with her into the soft clover, make love to him with all the passion and love that burned inside her.

Their kiss was all-consuming, communicating everything that words couldn't express. How much they'd feared losing each other, that they never again wanted to part.

"You realize, don't you, that we cannot stay at Winford together tonight without Lady Arden," she murmured, trailing kisses along his jawline.

He groaned as she softly nipped his throat. "I'll go to the inn."

"Won't that look odd?" she whispered against his smooth, hot skin.

"Do you have a better idea?"

She lost her mind and the thread of the conversation as he kissed her once more.

Emerging some time later from another heated interlude, they continued walking down to the stables.

Georgie glanced over her shoulder. "I hate to think of him in that house."

"Oh, he'll be gone by morning," said Beckenham indifferently. "He knows there's nothing here for him now." He hesitated. "One thing has always puzzled me. How *did* he get that ringlet of yours?"

She'd have read an implied accusation in that question six months ago. Now, she knew he believed in her innocence, trusted her. The knowledge was a warm glow in her heart. "Pearce told me that, actually, when I went to see him at Montford's ball. He bribed my hairdresser to give it to him. Can you believe it?"

"There is certainly no end to his cunning," said Beckenham.

"Another reason to wish Cloverleigh were mine," she sighed. "I'd have taken great delight in evicting him."

"As to that," said Beckenham, "you will never guess who called on me in Bath this morning."

"Who?"

"Young Lord Hardcastle. With your sister in tow."

"What?" She'd been so wrapped up in her own troubles, she'd forgotten all about the identity of the mysterious "He" in Lizzie's letter to Violet.

Beckenham's mouth quirked up at the edges. "A very earnest young man."

"I don't believe it," said Georgie, putting her fingertips to her temple. And yet it all made perfect sense. "How utterly stupid I've been! And how cunning of *her*. The little wretch. She didn't give so much as a *hint. . . .*"

"Your sister is a deep 'un, isn't she?" Beckenham said it in a tone of admiration. "You wouldn't credit it.

She presented it all as Hardcastle's plan, but of course I knew that was nonsense. It was all her."

Georgie recalled Violet's note. "She said she'd discovered a way for us both to get what we want. What did she mean? Oh, Marcus, tell me! Don't keep me in suspense. She wants to marry him, doesn't she? But he hasn't a feather to fly with!"

"I'm trying to tell you, but I must point out, Georgie, that I'm hard-put to get a word in edgewise."

"Oh." She blushed. "Sorry. Do go on."

"Thank you. Your sister has proposed a swap. Your inheritance for hers. Thus, you have Cloverleigh and she becomes the well-dowered bride Hardcastle needs to restore his estate."

Georgie frowned. "That is ludicrous. My portion is generous, but it can't compare with the value of Cloverleigh."

"I would, of course, be prepared to make up the difference," said Beckenham. "We shall be partners, Georgie. Think of it."

The notion appealed so strongly to her that she glowed up at him. Trust Beckenham to know how much she wanted equal footing with him when it came to Cloverleigh. A partnership. Yes! Even if it could not be done legally, they would be partners in fact and deed.

"You approve of Hardcastle's suit, then?" said Georgie, surprised.

"I cannot approve of the clandestine way they've conducted their romance," said Beckenham. "But I believe they are genuinely in love. Hardcastle is young, but his character seems steady enough. He is determined to haul his family out of the mire and Violet's fortune would help him do it. Lucrative as Cloverleigh is, he doesn't need another property to run—he needs money."

Beckenham cleared his throat, a little self-consciously, Georgie thought. "He has even asked my advice on a few matters."

Georgie smiled. She acquitted Hardcastle of shrewd calculation but there was no better way into Beckenham's good graces than to ask for his advice.

She stared at him wonderingly. "It all seems too good to be true. There must be some drawback we haven't thought of yet."

"Trust that we'll overcome any obstacles," said Beckenham, drawing her closer again. "We overcame everything that stood between you and me, didn't we?"

"We certainly did," she whispered before his mouth took hers.

Heedless of propriety and convenience, they sank together to the ground, pleasuring each other, loving each other. Their spirits soared and flew, over the fields, through the bluebell wood, sinking into the ground that was their heritage, their lifeblood, the very breath in their lungs.

"You will burn that letter, Beckenham, won't you?" said Georgie as they lay together in the moonlight.

"I rather thought to use it as a reference," said Beckenham. "Some of the things in that letter astonished even me. Would you really like me to—" He leaned in to whisper in her ear.

She gasped, flushing. "Did I write that? No! You are teasing me."

"If I am to supplant Pearce as the greatest lover ever, I need to know these things." He said it with so much tender amusement in his voice that she couldn't be angry. How wonderful to hear him so carefree and frivolous.

"Well," she said, trailing her fingertip down his chest,

"if you truly wish to be the greatest, my lord, you will have to get in an awful lot of practice."

"Is that so?" Beckenham captured her hand, turned it up to press a kiss in the center of her palm. "I suppose one must make heroic sacrifices to achieve true greatness."

Epilogue

The wedding was meant to be a quiet, private affair. But somehow, the groom's extensive family had caught wind of the appointed day. Calendars were swiftly rearranged, luggage packed, children and servants bundled into various vehicles, and they all descended en masse upon Winford.

Carriage after carriage bowled up the drive, disgorging Beckenham's kin. The more outspoken of them demanded to know whether Beckenham had run quite mad? Did he truly mean to wed that dreadful Georgie Black? Or was this some sort of jest Montford was trying to play?

That the duke rarely made jokes only added to the mystery of it all.

"We are positively overrun with Westruthers," said Georgie, glancing out the window. "Oh, look. Even the devilish Davenport has arrived. Do you think they've all come to forbid the banns?"

Her voice was light, but Beckenham knew her better than to believe she was sanguine. His cousins had largely placed the blame with Georgie for the dissolution of their engagement the first time. Unfairly, he knew now. If he'd been more cognizant of his feelings for Georgie, if he hadn't been too proud to express them, the incident with Pearce might never have occurred.

He came up behind her and put his arms around her waist, kissing her cheek. "Do you mind so very much?"

"They all hate me." She sighed, settling back into his embrace. "But if it makes you happy to have them here, I don't mind."

"They'll come around," he said. "When they get to know you, they cannot fail to do so."

He *was* happy—overjoyed, in fact—to have his family here. He'd agreed wholeheartedly with Georgie that they should marry swiftly and discreetly. He didn't wish to be the focus of the Ton's gossip and speculation.

Lydgate, Xavier and Xavier's sister, Rosamund, and their other cousins, Cecily, Jonathon, and Jane were as close to him as siblings. Yet, he hadn't known he wanted them there until they descended upon him. The girls brought their spouses, not to mention their numerous offspring, with them. Jonathon brought his new wife, Hilary, for whom Beckenham had developed a fondness, too.

The disused nursery was in pandemonium as nannies and nurses struggled to keep order. Beckenham was happy to leave them to it.

Suddenly, he wondered what the house would be like when he and Georgie filled the nursery with babies of their own.

He nuzzled her ear. "While everyone else is occupied getting settled, might we—?"

But the suggestion that had already brought a flush to her cheeks and a sparkle to her lovely eyes remained unspoken as Lydgate strolled in, a bat tucked under his arm. "Fancy a game of cricket on the lawn, Becks?

Constantine and I have pledged to get the boys out of everyone's hair."

Beckenham turned. The constraint between them since that day in Bath seemed to hang in the air. But if Lydgate was prepared to extend the olive branch, in the form of a bat made from willow, then Beckenham wouldn't refuse to grasp it.

"Capital notion," he said with an apologetic glance at Georgie.

She tilted her head. "Can anyone play, Lydgate? I am no bowler, but my batting average is *not* to be sneezed at."

Some time later, when he and Lydgate stood conferring over the condition of the pitch, Beckenham said, "I owe you an apology. You were right. About Pearce, I mean."

Lydgate gave a curt nod. "Gracious of you. But I'm the one who owes the apology. I shouldn't have spoken about Georgie that way. Within five minutes of seeing you together, I saw I was wrong."

And so it was, that rather than taking three hours to primp for her wedding, the future Countess of Beckenham grew windblown and apple-cheeked, playing cricket with the Westruther relations on the manicured lawn of Winford.

Cecily, Lady Ashburn, who had always loved Beckenham best and thus, had long been Georgie's sternest critic, said to her cousins, "Very well, I admit it! I came here ready to scratch her eyes out. But even *I* cannot possibly cavil at this marriage. Only look how happy she makes him. He is a different man."

Indeed, everyone saw that Beckenham appeared less grave, walked with a lighter step, laughed often. Georgie was up to bat, with Beckenham bowling. He exchanged smiling taunts with her as he passed the wickets, tossing the cricket ball from one hand to the other.

"Only look at *her*," said Jane. "She positively glows."

"She's as smitten as he is," Rosamund agreed, sighing. "I do so love a romance."

That evening at five o'clock, Marcus Edward Charles Westruther, fourth Earl of Beckenham, married Georgiana Mary Black in a quiet, private ceremony in the drawing room at Winford.

Rosamund whispered to her brother, "My dear Xavier, am I to understand this marriage has *your* approval?"

Steyne slanted an enigmatic glance at her, then returned his attention to the couple. "Hush. They are making their vows."

At the end of the ceremony, Lady Arden heaved a sigh of relief. "Thank Heaven *that* is done and dusted at long last!"

The Duke of Montford raised his brows, an ironic gleam in his eye. "You claim the credit for bringing this off, I gather."

"No," said Lady Arden dryly, watching her younger charge, Miss Violet Black, proudly show her betrothal ring to the other ladies present. "*That* honor belongs to someone else, I believe."

"All's well that ends well," said Violet as she and Smith helped Georgie prepare for bed that night.

"Truly, you ought to take over Lady Arden's role as the family matchmaker," said Georgie. She'd had many words to say to Violet, both on the subject of her clandestine romance with Hardcastle and on her recent flight to Bath.

Tonight, however, she could only be grateful to her devious sister. If Violet hadn't intervened, Beckenham might even now be walking down the aisle with Priscilla Trent.

Violet kissed her cheek, then flung her arms around her. They squeezed each other hard.

"Be happy, dearest," whispered Violet.

"You, too," said Georgie, blinking back sentimental tears.

And when Beckenham finally joined her, she slid her hands into his hair, brought his head down to her, and kissed him with all the joy in her heart.

"At *last*," she said on a sigh. "I'm afraid I'll wake up and find it was all a dream."

His dark eyes were full of tender laughter. "There won't be much dreaming here tonight—not if I have anything to say about it." His voice deepened to a husky growl. "Now that I don't have to sneak away, I am going to love you until you forget your own name."

"But I like my new name very much," she replied. "Georgiana Westruther, Countess of Beckenham. It sounds well, does it not?"

"It sounds absolutely perfect," said the earl, and he swept his countess into his arms and strode to the marital bed.

Read on for an excerpt from
Christina Brooke's next book

The Wickedest Lord Alive

Coming soon from St. Martin's Paperbacks

Waves of heat broke over Lizzie's body, alternating with showers of ice. For the first time in her life, she thought she might faint.

He had found her. Dear Heaven, what was she going to do?

"Well, don't just stand there like a looby, gel!" said Lady Chard, flapping her hand in a beckoning gesture that made the drapes of flesh beneath her arm wobble. "Come in and let me make you known to my guests."

Years of dissimulation came to Lizzie's rescue. She inhaled deeply, filling her lungs with a calming flood of air, and sank into a curtsy as Lady Chard made the introductions.

"*Miss* Allbright." Steyne's tone was drily ironic, his bow a mere inclination of the head that clearly expressed disbelief.

Lizzie made a small production of relinquishing her basket and book to the butler—so much for *Sense and Sensibility*—then propelled herself by sheer force of will toward the grouping of chairs around a handsome Adam fireplace where the small party stood. She sat opposite the two gentlemen, while Lady Chard sank into the armchair in a cloud of black silk.

Terror gripping her insides, Lizzie braced herself for exposure. There seemed no way to prevent the marquis from revealing the truth. He had her trapped like a rabbit in a snare.

She'd deny everything, claim she'd lost her memory and refuse to believe anything he said was true.

But she couldn't see a way out of the trap. Legally, he had the power to command her, whether she remembered him or no.

Her mind seethed with plans and her insides roiled with apprehension, but rather than denounce her, the marquis simply scrutinized her closely. He remained stonily silent while Lord Lydgate—a distant cousin of his, she gathered—made elegant conversation.

"I was just saying to Lady Chard what pleasant countryside you have here, Miss Allbright," said Lydgate, with his easy smile.

Lizzie warmed to him, for this slice of Sussex was in no way remarkable. In fact, for her, its lack of attractions of any sort was a great part of the region's charm.

She managed to reply, "I like it, certainly, but I fear there is little of interest here for the fashionable set. We live very quietly in Little Thurston."

"Aye, that we do," said Lady Chard. "So if you young rapscallions have a notion of kicking up a dust here, you won't be received kindly, mark my words."

Lydgate did his best to look wounded, but his blue eyes danced. "Lady Chard, you will give Miss Allbright an entirely false impression of us."

Steyne did not even bother to acknowledge their sallies. His cold, bright gaze fixed on Lizzie.

Her cheeks heated but she worked hard to appear unconscious of his piercing stare. Steyne made no attempt to denounce her on the spot, so she tried to relax and respond while Lord Lydgate gently steered the conversation.

"Is that a *smut* on your nose, gel?" demanded Lady Chard, breaking in unceremoniously upon Lord Lydgate's discourse. Her sharp eyes narrowed as she leaned toward Lizzie for a better look.

Oh, plague it! Lizzie's hand flew to her face. She rubbed at her nose with her fingertips, flushing with the fire of humiliation.

"Hmph!" Lady Chard's shrewd old eyes surveyed her. "And your hair's all anyhow. You've been sweeping and scrubbing over at the Minchins, I dare swear. In my day, we gave them alms and that was the end of it."

Any money that came the Minchins' way would be spent in the taproom at the local inn, as well Lady Chard knew.

"Is that so?" said Lizzie with innocent surprise. "Then I suppose it was not you, ma'am, who sent little Janey Minchin a doll for her birthday only last week."

Lady Chard hunched a shoulder. "I don't go cooking their dinner for them, at all events."

"No more do I," said Lizzie briskly, uncomfortable with this talk. Mr. Minchin might be a drunkard, but his wife was a proud woman, who would not appreciate the family's circumstances being bandied about in my lady's drawing room.

She sought a means of changing the subject, but for the first time since he'd said her name, Steyne spoke. "Perhaps Miss Allbright would like to go upstairs to freshen her appearance."

That made her flush more hotly than before. With what dignity she could muster, Lizzie stood. "No, I thank you. Indeed, I must be going now."

The gentlemen had risen when she did. Lydgate

glanced at Steyne as if he expected something, but the marquis merely dealt her another of his ironic bows.

The viscount started forward to take her hand, saying, "My dear Miss Allbright, I hear there is to be an assembly tonight. Would you honor me with the first country dance?"

Her head jerked up at that. Oh, but this was worse than anything! They were coming to the ball? And if she agreed to a dance with Lydgate, would she not be obliged to take the floor with the marquis, too?

Recalling all too vividly the last physical contact she'd had with Lord Steyne, she nearly shuddered.

"I am engaged for the first three sets, my lord."

"The fourth, then," Lydgate said promptly. He really did have an enchanting smile. It was a pity his relation hadn't an ounce of his warmth.

"Thank you. I'd be delighted," she murmured.

Without looking at Steyne, she turned to go.

"Miss Allbright." His cut-glass accents sliced the air.

Again, she halted and looked back, and for the first time, she met his gaze squarely.

There is a plummeting sensation one feels as one wakes suddenly from a deep sleep. Lizzie experienced that now. It seemed to her that she plunged headlong into something dark and dangerous.

With difficulty, she found her voice. "Yes, my lord?"

"Save me the supper waltz."

The command was so peremptory, it set her teeth on edge. Striving for her most affable tone, she said, "I fear I am now engaged for every dance, my lord."

"Ha!" said Lady Chard, clapping her hands. "There's one in the eye for you, sir. You ought to have been quicker off the mark."

His eyes narrowed. He had not expected her to react with spirit to his command.

She couldn't resist adding sweetly, "But do not fear that you will be without a partner, Lord Steyne. I am sure I can find *someone* for you to dance with."

To her surprise, a gleam of amusement briefly lit his eyes. "Until tonight, Miss Allbright."

The words were invested with so much meaning, it was all she could do not to pick up her skirts and sprint from the room.

"I think she likes me," said Lord Lydgate as they left Lady Chard's and mounted their horses.

"Lady Chard?" said Xavier, deliberately misunderstanding him.

"No, the divine Miss Allbright, of course," said Lydgate. "You never told me how pretty she is."

Xavier threw him a scornful glance. Truth to tell, he'd spent the entire visit quelling the urge to lean in to Miss Allbright and wipe the smudge from her elegant little nose with the pad of his thumb. Even when she'd rubbed at her face, she'd missed the spot. His suggestion that she refresh herself had sprung from a desire to remove temptation from reach, rather than any wish to improve upon her appearance.

Of course, being female, she'd taken his suggestion as a criticism, and that was just as well.

"You think her pretty?" said Xavier, investing his tone with indifference he only wished he could feel. "I would not have said so."

In fact, he did not consider the lady who called herself "Miss Allbright" to be pretty, nor even beautiful. Those banal epithets did not begin to do her justice.

"You are trying to provoke me," said Lydgate.

"No, I am refusing to allow *you* to provoke *me*," Xavier calmly replied. "You will not flirt with my wife, Lydgate."

"Until you claim her as such, I say she's fair game for flirting," said his irrepressible cousin with a grin. "I still don't know why you left her to kick her heels in this backwater for eight years."

Xavier made no immediate answer. It was true that after his first, fruitless search, he'd had little trouble locating his new bride. She'd been clever in her attempts to cover her tracks, surprisingly resourceful for a girl her age. But he'd had resources at his disposal of which she could never dream.

Yes, he'd found her, but he'd left her quite alone. He'd judged her far safer with the kindly vicar than with him.

Now, he said, "There seemed no urgency. She was very young."

"You mean you wanted to go on raising hell without a wife to plague you," said Lydgate.

"Now there, Lydgate, you are lamentably wide of the mark," said Xavier. "But do go on. Enlighten me as to my motives. You are nothing if not entertaining."

As their horses walked, Lydgate narrowed his eyes, and a shrewd look came into his face that his family had learned to mistrust. "You profess to be the Devil himself when it comes to sin. You throw orgies to rival the Hellfire Club—"

"Now there, I must protest," said Xavier, holding up one gloved hand. "My orgies never involve vulgarity, and I find black masses and the like utterly ridiculous."

"—and yet you rarely take part in those orgies yourself," continued Lydgate as if he had not spoken. "In you, my dear cousin, I detect strong ambivalence. When obliged to marry this Miss Allbright, you did not wish to mend your ways, but you wanted to protect your wife from your world. Perhaps, even, from yourself."

Xavier found that his jaw was rather too tightly clenched. He ought never to forget that Lydgate possessed a keen mind beneath all that hair.

"How is that so far?" asked Lydgate.

Deliberately, Xavier relaxed his facial muscles. "Like a bad play. But pray continue."

Lydgate's voice gentled. "Now you find yourself in sudden need of a son, a necessity which never seemed likely before."

He had braced himself for some allusion to Jack and Charlie, but he felt the anger rise up anyway. Not at Lydgate, but at a cruel, perverse Fate, which had seen fit to take two blameless little boys while allowing corroded souls like his own to live on. He would have died to spare his cousins from the fever that took their young lives, but he'd long ago learned the futility of such bargaining. He might as well hold black masses for all the good that would do.

In a more forceful tone, Lydgate added, "You cannot allow Vincent to step into your shoes, nor that scurvy boy of his. You need a son."

Coldly, Xavier said, "Either that, or I can simply ensure that my wicked uncle and his blasted spawn predecease me."

Lydgate tilted his head, no doubt considering ways and means. "Something could be contrived."

Xavier snorted. "Do not trouble yourself. I don't want blood on your hands on my account."

"Oh, I shouldn't think we'd need to murder 'em," said Lydgate cheerfully. "No, I mean perhaps we might produce an entirely new heir. A long-lost brother, perhaps?"

"Dear God, wasn't Davenport's resurrection enough?" Another relative, Jonathon Westruther, Earl of Davenport, had staged his own death for reasons which Xavier privately thought nonsensical. If the fool had thought to come to Xavier for help, he would not have needed to take such drastic measures. It was Xavier's practice never to interfere with his relations if he could avoid it, but sometimes one was obliged to make an exception.

He waved a hand. "Forget finding a new heir. Even I balk at perpetrating such a fraud. My ancestors would spin in their graves."

"Very well, then," said Lydgate. "So. Unbeknownst to everyone, from your nearest and dearest to the Ton's wiliest matchmaking mamas, you already have a wife. *Ergo*—"

Xavier cut him off. "I think we shall leave the rest unsaid."

He never spoke of his *affaires*, not even with Lydgate, but he found himself particularly reluctant to discuss his admittedly obvious intentions toward his marchioness. In fact, he began to wish he'd never allowed Lydgate to accompany him to Little Thurston. But his cousin knew Lady Chard well enough to make visiting her their excuse for coming. Xavier had no legitimate reason to be here.

No reason but to bed his wife.

His naïve, deceitful, pert, and damnably alluring wife.